THE TENNIS PLAYER FROM BERMUDA

The TENNIS PLAYER From BERMUDA

FIONA HODGKIN

Copyright © 2012 by Fiona Hodgkin

All rights reserved.

This is a work of fiction. Names, characters, places, and incidents are imaginary or mentioned in a purely fictional context. Any resemblance to actual persons or events is entirely coincidental.

www.thetennisplayerfrombermuda.com

First Edition

ISBN 978-1-938-02213-5

Contribution to design of 1962 map of the All England Club by Adrian Montoya of MICA.

Copies of this novel are available from:

McNally Jackson Books
52 Prince Street
New York, New York 10012
(212) 274-1160

http://www.mcnallyjackson.com/bookmachine/tennis-player-bermuda

Published in the United Kingdom by Troubador Publishing Ltd.
ISBN 9781780882215
www.troubador.co.uk/book_info.asp?bookid=1795

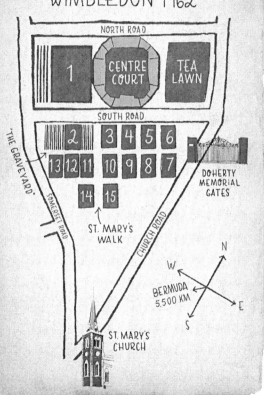

PART ONE

BERMUDA

AUGUST 1961
CORAL BEACH & TENNIS CLUB
PAGET PARISH, BERMUDA

I tossed the tennis ball high and out, cocked my wooden racket deep behind my shoulder, went up on my toes, whipped the racket forward, slammed the ball and ran toward the net.

Rachel Martin – *Mrs* Martin to someone my age – returned my service with her forehand, hard and low, to my feet.

I was already into the deuce service court alongside my father, and I bent down, so low my right knee was almost on the clay, and half volleyed, a bit too high, but angled away from Mrs Martin toward her husband, who was her mixed doubles partner. Usually, I would hit to the woman in mixed doubles, but Mrs Martin was a much stronger player than her husband. Earlier that summer, she had been a finalist in the Bermuda ladies' singles championship match. So when I could, I hit to Mr Martin.

He got his racket on it, just barely, and hit to my father in the ad service court, but I yelled "Mine!" and backhanded a hard volley straight down the centerline between the Martins. Our point.

Father bent his head down beside my cheek. "Rachel's forehand is so good. Why serve to it? It's match point, let's be careful," he said quietly. I didn't tell him what I thought, which was that I could volley her returns from either wing easily. He would regard that as cheeky. Instead, I smoothed down my tennis skirt and whispered, "I'll go down the middle to Mr Martin."

I went back to the baseline. I saw Father line up a bit closer to the far side. He was trying to fool the Martins into thinking that I would go wide again. I didn't bounce the white ball. Mrs Martin felt that bouncing the ball before serving was an affectation and had told me not to do it. I just set up, tossed, served, and ran forward. My serve hit the tape on the service line exactly and skidded a bit before coming up. Mr Martin bobbled his return and hit a lob, high but not deep.

"Mine!" I yelled. I backed up a few steps, set up, left index finger picking out the ball against the Bermuda sky, right elbow up, racket head brushing my back, kicked my left leg out for balance, and swung hard – what Bud Collins would call a 'skyhook.' The ball went fast down the line between the Martins. Neither of them got near it.

Game, set, and match to Dr. Hodgkin and his daughter, Fiona. I was 18, and that summer I was the ladies' singles tennis champion of Bermuda.

July 1957
Coral Beach & Tennis Club
Paget Parish, Bermuda

My parents both loved tennis and played often, usually at the Coral Beach & Tennis Club on South Road, but they were not what today we would call 'tennis parents.' I was their only child, and they began teaching me to play when I was perhaps five or six. The thought of pushing me to play tennis would not have entered their minds. I never had a paid coach; my parents would have felt that paying for a coach was unsporting and Not Done. Still, I loved tennis from the start. I just wasn't good. Father and I would play as mixed doubles partners on weekends and have great fun. When I served, even though I would hit a child's puffball over the net, Father would yell, "Come up, come up! Don't stay back!"

In July of 1957, I had just turned 14, and on my own I entered a girls' tournament at Coral Beach. I had never played in a tournament before. I knew all the girls who had entered, and perhaps one of my friends said she would enter if I would as well. In any event, I entered.

Private autos had been legal in Bermuda since just after the second war, but my parents, like many Bermuda families, did not own an auto until the mid-1960s or so. We rode pedal bikes, or took the ferries or the bus when we moved around. So my friends and I cycled to Coral Beach on a Saturday morning for the tournament, with our rackets in the baskets of our bikes.

I played two matches in the morning and won both. The Club served us lunch – cheese sandwiches and Coca-Cola – on the terrace above the courts along South Road. Then, after lunch, I was to play Sara Martin.

Sara was further along in puberty than me – I was quite envious of her – and larger and stronger. I didn't know this at the time, but Sara's mother, Rachel Martin, had played at Wimbledon in 1939, the last Wimbledon before the war. As a 14-year-old in Bermuda in 1957, it's possible I hadn't yet heard of Wimbledon.

Sara blasted me off the court. I would serve and run to the net, and Sara would easily hit the ball past me. She won 6-0, 6-0. Sara went ahead to play two more matches and win the girls' side of the tournament. Her mother had taught her to play tennis well.

Later that afternoon, I was sitting on a metal folding chair in the ladies' dressing room at Coral Beach. I had my head in my hands. I was sobbing because I couldn't bear losing. Mrs Martin walked into the dressing room, looking for me.

"Miss Hodgkin, why are you crying?" I looked up at her but couldn't answer. She was wearing a simple, white tennis dress that looked so old it was almost ragged. Just above her left breast, a small, faded Bermuda flag was sewn onto the dress.

"Your father has ruined your game by making you play mixed doubles with him. Come to the net, that's all you do."

I was still sobbing. "I like playing with Father."

"In singles, you must stay close to the service line. Don't come to the net unless the ball lands quite short."

"I like coming to the net."

Mrs Martin snorted. "You don't have the service to support a serve and volley game. You have to stay back."

I kept sobbing.

"Stand up," she said. She reached down and took hold of my arm. "We're going down to the courts."

She marched me down the steps to the lower courts. No one else was there; the tournament was over. The only bicycles leaning against the wall were Mrs Martin's and mine. She picked a tennis ball up off the court.

"Toss this," she said.

"I don't have my racket."

"I didn't ask you to hit it. I want you to toss it."

I tossed the ball, and it landed at my feet.

"Pathetic. It went straight over your head."

She reached under her tennis dress and pulled out a ball she had tucked into her tennis knickers. She raised her left arm with the ball in her hand, and when her arm was fully extended, she simply opened her fingers and let the ball's momentum carry it up. The ball went up about two meters and landed well out into the court.

"Like that," she said.

"But I can't – " She interrupted. "Toss it."

I did.

"Better. Again." I tossed another ball. "Higher. Farther out." I tossed again. "Better."

"But I can't hit it that high and out!"

She glared at me. She must dislike me, I thought, but I had no idea why.

"If you want to follow your serve in, you'll have to toss the ball high and out, and then extend your arm to hit it. You're not strong enough to do it any other way. Now try tossing it high and out and then hitting it."

I found my racket. I stood at the baseline. The sky was the blue that you see only in Bermuda. There was a farmer in a horse-drawn cart, slowly moving along South Road. Other than the hooves of the farmer's horse clopping on the road, and the barely audible waves landing on Coral Beach far behind me, the court was silent. Mrs Martin looked grimly at me. I set up, took the white ball and tossed it.

I drew my feet together and whipped my arm forward and out. I pulled the racket through as hard as I could and hit the ball with all my weight. The ball skidded on the tape of the service line of the opposite service court and then hit the concrete block wall at the back of the court, just under South Road. It ricocheted high in the air and finally landed back in the court. I turned to look at Mrs Martin.

She looked back at me for a few moments. It was as though I had confirmed something bad about myself that she had already suspected, but I had no idea what it could be.

"Like that," she said finally. She said nothing more, turned on her heel, took her bike and left.

I was alone on the courts. I gathered about twenty balls that I found on the courts and practiced my serve until dusk came. Then I rode my bike home.

A week or so later, Mrs Martin called Mother and arranged to play tennis with me one afternoon. Over the next four years, until I left the island for college at Smith, we played tennis with one another four or five times a week, and more often during school holidays, but she usually arranged these meetings through Mother.

Mrs Martin was careful to avoid any appearance that she was coaching me; that was Not Done. For boys on a football or cricket team, yes. For a young lady like me playing tennis, no.

But she was coaching me, though her style of coaching was unorthodox. She cared nothing for drills or exercises. We warmed up – she called it 'knocking up' – for ten minutes, and then we played a match. After a year or so, I would sometimes win one of the first two sets and then we would play out three sets.

She cared little about the form of my strokes, whether I was using an Eastern grip or was simply hanging on the racket handle any way I could. Occasionally, she would reach over the net and twist my racket in my hand, or bend my elbow up and say, "Like that."

She was reserved and quiet, and I eventually realized that she was extremely shy. She spoke little and had almost no sense of humor. She took the game of tennis with a deadly seriousness.

The first time we played, I either hit the ball into the net or made some other error, and I said out loud, "Oh, no!" At the next changeover, she was drying her hands with a towel when she said softly, "Never speak or make an unnecessary noise during play. It is unfairly distracting to your opponent."

I slowly learned that what fascinated her was strategy, although she never would have used that word. During one changeover, she asked, "Why did you lose that last point?"

She had made a backhand winner that she hit so hard any

full-grown, accomplished player would have struggled to reach and return. I had no chance whatsoever. "Your shot was too good."

"No." She picked up a ball by pinching it between her tennis shoe and her racket head, popping it up into the air and catching it with her left hand. She tossed it into the court. It landed just beyond the service line and about half a meter inside the sideline. "That's where your shot landed." She popped up another ball and then tossed it. The ball bounced exactly on the baseline. "If your shot had landed there, my return probably wouldn't have been a winner. I would have returned the ball, certainly." She looked at the court, and I could sense that she was replaying her shot in her mind. "Possibly a winner. But unlikely."

"You mean I lost because my shot was too short?"

"In part. But why was it short?"

"I should have hit it harder."

"No. Where were you when you hit the ball?"

I pointed in the general direction of the deuce service box on my side of the court. "There." I had no idea where I had been in the box.

"No." She popped up another ball and threw it softly into the deuce box. It bounced precisely on the centerline two meters back from the net. "You were there. Let's resume play."

I had already learned it was useless to ask her to explain.

One rainy afternoon, when we couldn't play tennis, I walked over to Mrs Martin's house and knocked on the screen door to her kitchen. She let me in, made me a cup of tea and sat at her kitchen table. I sat beside her. Mrs Martin took out a scrap of paper and a pencil and began drawing a rough diagram of a tennis court, with lines showing the paths a ball might follow.

"After being struck by the racket, the ball gradually begins to slow," Mrs Martin said. "But it slows at a faster rate before it goes over the net."

"Why?"

"Air resistance is proportional to the square of the speed of the ball. There's much more air resistance when the ball is traveling faster."

"Oh."

She sat quietly looking at her drawing of a court.

I asked, "What if I put topspin on the ball?" I had just learned how to make the ball spin, and I had been experimenting with this new skill.

"Because of the Magnus effect, topspin makes the ball curve sharply down to the court."

"Oh." I had no idea what she was talking about.

"A ball that spins in the direction of its travel creates a whirlpool of air and is forced downward. Isaac Newton realized this in 1672 while he was watching tennis at Trinity College, Cambridge. Real tennis, of course. Lawn tennis wasn't invented until the 1870s."

I'd never heard of 'real tennis', which later I learned had been played on enclosed courts for centuries.

For that matter, I'd barely heard of Isaac Newton.

She continued. "The spin of the ball affects its trajectory, not its speed. Until it bounces."

"What about after it bounces?"

Mrs Martin shrugged. "Depends on the court. On grass, there's not much friction between the ball and the grass, so the bounce doesn't slow the ball much. On clay, there's more friction and the ball slows more. Grass is a fast court, clay is a slow court."

"With topspin, I feel the ball doesn't slow after the bounce."

"It slows, usually. Just not as much as a ball hit flat, without spin."

"Why not?"

"When a ball hits the court, friction slows the bottom of the ball but not the top, so the ball begins to spin in the direction of its travel. But a ball hit with topspin is already spinning in that direction. So friction converts less of the speed of the ball into spin."

I was fascinated. "How do you know all this?"

"I thought about it a great deal when I was your age."

"Oh."

She took the scrap of paper on which she had drawn a court and drew an 'X' on the ad court baseline, right at the corner with the sideline.

"That's you."

Then she drew two lines, one following the ad court sideline, across the net, and down the deuce court sideline of the opposite court, and the second going crosscourt over the net to the ad court baseline.

"You would hit down the sideline," she said, pointing to the first line, "when your opponent is out of position. Here. Or here." She drew two 'Os,' one on the ad side of the baseline, the other in the ad service court. "From these positions, your opponent might not reach a down the line shot."

Then Mrs Martin asked, "Where would you hit when your opponent is well positioned?"

"I know!" I practically yelled. "I would hit crosscourt, and I know why, too. Father told me. The net is lower in the center, and a crosscourt ball goes over the center of the net."

She snorted. "Incorrect."

I was crestfallen.

"Miss Hodgkin, I spoke without thinking. I did not mean to sound as though I was contradicting your father."

"It's all right. But the net *is* lower in the center. Doesn't that make it an easier shot?"

"Which of the two lines I've drawn is longer? Down the line? Or crosscourt?"

I put my finger on the crosscourt line.

"Correct. It's longer by more than a meter, but both crosscourt segments are longer. The segment before the line intersects the net is longer, as is the segment after the intersection."

I was mystified.

"Over which segment does the ball slow at a faster rate?"

I put my finger on the segment before the intersection with the net.

"Correct. So you're hitting the ball a longer distance, and it's slowing at a faster rate before it reaches the net."

She paused. "When I was your age, I spent weeks at Coral Beach, on the court by myself, hitting balls and thinking about this problem. The net is lower in the center, which is an advantage to hitting crosscourt, but this advantage is basically negated by the greater force and the wider angle of attack needed to make the ball travel a longer distance and still clear the net."

"So I should hit down the line?"

"No, not when your opponent is well positioned. You were correct to say that crosscourt is the proper shot in that situation. It just doesn't have anything to do with the height of the net."

"So why do I hit crosscourt?"

"Because the second segment of the crosscourt line is also longer."

"You mean the segment after the net?"

"Correct."

"Why does that matter?"

"Because a longer line crosses a larger area." She put her finger on her drawing. "Look at all this space in the ad court you have to make a crosscourt shot."

"So I should hit crosscourt to just within the lines?"

"No."

"Father told me to aim about half a meter inside the lines, to be safe."

"I told Sara the same," Mrs Martin said. "But I want you to aim for the outer edge of the line. Not the line itself – the outer edge."

"Why?"

Mrs Martin had a pained expression on her face; I worried that something must be wrong.

Finally, quietly, she answered. "Because you are one of only two girls I've ever seen with the natural ability to hit the exact outer edge of the line, almost every time."

After I had played tennis with Mrs Martin for a year or so, I asked Mother about Mrs Martin's tennis career.

"Go ask your father, he knows about it."

I found Father in our sitting room, where we spent most of our time together as a family in our house – 'Midpoint,' it had been named for 200 years or so. There was no air conditioning in private homes in Bermuda at that time, and the sitting room was the coolest part of our house. The incredibly thick masonry walls and our water tank, which collected rainwater from our whitewashed limestone roof, kept it cool. The water tank was just underneath the sitting room and acted as a passive and quite effective cooling system. As in most old Bermuda homes, the plaster ceiling simply followed the inside pitch of the roof, creating the famous Bermuda tray ceiling.

From the windows on the north side of the sitting room we had a spectacular view of Hamilton Harbour below us, which no doubt is why Midpoint had been built in precisely that spot.

Mother and Father kept the back issues of their medical journals stacked on the floor of the sitting room. When Father decided he needed to see an article from an issue of *The Lancet* from a year or so year earlier, he would try to slide it gently out of the stack, but usually the entire stack would come crashing to the floor. In her favorite chair, Mother spent evenings writing notes in her patients' medical charts, which she kept in neat piles on the floor.

Father said, "Rachel? She was an honor for Bermuda in tennis, before the war. When she played overseas, she would sew a small Bermuda flag on her dress, just above her left breast. That pleased us all."

He thought for a moment. "Rachel was invited to play at Wimbledon in '39, the last championships before the war.

She was only about 19 then. Rachel went all the way to the final. She lost in a long match with Alice Marble. It was a chilly, rainy day. Early July, but you know London weather. Rachel pulled on a sweater during the match, but she couldn't have been comfortable. She wasn't used to the cold."

"How do you know it was cold?"

"I was there. I had just begun my medical internship at Guy's Hospital in London, and Rachel found me a ticket for the players' box. I got the afternoon off from hospital and took the Tube to Southfields. Rachel had no family in London except me" – Father and Mrs Martin were cousins – "and I thought I should be there for her. I sat beside Teach Tennant, Marble's coach. Teach is probably the greatest tennis coach ever, except for Rachel."

"What happened in the match?"

"It lasted from two in the afternoon until it was almost dark. They suspended play, twice, I think, for rain. Difficult conditions. I can't recall the score, but the last two sets went to extra games. Rachel played so well. She held off several championship points in the third set before she lost. She came close to winning. If the third set had gone on a few more minutes, the umpire would have had to suspend the match for darkness.

"It started to rain again, hard, just after Marble won. Rachel was just standing there, beside the umpire's chair, in the rain. I went down to the court, but a Coldstream Guardsman stopped me. I told him I was a physician, and he let me through. I walked over to her in the rain. She was crying. The groundskeepers had taken down the net and were pulling the tarp over the court. I told Rachel we needed to get out of the rain, and I led her over to the players' entrance to Centre Court, just under the Royal Box. Teach was just coming back out. She was looking for Rachel. Teach took Rachel to the ladies' dressing room.

"The London newspapers were full of it the next morning. Everyone in Bermuda was proud of Rachel. After the war, Rachel and Derek" – Mrs Martin's husband – "moved to London for some years because of his position with Butterfield's" – Butterfield's was our bank in Hamilton – "but by then she had her family and she never went back to international competition."

The next morning, Mrs Martin and I played at Coral Beach, and afterwards I asked, "Did you learn to play tennis here?"

"No. These courts weren't laid down until after the war." We were on one of the upper courts. "I learned on the lower courts, down by South Road."

"Who taught you?"

"My parents."

"But you must have had someone who showed you to play well."

"Miss Hodgkin, you just lost our match 6-2, 6-1. Why are we discussing the ancient history of tennis in Bermuda? Why not think through why you lost?"

"I apologize."

She snorted. "Don't apologize. Win."

"It's just that I know you played at Wimbledon, and I wanted to know more about that. How it happened. How you learned. That's all."

I was ready to cry. I was still a child, really. She never meant to hurt me, but she could be mean.

She cocked her head to one side. She was thinking. "The

only person who can tell you anything about playing tennis is yourself. All the fancy people who say they can teach you how to be a tennis champion are wrong, and most of the things they tell you are wrong. You'll have to find out by yourself. There's no other way."

She walked away toward her bicycle.

"I know you had to play the final in the cold. And it was raining." I wiped my eyes with the sleeve of my tennis dress.

She turned and stared at me. "You've been talking to your father. It was cold and rainy on Centre Court that afternoon." She left.

When I was 16, my parents and I were invited to a Christmas party at the Martins' home, and there I saw an old book on a table: *Match Play and the Spin of the Ball,* by William T. Tilden. It would be an understatement to say that this book had been thoroughly read. It looked as though the dog had been after it. On the flyleaf was scrawled, "To Rachel, with admiration. Bill." I started reading the book but quickly closed it, because I could see that almost every page carried Mrs Martin's handwritten notes in the margins.

I found Tilden's book in the Bermuda library, took it home and neglected my schoolwork for one evening to read it cover to cover.

The next day, before we played, I said to Mrs Martin, "I saw a book at your house by William Tilden. I checked it out of the library. He says that a baseline player with a good return of service will usually defeat a serve and volley player."

She nodded. "Big Bill thought a strong return would more often than not pass a player at the net."

"You knew him?"

She nodded again. "I met him at the Australian championships at Kooyong. Just before the war."

After a moment, she said, "Big Bill went to Berlin, to the Rot-Weiss Club, to coach the German Davis Cup team. In 1937. Before I knew him. He regretted going to Berlin. At least, I hope so."

"What's the 'Rot-Weiss Club'?"

She didn't answer; she was in a reverie.

"Was he right about baseline players? That they defeat serve and volley players?"

She snapped back to the present. "Miss Hodgkin, are we going to devote the entire afternoon to chatting about Bill's various theories?" She tossed her old wooden racket onto the court.

"Rough or smooth?" She meant that I should call whether the knots in the gut would land 'rough' – meaning that the side with the gut sticking out of the knots would point up – or 'smooth.'

At a changeover, while she was drying her hands, I asked, "Should I switch and start staying on the baseline?"

"No."

"You think I'm too small."

"No. There are women baseline players with your stature who play effectively. You would have to play with intelligence from the baseline, but you do play intelligently." This was one of Mrs Martin's rare compliments.

"So why shouldn't I think about switching to the baseline?"

She thought for a moment. "The baseline and the net each has advantages, but the principal advantage of playing from the baseline is time. Compared to the net, you have an additional half-second, maybe less, at the baseline to plan your shot."

She seemed to regard an additional half-second as the tennis equivalent of a long weekend in the country. "Let's resume play."

For once I had to have an answer, and I put my hand on her arm. "Please tell me what you mean."

"At the net, you can't plan. There's no time. You rely on instinct and confidence. A player at the net with good instincts and confidence may have been easy for Big Bill to pass, but not so easy for the rest of us. But confidence is essential at the net."

I felt I was the least confident person on the planet. I was a small, awkward teenage girl. "Am I confident? Do you think I'm confident?"

She cocked her head to one side. "Your mother, and both your grandmothers, are medical doctors. I'm certain that during their medical training, and after, they were made to feel unwelcome because they are women in a male profession. They cared not the slightest. Each of them had confidence in herself."

She paused. "You may have some of their confidence. Let's resume play."

I won the Bermuda girls' singles championship in both 1958 and 1959, both times against older girls, and both times easily.

But Mrs Martin did not come to watch my matches. That might have been misconstrued by some as coaching. Everyone knew she played tennis with me, but she wanted to make it appear that we merely played an occasional social game together, which was nonsense and everyone knew it.

She may not have admitted even to herself that we had a complicated, intense, private, and competitive relationship with one another. I don't mean to suggest that it was in any way inappropriate by today's standards; it wasn't, but I depended on her, and in some way I'm sure she wouldn't admit, and may not have even realized, she depended on me.

But I wasn't sure, and now decades later I'm still not sure, whether at that time she liked me.

I owe her so much and today, while she is quite elderly, and I am in my late 60s, we are close friends. I shop for her groceries, and we walk together slowly on quiet lanes in Paget and chat about our families. But when I was a girl it was as though she felt obligated to show me the way I might become a champion – even though she was plainly reluctant to do so. For what possible reason, I couldn't imagine.

We never talked about it.

She rarely talked about anything.

But we both knew we were watching sand flowing down through an hourglass.

For years, she won 6-0, 6-0, every time. Then it was often 6-2, 6-2. Later it was 6-4, 6-4, and a few times 6-4, 4-6, 6-4.

It was only a matter of time. But I had never defeated her.

June 1960
First Round Ladies' Singles Tournament
Tennis Stadium
Montpelier Road
Bermuda

There were no rules about entering either the Bermuda girls' tournament or the main tournament. Most young ladies played in the girls' tournament until they went away for university to England or the States, and then they either stopped playing altogether or moved to the main tournament. There was no set age limit. You entered the tournament in which you wanted to play. In June 1960, I entered myself in the main tournament. Only after I had entered did I learn that the youngest, unseeded player was always paired in the first round with the top seeded player, who in 1960 was the defending champion, Mrs Martin. That meant I would play her in the first round.

At the time, this seemed a horrible mistake. Looking back, though, I'm not sure it was a mistake. It may have given me the career in tennis I had.

Mother's response was simple: "You must withdraw from the tournament." I said no. Father, the diplomat, asked for a word with me alone.

He began by calling me 'sweetheart,' which was his

softening up move. It usually worked. But it didn't this time. I said I was staying in the tournament.

"Fiona, Rachel is a tennis player with an international reputation. She is extremely competitive. I've known her all her life. She cares for you, a great deal, but you must understand if you challenge her in public competition she will crush you. And she'll be entirely justified. No one will criticize her in the slightest."

"I will play her and win."

"Fiona, Rachel is undoubtedly the best tennis player to ever live on this island. You must be realistic."

"I will win."

"I'm sure you will win over her, some day, and maybe some day soon. But not this year. Wait until you're 18, next year. Play her then."

"I'm playing her next week." And that was that.

After my brief first round match, the Hodgkin family and Mrs Martin met in the ladies' dressing room in the tennis stadium near Hamilton. It was highly unusual for Father to be in the ladies' dressing room, but the lady players, under the circumstances, all decided to be somewhere else until this particular meeting of parents, child, and defending champion had ended.

I was not merely crying; it would be more accurate to call it uncontrolled wailing.

Mrs Martin, after she won the match, 6-1, 6-0, had been furious and brutal. She called me a coward in front of my parents – who had not come to my defense. It is possible that, contrary to her bedrock principles, Mrs Martin had given me the only game I won in order to encourage me. If so, it hadn't worked.

In the dressing room, Mrs Martin was still angry and even more specific in her accounting of my shortcomings.

"You capitulated in the second set. You failed to even try. Why bother walking out onto the court?"

"I couldn't win," I said through my tears.

"How the devil do you know?" she snapped. "The match isn't over until the last point is played. You gave up."

"I just want you to play tennis with me, still. I have to play with you."

"I can't play with a coward."

"I'm not a coward."

"You have the skill. You're intelligent on the court. But you don't have the character to win. You're weak."

And then her *coup de grâce*: "You'll never be a champion."

I wailed.

Mother interrupted. "I think we should talk about whether Fiona should continue playing tennis at all. Perhaps another sport would be better for her."

Mrs Martin was a little calmer now. She had never called me by my Christian name, at least not since I was a baby. But now she turned to me and said, "I think that is something only Fiona can decide."

She said good day to my parents and walked out.

I didn't play tennis for a month. I worked for Mother and Grandfather filing their patients' charts. I talked to no one. I was humiliated, and everyone on Bermuda knew it. I was miserable. In the late afternoons, I would cycle to some deserted beach and sit on the sand watching the Atlantic. I thought about leaving Bermuda; we had plenty of relatives in both the States and England with whom I could live.

Finally, one Saturday afternoon, I put on a tennis dress, took my racket, and cycled to the Martins' home, but they were not there. I went to Coral Beach and found the Martins playing mixed doubles with another couple. I waited until they came off the court, and then approached Mrs Martin and asked if I might have a word.

"Of course," she said and sat down in a wooden chair.

I sat in a chair next to her.

I said, "Perhaps you're tired after your match."

"It was a social doubles match. It wasn't tiring."

"Would you be willing to play a match with me?"

"Certainly. Let me go to the dressing room and wash my face. I'll meet you on one of the upper courts."

It lasted almost three hours. By the second set, all the players on the other courts had abandoned play to watch our match. I'm sure the older tennis players watching us were thinking, "This is an important match for Bermuda."

She was so strong and hit her groundstrokes so hard that I thought, 'What could she possibly have been like when she was younger?' I took the first set 14-12; there were no 'tie-breaks' in those days – we'd never heard the phrase 'tie-break' in tennis scoring.

She fought every point of the second set, but by then she was tired. She should have put this match off until Sunday morning, when she would have been fresh. Then she could have pulled out the second set. But we both knew this was it. She was desperate to break my service early in the second set; she hit every ball viciously hard. This was her only chance. If the second set went into extra games, she would fade.

I was 17; she must have in her early 40s then. She knew I could play all afternoon and until it was dark. She had to break me, get this set behind her, and then the third set – well, she would deal with the third set when she got there. But she didn't have the chance.

With the games 6-all on her serve, she drove a backhand long, only by a few centimeters but still long, and made it my advantage in the game. I won the game, breaking her serve. I looked across the net at her; we both knew it was over. She still fought every point; she tried to get the break back; she would never concede. But I kept the break. Finally, I took the second set and the match.

I had beaten her. Not in competition. Not yet. And not when she was fresh. But I had beaten her.

When I came to the net to shake hands, she refused my hand.

Instead, with perhaps 30 people watching us from the sidelines, with the net between us, she put her arms around me, pulled my head to her chest and kissed the top of my head. "You're wonderful; I'm so proud of you," she whispered. I felt her tears falling on my forehead.

SATURDAY, 1 JULY 1961
MY EIGHTEENTH BIRTHDAY
LADIES' SINGLES CHAMPIONSHIP FINAL
TENNIS STADIUM
MONTPELIER ROAD
BERMUDA

The next year, I met Mrs Martin in the finals of the Bermuda ladies' singles championship in the old tennis stadium outside Hamilton. She, as the defending champion, was seeded first; I was seeded second. Every seat was filled, and spectators spilled out onto the sides of the court. She served first, and I took her first serve of the match and hit it for a winner back down the line – the ball just barely touched the baseline and then bounced off the back wall and hung in the air for seconds before it finally landed back in the court.

I wanted everyone there to remember this match forever.

It was a hot Bermuda day, but I felt so cold my hands were shaking between points. I fired volleys to her forehand just to show that I could catch her shot with my racket, drain the ball's terrific kinetic energy with my hand and forearm, and then sharply angle my volley softly into her service box for a clear winner.

I served ace after ace and volleyed winner after winner; I

took service game after service game at love. I hit only for the outer edges of the lines; I took ferocious, insane chances and came out on top each time. In the second set, I started following in my return of her first serve to volley winners.

I wanted to crush her, and I wanted everyone in Bermuda to watch me do it. She fought back; she would never give up; but I overwhelmed her.

Ahead 4-love in the second set, I lunged to volley one of her shots, got too far out over my feet, fell, hit the court, and lacerated the distal surface of my left elbow. I was bleeding, and suddenly there was blood all over the side of my tennis dress. I walked to the sideline and found a towel to stanch the blood. I looked up and saw Father starting down the steps of the bleachers toward the court.

"No, Father. Stay where you are," I called loudly.

The chair umpire, George Michaels, said from the chair, "Miss Hodgkin, perhaps Doctor Hodgkin or Doctor Wilson should look at your arm before you resume play." My mother used her maiden name, Wilson, in her medical practice – which was practically a scandal in those days.

"Mr Michaels, I am ready to play now." I picked up my racket and walked back to the baseline. Mrs Martin, across the net, was expressionless.

It was over in 34 minutes. 6-1, 6-0.

I walked to the net, shook hands with Mrs Martin, and went to pick up a towel to hold to my elbow. Mrs Martin said nothing to me. The spectators, even my parents, were silent. There was no applause. I didn't care. I knew the spectators thought I hadn't been sporting.

It was one thing to win a match handily. That would be acceptable. It was quite another for a young girl like me to appear to dominate an older, respected player. That was Not Done. To make it even worse, I had played with an obvious grim fury. I knew Mother and Father would disapprove.

But I had won; I was the champion; that was all I cared about.

Mr Michaels fussily arranged a small table on the court with the two cheap pewter plates that were the prizes for the finalist and the champion. Mrs Martin and I stood side by side. I was still holding a towel to my elbow. Mrs Martin walked forward and brushed past Mr Michaels, who was attempting to award her the finalist plate. Instead, she walked to the center of the court, folded her arms over her chest, and looked out at the spectators.

Everyone in the stadium, still silent, stood up together at once. In Bermuda, in those days, this was a mark of immense respect.

As a teenager – back then she was 'Miss Rachel Outerbridge' – she had sailed on a steamship to Australia by herself. She was determined to become an unbeatable tennis machine, but she had almost no money. During her first week in Melbourne, she lived, homesick and lonely, in a decrepit rooming house in St. Kilda, ate only cheap Greek bread, drank tap water, and rode the No. 16 tram down Glenferries Road to Kooyong.

But when she played in the second round of the Australian championship on the lawns at Kooyong, Nell Hopman watched. Nell had just won her own second round match. Nell turned to her husband. "Who *is* that girl? What's that flag on her dress?"

That afternoon, Nell and Harry found a wealthy family in the Toorak neighborhood to take in Rachel. For her first two days with that family, Rachel told me decades later, all she had done was eat.

And Nell, being Nell, had taken Rachel's pocketbook without asking, rummaged around in it and – just as Nell expected – found no money. So she had the Lawn Tennis Association of Victoria give Rachel some spending money. This is what Rachel told me she remembered most: that the LTAV had given her money for her pocketbook.

Rachel was the youngest Australian ladies' singles champion until Margaret Smith, two decades later. An old black and white photograph of Rachel, taken just after she defeated Nell in the final, shows a shy young girl clutching her racket to her chest. The framed photo still hangs in the members' bar in the Kooyong clubhouse.

The news that Rachel had won the championship at Kooyong flashed to Bermuda in the middle of the night, and the next morning all Bermuda was on Front Street, cheering. Her anxious parents sent her a telegram congratulating her but urging her to come home to Bermuda.

She could afford to send only a one-word telegram in reply: WIMBLEDON.

I thought, 'What would she have done for Bermuda in tennis if the war hadn't come?' I think everyone else there that day had the same thought.

Mrs Martin turned away from the spectators, and Mr Michaels, relieved that she was finally going to accept her finalist plate, picked it up from the table.

"George, will you kindly forget those silly plates?"

She walked back to where I was standing. I tensed, expecting she might slap me across the face. Instead, she gently put her arm around my shoulders and walked with me back onto the court. I stood there with my hand holding the towel against my left elbow, with bloodstains on my dress, and Mrs Martin's arm around me. The crowd was completely silent.

Mrs Martin was at least four inches taller than I. She leaned her head down and kissed my cheek.

Then she said, loudly enough for everyone to hear, "Miss Hodgkin, that match was quite well played. Bermuda should be proud of you. I am."

The whole stadium suddenly exploded with cheers. My parents forgot themselves to such an extent that they actually hugged one another in public and began yelling together, "Fiona! Fiona!" Everyone took up crying out my name.

Mrs Martin turned to me and said quietly, "Now we need to ask one of your parents to look after your arm."

Sептember 1961
Paget Parish
Bermuda

From today's perspective, my application to enter Smith College appears ridiculously simple. It consisted of a brief letter in late 1960 from Mother to Thomas Mendenhall, the then President of Smith, noting that I, Miss Fiona Alice Ashburton Hodgkin, of Paget, Bermuda, would be 18 years of age on July 1, 1961; that I was the granddaughter of Fiona Alice Wilson, née Ashburton, M.D., Smith class of 1912; that I was the daughter of herself, Fiona Alice Ashburton Hodgkin, née Wilson, M.D., Smith class of 1935; and that I would appreciate the opportunity to matriculate at Smith in the fall of 1961.

Mother, perhaps unnecessarily, added that I would pursue a pre-medical course of study at Smith.

Professor Mendenhall replied in an equally short letter to Mother stating merely that I would room in Emerson House (where Mother had lived), that classes would begin on Tuesday, September 5, 1961, and finally, that Mother would receive the college's statement for my fees and tuition.

And that was that.

Bermuda families, even today, are frugal. We are so

isolated, and much more so then than now. I was not surprised when Mother, who was helping me pack for Smith, lugged out storage boxes of her own winter clothes from Smith for me to take to Northampton. The clothes were outlandish and hideous. The winter boots were enormous, the sweaters incredibly thick; I could not imagine what it would be like to wear them. I had never seen snow except in cinemas and photographs. I did know what snow was: it was white and cold.

The day before I left Bermuda to fly to New York on my way to Smith, I went to see Mrs Martin. She was hanging her family's laundry to dry on a line in their garden. She saw me getting off my bicycle, and she put down the laundry and waited for me to walk through the garden to where she was standing.

"I leave tomorrow. I came to say goodbye – and to thank you."

"I appreciate you coming to see me."

She didn't say anything more. I waited and finally said, "Could we sit down?"

We sat down on the grass. She took my hand and held it. I was happy just sitting with her.

After a minute, she said, "You play at a level that, in a few years, will give you a place in international competition."

"You did as well."

"A long time ago."

"I want to do as well as I can at tennis."

"You want to win Wimbledon."

She was exactly right. "I can't expect it to happen for me."

She snorted. "We spent years on tennis courts so you could predict you can't win?"

"You didn't win."

"I didn't. I wanted to."

"But the weather was terrible, and you were all alone in England."

"I wasn't alone. I was with a young man. A German tennis player from Berlin." She hesitated. "I met him at Kooyong."

"You were seeing him?"

"Well, 'seeing him' is the polite way of saying what I was doing. The evening before I played Alice, he broke up with me. I never saw him again."

She stopped. I thought this was all she would say, but then she started again: "Later, I heard we shot down his bomber over the Channel in the Battle of Britain. He drowned."

She paused for a long time. "Or so I heard."

"Why did he break up with you?" I couldn't help asking, but I had crossed a line. This man broke up with her the evening before her Wimbledon final? I was dumbfounded.

"It made no difference. My match with Alice would have turned out the same anyway."

"How can you know that?"

She didn't answer. She leaned over, put her arm around me, and pulled my head against her chest, with her hand holding my head to her.

She held me for a few moments. "It's tomorrow, then?"

"Yes."

She stood and brushed off her skirt. She didn't say goodbye. She turned and went back to her laundry, and I took my bicycle and went home.

September 1961
Smith College
Northampton, Massachusetts

I loved Smith, but I had never been away from my parents before. Although they went home to England on holiday every three or four years, they always took me along. I say they went 'home' to England because that's what they would say, but both of them were born in Bermuda. Both of my grandfathers were born in Bermuda as well. And Mother's mother was an American. As a child, I began calling her 'American Grandmother.' Only Father's mother had been born in England. Naturally, I called her 'English Grandmother.'

I was terribly homesick for Bermuda.

In the 1880s, Smith had been one of the first American colleges to have a tennis team, and tennis had been a fad among Smith students. The Upper Campus had been covered with grass courts with narrow strips of fabric for the lines, which were held down to the grass by – what else? – hairpins.

The first day of practice for the Smith tennis team was

several days after classes began in September. I was a few minutes late to practice because my chemistry laboratory ran long, and when I got to the courts, about eight young ladies, from first years to seniors, were already running in a circle on one side of the court while a young man standing on the opposite service line – the team's coach, I learned – was feeding them balls from a large basket. He must have told the girls to hit the balls deep, because they didn't seem to be hitting the balls back to him. Instead, they were spraying the balls all over the court.

The coach kept calling out, "Good! Good shot! Keep at it!"

This was a different approach to tennis than that employed by Mrs Martin.

He caught sight of me in my tennis dress, waved his arm, and yelled, "Hi! Come join in!"

I dutifully inserted myself into the circle of girls. But when my turn came, the coach accidentally fed me a ball that nicked the net cord and then dropped softly into my side of the court close to the net. It bounced up only 10 centimeters or so.

I was already there. Both my right knee and the lower rim of my racket grazed the court surface as I half-volleyed the ball. I didn't try to do anything with it; I just flicked it over the net to the coach.

He looked at me for a moment, and then I returned to the circle of girls.

On my next turn, he hit the ball straight to me. I took two small steps back, swung my shoulders around so I was perpendicular to the net, took my racket back low, and hit the ball with heavy topspin. It flew a meter over the net but then fell sharply and just touched the baseline. I had hit the ball so hard that it drove itself halfway through one of the gaps in the chain-link fence at the back of the court.

The coach held up his hand to stop the circle of girls. "Can you do that again?"

"I think so."

The coach hit me a hard backhand, with a bit of backspin so that the ball, he thought, would bounce up at steeper angle than I expected. But I didn't bother letting it bounce. Instead, I closed in and volleyed his shot. I let my forearm recoil to drain most of the pace from the ball, which popped back over the net and landed at his feet.

The coach hit back a high, deep overhead.

I drifted back, used my left index finger to fix the ball as it fell back toward the court, and hit an overhead back to him.

He popped the ball up again, and I adjusted my position, set up, and again just hit the ball back to him.

This time he lobbed the ball high and to my backhand. I had to turn around so that I was facing my own baseline. I looked up at the ball, jumped, and swung over my shoulder. The ball landed at his feet.

The coach and I were both laughing. My Smith teammates were standing beside the court with their mouths open.

He hit another overhead high into the air over the court. Still laughing, I made a show of bouncing from one foot to the other as though I were trying to decide which direction to smash the ball. Finally, while the ball was still on its trajectory over the court, I pointed with my left hand and yelled, "Your ad court!"

I let the ball bounce. It went well above my head. I

smashed it. The coach had moved to his ad court and, though he lunged, the ball whipped past him. It barely nicked the outside of his ad court baseline.

He looked back at the fence. Now there were two balls stuck in it. The coach motioned for me to meet him at the net. "Are you an amateur? You can't play on the Smith team if you're a professional."

"I'm an amateur."

"I've never seen you before. You must be starting your first year."

"Yes."

"What's your name?"

"Fiona Hodgkin."

"Well, Fiona, you're playing in the number one position on the team. Come over to this side of the net and feed balls to your teammates. I'll move over there and help them with their ground strokes."

A minute later, I was standing beside the basket of balls and feeding them to my teammates. I was yelling, "Bend your knees! Good shot! Drop the racket head! Let's go, Smithies!"

March 1962
Spring Holiday from Smith
Paget Parish, Bermuda

Smith kindly rearranged my classes to give me a full two weeks of spring holiday, and I took an airplane home from New York's Idlewild Airport. When I landed at Kindley Field, my parents were waiting for me; I was thrilled to see them. We took a taxi from the airport, and so I was quickly at Midpoint and back in my own room.

The next morning, I met Mrs Martin at Coral Beach for a tennis match. We embraced, and I said, "I missed you so much."

She said, "Let's knock up."

"Yes, but first I have to tell you about all the different drills we do in tennis practice; they're quite humorous." I said this just to hear her reaction.

She snorted. "After our match perhaps."

But it was wonderful to see her and to play against her again.

On my second evening at home, I was having tea with my parents, when Mother said that she had spoken that day by telephone with Mrs Pemberton in Tucker's Town, who said that her nephew, Mark Thakeham, was visiting from England for the school holiday.

"She's putting together a mixed doubles party for young people tomorrow afternoon, and she wanted to know if you could come join them."

Mrs Pemberton's home was called 'Tempest,' and it had a private grass tennis court, one of only two in Bermuda, at least to my knowledge. In the past several years, Mrs Pemberton had invited me to play there four or five times, and I had always accepted, just to have the experience of playing on grass. It is difficult, even if one is wealthy, to have a grass tennis court in Bermuda. Our climate is not well suited for it. Tennis players look at the beautiful greens on our golf courses and think, "This is the perfect place for a lawn tennis court."

The golf greens, though, support a few people each day who walk, slowly, across them to hit, gently, a small ball that rolls softly on the grass.

A tennis court has to put up with someone like me dragging a toe across the same foot of grass probably 80 times in a single match and then pounding along exactly the same path each time toward the net. Even in England, with consistently cool temperatures and plenty of rain, and as small as I am, I can damage a grass court in a single match.

In Bermuda? With inconsistent rainfall and hot temperatures? A grass court doesn't work well.

But, for all that, the grass court at Tempest was perfect and beautiful, probably because it was rarely played upon. It was for display, not tennis. Mrs Pemberton was not Bermudian, and she did not live in Bermuda. She was from England and stayed at Tempest only on holiday.

Father spoke up. "I served with Ralph Thakeham in the war. First-rate physician. First-rate officer, for that. Now a well-known senior medical consultant in London. He's 'Viscount Thakeham,' of course, but Ralph never uses the title. His patients call him just 'Doctor Thakeham.' He's the younger brother of our Mrs Pemberton in Tucker's Town. I hear good things about the young Mark Thakeham. He's fourth year medicine at Cambridge, and he played tennis for Cambridge."

My parents had been mixed doubles partners for many years, and they knew how to coordinate with one another. I recognized a planned, combined attack at the net. They must have discussed this in advance of raising it with me.

"I told Mother I would help in the clinic tomorrow."

"Oh, Fiona," Mother said. "You're home on holiday. Go to Tempest and enjoy yourself."

I said I would go, and Mother left the table to ring Mrs Pemberton.

I took the bus to the Mid-Ocean Club and then walked about 15 minutes to Tempest. I was met at the door by the housekeeper, who took me down to the grass court. The setting was beautiful, even by Bermuda standards, which in terms of natural beauty are about the highest in the world. The grass court was on the edge of a cliff, looking over the Atlantic to the southeast.

When you tossed the ball for your serve from the north end of the court, the last thing you saw before hitting the ball was the sharp horizon far out on the Atlantic. Looking exactly in that direction, there was nothing except the blue water of the Atlantic – and I mean *nothing* – between you and Antarctica, about 13,000 kilometers away.

In the other directions, the court was so well protected by Bermuda cedars and oleanders that the prevailing wind from the west usually didn't affect play. This grass court is still there today, and it must be one of the most spectacular tennis courts in the world.

It belongs to me, now.

I knew all the young people there except one, who I thought must be Mark Thakeham. There were seven people, plus me, evenly divided between girls and boys, so the plan must be for some ghastly round robin, mixed doubles play. I would rather have swallowed a lizard. I said my hellos to my friends, and Mrs Pemberton swooped down to introduce me to her nephew.

I realize how silly this sounds today, because my daughters roll their eyes when they hear me talk about it. But in 1962, in Bermuda, an 18-year-old girl like me could speak appropriately on a social basis with a young man she did not know only if and not until she had been introduced by an adult. I swear it's true.

Mrs Pemberton said, "Miss Hodgkin, may I introduce you to my nephew, Mark Thakeham?"

Mark said, "It's nice to meet you, Miss Hodgkin. I'm told you play tennis."

"Mr Thakeham, welcome to Bermuda. Have you been on our island before?"

"Never. I'm probably not the first person to say this is a beautiful place. So is it true that you play tennis?"

"I do play, Mr Thakeham, but not as well as I would wish."

Mark had strikingly good looks, with strawberry blond

hair, and that classic English complexion. He was attentive and polite, with an aristocratic English accent. He was plainly intelligent. He asked me about Smith — only approximately one percent of the members of Mark's social class in England at that time would have heard of Smith, so he must have been briefed on me in advance — and he asked what course of study I was pursuing.

"My parents are both physicians, and I hope to be one as well, and so I am what we in the States call 'pre-med.'"

"I am planning to be a physician myself, Miss Hodgkin. I think our fathers served together as doctors in the war."

"That is my understanding as well," I said.

Mark surprised me. When I said I wanted to be a physician, men reacted with derision and women at best were skeptical — this was 1962, remember. Even people who knew my mother and grandmothers, and therefore understood that my career in medicine had been decided the moment I was born, were still quite uncomfortable with the idea. Mark, though, seemed to feel that my plan to be a physician was nothing out of the ordinary.

But maybe he had been advised that this was just the way I was and to accept me on my own terms.

To me, this had the earmarks of a setup. Some people, including my parents, had apparently reached the conclusion that this toff and I should meet, and maybe one thing might lead to another.

"Mr Thakeham, I was told you played for Cambridge?"

"Yes, Miss Hodgkin." He laughed. "But understand that the university has only an informal team. It's just club play. I'm told you are a superb player, and you shouldn't expect much from me, I'm afraid."

"Mr Thakeham, I know we're planning to play some mixed doubles this afternoon, but would you consider playing a match of singles against me first?"

"I'll certainly play against you if you will please call me Mark."

"Then I hope you will call me Fiona." The social convention in Bermuda at the time was that, because we were close in age – Mark was about four years my senior – we could, by mutual agreement, decide to use our Christian names for one another.

So while the others were still chatting, and before the round robin, or whatever other awful scheme – probably something dispensing with advantage scoring – was organized, Mark and I walked out onto the beautiful grass and knocked up.

After a few minutes, I stopped, casually tossed my wooden Maxply racket onto the grass, and asked him, "rough or smooth?" Mark said "rough" and won, so he would have the first serve. I looked up to see where the sun was shining and decided I wanted to receive on the north end of the court.

Mark served, hard. It wasn't placed well – it bounced smack in the middle of my deuce service court – but all I could do was block his serve back. He came in on my weak return and blasted a forehand deep into my ad court. I wasn't anywhere near it. I felt as though I was playing mixed doubles, but without my male partner at the net to cut off shots like that.

As I walked over to the ad court, I told myself that Mark just wanted to show me how strong he was, and that now he would slow down. But no. His next serve was faster than his first, though again not well placed. I got my racket on it but made another weak return. Again, he hit a strong forehand crosscourt. I got to it, barely, but only clipped it with the rim of my racket. The ball glanced off into the oleanders.

My girlfriends were watching us and giggling. One of them called out, "Careful, Mr Thakeham. Our Fiona doesn't care to lose."

30-love. I went back to my deuce court. I was inwardly fuming. This time Mark's serve was well placed, right down the middle, and even harder. I hit it with my backhand, but late, so the ball popped up and floated over the net. Mark was waiting for it. He smashed it.

I motioned to him that I wanted to talk at the net.

"Mark," I said, "I'm about seven stone seven." I meant that I weighed 105 pounds. "I'll guess that you must be 13 stone. And you're fit. Have we established to your satisfaction that you're the more muscular player?"

He grinned. "You said you wanted to play singles."

I turned away from him. Over my shoulder, I said, "Not any longer."

As I walked off the court, he jumped over the net and took my arm.

"Fiona."

I shook his arm off. I regretted agreeing to come to this tennis party.

I went and sat down with my girlfriends. They had concocted a complex round robin mixed doubles format with games to five points, no ad scoring, one team serving all five points. The winning team then would sit out. It made no sense to me. Luckily, I was able to avoid being paired with Mark. I noticed that during the round robin his serves were good, but he didn't try to overpower anyone.

After tennis, the housekeeper served tea on the lawn beside the court. After we had tea, I looked at my watch. All the others lived in Tucker's Town or close by in St. George's parish, so they could bicycle home, but the last bus back to Hamilton left in half an hour, and I needed to be at the Mid-Ocean Club to catch it. I stood and said to the group that I needed to leave for the bus, and that I would go inside and thank Mrs Pemberton for inviting me.

Mark said, "Fiona, don't leave yet. I'm sure my aunt would loan me an auto to drive you home."

"Mark, that's kind of you, but my parents probably would prefer I took the bus." I left before he could reply.

When I walked into the sitting room in Midpoint, Mother was writing notes in the charts of patients she had seen that day, and Father was reading *The Lancet*.

Mother said, "Fiona, it's good to see you. Did you enjoy the party?"

"Yes, Mother." I sat down and picked up *Life* magazine.

I saw them glance at one another.

"Have you had your tea?" Mother asked.

"Yes, Mother. I had a good tea at Tempest."

Father said, "Sweetheart, did you meet young Mark Thakeham?"

"Yes, Father."

They glanced at one another again.

"Well?" Father asked.

I was leafing through the magazine. "I didn't care for him."

Mother bent over her charts, and Father went back to *The Lancet*.

After a minute or so, Father's curiosity got the better of him. "Why not?"

Mother glared at him, and he went back to the article on the new Sabin polio vaccine he was reading.

The next day, I was filing charts in the clinic Mother shared with my grandfather. One of my girlfriends, who had been at the tennis party the afternoon before, came in through the screen door of the clinic. She was agog about Mark.

"Fiona, after you left, he asked Mildred to go out with him. He borrowed a roadster from Mrs Pemberton and took Mildred to St. George's for pints at the White Horse."

"Good for her." Mildred was quite good looking. This boy was going to cut a wide swath in Bermuda in the two weeks he was upon us.

"Mark's father is Viscount Thakeham."

"So I've heard."

"You don't seem interested."

"I'm not," I said, slamming shut a file drawer of patient charts.

"Mark likes you."

"Why in heaven would you say that?"

"When you left just after tea, he kept asking us about you."

"Then why did Mildred go out with him?"

"Who wouldn't? He has use of an auto. He's cute. And his father's a viscount."

Later that afternoon, the screen door opened and then slammed shut.

"I'm sorry," Mark said. "I didn't know it would shut so quickly."

Then he said to me, "Hello, Fiona."

"Hello yourself." I turned back to my filing work.

Mother happened to come to my desk with several patient charts. "Fiona, take these home, will you? I need to write some notes in them this evening."

She noticed Mark. "May I help you?"

I said, "Mother, this is Mark Thakeham. Mark, this is my mother, Doctor Fiona Wilson."

They shook hands. Mother said, "Mr Thakeham, I've met your parents on two occasions in England. You're a medical student at Cambridge, I'm told."

"Yes, Doctor Wilson, I'm in my first clinical year."

Mother looked at Mark, and then at me.

"Well, I have patients waiting for me. Good luck in the clinic, Mr Thakeham."

Mark said, "Fiona." Then he stopped.

"Yes, Mark? I have work to do."

"Fiona, I apologize to you. I know I was rude to you when we played."

"Apology accepted. And thank you for coming to see me."

"Fiona, perhaps we could play tennis tomorrow?"

"I have a match already." I was meeting Mrs Martin at nine the next morning at Coral Beach. "Perhaps you might arrange to play with Mildred."

"Well, news must travel fast."

"It's a small island."

"You and I might play just a set after your match tomorrow? Or we could meet for lunch."

Now I felt that I was the one acting impolitely. After all, he was a visitor to Bermuda.

"My match is at Coral Beach. But I'll be finished by 10:30 or so. If you want, we could play after that. You'd have to come to Coral Beach. Do you know where it is?"

He didn't, but I showed him on a small tourist map.

The next morning, when Mark arrived at Coral Beach, I introduced him to Mrs Martin. She said to the two of us, "Would you young people mind if I watched a bit of your match?"

This was meant for Mark, not me, and Mark replied that he would welcome having her as a spectator. I hadn't explained to Mark who Mrs Martin was for me.

Then Mrs Martin said to us, "I take it your match will be merely social?" Translated into today's English from the language of early 1960s Bermuda social conventions, she was asking whether she might coach me while I played Mark.

I turned to Mark and asked, "Mark, would you mind if Mrs Martin spoke to me during our match? Please don't hesitate to say if it might distract you."

This bewildered Mark. "It wouldn't distract me in the slightest. Not a problem for me." So Mrs Martin sat on a bench beside the court, and we began our match.

Mark served softly to me in the first game. I noticed that Mrs Martin's forehead was furrowed, as though she were puzzled.

At the changeover, she said to Mark, "Are you intentionally backing off your serve?"

"Perhaps a bit."

"No. Hit the best serves you can."

He looked at me, and I shrugged.

In Mark's next service game, he began sending hard, fast serves over the net, and I either didn't get my racket on them or, at best, blocked them back.

Mrs Martin signaled that she wanted to stop play. She walked over to me. "Don't block his serve. Stroke through your return."

"I can't, at least not on his first service. He hits it too hard."

She snorted. "Nonsense. You'll play plenty of women in international competition with more effective serves than this young man. Don't give him any more lollipops."

This was her term for a soft return: a 'lollipop.' She didn't approve of lollipops.

I tried moving back well behind the baseline to return his first service. I glanced over and saw Mrs Martin shaking her head. She didn't approve of standing behind the baseline. On his next serve, I held my ground at the baseline. Mark had little control over his serve. He could make the ball land in the service box, and hard. Whether it went wide, straight down the middle, or directly into my body, was mostly a matter of chance. But the ball certainly came over the net fast.

Mark served to my deuce court. I saw the ball was going to be down the centre line, to my backhand. I took the throat of my racket in my left hand and pulled the racket well back and down. But his serve was so fast I connected with the ball late, probably just a few centimeters in front of me, and my return went wide and landed well out.

I looked over at Mrs Martin. She was nodding. I guessed what she was thinking: 'Better to try, and hit it out, than not to try at all.'

I walked across to my ad court for his next service. I set up on the baseline. Mark tossed and hit a remarkably fast serve, which again went straight down the middle. A beautiful serve. It kicked up above my shoulder. I took the ball with my forehand, above my shoulder, as hard as I could swing, and sent the ball crosscourt into his deuce court. I hit the return so hard and flat that Mark didn't get within a meter of it. A clear winner.

I looked over at Mrs Martin.

She said, "Like that."

No more lollipops.

Mrs Martin left for home after our first set, and then Mark and I played two more. That was a total of six sets for me that morning, and I was done in. I had to shower before lunch, so I pointed Mark in the direction of the balcony overlooking the Atlantic where we would have lunch, and I went to the dressing room.

My hair was wet when I arrived on the balcony and sat down with him. "I hope you don't mind my hair being wet. To dry it would delay lunch by probably an hour."

"Your hair looks beautiful wet."

I had no idea what to think about that.

The waiter came and we ordered. Mark began to ask, "Who on earth – "

I put my hand on his forearm to stop him in mid-sentence. "I should have warned you about Mrs Martin. But I had no idea she would stay to watch us play."

"Who is she?"

"Well, really, she's my coach, but since on Bermuda it's considered unsporting and Not Done for a young lady to have a tennis coach, Mrs Martin would never think of herself as my coach."

"What would she say she is?"

"She would say just that she and I play tennis together. She's my father's cousin, so we're related. She's a wonderful person and good to me, but she's a bit of a character. She reached the singles final at Wimbledon just before the war."

"Wimbledon? Can you beat her?"

"Yes. For years I couldn't, but now I haven't lost to her for a year or so. But her play is at an international level, still."

"How long has she been coaching you?"

"Well, longer than four years."

"How often do you play with her?"

"On spring holiday, we've had good luck with the weather, and so we've played every morning. She thinks the tennis coach at Smith has given me some bad habits, and she's trying to fix them in the short time before I go back to school."

"What bad habits?"

"She thinks the Smith coach is making me play more cautiously and to work the percentages. He's influenced by Jack Kramer a great deal."

"So Mrs Martin doesn't believe in playing the percentages?"

"No, she doesn't." I thought for a moment. "I think she believes in playing each point as though your life depends on winning it."

After lunch, we walked down the steep staircase to the beach, took off our shoes, and walked along Coral Beach together.

"This must be the most beautiful beach in the world," Mark said.

"Most people would say this isn't even the most beautiful beach in Bermuda."

"Which beach is the best?"

"Oh, probably one of the beaches farther along the South Shore. Warwick Long Bay is where I usually go to swim."

When we reached the end of the beach, we sat down on the rocks facing one another and talked for two solid hours. We compared notes about pre-med at Smith versus the medical course of study at Cambridge, and he warned me about how difficult he had found organic chemistry. I would be taking organic chemistry in the fall. Mark told me about his first clinical rotation in medical school, which was fascinating. Someone must have taught Mark to make conversation: he expressed an interest in me, a girl, which was just about unheard of in my limited experience with boys. And he seemed to take what I said seriously. I couldn't recall any boy ever taking me seriously.

By the time we walked back to the staircase, and climbed up to the balcony, it was almost four o'clock. Mark said, "May I drive you home?"

"No, I have my bicycle here."

Mark waited a moment. I was looking at him. He said, "Perhaps this is a bit forward of me, since we've seen each other today. But might I see you again tomorrow?"

I didn't reply.

He said, "We could arrange something without Mrs Martin."

I didn't reply.

"I haven't seen much of the island."

"Oh, I don't know. You've explored the pub in St. George's."

He grimaced. I knew I had been a shrew, so I said, "We could go to Gibbs Hill Lighthouse tomorrow. It's one of my favorite places. We can take the bus from Hamilton."

"I've been using a roadster that belongs to my aunt. I could pick you up and drive you there."

"Mrs Pemberton owns a roadster? I'd be surprised if she can drive."

"She can't."

"Why does she have a roadster, then?"

"She and my father have an interest in British Motor. MG is part of British Motor. Aunt and Father thought having one of the MG roadsters in Bermuda would spark interest in MG autos here."

"It hasn't worked."

"Unfortunately, you seem correct in that."

"I'll make us a picnic lunch. If you could pick me up at home at, say, noon, we could go to Gibbs Hill Lighthouse and climb to the top to see the view. Then we could have lunch on the lawn there."

"That sounds perfect. Where do you live?"

March 1962
Spring Holiday from Smith
Spittal Pond
Smith's Parish, Bermuda

The next morning saw pouring rain all over Bermuda, so the Gibbs Hill expedition was off the calendar. I worked in Mother's clinic, but in the early afternoon Mrs Pemberton rang Mother and invited me to tea later at Tempest. She offered to have Mark come collect me, but Mother declined. I could easily take the bus.

I sat on the bus on the slow ride in the rain to Tucker's Town telling myself not to become attached to Mark. He was probably bored to distraction staying at Tempest with his aunt. He couldn't possibly like me. He was an exceptionally handsome boy; no doubt he had his pick of girls. He was probably just fitting me in between visits with Mildred.

But when I got off the bus at the Mid-Ocean Club, Mark was standing there waiting in the rain under an umbrella. Despite the talk I had given myself on the bus, I thought it unlikely a boy would wait in the rain for a girl unless he liked her at least a bit. I had my own umbrella, but while we walked to Tempest, Mark put his arm around my shoulders and held his umbrella over both of us.

While we were having tea, the rain cleared, and the evening became clear. Typical Bermuda weather; it often changes back and forth between rain and bright blue sky several times a day. Again, I was bumping up against the time for the last bus back toward Paget from the Mid-Ocean Club, but, once again, Mark offered to drive me home. This time, I accepted and asked his aunt if I might use her telephone to ring my parents to tell them I would be home later than the last bus.

It was still quite light when we drove off from Tempest in the MG; Mark had the hood down. We swept along South Road past what must be some of the most perfect ocean views in the world.

When we drove past Knapton Point, I said to Mark over the wind, "Do you want to stop and see Spanish Rock?"

"What is it?"

"It's a flat rock above the Atlantic. A sailor carved some letters, a cross, and the year 1543 into it. We've always called it 'Spanish Rock,' but someone in Portugal now says the sailor was probably Portuguese. Perhaps we should call it 'Portuguese Rock' instead."

"Is it authentic?"

"You mean, was it really carved in 1543? I don't know, but the first settlers in Bermuda saw the carving, so it's been there a long time. The person who carved it must have been one of the first people on Bermuda. Do you want to see it?"

"Certainly. Where is it?"

"Just ahead, at Spittal Pond. Turn off here to the left."

Mark turned and brought the MG to a stop in a cloud of gravel dust at the entrance for Spittal Pond. We walked down a steep, rough path and then along a sandy track beside the pond. I told Mark, "The pond isn't really fresh water. It's a bit salty. We don't have much fresh water on Bermuda, except the rain water we collect on our roofs. Let's go this way, to the left." We hiked up a hill through thick brush to the top, where we had a spectacular view of the Atlantic waves crashing against the rocks of the South Shore and sending salt spray up almost to where we were standing.

"Down there," I said, pointing for Mark.

We scrambled down through the brush to a large, flat rock overlooking the waves. The rock was defaced all over with carvings. I said, "An American thought the carving, I mean the one from 1543, was going to be eroded away, so he made a plaster mold of the carving, and then covered it with a bronze impression. That was sixty years or so ago."

I stood looking out at the Atlantic.

Mark asked, out of the blue, "Were you homesick when you were in the States?"

"Terribly homesick. All the snow was a shock to me. And I missed my parents. I grew up in Bermuda, it was all I knew until I went away to the States. Well, I'd been to England several times but always with my parents."

Then I asked, "Did you grow up in London?"

"No. Not really. I spent most of my time before I went off to Harrow at our country house in Hampshire. We have a dairy farm there. When my father joined the Royal Navy at the start of the war, he moved Mother and me, and my nanny, to our country house. I had just been born, actually, so I don't have any memory of it."

"Do your parents live in Hampshire?"

"Well, Father's medical practice is in London, and we have a home in Hyde Park Gate. But it was bombed in

October 1940, during the Blitz, and we couldn't live there again until I was about 10 or so. Father couldn't get a license for the building materials right after the war. But finally he was able to have it all put right. Mother and Father still live there. They spend long weekends in Hampshire during the summer."

Mark looked down at Spanish rock and pointed to the bronze impression. "This must be the bronze cover?"

"Yes," I said. The impression showed a crude R and a P, with a cross and the year 1543. "This fellow in Portugal thinks the R and the P stand for the King of Portugal, and that the sailor who carved it was claiming the island for his King."

We turned away from the rock, went as close to the edge of the cliff as I was willing to go, and looked down into the impossibly clear, blue water, with waves blasting against the rocks.

It was getting on to dusk. We walked back to the sandy track toward the MG, and Mark took my hand in his as we were walking. Once we reached the roadster, he said, "You'd better tell me again how to get to your home, because I'm lost."

I pointed him back onto South Road. He made the turn into our lane and pulled over in front of Midpoint. He jumped out and opened the door for me.

"Fiona?"

"Yes, Mark?"

"We had talked about a picnic, before the rain came. Are you still willing to stand me for a picnic? Perhaps tomorrow?"

"Yes. At Gibbs Hill. I'll make a lunch for us. When will you collect me?"

We agreed on noon. He reached behind my head and

tugged gently on my ponytail to tease me, then jumped into the driver's seat and roared off.

It was almost dark. I stood there for a moment in front of Midpoint. Mark hadn't tried to kiss me goodnight, and I couldn't decide whether I was relieved or disappointed.

March 1962
Spring Holiday from Smith
Gibbs Hill Lighthouse
Southampton Parish, Bermuda

There was a bowl of Bermuda fish chowder in our refrigerator, which our housekeeper had made the day before, and it had been delicious when my parents and I had it last night. I took the left over chowder and poured it equally into two glass jars. And spoons. Then I made sandwiches with Irish cheese, the year's first lettuce from our garden, and Portuguese bread our housekeeper had baked. What else? A thermos of coffee. Then I baked oatmeal cookies, and wrapped them in two cloth napkins to keep them warm. Finally, an old sheet from the bottom of Mother's linen closet. I put all of this in a flower basket that Mother used to collect cut flowers in our garden. Then I sat down and waited for Mark to collect me.

When he did, I walked out with my basket, and he said, "Fiona, you're a beautiful girl."

I was startled; no one other than my parents and grandparents had ever said anything remotely like this to me. I didn't get compliments often, or really even at all. My figure was athletic and boyish, and even at age 18 my breasts were small. My parents liked me to keep my hair long. It was straight and light brown, and since I was a small girl it had hung down to the small of my back.

I loved hearing him say that I was beautiful. I said, "I'll give you exactly 15 minutes to stop talking nonsense like that." He laughed.

It was a perfect Bermuda morning after yesterday's rain, and Mark had the hood on the MG down. We drove along Middle Road and pulled alongside the road near Gibbs Hill.

"Let's take the basket and leave it at the foot of the lighthouse," I said. "We'll climb the stairs to the top and then have lunch."

As a girl, I must have climbed to the top of the lighthouse dozens of times – 185 steps up each time. As we went up the steep, narrow staircase, Mark said from behind me, "Now I know how you came to be so fit, if this is your idea of a pleasant way to spend a morning."

I laughed. "When I'm here by myself, I usually run up the stairs."

"Why am I not surprised?"

The view from the top was terrific. We could see most of the island, and the Atlantic on three sides of the island. It was such a clear morning that we could pick out on the horizon the tiny fishing boats that sailed out of St. George's.

"When was this built?" Mark asked.

"Every school child in Bermuda knows that the lighthouse gave its first light the night of May 1, 1846. The iron column of the lighthouse was made in England and then bolted together here."

Later, we walked to the edge of the tiny lawn below the lighthouse to a spot where there was a bit of shade. I spread out the sheet on the grass, sat down on it, smoothed out my skirt, and began pulling food from the basket. Mark sat down across from me. We ate and talked. We finished the chowder and sandwiches, and I poured him a cup of coffee.

"I hope you don't take milk. I entirely forgot milk. I never drank coffee until I got to Smith, but tea isn't easy to find in the States, so I started drinking coffee."

We talked for a long time, and then he leaned toward me and drew his finger across my left cheek. I just looked at him, with my hands on my skirt in my lap. I was totally naïve, but even I realized what was about to happen.

I had been kissed only once. That had been after a mixer at Smith – a 'mixer' being a chaperoned party with boys imported from nearby colleges. I liked that boy well enough, but he had not the slightest idea of what he was about. I had the sense that Mark was going to be different, and he was.

He put his hand under my chin, lifted my face up slightly, and kissed me. I didn't kiss him back, but only because I was so clueless that I didn't know I was supposed to respond to him. He pulled back and shifted himself on the sheet so that he was sitting beside me. He picked up my hands and put my arms around his neck.

"It's customary," he said, "for a girl to show some sign she likes being kissed. If she does."

I laughed. "What sign would you like?"

He kissed me again, and finally I tumbled to the idea that this activity demanded joint participation. But I said, "This is crazy. We're out in the open. A taxi full of tourists could show up anytime." He smiled and kissed me again. The potential for the arrival of tourists bothered him not a wit.

Then he put his hand gently under my breast. I

The Tennis Player From Bermuda

immediately jerked back and brushed his hand away. Nothing like that had ever happened to me.

"Are you all right?" he asked.

"Yes, of course. You startled me, that's all."

He put his arms around my shoulders and pulled me to him. I put my face against his chest. I liked being there. After a moment, he lifted my face and kissed me, and then he put his hand back on my breast. I clamped my hand around his, but I didn't move his hand away.

"Mark, I like that, but it makes me uncomfortable."

I was sending mixed messages here, since I kept my hand on his, but I was new at all this. He slowly moved his hand away but not before squeezing me, gently. I had never felt anything like that before. It was amazing. I buried my face in his chest again, with my arms still around him, where I was prepared to remain as long as possible. Tourists or no tourists.

He drove me home. It was late afternoon. We stood beside the MG, talking and holding hands, for so long that Mother finally came along walking home from the clinic, in her long, white lab coat.

I dropped Mark's hand.

Mother said, "Hello, Mr Thakeham. What have you young people been doing this afternoon?"

I answered quickly to avoid the possibility that Mark might say something not appropriate. "I took Mark to see Gibbs Hill, and we had a picnic lunch at the lighthouse. He's just brought me home."

Mother looked up at the sky to see where the sun was

over the horizon toward Dockyard. I could tell she was thinking that our picnic seemed to have lasted quite a long time, but she didn't raise the issue.

Instead, she invited Mark to come for tea the next afternoon, said goodbye to him, and went inside to begin making tea for Father.

When I walked into Midpoint, I went to the kitchen to help Mother. For a minute or so, she was silent.

Finally, she said, "I thought you didn't care for Mark Thakeham."

"I've changed my mind."

MARCH 1962
SPRING HOLIDAY FROM SMITH
'TEMPEST'
TUCKER'S TOWN, BERMUDA

Mark and I played three hard sets on the grass court at Tempest, then we changed into our swimsuits and dived into the salt water pool. His aunt was shopping in Hamilton and the housekeeper was off, so we had everything to ourselves.

I was sitting beside the pool with my legs in the water when Mark came up for air just in front of me. He folded his arms over my knees, and I leaned over and kissed the top of his head. He looked up at me and suggested that we go inside the house, to his room, and become lovers.

A week before I had not even known he existed, and now instead of slapping him, which is what I ought to have done, I found myself thinking that he had come up with a thrilling, fascinating, and frightening idea.

But good judgment got the better of me.

"We're going to do no such thing. Put it out of your mind." With that, I placed my hand on top of his head, pushed him off my knees, and played at holding him under water for a second or so before releasing him.

He came up for air, then pulled himself up on the side of

the pool and sat beside me. "I can't get it out of my mind, and I don't think you can either."

He was right about my part of that, at least.

"What's in my mind is my business. I have a question for you: have you ever slept with a girl?'

"That's certainly a personal question."

"Mark, you just asked me to sleep with you in the same tone of voice you might use to ask if I take milk in my tea. I think I'm entitled to ask a personal question."

He smiled ruefully. "Well, yes, I have slept with a girl before."

"More than one? How many?"

"Another personal question."

"Answer it honestly, and I'll leave off personal questions, at least for awhile."

"Two or three, I suppose."

I didn't think he was exaggerating. If anything, I thought he was minimizing the truth to make himself look less of a philanderer in my eyes. I took 'two or three, I suppose' to mean 'four or five.'

"I'm not adding myself to your list. But I do think we need to get you and your English complexion out of the Bermuda sun."

I stood up, reached down to take his hands and helped him stand. Then I led him over to a chaise longue on the grass that was in the shade of a large tree. We stretched out beside one another, and he put his arm around me.

After a few minutes, he reached up and pulled down the shoulder strap of my bathing suit and uncovered one of my breasts. I held my breath for a moment. He took my breast in his hand and then kissed me there, and the feeling was so wonderful that it frightened me. I put my hand on the back of his head and wove my fingers through his hair. We stayed like that for a minute or so, then I pulled my strap back up onto my shoulder. He didn't resist; he just reached over and playfully tugged at my ponytail.

We didn't talk while we were on the longue together; we may have even dozed for a bit. But Mark and I were expected at Midpoint for tea, so finally we got up and went to change into our clothes – separately.

After tea, Mother and I washed the dishes while Father and Mark went into the living room. There Father poured a Black Seal rum for himself, plus one for Mark. This was unusual; my parents normally didn't drink alcohol because of the risk that one of them might be called to hospital unexpectedly. But now Father and Mark, who were both Cambridge men, sat down with their rum and began seriously debating the Tories versus Labour.

"Macmillan is fundamentally sound," Father said.

"If Gaitskell steps down, though," Mark replied, "and Labour is led by Wilson, then Macmillan will have a tussle on his hands."

Mother and I, in the kitchen, laughed softly to ourselves while listening to them. Neither of them had a clue about politics. Mother leaned over to me and whispered, "Where *do* we find these silly men?"

It was thrilling for me to have her treat me, almost, as an equal.

MARCH 1962
SPRING HOLIDAY FROM SMITH
AMERICAN GRANDMOTHER

The day before Mark left Bermuda for England, English Grandmother gave a formal ladies' lunch in my honor at her home, which was less than 20 meters or so from Midpoint. The two houses had shared a garden for – well, for longer than anyone in Bermuda could remember.

English Grandmother's lunch was the reason I wasn't having a goodbye lunch somewhere else with Mark.

American Grandmother's idea of a formal ladies' lunch in my honor would have been to walk with me down to Hamilton Harbour and buy a freshly grilled fish, wrapped in newspaper, from one of the fishermen. Then she and I would sit down on the seawall around the harbour and dangle our feet in the water while we picked the fish apart with our fingers and ate it.

To American Grandmother, when I was young, this would be an opportunity to teach me the names of the bones in the foot, or the muscles in the hand, or how to take my pulse. Aside from her family, American Grandmother was interested only in medicine: she didn't garden, she sewed and mended only when essential, her house looked as though a hurricane had just passed through, and she was a truly terrible cook.

But she was an extraordinary physician.

When she was a girl in Massachusetts, she told me, somehow she had heard about Mary Elizabeth Garrett of Baltimore, who, in the early 1890s, had given a large share of the money needed to start the Johns Hopkins School of Medicine. In doing so, Garrett had extracted the painful promise from the Hopkins trustees (all male, of course) that women would be admitted to the medical school 'on the same terms as men.' American Grandmother couldn't recall how or when she had heard Garrett's story, but she had instantly decided to become a doctor.

I gather her parents (my great-grandparents) were at first amused that young Fiona wanted to attend medical school. When American Grandmother excelled at chemistry at Smith, they were less amused, and in 1912, when she was accepted at the Johns Hopkins School of Medicine, they were horrified – which bothered American Grandmother not the slightest.

American Grandmother became one of the first researchers to explore the biochemical basis of the menstrual cycle. In 1915, in her third year of medical school, she published a groundbreaking paper in *The Boston Medical & Surgical Journal* – then, as now, one of the leading medical journals, although today it is known as *The New England Journal of Medicine*.

For a woman medical student in 1915, life didn't get better than that.

I have an old, yellowed reprint of her paper: 'Ovulation and the Luteinizing Factor. Ashburton FA. From the Johns Hopkins School of Medicine.' In the paper, she explained how she had drawn a blood sample from a "human female volunteer" each day of the volunteer's cycle.

"How did you find a volunteer?" I asked.

"It was me!" she laughed. "By the third week, my left arm looked like a pincushion from all the needle sticks!"

No doubt she had a great future in medical research ahead of her at Hopkins, but she happened to visit Bermuda on holiday, where, by chance, she met a young doctor, who would become my grandfather. Apparently without a backward glance, American Grandmother chucked her career at Hopkins to marry him and practice general medicine on Point Finger Road in Bermuda. (Good for me, since otherwise I wouldn't be here to tell you this story.)

I once asked her why she had done it. At the time I asked, my daughters were her great-granddaughters. Without hesitating, she replied, "Because your grandfather was quite sexually attractive."

As the ladies' lunch in my honor was at long last drawing to a close, I heard the roar of Mark's MG pulling up in front of Midpoint. I quickly kissed Mother, then American Grandmother, and finally English Grandmother.

"I have to leave," I told them.

MARCH 1962
SPRING HOLIDAY FROM SMITH
MID-OCEAN CLUB BEACH, BERMUDA

Earlier that spring, I had gone to Boston with four of my friends from Smith – all of us were in Emerson House – on a shopping expedition. I bought several sensible knickers and two nice blouses, and then, under the influence of my friends, a two-piece swimsuit. Certainly not a bikini, but at least it had a separate top and bottom. Today, none of my granddaughters would consent to be seen even dead in this swimsuit. It was quite modest, and they could easily make three of their bikinis out of one of this swimsuit. But for me, then, it was daring.

I had never worn the swimsuit outside the fitting room of the store in Boston, and I seriously doubted Mother would let me out of the house wearing it. I had stuffed the swimsuit into my beach bag with a couple of towels so Mother wouldn't see it. I would change at the Mid-Ocean Club.

Mark and I had the beach entirely to ourselves that weekday afternoon. By the time I emerged from the dressing room, still tugging at the edges of the swimsuit trying to make sure it was covering everything that absolutely had to be covered, Mark was already on the beach. He turned around and was dazzled. He took my hand, and we walked toward the ocean.

"What have I done to deserve this amazing swimsuit?" he asked.

"Don't get any ideas. I don't want you trying to remove any part of it."

"There aren't many parts to remove. One would have to be selective."

I laughed. "That makes it easy; just stay away from it."

"I would never do anything improper with your swimsuit."

"Excuse me? What exactly happened at Tempest?"

"I don't recall any objection made to my conduct."

"Perhaps not, but today, behave yourself."

We dived into the water, which at that time of year was still cold, and we splashed one another. I swam toward the reef, and Mark swam up beside me; he was a strong swimmer. Eventually, we turned around and swam back to the beach. We walked up toward the wildly jumbled rocks at the top of the beach, and Mark spread a towel on the sand for us. I sat down and ran my hands through my ponytail to squeeze out the salt water.

Mark sat down beside me, put his arm around me, and then spread another towel on top of us, which felt warm and comfortable.

He kissed me, and all I could think about was that he would leave tomorrow. How many thousands of kilometers away would he be? I'd probably never see him again.

Mark reached below me, put his hand under my bottom, lifted me up, and dropped me between his legs, so that I was leaning back against his chest. I was scared at first, but then I found that leaning back against him, with his arms folded around me, was quite nice. I closed my eyes, and if I could have stayed like that for a long time, that would have been fine with me. Mark tucked the towel around me.

Then I was shocked when he pushed his hand under the front of the bottom of my swimsuit. I instantly went rigid, and I kept my eyes shut, but I didn't say 'No,' and I didn't grab his hand. But I did clamp my legs together.

He whispered, "I'm just going to touch you, don't worry, that's all."

After a moment he said, "Fiona, this won't work unless you move your legs apart, just a bit."

I spread my legs maybe a centimeter.

He laughed. "Fiona, it just can't happen unless I can put my hand between your legs. I promise you it will be all right. I'm only going to touch you; nothing more."

I spread my legs just a bit more. Mark touched me, lightly, but it felt like a small electric shock. I yelped, grabbed his hand, twisted away from him, and gasped for breath. He held me for a moment, and kissed me on the top of my head.

"Fiona," he said, pulling me back against his chest again. "It might be more comfortable for both of us if you took off the bottom of your swimsuit."

"I'm not going to do that."

"Fiona. Lift yourself up and pull off the bottom. It will be easier that way."

I was frightened, but I wanted him to touch me. "Don't look at me."

"I won't," he lied happily.

I pulled the towel back over me, reached down, and took off the bottom of my suit. I thought, 'I must be crazy to do this.'

I leaned back against him, holding the towel around me, and kept my eyes shut. He began touching me, gently, and it was instantly clear that he knew exactly what to do. At the end I cried out so loudly that I probably alerted everyone in Tucker's Town that I was there with Mark.

That moment, Mark could have made love to me without a word of protest from my side. Instead – to give the devil his due – he just held me for a minute or so, and then he stood up. He folded my legs so that they were in the shade of the rocks and out of the Bermuda sun. He put the towel over me and leaned over and kissed me on my forehead. I still had my eyes shut.

Then he walked down to the Atlantic and dove in. Mark, thoughtfully, was going for a swim so that I could have a few minutes alone to pull myself together.

When he came back, dripping wet, I had reassembled my swimsuit, and I was sitting with my back against the rocks. If that was just Mark touching me, what on earth would it be like to make love to him? He sat down beside me and put his arm over my shoulders.

I said, "I should have made love to you yesterday. You'll be on your way to England tomorrow, and I'll kick myself for not going to bed with you. But I'm so scared of making love."

"You're scared? What about me the first time? You think I wasn't scared?"

"Why would you have been scared? I would have thought it would be the girl who would be scared."

"I was scared out of my wits because I had no idea of how it was supposed to be done. And the young lady – it was her first time, as well – was absolutely no help. She kept saying, 'Mark, what *are* you trying to do?'" He said this mimicking a girl's higher pitched voice, with a slight accent I couldn't place.

I had to laugh at him.

Mark went on. "It was a complete embarrassment for me, and I'm sure the young lady wished she had picked someone experienced to sleep with for the first time. You know how I touched your clitoris just now?"

I'm sure my face turned red, but I nodded. I've subsequently found that in matters of human anatomy medical students are carelessly blunt.

"Well, my first time, I didn't know there *was* a clitoris. No idea."

"You seemed to have learned all about it."

He laughed. "Is that a compliment?"

I smiled. "Yes, it is. Was she your girlfriend? I mean, the person you slept with the first time."

"Yes."

"She must not still be your girlfriend, because you told me you've been with more than one girl."

"No, we broke up" – he stopped to think – "in the summer of 1959."

"Why did you break up?"

He shrugged. "She wanted to see someone else. But she's still a good friend of mine. I hope you'll meet her some day."

Meeting Mark's first lover was not going to be high on my list of social priorities, but I didn't tell him that. Then I had an uncomfortable thought. "Do you have a girlfriend now?"

"Not in England."

I didn't like the qualified sound of that answer. "Do you have a girlfriend somewhere else?"

"I seem to have acquired one in Bermuda."

I was so pleased I practically glowed.

After that, we walked along the beach together. Mark put his arm around my waist and, in a proprietary sort of way, tucked his thumb under the waistband of my swimsuit bottom.

The day Mark was leaving Bermuda, I was working for Mother and Grandfather in the clinic. Mark was having lunch with his aunt in Hamilton, and her driver was going to take him to Kindley Field later that afternoon. Mark said he would stop at the clinic after lunch to say goodbye. When I saw him pull up in front of the clinic and park the MG on Point Finger Road, I promised myself that I absolutely would not cry.

I smoothed my skirt down, checked the mirror to make sure my ponytail was neatly tied back, and walked outside. There couldn't be a more public spot in Bermuda. Mother's clinic was just across the street from hospital, and people were everywhere. Not the ideal place for goodbyes. Mark got out of the MG and put his arms around my shoulders. I put my arms around his waist, and we kissed. I was making myself the talk of Point Finger Road.

I said, "We'll never see each other again." I was keeping my promise to myself not to cry, but it was a close thing.

"Certainly we'll see each other again."

I leaned my forehead against his chest. "Doubtful. I'll be in the States, and you'll be in England."

"Not doubtful." He lifted up my chin with his hand and smiled at me. "I promise you we'll see each other again."

With that, he kissed me a final time, pulled lightly on my ponytail, got in the MG, and drove off. I stood there alone and disconsolate.

Mother came through the door of the clinic in her white lab coat with her stethoscope hanging out of the pocket. I expected her to scold me for making a spectacle of myself in public. Instead, she stood beside me and said quietly, "I know exactly how you feel."

Then she took me by the hand, led me back inside and began making me a cup of tea. I started crying. "You said you know how I feel. What did you do?"

"There's nothing to do. You put one foot in front of another." She handed me a tissue and kissed me on my forehead. "Now, stop crying. I have patients waiting for me, and you have work to do."

April 1962
Smith College
Northampton, Massachusetts

Three weeks after I returned to Smith from spring holiday, Mother wrote me a letter that I received on a Thursday evening, when I arrived back at Emerson House from tennis practice.

This was unusual; Mother and I wrote one another every Sunday afternoon. This was a tradition that Mother and American Grandmother had started when Mother began at Smith, and Mother and I had decided to continue it. It took the mail about a week to travel in either direction from Bermuda. So normally I received a letter from Mother on Monday or Tuesday, which she had written on Sunday the week before – usually with a quick note from Father at the end of her letter. But I had already received a letter from her earlier that week, and now here was a second letter. I was a little concerned, though if anything were seriously wrong she would have telephoned me. A telephone call was not easy, and it was expensive, but occasionally we would speak by telephone.

I opened the letter and got incredibly wonderful news. Mark's mother, Lady Thakeham, had written Mother to invite me to London for the season of parties in June, and Mother was asking me if I wanted to accept.

Actually, Lady Thakeham's invitation was to just one party, which the Thakehams were giving for Mark's younger sister, Catherine. Lady Thakeham, though, told Mother that, once it became known that I would be in London, I would likely receive invitations to many other parties. Mother said in her letter to me that this was certainly true. I would need an escort, but Lady Thakeham said that Mark would be willing to escort me unless I had some other young man in mind. (Reading this, I knew that Mark, as a joke on me, had suggested to his Mother that I might prefer someone other than him as an escort.)

Mother also told me that Lady Thakeham had invited me to stay with them, but she also knew that I had family in London, and that I might prefer to be with my own family, and if so that was completely agreeable. (Since my London relatives were elderly great aunts, this would be an easy choice.) Finally, Mrs Thakeham had said that she understood I was interested in tennis, and since Wimbledon would be on during June, it might be possible to find tickets for Centre Court one or two afternoons during the fortnight.

Mother went on to say in her letter that, if I wanted to accept the invitation, Father would have to make my travel plans and establish credit for me at the Butterfield's bank office in London, that she would have to reply to Mrs Thakeham, and she and I together would have to think about my clothes for the parties. So, if I wanted to accept, it might be best for me to telephone home.

There was one telephone in Emerson House, down in the front hallway, and I was dialing the international operator about two seconds after finishing this extraordinary letter.

The best part was that, obviously, Mark had put his mother up to this scheme and must have done so promptly after returning to London. I had not heard from Mark since we parted in Bermuda. He had asked for my address at Smith, and I had given it to him, but I pointedly did not ask for his address. Not having a letter from him in three weeks, I had almost decided he simply didn't want to write me. Now, it seemed, he had done something better than write; he had arranged to keep his promise that we would see one another again.

The invitation also solved an unspoken but real problem in the Hodgkin household, which was that at some point I would have to make an appearance at the London season. Both Mother and English Grandmother had done so.

I was about to turn 19, and our English relatives would expect that this year, or next, or at the latest when I was 21, I would spend the season in London, going to parties and perhaps finding a husband from a good English family. Back in the 1930s, American Grandmother had taken Mother to the season; that must have been an interesting cultural clash. But I couldn't go to the season alone. That was Not Done, and it was always difficult for Mother and Father to close their clinics and leave for England on holiday.

I finally was able to ring our home in Paget, and Father answered. When he heard me on the line, he said, "I told your mother that you were far too busy with your studies to run off to London for the month of June." And we both laughed.

When Mother came on, she seemed most concerned about my clothes, which surprised me. Mother normally cared little about clothes, and, in any event, I had plenty of nice things. But she said, "Fiona, you have no idea about the season." And she was right about that. So Mother wrote Lady Thakeham, thanked her for the kind invitation, and said I was pleased to accept.

And that was that.

Smith for me that spring was a blur of chemistry labs, calculus, and tennis. I received a letter from Mark, which pleased me a great deal. It was just a page and a half of scribbled comments about his clinical work in medical school, but just after his signature, he added a postscript: "Heard that my mother has invited you to stay with us in June; what a coincidence given that you and I just met in Bermuda a few weeks ago; hope you can accept."

May 1962
Exhibition Match with Claire Kershaw
Longwood Cricket Club
Chestnut Hill, Massachusetts

By the end of April, I was ranked number one in singles tennis among girl college students in New England. My ranking led to an invitation for me to play early in May in a ladies' tournament one weekend at the Longwood Cricket Club, on grass. Longwood was in Chestnut Hill near Boston. I arranged to stay with my cousins in Boston for that weekend, and late Friday after my classes, I took a Greyhound coach to Boston. There would be three rounds on Saturday, and then the final would be on Sunday morning.

But there was a surprise: when I arrived at Longwood Saturday morning, I learned that, on Sunday afternoon, the winner would play an exhibition match against Claire Kershaw. I recognized that name instantly. Kershaw had won the singles championship at Wimbledon in 1960 and 1961. I had seen her only in newspaper photographs. She had been 25 and recently married when she won Wimbledon her first time. Now Kershaw must be close to 27.

At the end of 1961, Lance Tingay, the tennis correspondent of London's *Daily Telegraph* newspaper, had ranked Kershaw the number one woman player in his World Rankings. Before the objective, computerized rankings began in 1973, Tingay's World Rankings in the *Daily Telegraph* were considered authoritative.

I asked the referee what Mrs Kershaw was doing here, and he told me that she was on a tour of America before defending her championship at Wimbledon.

When I was handed the draw, I saw that I knew most of the players. I had beaten all the ones I knew, and I had been seeded number one. With luck, tomorrow afternoon I would play the defending Wimbledon champion. My knees went weak as I thought about it. I didn't lose a set on Saturday; I can't recall how many games I lost but not many.

When I went home to my cousins late that afternoon, I was trembling. I could barely talk. All I could think about was playing Kershaw.

'Please don't let it rain on Sunday afternoon,' I thought. I wolfed down dinner and went straight to bed, where I tried to force myself to sleep.

Sunday morning in the final, I played an older woman I didn't know. She was a good club player but not at all a threat. I tried to keep it interesting for the spectators, but mainly I wanted to keep myself as fresh as possible to play Kershaw. After winning the final, I went to the showers and turned on the hot water. I was always amazed by the amount of water, and especially hot water, that was taken for granted in the States. In Bermuda, we had only rainwater, and we heated little of it.

There was a buffet lunch in the Longwood clubhouse before the exhibition match with a crowd of people, all there to watch Kershaw play. I got myself a salad and sat down at table with the tournament referee; I knew no one else. The players I knew had lost the day before and gone home.

A young woman sat down with us. Her hair was so blond it was almost silver; she kept it brushed back and held in place with a simple barrette. Her face was lovely, with large, pale blue eyes, and an impish grin. Her elegant white tennis dress had a matchbox skirt, with narrow, light blue ruffles on the seams. On the hem was embroidered in tiny blue script, 'Teddy Tinling.'

She wore a thin, plain gold wedding band but no other jewelry, not even earrings, and, unusual for that time, no makeup. Well, perhaps there was a trace of cream on her cheeks to ward off the sun. But nothing else.

She wasn't a large woman, but when she made even a simple movement – reaching for the pepper shaker, for example – it was impossible to miss the muscular power behind her limbs. Still, she was quite feminine.

The way she chatted with the referee was so friendly and outgoing that she might have been mistaken for an American, except that her upper class English accent gave her away. This, it dawned on me, was Claire Kershaw, and the idea that I was sitting at the same table with someone who had won Wimbledon – twice – was just incredible to me.

The referee turned to me. "Well, here's your opponent this afternoon!"

Kershaw stood up and reached out her hand. "I'm Claire."

I shook her hand. "I'm Fiona Hodgkin."

Claire burst into a smile. "I thought it might be you when I saw you just now! Fiona, I've heard so much about you!"

How could a Wimbledon champion possibly have heard of me? I was bewildered. But then a group of ladies descended on Claire for autographs and photographs, and I didn't have the chance to talk to her again before our match. In those days, tennis outfits for ladies in the States (and Bermuda, for that matter) were usually shapeless dresses, or blouses with pleated skirts that, unfortunately, tended to emphasize the hips. Claire's carefully tailored dress with its blue ruffles was a sensation at Longwood that afternoon.

Once we were on the court, Claire casually tossed her racket onto the grass. I called it smooth and won the serve. Once we began playing, it was obvious to me that, as they say in the States, I wasn't in Kansas anymore. Claire played effortlessly, with complete grace, and her style was perfectly balanced between the baseline and the net.

She put huge topspin on the ball with each groundstroke, and the ball would sail a meter over the net before dropping like a rock. I practically had to scrape her shots off the grass. She was patient, consistent, and happy for each point to go on until, at last, she would hit a winner.

And she was casual. She chatted with the spectators on the changeovers. Claire knew how to warm up the crowd and charm everyone. She wanted to entertain the spectators; that was the whole point of this match. Claire wasn't even taking it seriously. I was there only as a foil, so she could delight the crowd, which infuriated me. I was not about to roll over for this show.

Today, I know the custom that often governs exhibition matches, which is that they don't go to three sets. The matches aren't fixed. It's just that the player who wins the first set usually then, by convention, wins the second set, so that both players can catch the late afternoon flight out of wherever the exhibition is played. And the second set often features trick shots to amaze the crowd. At the time, no one had explained any of this to me – and it might not have made any difference even if someone had.

I lost the first set 6-4, because I made two stupid errors when I was serving in the seventh game with the games even at three apiece. Claire took advantage of these errors to break me and then take the set. I decided I wasn't going to let that happen again.

Early in the second set, on Claire's serve, I took up my usual spot a meter from the net. Claire hit a beautiful passing shot down my ad court line. I lunged for it, caught it with my backhand, punched it back crosscourt to her ad court corner, and drifted toward the centerline. Claire reached my shot and hit a topspin forehand that made the ball drop over the net right at my feet. I half-volleyed it back; I was so low to the grass that I found myself looking *up* at the net cord. Claire sent up a deep lob. I ran back, with no time to set up, jumped, and smashed the ball. It wasn't pretty, but it got the job done. Claire got only the rim of her racket on the ball, and it ricocheted into the crowd.

This put me ahead in the score, 30-15, and I went on to break Claire's serve.

At the next changeover, she wasn't chatting with the spectators. This was all business now. Claire had no intention of going three sets in an exhibition match with an unknown teenager from nowhere. But that's what happened. She couldn't get the break back, and I took the second set.

In the third set, I came to the net on almost every point and punched volleys into the corners of Claire's court. But, on my serve, I hit a forehand volley that went wide, and she went ahead in the game. That was all she needed; if you gave

The Tennis Player From Bermuda

her the slightest opening, she would make the most of it. She won the third set 8-6, and so the match, but only by making an enormous effort.

The crowd was sophisticated enough to know this wasn't the match they were supposed to see, and this was confirmed at the net when Claire shook my hand but then put her arms around me and hugged me over the net. Claire was emotional; she whispered straight into my ear, "You're everything I heard you were."

A few minutes later in the dressing room, Claire sat down beside me. She hadn't taken a shower yet; she was toweling the sweat off her arms. She said, "That third set was something. Great for the Longwood members to see a real match."

"I'm sure you gave me the second set to make it interesting."

She laughed. "I didn't give you anything. My plan was to take the second set, sign a few autographs, and head back to my hotel."

Then Claire said, "Rachel Martin told me about you."

I was astonished. "Do you know Mrs Martin?"

"Rachel was my coach for four years or so when I was a teenager."

"That couldn't be! She and I listened together to the BBC shortwave broadcast of the final last year at Wimbledon when you won. She didn't say she knew you."

"We're certainly talking about the same lady. Only Rachel would not think to mention that."

"How did Mrs Martin become your coach?"

"She and her husband spent the weekend at my parents' country house when I was, I guess, 14. Her husband worked in the City for a few years in the '40s and early '50s. We have an old grass court, and Rachel watched me play with my brother. After we finished, she asked my mother if she could play with me. We played a couple of times that weekend. After that, Rachel arranged with Mother to play with me in London maybe four or five times a week. Sometimes we played on grass at Queen's. Other times on a covered wood court."

I felt a chill. This was so much like what had happened after I served for Mrs Martin the first time. I remembered something Mrs Martin had said to me years ago: I was one of only two girls she had seen who could hit the outside edge of the lines exactly, almost every time.

Claire Kershaw must be the other girl.

Claire went on. "I had never been especially keen on tennis, because I disliked all the drills."

"But Mrs Martin doesn't use drills."

"That's right. No drills. By the time she went home to Bermuda, I was wild for tennis, and then my parents found another coach for me. I didn't like that coach and dropped him after a couple of months. Never had a coach again. But Rachel and I still play together whenever she's in London."

"How did she tell you about me?"

"Rachel and I exchange letters two or three times a year, and last Christmas I mentioned in my note to her that I was going to tour the States in the spring. She wrote back a long letter and asked me to make a point of watching you play, which I planned to do while I'm here. But I didn't know I would wind up watching you from across the net."

"What did she say about me?"

"She said that you have a bad case of the serves and volleys. Was she ever right about that!"

Claire laughed but then paused. "Rachel also said that you might win Wimbledon within the next four or five years. After this afternoon, I think she might be right about that as well. Rachel says that what you need is experience in international competition. You need to get out of Bermuda and out of college competition, in other words."

I was stunned; I couldn't speak.

"So," Claire asked. "What are your plans?"

"Both my parents are physicians, and I hope to go to medical school."

"Good for you! But, actually, I meant more where are you going to play this summer?"

"I don't have any plans to play this summer. I'm going to be in London for the season. My boyfriend is English, and his family invited me to stay with them in London. Did you ever do the season?" I could tell by her accent that she was from a family that would have made certain she was at the season.

"I did, the same year I made my first appearance at Wimbledon. That was 1956. I met my husband, Richard, at a party that season, although it took us years to get married. Because of my tennis, I didn't drink at the parties. I'm probably the only person ever to get through the season sober!" She laughed.

"When did you get married?"

"In 1960. This year will probably be my last Wimbledon. I've been there six times so far. I'd love to win again before I give up competition."

"Do you think you'll win?"

"I have to get past Margaret Smith first. She hasn't yet won the singles at Wimbledon. Lucky for me, last year

Margaret lost in the fifth round to Christine Truman. But now the London bookies are giving highwaymen's odds of six to four on Margaret to win the singles this year. I've played her three times in competition, all three times on grass, and I lost twice. I lost to her at Kooyong just a few months ago."

"Why would you give up competition?"

"I want to have a family. I could still compete after I have children; I know some women who do. I talked to Kay Menzies about it."

"Who is she?"

Claire stared at me in disbelief. "Kay Stammers Menzies. The best English woman player before and after the war. Older than me but a good friend. She had her family during the war, then led our Wightman Cup team."

"Oh."

"But I don't think I want to keep playing if I can have a baby. Too much travel, for one thing." Claire leaned over to me and said softly, "Richard and I are already trying to have a baby. I thought that, even if I were lucky enough to get pregnant, Wimbledon would be so early for me that being pregnant wouldn't make any difference."

"Won't you miss tennis?"

"No, not if I can have a family."

I was silent. It was hard for me to imagine giving up tennis, I mean in competition.

Claire knew what I was thinking. "Fiona, do you know what I did after I won the final in 1960? I went out with Richard, my brother, and my parents and celebrated at the Wimbledon Ball. But we went home quite early because I was tired."

She laughed. "Actually, we were *both* tired. Richard claims it's much harder to watch a Wimbledon final than to play in one. And then, Sunday morning, I woke up and boiled him an egg and made tea for his breakfast. It was the same as always. I had gotten what I had wanted for years, but everything was just the same. I mean, there's all this, now." She smiled. "Exhibition matches with girls from Bermuda. But nothing really changed. I won't miss it."

She thought for a moment. "I want a family now."

Then she changed the subject. "Tell me about this boyfriend."

"I only met him a month or so ago. He came to Bermuda to visit his aunt there on holiday, and I was set up with him."

"Set up?"

I thought that maybe I had used an exclusively American expression. "I just mean that apparently it had been arranged that I should meet him."

"I know what 'set up' means. I'm not a dinosaur. How were you set up?"

"I don't know exactly, but his father and my father served together in the war, in the Royal Navy, and they're friends. I had the feeling that everyone had decided I should meet him. When I did, then my parents basically let me see him whenever I wanted, which was all the time. That's unheard of for them."

"You must like him."

"A great deal."

"Did you sleep with him?"

"Claire!"

"Yes, yes, it's a personal question, I shouldn't ask, it's private, I'm awful. What's the answer?"

"No. But maybe I should have."

"Have you ever slept with anyone?"

"No."

"Well, as soon as you're on the international tennis circuit, the men players will fix that, for sure, and quickly." Claire said this bitterly.

"Did you sleep with anyone before your husband?"

She shook her head ruefully. "Fiona, I was already on the circuit, and by myself, when I was your age. By the time Richard finally got around to proposing to me, I had gone through most of the men on the circuit and was about to start in on the Wimbledon ball boys."

Then she asked, "What's this boyfriend like?"

"He's good looking. He's a medical student at Cambridge, so he's older than me."

"So he doesn't push you into things? He must not, or you'd already have been in his bed."

I nodded. "Well, I seem to do almost anything he asks. But I don't think he pushes me, at least not too much. He's about right, I mean in the way he treats me." I smiled. "Claire, he's wonderful."

She laughed. "We'll see about that."

Then Claire switched subjects again. "Fiona, will I offend you if I say something about your game?"

"I'd want to hear anything you say about my game."

"There were only two important games in our match. The two games when I broke you."

"Yes."

"If you had won either of those games, we'd probably still be out there, or maybe you would have won by now. You think so?"

"Yes."

"You know what I think? You got behind in the score on your serve, and you got impatient. Because you were impatient, you made mistakes. I don't mean to lecture you, I hate it when people do that to me, but that's what I think."

"I know what you're saying. You're right."

"You play so quickly on your serve. I know where that comes from. Rachel plays so quickly. Play has to be continuous, sure. But still, you usually serve less than 10 seconds after the previous point. Slow down, catch your breath, think, plan the next point."

At that time, the Rules of Lawn Tennis required play to be "continuous," including between points, so the server wasn't given time to reach for a towel or bounce the ball endlessly before serving. It wasn't until 1979 that the server would be allowed 30 seconds (later cut to 20 seconds) to serve. So, in 1962, play in international competition was much faster than today.

Claire smiled. "I'm not going to tell you to bounce the ball on the court while you're taking your time. I know that's against Rachel's rules."

"But to serve quickly can put pressure on your opponent."

"Maybe. Maybe a few women feel the pressure. For most of them, though, it's like trying to put pressure on a rock. They don't care, and it doesn't affect them."

Now I switched subjects. "Were you serious when you said I might win someday at Wimbledon?"

"There's so much that's pure luck, good or bad. The weather can be terrible. We always say we should re-schedule Wimbledon and hold it in the summer!'"

I frowned. "Wimbledon is in the summer."

Claire sighed. "It's a joke, Fiona."

"Oh."

"You can wake up one morning sick. Or you can wake up one morning with your period and feel awful. An opponent can have a great day. You can have a bad day. It's two long weeks. Unless you have a bye for the first round, it's six matches in a row just to get to the final. It's exhausting, it really is exhausting. Anything can happen. And you know Centre Court."

When she said this, I thought, 'No, I don't know Centre Court, but I plan to learn all about it.'

"It all happens so quickly, and then it's over. All that matters is who wins the last point. So you never know." She stopped for a moment. "But, yes, I think you might win Wimbledon. For one reason: you're extraordinary at the net."

She paused again, thinking. "You may be one of the best ever at the net. That's what Rachel thinks, and maybe she's right. But it's too soon to know. Maybe you'll collapse in international competition. Rachel is worried about that, because you've been cooped up in Bermuda and at college in the States. You certainly take too many chances. That's Rachel's influence, to go all out. She's never liked being cautious. But still – the question is how you'll do in international competition."

We heard a knock on the door, and Claire yelled, "Come in!"

The club steward poked his head through the door. "Claire, could we ask you to come back out on the court for some photographs with the members?"

"Yes, I'll be right there." Claire turned to me, smiled, and held up her index finger. "Be careful what you wish for!" She walked to the door, stopped for a moment, then turned around to me.

"Fiona, you're an amateur; am I right about that?"

"Of course."

"Have you ever played in a tournament where a professional was also playing?" She was referring to the ridiculous rules that governed whether a player could be considered an 'amateur.' Even if you had merely played in the same tournament with a professional, you could be disqualified from amateur competition.

"No. Last year I saw Pancho Gonzales beat Frank Sedgman, when Jack Kramer brought them to Bermuda. My parents took me to see them play. But I didn't even meet them. I've never played with a professional."

"You'll be in London the week of June 18?"

"Yes. I'll be at the season."

She walked back to the bench and sat down beside me. "You could play at Roehampton that week. If I could get you an invitation, would you play?"

"Yes, I'm sure I would enjoy it." I had never heard of Roehampton. I had no idea what Claire was talking about.

"The draw is probably already set. Everyone fights for an invitation. The LTA would have to submit an entry form for you. That's all right, they probably consider Bermuda to be part of Great Britain. Don't get your hopes up; I doubt I can make it happen. Tomorrow morning I'll send the Committee a telegram about you. But remember, every woman in tennis wants to be at Roehampton. I'll do my best. Will you give me your address?"

I pulled my notepad from my pocketbook, tore off a page, wrote my address at Smith, and handed the page to her.

She got up and walked to the door to go have her photograph taken with the Longwood members.

"Claire, what is the 'LTA'?"

She turned and stared at me. "The Lawn Tennis Association. They run amateur tennis in Britain. I don't really know how they submit the forms. They do it for me, I guess, more or less automatically."

"They might submit a form for me? To where?"

Claire laughed. "To the All England Club, silly. For Wimbledon."

I sat staring at Claire with my mouth hanging open.

It finally dawned on Claire that I wasn't conversant with the process for selecting the qualifiers for the singles draw at Wimbledon. "Fiona, Roehampton is the week before Wimbledon. It's the qualifying competition. That's how I qualified for Wimbledon, my first time. The All England Lawn Tennis Club Committee of Management, in its infinite wisdom, and after consulting with the Referee, Colonel Legg, may invite you to play at Roehampton. There are three rounds at Roehampton. It's brutal."

She laughed again. I had the sense that Claire had enjoyed Roehampton thoroughly.

"The women who win all three rounds get unseeded spots in the Wimbledon draw." She leaned over and kissed my cheek. "I'll send the Committee a telegram first thing in the morning. I'll tell them to see what you can do. But they probably won't listen to me."

Claire left for photographs with the Longwood members.

To me, then, Wimbledon was merely a shimmering dream. I had seen it only in smudged black and white newspaper photographs showing legendary players, like

Angela Mortimer and Maria Bueno, on Centre Court. I had heard matches at Wimbledon only over crackling, short wave BBC radio broadcasts: *"Crosscourt. Point to Miss Mortimer. Good show by the girl from Devon."*

I sat on the dressing room bench, trying to breath slowly. I might, just possibly, have a path to Wimbledon.

May 1962
Smith College
Emerson House
Northampton, Massachusetts

Two weeks after I played Claire at Longwood, I was at Smith waiting for an afternoon chemistry lab to get started, when a girl from Emerson House came in and told me that I had received a telegram. She had seen it when she had gone back to the house for lunch. I instantly cut the lab, ran as fast as I could along the path under the trees back to the house, burst through the door, found my telegram on the front hall table, and tore it open.

Western Union

FIONA HODGKIN
    CONFIRM SOONEST ENTRY JUNE 18 QUALIFYING ROEHAMPTON STOP CONFIRM AMATEUR STATUS STOP

        THE COMMITTEE
        ALL ENGLAND LAWN TENNIS CLUB

I screamed at the top of my lungs, "YES! YES!" I was jumping up and down in the hallway.

The house matron came out of the kitchen. "Fiona, a young man must have proposed to you. That's the only thing that could make you so happy. Congratulations!"

Mother was Not Pleased.

I had written her immediately with the news about Roehampton, told her I had accepted the Committee's invitation by a reply telegram, and generally made it clear that this was the most wonderful thing that could have happened.

It never entered my mind that Mother would not see it that way.

She telephoned me during dinner one night at Emerson House. "Fiona," she began coldly. "By agreeing to play tennis in London, you've put yourself and me in an awkward position. Lady Thakeham is likely to feel, and would be justified in feeling, that we have taken advantage of her invitation in order to have you enter a tennis tournament."

I had not thought about this, and I regret to say Mother was correct on this point.

"Also," Mother continued, "this isn't a step you should have taken without discussing it first with your father and me. I'm unhappy that you did this on your own."

I had never thought to talk with Mother about this; I had been too excited. Again, unfortunately, she was in the right about this.

"I think you need to withdraw from this tournament in London."

I hesitated and then decided on a strategic retreat. "Mother, you're exactly right, and I apologize to you and

Father. I was excited about this, and I acted without thinking. But the tournament will only be a day, at most two. I'm sure I'll lose in the first or second round. It won't interfere with anything I'm doing with the Thakehams."

She had anticipated my retreat. "No. I talked with Rachel Martin today, who is as surprised as I am. But she tells me not to count on your losing. She expects you'll be in it until the end, or near the end."

Thanks a lot, Mrs Martin, for all your help here; you can't be bothered to tell me that I'm any good, but you seem to advertise me widely to everyone else.

"Mother," I said, "I do apologize, but I will write a letter to Lady Thakeham tonight, a long, polite letter, and mail it in the morning. I'll tell her I did this without asking you, which I sincerely regret, and I'll promise her Roehampton won't interfere with the season. And if it does, I'll simply withdraw. I'll tell her I had no idea about this tournament when you accepted her invitation to stay with them, which is true."

When I said this to Mother, I thought that what I should really do tonight is a calculus problem set, but I put that aside for the moment. The important thing was to hang onto my place at Roehampton. Mother was entirely capable of saying simply that I wasn't playing tennis in London. That would be that. If she decided I shouldn't play at Roehampton, it would be hard, probably impossible, to change her mind. I doubted I could persuade Father to take my side on this.

But I had one major psychological advantage over Mother, which is that I was her only child. I have no idea why my parents didn't have more children; they certainly didn't seem to have the slightest difficulty having me, and they both loved children. But I was their only child, and that meant, in my experience, that neither of them could be angry or upset at me for long. I could tell Mother was at least a bit mollified by my apology.

So I went at Mother again. "I'll write Lady Thakeham tonight, and I promise you I'll make it right with her, and while I'm in London I'll behave so that she will be happy to have had me visit."

Mother said, "Fiona, will you write me tonight and tell me you've written Mark's mother?"

"Yes, Mother."

"And you'll apologize to her?"

"Yes, Mother, I will."

"And you'll tell her you'll withdraw from this tournament if it interferes in any way with your obligations to her family?"

"I will say that explicitly to her."

"Then please do so. And, Fiona, you really must talk with us before you decide on something like this."

"Yes, Mother, I will."

And so we told one another that we loved each other and said goodbye.

Roehampton and Lady Thakeham didn't turn out exactly the way I promised Mother they would.

September 2011
All England Club Wimbledon
London, England

When I told Claire I was going to write this story of my tennis career and how I met my husband, she wasn't enthusiastic. She and I are both old now – I'm in my late 60s, and Claire is almost 76. It had happened so long ago, why go back into all that? That was Claire's thinking.

Claire had published her own tennis autobiography soon after she first won Wimbledon in 1960. An autobiography was one of the few accepted ways for a successful amateur to make money from tennis. But Claire hadn't written a single word of that book – except for the preface. She wrote the preface herself.

Claire explained in the preface that, when she had told her husband, Richard, about her plan to include the louche details of her love affairs with men players when she was a single girl on the international tennis circuit, Richard objected. Then, Claire wrote, Richard engaged a young literary lady from a good English family to ghostwrite a proper tennis autobiography for Claire.

The ghostwriter, naturally, asked to interview Claire, and so Claire had invited her over to the flat. In her preface, Claire wrote: "She was an aspiring novelist; she was charming; she preferred Earl Grey tea; she knew nothing about tennis."

Claire's tennis autobiography had been a runaway best seller in England.

I was in London to give a paper at a pediatric medical conference, and I was staying with Claire and Richard. At breakfast, I asked Claire if she'd kept a copy of the telegram she had sent to the Committee about me in 1962.

"No, I didn't. I just scribbled something down on a Western Union message pad in the hotel in Boston that morning. I didn't think to keep a copy."

"You must remember what you said about me to the Committee."

"No, I don't. Anyway, it's a mistake, this idea of writing it all down."

I persisted. I had decided to write my story, and I was going to do it.

Finally, Claire said, " The All England Club hasn't thrown anything away, ever. So they'll have my telegram. Just speak with the Club's Secretary."

That morning I rang the Club. The Secretary said, "It's Doctor Hodgkin, isn't it?"

"Yes. I regret that you and I haven't been introduced. But if you please. There was a telegram in 1962, about me. If it still exists, may I see it?"

"A telegram?"

"To the Committee of Management," I said. "From Claire. I mean, from Mrs Richard Kershaw. About me."

The Secretary told me to come around to the Club, and he would meet me at Gate 5. We would see, he said, if the telegram could be found in the files.

I took the Tube to Southfields and walked under my umbrella in the rain down Church Road. I hadn't been to Wimbledon in many years, and all the new gates confused me. But surely the 'Gate 5' the Secretary directed me to must be the old South East Gate, the main entrance to the Club?

Good to his word, the Secretary was standing at the gate under an umbrella.

"Where are the Doherty Gates?" I asked.

"Oh, they're down at the south end of the ground now. Have been since 2006."

The Doherty Memorial Gates, made of black wrought iron, with the letters 'A.E.L.T.C.' in bright gold leaf, had stood at the South East Gate since 1931. They had been given to the Club by Rev. W. V. Doherty in memory of his brothers, Reggie and Laurie, who between them had won Wimbledon nine times – Laurie won five times in a row, 1902 to1906. The Committee approved the design of the Gates in October 1930, and they had been bolted to the masonry gateposts the next year.

"Why in heaven would the Doherty Gates be moved?"

"My dear Doctor Hodgkin, the lorries, of course."

"The lorries?"

"When Centre Court was rebuilt. For the new retractable roof. The construction lorries were too wide for the old gates."

"But no one ever goes to the south end of the ground! No one would see the gates."

"Oh, the Committee put quite a nice little plaque down there. In the wall beside them."

Once we were in his office, the Secretary summoned a young clerk. "Simon, we want a telegram from 1962, it will likely be on an old Post Office Telegram form, probably quite short, telegrams were expensive. From Mrs Richard Kershaw to the Committee."

I interjected. "She may have signed the telegram 'Claire Kershaw,' or even just 'Claire.'"

"Just so," the Secretary said. "Off you go, then, Simon."

The Secretary suggested that I wait in the members' buffet in the Millennium Building, on the other side of Centre Court, while Simon conducted his search.

In September, on a chilly, rainy London day, the buffet was as cold and closed as a tomb. The lone attendant gave me a cup of tea, and I took it out on the covered balcony, which had a view of the outer grass courts and, in the distance, on a hill, in the mist, the old spire of St. Mary's Church.

On a sunny day during the Championships, this balcony would be a splendid spot from which to see the milling crowds, the brilliant green grass, the tennis players fighting to stay in the draw, and the blooming hydrangea. Now, though, the nets were down, the umpires' chairs gone, the hydrangea pruned back to the old wood, and the only sign of life was a single groundskeeper wearing a yellow rain slicker who appeared to be merely looking forlornly down at the grass.

I stood there, lost in thought.

Simon, the young clerk, appeared after about an hour. He coughed, politely, to gain my attention. I turned around.

"Doctor, is this possibly the telegram for which you are looking?"

I went back inside the buffet and sat down at a table. The telegram was crinkled, and I held it down with my fingers spread to flatten it. The strips of type that had been pasted onto the form were peeling off.

Post Office Telegram

THE COMMITTEE
ALL ENGLAND LAWN TENNIS CLUB

DEAR DARLING BOYS STOP YESTERDAY EXHIBITION MATCH LONGWOOD BOSTON GRASS FIONA HODGKIN 18 YEARS BERMUDA AMATEUR SINGLES CHAMPION STOP COACH AMATEUR RACHEL OUTERBRIDGE 1939 SINGLES FINALIST STOP FH SWEET YOUNG BALL OF ENERGY STOP YOU MUST LIST FH FOR ROEHAMPTON STOP FH ADDRESS EMERSON HOUSE SMITH COLLEGE NORTHAMPTON MASS US STOP I PROMISE TO SLEEP WITH EACH OF YOU UPON RETURN ENGLAND STOP SEPARATELY OF COURSE STOP

The telegram was signed with a single word: CLAIRE.

I burst out laughing, which startled Simon. In 1962, the members of the Committee were all men, with an average age of probably 75. (The first woman on the Committee would be Virginia Wade, but that wouldn't happen until 1982.) In their dreams, the Committee members no doubt wished the beautiful Claire actually meant to sleep with them.

But they had obediently put me down for Roehampton.

In the rain, under my umbrella, I walked back to Gate 5. The young security guards at the gate wore bright orange jackets and had coiled wires from their radios running under their collars to earphones. They must have been told who I was or, more accurately, who I had been before they were born, because they quietly stepped aside as I approached.

I stood at the gate for a moment, looking across Church Road at the Wimbledon golf course.

Then, instead of turning left, back to Southfields, I turned right and walked toward to the point where Church Road met Somerset Road, at the south end of the Club's ground.

I wanted to say hello to my poor old friends, the Doherty Memorial Gates.

SATURDAY, 9 JUNE 1962
MIDPOINT
PAGET PARISH, BERMUDA

The day before my flight to London, Mother was helping me pack. We were going to have a family dinner that evening with my grandparents to say goodbye for a month.

While we were in my room, surrounded by piles of clothes, Mother said, "Fiona, during the season in London, many young people drink too much at the parties and do not conduct themselves well; in fact, quite badly sometimes. Drinking is a risk for girls – I mean drinking alcohol."

I was glad she had cleared that up for me.

"Your father and I are sending you off for the season because we can count on you to show good judgment and to conduct yourself well. Can we rely on you?"

"Yes, Mother." I predicted to myself what was coming next. Mark Thakeham. And I was right.

"I know you like Mark a great deal. And he seems to like you. Maybe over the next few years you'll have a friendship that's important to both of you. If that happens, all well and good. But Mark is four years older than you, and I'm confident he's sexually experienced. Perhaps quite so."

She was right about that, I thought.

The Tennis Player From Bermuda

"You, I take it, are not sexually experienced?"

"Uh, well, not very."

She sighed. "I meant my question to ask whether you've had sexual intercourse." She had been a physician for a long time and didn't shy away from biological facts.

"No."

Mother looked at me. "But something close to it, I think," she said.

I said nothing.

Mother arched her eyebrow. "Well?"

"Mark touched me once." I dreaded telling her what I was talking about, but to my surprise she seemed to know exactly what I meant.

"And that's all?"

"Mark said he would just touch me, nothing more. That's all he did."

"Well, good for you, Mark Thakeham," Mother said softly. She sounded a bit surprised at the show of at least partially responsible conduct from this quarter.

Then she asked, "Do you plan to sleep with him while you're in England?"

I hesitated. "I don't think so."

"Good. I don't want you to. Fiona, I know how tiresome it is at your age to have adults always saying that you're too young to do this or that, but here you really are too young. I want you to wait."

"I won't sleep with him while I'm in London."

"Good."

"But maybe someday?"

"Fiona, if in two or three years you decide this is what is right for you, and you protect yourself with a contraceptive, then go straight ahead. But when you decide to start, do it on your terms, not on Mark's terms, or on some other boy's terms. And not now."

"I promise that's what I'll do."

"Good. So I don't need to take you to the clinic in the morning and fit you with a diaphragm. Am I right about that?"

"I don't need a diaphragm," I almost whispered.

The idea of having Mother fit me with a diaphragm made the blood drain from my face. I knew about contraception because, a year or so earlier, while I was on a walk in Paget with American Grandmother, she had told me, in great and embarrassingly graphic detail, how to use a diaphragm. Then, having built up a full head of steam on the subject of human reproduction, American Grandmother had gone on to explain the biochemistry of the menstrual cycle.

It was extremely interesting, and when I had arrived at Smith I found, to my surprise, that I was far better informed that most of my classmates.

"And when the time comes," Mother said, "don't hesitate to ask me for help with a contraceptive. Or ask American Grandmother, if you feel more comfortable talking to her."

We both laughed; we knew that if I so much as said the word 'sex' to American Grandmother, she'd have me on her examining table within five minutes.

Mother said, "Now, which of these tennis dresses do you want to pack?"

"How old were you when you married?"

Mother did not like the implication behind this question in the slightest. "I was 27, almost 28, so nine years or so older than you are now. I was a medical doctor in practice. Your father was serving on a Royal Navy destroyer in the war, and I knew I would be lucky to see him again."

"Were you sexually experienced then?"

"That's an impudent question, and I shouldn't answer it. But I will. You've been honest with me, and so I should be honest with you. Yes, but only with your father. While I was in medical school, I decided it was time I should take him to bed."

Mother chuckled but almost just to herself. "When I did, I couldn't tell whether he was more surprised or thrilled."

She paused, probably thinking that she shouldn't make this sound to be so much fun. "But I protected myself. Contraceptives were difficult to obtain in the States, but I went to the Baltimore Birth Control Clinic, where there were five women physicians. One of them fitted me with a diaphragm. When I said I was a medical student at Hopkins, she told me to get to work in the clinic. This was the Depression; almost no one had money, but I replied, 'Oh, no, I can pay for the diaphragm; I don't need to work to pay the fee.' The doctor said, 'You don't understand. We need the help.' So I volunteered three evenings a week at the clinic."

"But how did you see Father? You were in the States, and Father was in medical school at Cambridge."

She smiled. "We found ways to meet twice a year or so. And for the two days we were together after our wedding, before his destroyer left Bermuda, I didn't use a contraceptive. I wanted to have his child, and I did."

She reached over, took my chin in her hand, and playfully waggled my head. "Obviously."

"Now," she said with relief, "back to packing."

Sunday, 10 June 1962
Coral Beach & Tennis Club
Paget Parish, Bermuda

My flight to London did not depart until the evening, so early the next morning I played a match against Mrs Martin and won in two sets.

Afterward, she sat down on a bench beside the court. She was thinking, with her head cocked to one side.

After a few moments, she told me to sit down. Then she said, almost in a whisper, "I didn't mean for Claire to arrange for you to play at Roehampton, not this year anyway. She's so headstrong. I wouldn't have written her about you if I'd thought she would do this. You should wait one or two years. Not now."

"Are they that much better than I am?"

"No. But most of them are older and more experienced. It will be different than anything you've done, and harder. Much harder."

"How old were you?"

We both knew that in June 1939 she had been my age now.

"Yes, but I had played in international competition before. I knew what it is like."

"I played Claire."

She shook her head. "In an exhibition, not competition."

"You think I can't win."

"No. I think you might win. But this year, when you're so young, winning will take so much it will change you. Maybe not for the better. Especially because you'll have to do it alone."

It dawned on me that she was thinking of herself. "Did that happen to you?"

She nodded.

I thought for a moment. "And maybe Claire as well?"

"Claire had a difficult time on the circuit. I wasn't there to help her. I couldn't leave my family."

"You can't imagine how much I want this."

"I know exactly how much you want it. But go to the parties for the London season, watch some matches at Roehampton and Wimbledon, come home to Bermuda, and then we'll prepare for next year. Now is too early."

"I have to do this."

"You'll be a long way from home. I won't be there to help you." Mrs Martin was speaking so softly I could barely hear her.

She straightened up. "I'll talk to your parents and suggest you take time off from college to play at Kooyong this winter. I might even be able to come with you. Then next year you'll have experience with international competition."

The odds that my parents would agree to my taking time off from Smith to play tennis in Australia were vanishingly small. I put both my hands around her left hand and held it.

"I have to do this now. I know I can win. I won't let anything happen to me."

She used my Christian name. "Fiona, I haven't prepared you for this. It's my fault. I know I'm difficult. I'm weak. I haven't helped you. Now you're going to play at Roehampton, and I haven't shown you what it's going to be like."

She began crying.

I put my arms around her; she was so important to me. "Rachel, that's nonsense. You've done everything for me. Look, I love tennis. This is what I want. And if I can get it, the only reason is you. Please stop crying, because if you don't stop, then I'll start crying."

She had her head on my shoulder. "I've been terrible for you. I haven't taught you anything you'll need."

"Rachel, stop. You've always told me that you can't show me what I need, that I have to find it by myself."

She nodded. Then she wiped her eyes with the back of her hand, stood, and walked to her bicycle. She lifted something wrapped in tissue out of the basket. She came back to me.

"I want you to have this." She held it out to me.

I took off the tissue. It was an old tennis sweater. A long time ago, it had been white, but now it had faded to beige. There were narrow navy and green borders at the neck and cuffs. The cuffs and the hem were coming a bit unraveled. Over the left breast was embroidered 'KOOYONG,' and just below that were crossed tennis rackets and 'EST. 1892.'

"Nell and Harry Hopman gave me this sweater. I wore it in my third set against Alice on Centre Court."

"Rachel, you shouldn't give this to me."

"It can be chilly in London in June. I'll feel better if I know you have something warm to wear."

"Claire is bound to see me wearing this. She might feel you could have given her your sweater."

"Claire will understand." Rachel paused. "She's probably known since she played you at Longwood."

I had no idea what Rachel meant.

I held the sweater to my chest. Rachel leaned over and kissed me on top of my head. "Good luck, Fiona."

She walked back to her bicycle and left me alone on the court. It happened to be the same court where I had served for her the first time, years before. I sat on the bench thinking for several minutes. Then I got up and bicycled home. Neither of my parents was there; we had called a taxi to Kindley Field for five o'clock. Now it wasn't even yet noon; I was all packed. I still had time.

First I put Rachel's sweater into one of my suitcases. Then I left Midpoint and walked down to the dock at Lower Ferry and waited for the ferry across the harbour to Hamilton.

Once I got off the ferry near Albuoys Point, I began looking in the shops on Front Street that catered to tourists and the passengers on ships calling at Hamilton. It took me 20 minutes or so to find what I wanted. In a small, dark shop, there was a bin of miniature cloth flags glued to short sticks of wood, a bit longer than a matchstick. I think these little flags were meant to be stuck in the tops of cakes for celebrations.

I was taking five tennis dresses to London; I bought five of the small flags. These flags had the Union Jack in one corner, with a coat of arms showing a shipwreck and a lion, all against a bright red field.

They were the flag of Bermuda.

On the ferry back to Lower Ferry, I stood at the railing

looking out at the blue water and the Bermuda fitted dinghies with their triangular sails racing across the Great Sound. I had lived almost my entire life beside this harbour. Now I was going to sew these flags onto my tennis dresses, just above my left breast. I was determined, one way or another, whatever it took, to win all three rounds at Roehampton – and qualify for the Wimbledon draw.

Whatever it took.

Part Two

LONDON

Monday, 11 June 1962
16 Hyde Park Gate
Kensington
London, England

When I came through the barriers after passport control and customs at Heathrow, I was clutching just my tennis rackets, a paperback copy of Vera Brittain's *Testament of Youth* I had read on the flight, and my pocketbook. I had checked as baggage everything else. I was groggy and rumpled after the bumpy 10 hour flight from Bermuda, which had been on a BOAC turboprop aircraft, not a jet. There had been a time when I thought I'd never see Mark again, but now he was standing right there, on the other side of the barricade. I didn't have to go to him; he jumped over the barricade and hugged me.

And then he kissed me.

Originally, the Thakeham family was Dutch and certainly not named 'Thakeham.' Mark's ancestor, Marcellus ter' Joopt, came to England with William of Orange at the time of the English Revolution in 1688. ter' Joopt amassed a large fortune after arriving in England – how exactly isn't known – and then retired to Hampshire with a young bride from an aristocratic English family.

ter' Joopt sensed that his Dutch name might not be ideal for an upwardly mobile family in England. He noticed that the house he had purchased in Hampshire, which was called 'Thakeham House,' had a perfectly good English name. And for good reason: the house had been built a 100 years before by one of Queen Elizabeth's courtiers.

So, one day, ter' Joopt simply changed his name to 'Thakeham,' and the next day, William made him the first Viscount Thakeham

Basically, my boyfriend had been named after a house.

For longer than a hundred years, the Thakeham family was content in Hampshire. Dutch thriftiness and industry ran in the family – the Thakehams conserved and increased their fortune. No drunken, gambling wastrels in this family. Mostly, the men were physicians.

In about 1830, the sixth Viscount Thakeham decided to build a fashionable London residence (though he retained Thakeham House). The Campden Charities were then attempting to develop Hyde Park Gate just south of Kensington Palace, and Viscount Thakeham bought a lot and built an unusual, red brick, L-shaped house that was now entirely overgrown with Boston ivy. The front door was an arched lattice of frosted glass and wood.

Hyde Park Gate is actually two streets, side by side, with the same name. The more famous street is to the east, with the house where Virginia Woolf was born, and the house where Winston Churchill died. Generations of London cabbies have called the other street, just to the west, the

'Frying Pan,' because it leads to a circular drive around a small sylvan park surrounded by a rustic wooden fence. The street looks like a frying pan.

The Frying Pan always has a London bobby casually standing at the entrance on Kensington Road, because several of the greatest families in England, including Mark's, make their London homes there.

It was to 16 Hyde Park Gate that Mark took me after I landed at Heathrow.

We were met at the door by a slender, middle-aged lady who said, "Miss Hodgkin. I've heard so much about you from Mark. I'm Myrtle Hanson. Mark, bring Miss Hodgkin's luggage upstairs. I'm putting her in the second rear bedroom."

The three of us climbed a magnificent curved staircase with a wrought-iron balustrade with the initial 'T' worked into the intricate design.

"Here you are," Miss Hanson said. "I thought you'd be comfortable here because this bedroom has its own bath and a nice view of the rear gardens."

We were in a large, airy room with two tall windows. Mark dropped two of my bags and went back downstairs for the third.

"When I first came through the front door, I thought you were Lady Thakeham."

Miss Hanson laughed but in a friendly way. "I was the nursery nurse for Mark from the time he was born and then the same for Catherine. Now I'm the housekeeper."

The Tennis Player From Bermuda

Mark returned with my third bag, dropped it, and dropped himself into a side chair in the bedroom.

Miss Hanson said, "Mark, your services are no longer required here. Miss Hodgkin has had a long flight and needs to rest before lunch."

He started to say something, but Miss Hanson cut him off. "Goodbye, Mark."

Mark gave me a rueful smile and left the room. I gathered Miss Hanson was more than a housekeeper.

Miss Hanson said, "Young Janet works for me, and she'll be here in a minute with a pot of tea for you. Then she'll unpack your bags and put away your clothes. You should wash your face and stretch out on the bed for some rest. Janet won't bother you. If you're tired, you may have lunch here in your room whenever you want, or Mark will be having lunch downstairs in an hour or so. Suit yourself."

She walked over to the side of the large bed and pointed to two small buttons on a brass plate set into the wall. The brass was highly polished.

"There used to be markings to show which button was which, but the markings wore away with the polishing before I got here."

I had the impression that, if Miss Hanson had been around then, the polishing would have been done more carefully.

She went on. "So, you just have to remember. The button on the left brings Janet until about nine o'clock in the evening. On Thursdays, her day off, it will be one of my other girls. The button on the right brings me, any time of day or night."

"I'm sure I won't call. I won't need anything."

"How old are you?"

"I'm 18. I'll be 19 on July 1."

Miss Hanson smiled. "You're a long way from your parents. Don't hesitate to call me." She left.

I learned later that, when Miss Hanson was 18, she had placed an advert in the magazine *The Lady*, seeking a position as a nursery nurse. She was engaged by Lady Thakeham, who was then expecting Mark. During the war, Miss Hanson worked in the dairy at Thakeham House, with Mark toddling along after her. Now, she managed both 16 Hyde Park Gate and Thakeham House, including the dairy, which, over the years, she had built into a large and profitable business for the family. Miss Hanson was regularly brought in by Doctor Thakeham to consult on the family's financial affairs – unlike Lady Thakeham, who was consulted only on the new wallpaper for the front hall.

Mark told me that once at Harrow he had been struggling a bit with mathematics, no doubt because of the competing demands of cricket. Miss Hanson taught herself basic calculus in a week and then began taking the Tube to the Harrow-on-the-Hill stop each weekday afternoon for a month. She would meet Mark in a tea shop, where she drilled him on equations for an hour. Mark no longer struggled in math.

I put my head on the pillow and was quickly asleep. I didn't even hear Janet unpacking my bags. I slept for two hours.

I met Lady Thakeham that afternoon at tea, which was in a long, narrow conservatory that extended out from the house into the rear garden. There were glass doors on each side that opened onto the garden. With the doors opened, I felt that we were practically outside, but with protection from the rain and the (occasional) sun.

Mark leaned over his mother and playfully kissed her on top of her exquisitely coiffed hair.

"Mark, please don't. You'll muss my hair."

Then she turned to me. "You must be Miss Hodgkin, child. Thomas Hodgkin's daughter. How kind of you to visit us from Bermuda." She said 'Bermuda' in the way that some people might say 'Antarctica.'

I was wary of her from the start. I said, "My parents and I appreciate your invitation to me."

"We are pleased to have you. And thank you for your kind letter to me about your plans for tennis."

Mark said, "Fiona's plans for tennis? We're going to Wimbledon for an afternoon the first week of the fortnight. Do we have tickets? Should I ring the Club?"

"Miss Hodgkin plans to play tennis for a day while she is with us. She wrote me a nice letter with all the details."

I hadn't written to Mark about Roehampton, mainly because he had been quite stingy in writing to me. So I had reciprocated. Now I thought that perhaps I should have prepared him in advance.

I hesitated. "Well, it may be for a day or possibly a few days."

Lady Thakeham, I sensed, knew that she had an opportunity to trap me, and she took it. "Miss Hodgkin, dear, where is it again you've been invited to play one afternoon?"

"The Bank of England Sports Grounds at Roehampton."

Mark was tucking into a crumpet when I said this, and he choked slightly. "Roehampton? You've been invited to play at Roehampton?"

Lady Thakeham smiled icily.

Mark managed to control his choking. "Fiona, did you say you're going to play at Roehampton?"

"Yes, I did."

"You mean the qualifying round for Wimbledon?"

"Yes."

"You're not serious," he said with a laugh.

"Mark," I said, maybe a little sharply, "I don't care for your tone. The Committee invited me to play at Roehampton. I wrote your mother about the invitation. I'm going to play the first round, and we'll see what we see."

"You could not possibly both compete at Roehampton and attend the season."

Lady Thakeham beamed.

"Claire Kershaw did."

"How do you know?"

"She told me."

"You know Kershaw?"

I was a mere colonial from Antarctica – excuse me, Bermuda – but I'd had enough. "Mark," I said stiffly, "I know Claire quite well." Perhaps this was stretching things a bit. "She was kind enough to find me a place in the qualifying round at Roehampton. I told Lady Thakeham in my letter that Roehampton would in no way interfere with my social obligations during the season. I was entirely sincere."

Again, stretching things a bit.

Mark was about to say something, but Lady Thakeham stopped him. "That's all settled, then," she said. "We should discuss our social obligations this week." She pulled open her datebook.

"Tomorrow, the Wilsons have invited Miss Hodgkin and

Catherine for tea" – the Wilsons were my cousins – "and that evening is the party for Marjorie Boynton at the Savoy. Wednesday, Catherine is giving a luncheon at Simpsons in the Strand for Miss Hodgkin, and then, my dear, that afternoon you have invited 12 young ladies here for tea. Don't be concerned, I've already arranged the details and sent invitations to your guests. That evening dinner is with the Ralstons, we'll return home to dress for the party for Alice Herbert, but I've promised Catherine that we will leave by one in the morning and have breakfast at the party for Harriet Rutherford – Lady Thornton asked Catherine if we could come. Thursday, lunch is at Claridge's with the Alstons, then tea with Mary Matthews, dinner with Lord Hawthorn at the Inner Temple, home to dress, then a dance at Grosvenor House for Hope McAllister. Friday, my dear, you and Catherine have invited 15 young ladies to an informal lunch here, then tea is with Anne Gofford and her parents. We're invited to dinner at White's by Lord Wilberforce, Princess Margaret will be there, so you'll want to dress especially well, and then there will be Mary Sanford's party, but we'll leave by midnight or so to have an early breakfast with Lady Crawford and her daughters."

I was stunned. Maybe Mark was onto something when he said I couldn't both attend the season and play at Roehampton. "Should I be writing this down?"

"No, dear child, there's no need. I will see that Harold takes you and Catherine to everything." I had no idea who 'Harold' might be. Lady Thakeham smiled, closed her datebook, excused herself, and swept from the room.

Mark was chuckling. "I told you."

"Maybe it's busy just this week."

"Next week is *worse*."

Miss Hanson came into the conservatory. "There is a telegram for Miss Hodgkin."

Mark looked at me quizzically. I opened the telegram:

POST OFFICE TELEGRAM

RECEIVED LONG LETTER RACHEL TELLING ME EXACTLY HOW TO PREPARE YOU FOR ROEHAMPTON STOP SHE APPEARS TO THINK I KNOW NOTHING ABOUT TENNIS STOP WE HAVE A LOT OF WORK TO DO STOP MEET ROEHAMPTON 11 TUESDAY MORNING STOP

CLAIRE

Mark held out his hand for the telegram. This was rude of him, but I obediently handed it over.

"So you do know Claire Kershaw. How does Kershaw come to know Rachel?"

"Rachel was her coach back in the late 1940s. They're friends."

Mark didn't say anything. He simply held the telegram in his fingers.

Finally, I said, "Mark, tomorrow I'll need to spend some time practicing with Claire."

Tuesday, 12 June 1962
Roehampton

"I can't be with you next week for the qualifying round," Claire said. "Eastbourne invited me to play there next week and sent along a nice packet for my expenses. So you'll be on your own."

We were standing in the Secretary's old, cluttered office in the clubhouse at Roehampton while credentials were checked, green eyeshades adjusted, papers stapled, applications stamped, notices issued, and procedures followed.

If Claire hadn't been with me, none of the Roehampton staff would have believed that I was actually on the Committee's list of players invited to compete in the qualifying round. But Claire navigated the system for me, and I finally received an impressive pass with the word PLAYER splashed across it in red ink. With this pass hanging around my neck, I could come and go at Roehampton as I pleased, get tea at no charge, and even try to schedule practice time on the courts.

Practice time wasn't a problem as long as I was with Claire. She politely asked the referee, Mr Soames, if she and I might have the use of a court for three hours or so. "Certainly, Mrs Kershaw. Which court would you prefer?" Two

Wimbledon singles championships carry definite privileges in the world of tennis.

When I first practiced with Claire, it was immediately apparent that she'd been coached by Rachel. Claire knocked up for 10 minutes and then threw her racket out onto the grass. "Rough or smooth?" she asked. Just like Rachel, she thought the best practice was to play a match.

On a changeover in our second set, I drank a cup of water with Claire beside me. She said quietly, "In my service game just now, at 30-15, just before I tossed the ball for my serve, you looked up at two people walking on the path from the clubhouse.

I couldn't recall. "Did I?"

"Yes. I won the point. And the game."

"Well, if I looked away, it was just a quick glance."

"You won't win, at least not at Roehampton, if you let your mind wander during a point, even for a half-second. Pull a curtain around the court in your mind so that it's just you and the other girl. If Rachel were here, you might glance at her, quickly, just for reassurance. But she won't be here. You'll be by yourself."

I was a bit shaken by Claire's lecture.

When we finally finished practicing, we walked back to the Roehampton clubhouse. Claire asked, "How's the season going? Found a potential husband yet?"

"My first party is tonight, but Lady Thakeham read me my schedule yesterday at tea, and I can't believe it. I don't have clothes for half the parties I'm attending this week, much less next week. How did you manage both the season and qualifying at Roehampton?"

Claire laughed. "It wasn't easy. But I had only my own

mother to deal with, and I didn't have a boyfriend. Well, maybe I did, but not someone I cared about. So it was easier for me. Are you buying new clothes?"

"Before I left home, Mother told me to go to shopping in London and buy an evening gown. I asked her for a budget, and she said, 'Use your judgment, but don't spend too much.' Which isn't helpful. How much does a gown cost?"

"Between £2 on Saturday morning in Portobello Road and £2,000 any day in New Bond Street. Somewhere in that range."

"That's about as helpful as what Mother told me. Where should I go to buy a gown?"

"Let's go shopping together, tomorrow. We'll practice early and then look for a gown. You should find one that will make people talk about you."

"I don't want people to talk about me."

"But that's the whole point of the season."

Wednesday, 13 June 1962
Teddy Tinling's Shop
Mayfair

"We'll start with Teddy," Claire said. "He doesn't design many evening gowns now, but let's see what he might have on offer for you."

"Who's Teddy?"

"Teddy Tinling. In the 1930s, a girl couldn't go to the season without at least a couple of Tinling gowns in her closet. After the war, Teddy mostly gave up on gowns because of the utility restrictions on clothes. He started designing tennis kit instead."

Claire was driving her white Alfa Romeo roadster with the hood down. She suddenly swerved to avoid hitting a young man who was crossing Ken High. Claire turned halfway around in the driver's seat and blew him a kiss as we roared down the busy street at about 120 kph.

"Maureen Connolly asked Teddy to make her wedding dress when she finally married Norman, and I did the same when I married Richard. But his main line now is tennis dresses."

She changed down to third gear as we whipped around the Wellington Arch and shot into Piccadilly. Claire's favorite speed in the Alfa was as fast as it could go.

I was desperately hanging onto a leather strap on the door. "Who in heaven taught you to drive? Or did you just teach yourself?"

"My brother taught me. He taught himself. He bumped into a few things at first, but then he got the hang of it. Now he races autos in his spare time."

Just off Berkeley Square in Mayfair, she found a tiny parking spot and wedged in the Alfa. Then she led me to a narrow townhouse, where she didn't bother knocking on the door. She walked in and called, "Teddy, it's me."

I gathered from this entrance that Claire was well known in the Tinling establishment.

From the back of the shop stepped the tallest person I'd ever seen. I guessed he was in his early 50s. His head was shaved entirely bald, and he was wearing a yellow shirt with an open collar, trousers with vertical mauve and white stripes, and white patent leather shoes. The effect was dizzying.

He and Claire embraced and kissed one another. He said, "Claire, *ma chérie*, you remind me so much of Suzanne. We should take *Le Train Bleu* to Cannes tonight. Together. Alone. The two of us."

Claire linked her arm with his. "I don't remind you of Suzanne in the slightest, but Cannes might be interesting. After Wimbledon perhaps. Now I need you to find a gown for my friend from Bermuda."

"Suzanne?" I asked, brightly.

Tinling glanced at Claire with one eyebrow raised.

Claire said, "My friend is young. But nice. Once you get to know her."

Tinling was skeptical.

"Teddy, please meet Miss Fiona Hodgkin. She's going to

play at Roehampton. You remember Rachel Outerbridge, Teddy."

Tinling nodded.

"Rachel coaches this girl."

This, I could tell, moved me up several notches in Tinling's estimation.

Claire turned to me. "Fiona, this is Lieutenant-Colonel Cuthbert Collingwood Tinling. Known to his friends, with one exception, as 'Teddy.'"

Teddy bowed slightly to me.

"The exception," Claire said dryly, "is Bud Collins, who calls Teddy 'The Leaning Tower of Pizazz.'"

I held out my hand to Teddy, but instead of shaking hands, he leaned forward and kissed my hand. "My dear Fiona, how delightful to meet you," he murmured.

Claire pointed to an old photo that hung on the wall. "Teddy is taller than even Bill Tilden was, and he's got a photo to prove it."

The photo showed a young Teddy, with a full head of slicked-down hair, beside Bill Tilden, who was wearing a trench coat and holding two rackets. Teddy was slightly the taller of the two.

"The verdict," Teddy said, "Tilden 1.8 meters; Tinling 1.9 meters. Actually, I think the measurement of me was wrong. I'm two meters. Claire, I must show you what I've made for Maria Bueno."

With a flourish, Teddy picked up from a cutting table a white tennis dress. The skirt had a pink lining so bright anyone who saw it would feel faint.

"I call this 'Italian Pink,'" Teddy said.

"Teddy, Maria's dress is lovely, but have you lost your

mind? If that dress makes an appearance on Centre Court, the Committee will have your head mounted on the Doherty Gates, as a warning to others."

"You've yet to see the matching panties."

"Don't show them to me. I want to be able to tell the Committee truthfully that I knew nothing about the panties."

"There's nothing in the rules or on the entry form that prohibits colour on ladies' tennis dresses."

"What about the sign in the ladies' upper dressing room?"

"It's gone. I took it down last week." He fished around in the fabric scraps on the table and finally held up a small, faded handwritten sign: *'Competitors are Expected to Wear White Clothing.'*

I asked, "How could you take down a sign that was in a ladies' dressing room?"

Claire explained. "Kay Menzies always wore Teddy's dresses, but one afternoon she couldn't get her zipper up. Mrs Ward tried but couldn't get it up either."

"Who's Mrs Ward?"

Teddy said, "She's the attendant for the upper dressing room. Been there since Worple Road, probably."

"So Teddy was in the hallway, banging on the door and yelling for Kay to get onto Centre Court. Finally, Teddy barges through the door, gets Kay's zipper up in one second, and hustles her out to the waiting room."

I looked at Teddy in shock. "You went into the ladies' dressing room?"

Teddy made an elaborate courtier's bow, with his incredibly long arms outstretched.

Claire said, "Maybe a couple of girls had to wrap towels around themselves. But the world didn't come to an end.

Since then, Teddy comes and goes as he pleases. He doesn't even knock. He makes all the tennis kit, so it's convenient to have him around."

I picked up the handwritten sign that Teddy had taken from the dressing room. "Why was there a sign like this in the first place?"

It must be hard to look sheepish when you're two meters tall, but Teddy did.

Claire said, "The sign was thumbtacked to the wall in 1949. Just before *l'affaire* Gussy Moran."

"But it had nothing to do with Gussy," Teddy objected.

"I know. It was the pink and blue hems you sewed on the dresses for Joy Gannon and Betty Hilton in '48."

Claire turned to me. "The Committee think they've fixed the 'Tinling Problem' with the sign in the dressing room when BOOM!" Claire flung her hands out to mimic an explosion. "Gussy Moran appears at Hurlingham the day before Wimbledon wearing panties on which Teddy had sewn lace around the bottom."

"Did anyone notice?" I asked.

They both looked at me as though I had just arrived from Mars.

"Everyone noticed," Claire said. "Including the photographers from *Life* magazine, who were all on their stomachs trying to get photos of the panties. The newspapers issued special editions on sightings of the lace panties. Teddy, what was it Louis Greig said about all this?"

"Sir Louis told the newspapers, 'Wimbledon needs no panties for its popularity.'"

"Sir Louis?" I asked.

"At the time," Teddy said, "Sir Louis was the Chairman

of the All England Club. I regret to say he has since gone to his reward in heaven, where I have it on good authority all white attire is required."

Minutes later, I found myself in only my knickers, standing in the middle of the room. I had my arms wrapped resolutely around my small bust. Teddy, Claire, and Mrs Hogan, Teddy's long time assistant, were unconcerned by my obvious embarrassment at being practically naked in front of them.

Teddy gave Claire a look that I could tell meant, 'Where did you find this girl?'

"Fiona," Claire said. "Please. Drop your arms. Teddy needs to fit a gown for you. In the unlikely event Teddy is overcome by lust, Mrs Hogan and I will protect you."

Reluctantly, I dropped my arms, and the three of them regarded my boyish figure.

Teddy said, "This young lady needs a gown cut with considerable décolletage."

Claire, who is well endowed in the bust department, was dubious. "Teddy, are you sure? Fiona doesn't have much décolletage to work with."

"Perhaps, but this girl reminds me of what Billy Wilder – Claire, you know, the movie director – said about Audrey Hepburn when he first met her."

"What was that?"

"'This girl, singlehanded, may make bosoms a thing of the past.'"

All three of them chuckled. I snapped my arms back around my chest.

At Teddy's direction, Mrs Hogan disappeared into the back of the shop and returned with a black, strapless, floor-length gown, which the three of them pulled over my head. Teddy and Mrs Hogan began sticking pins into the gown and occasionally, by accident, into me, while they fitted the gown.

They led me over to a floor length mirror. The gown was about five times more sophisticated and revealing than any dress I'd ever worn, and about 10 times more expensive. If the goal was to make people talk about me, this gown would make that happen. I instantly loved the gown.

After I wrote Teddy a bank draft on Butterfield's for an outrageous amount of money, Claire drove me back to Hyde Park Gate.

"You and Teddy were talking about Suzanne. Does she work for Teddy?"

Claire made a racing change and swung into Kensington Road. "Teddy meant Suzanne Lenglen. She won Wimbledon six times. Five times in a row, 1919 to 1923. She had jaundice in 1924, but she won again in 1925."

Claire narrowly missed swiping a bus.

"In 1919, Suzanne appeared on the old Centre Court on Worple Road in a short dress – and get this! – no corset."

"Well," I said, "she certainly couldn't play tennis wearing a corset."

"Think again. Suzanne was the first girl to play on Centre Court without wearing a corset. It was so shocking and immoral that everyone had to come watch her!" Claire laughed. "The Committee were scandalized, but they decided to build a bigger Centre Court on Church Road so more paying spectators could come see Suzanne."

Claire slowed slightly so I could wave to the bobby at the entrance to Hyde Park Gate to let him know I belonged there. "Bunny Ryan was Suzanne's doubles partner. They won the last match ever played on the old Centre Court. The BBC interviewed Bunny a month or so ago, and Bunny said every English tennis girl should kneel down and thank Suzanne for getting rid of corsets!"

"Did Teddy know Suzanne?"

Claire started to say something but then stopped. I wasn't a member of the informal Wimbledon family. Maybe I would be in a few years but not now. Not yet.

"Yes, Teddy knew Suzanne. Quite well."

That night, Harold drove Mark and me back from Miss Rutherford's breakfast after two in the morning. My Tinling gown wouldn't be ready for several days, but in any event I had half decided to save it for Catherine's party, which would be the Wednesday during the first week of Wimbledon. So I wore a party dress that dated from my days as a Bermuda teenage schoolgirl.

Until that evening, I had no idea that my parents were well known, and well liked, in London. Several couples I met said, "You're the daughter of Fiona and Tom, aren't you? It's wonderful to have you in London. You must come for tea next Tuesday." And they seemed sincere. Mark and I danced together, and I was quite aware that there were many girls watching who were envious of me.

Still, even at two in the morning, Mark felt that we had left breakfast a bit early, and I had been the one to suggest we say our goodbyes. I was tired. Mark was in the middle of a hospital rotation in London, but in those days medical school rotations, at least in England, and especially during the season, were relaxed affairs, not at all the frenetic, 18-hour-a-day marathons that they became just in time for me to start my own medical rotations.

If it didn't rain, I was meeting Claire at Roehampton to practice at 11 the next morning, or rather *that* morning, and I wanted to go straight to sleep. I had learned that practice with Claire was so exhausting that it made practice with Rachel seem like time spent reading a mystery novel at the beach. Claire was *serious*.

But I sensed my boyfriend was unhappy with me, and so I sat him down on a sofa in Dr. Thakeham's study and gave him the type of kiss that I hoped would make him feel better. It did, but it also made him feel that the idea of me going straight to sleep was premature.

"We should spend some time alone," Mark said. It was true that, since I had arrived, most of my time had been spent on tennis, and when Mark and I were together, we had been in the company of other people.

"Yes, definitely," I said. "But not tonight. I'm tired, and I'm meeting Claire at Roehampton in the morning."

"Fiona, is this friendship you have with Kershaw a bit too much of a good thing, do you think?"

I was taken aback by this. I had known Claire only a short time – two months, perhaps. She was older than me by almost eight years. I didn't think of her as my 'friend.' I was thrilled even to know her. I hadn't thought of it before Mark asked, but I suppose I had assumed that Claire was looking after me merely because Rachel had asked her to do so.

"I can't imagine that it's too much of a good thing. Claire's been very helpful to me. Rachel thinks highly of Claire."

Mark was astute enough to know that Rachel's endorsement was, for me, the final word on the subject.

"It just seems that tennis and Claire Kershaw have taken over your visit to London."

He was right about that. I leaned over and gave him another kiss. "Mark, my tennis this year is just a trial run. Some day, I hope to play at Wimbledon – and I hope you'll be there to watch. Let me have some fun at tennis this year, and I promise I'll be a good girlfriend for you."

He kissed me and put his hand on my breast.

I laughed and kissed him back. "Within reasonable limits."

"Fiona, everyone here is sound asleep. Let's go upstairs to my room, or the room you're staying in, and make love."

"Mark, I'm only 18 – "

"Almost 19," he said.

"Almost 19," I agreed.

"Fiona, I will take good care of you. I promise," Mark said.

"Mark, I know you would take care of me, but making love would be a big step, and I'm not ready to take it. At least, not tonight."

To give the devil his due, Mark took this in good spirit. He stood up and held out his hands. I put my hands in his, and he pulled me gently up from the sofa. I was so tired that I appreciated his help. And we went off to bed – separately.

In retrospect, I know I wasn't fair to Mark. I should have been straightforward with him, but I wasn't. I should have said, 'Look, Mark, I'm going to qualify for Wimbledon this week. I don't care what it takes – season or no season. Whatever it takes. Incidentally, I promised Mother I wouldn't sleep with you while I'm in London.'

The question in my mind now is, if I had been straightforward, and I had told Mark exactly the truth, would my life have turned out any differently?

MONDAY, 18 JUNE 1962
FIRST ROUND LADIES' QUALIFYING MATCH
ROEHAMPTON

For all my bold talk to myself about getting through the qualifying rounds, on the first morning of Roehampton, I was nervous and uncertain. My first match was scheduled for noon, but I learned that, at Roehampton, with so many matches to complete in only four days, and with London's usual rainy June weather – well, the 'schedule' was just a guess at which matches would be played, on which court, and when.

So, after delays, and rain, and mix-ups about courts, my first match in international competition started, not at noon, but after six that evening on a grass court that even the chair umpire said, charitably, was "damp."

Mark was at Roehampton to encourage me, but I knew that evening was a party at White's for his cousin, Jennifer Pemberton. I didn't have to be told that, for Mark, this was a party at which he absolutely had to appear. If my first round match finished in an hour, we could get to Hyde Park Gate, dress, and still arrive at Jennifer's party fashionably late.

My first round opponent was a Polish girl, Anastazja Banaszynski. In the dressing room, for six long hours, she tried to be friendly to me, but she spoke little English, and my Polish was non-existent. But I admired her. I kept thinking, 'How much courage must it take to come to England, without speaking the language well, I'm sure with almost no money, and from a Communist country, to play in the qualifying round?'

Anastazja had qualified for Wimbledon the year before at Roehampton, and I'm sure she was disappointed to have to try and qualify again. She had lost in the first round of Wimbledon in 1961. If she had been trounced by Claire on Ladies' Day on Centre Court, that would have been one thing. (Claire, in fact, had never played her.) But Anastazja had lost, in straight sets, on one of the outer courts to another unknown player.

The Committee had not invited her into the draw for 1962, but they had offered her another chance to qualify at Roehampton. Now I watched her in the dressing room. She weighed at least half again as much as me, and she was far stronger. But I guessed – correctly, as it turned out – that she could not match me in speed. I expected she could hit the ball incredibly hard, but, if I could get it back, and away from her, she wouldn't be dashing around the court and hitting a return. The court, though, with the weather we'd had that day, would be slippery – not good for me.

You cannot imagine the relief associated with the call at long, long last: "Miss Banaszynski, Miss Hodgkin, you're wanted on court, please." We walked together past the long line of 12 grass courts; we were to play on the far court. We knocked up, and then I tossed my racket down on the grass. Anastazja called 'rough' and won. She didn't know the difference in English between 'rough' and 'smooth,' but she had memorized the word 'rough.' When she called the toss in England, she always called 'rough.'

Anastazja served first. It went straight past me; her serve was unbelievably fast. I crossed to my ad court and set up again to receive. She served. I got my racket on it but just barely. The ball hit the rim of my racket and went wildly wide into the next court, where it disrupted play and forced the women there to play a let – in a match that, I'm sure, meant everything to each of them. This was the lowest form of poor play; I knew everyone was looking at me and thinking, 'What's this teenager from nowhere doing at Roehampton?' I went back to the deuce court. I was asking myself whether I should be at Roehampton.

Anastazja won the first game at love. I couldn't remember the last time I had lost a game at love. Then I served for the first time. Anastazja had a problem with my serve as well; she couldn't tell where I was going to place it, and even when she was able to return my serve, I was already at the net to cut off her return. She wasn't fast enough to get to my volley, most times.

With the games in the first set at 8-9, on my serve, the rain started. It was already close to eight o'clock. "Play is suspended," the umpire called while he was heaving his considerable bulk out of the chair. The courts at Roehampton had no tarps to cover them. The rain fell straight onto the grass. I rushed for cover and found Mark. He kissed me in front of half the tennis world – and I kissed him back.

At least I had a boyfriend.

Anastazja had seen me kiss Mark. Once we were in the dressing room, and drying off, she said, "You – " Then she stopped, trying to think of the English word. She pointed to the door of the dressing room.

"You mean my boyfriend?"

She smiled. "Yes. Boyfriend. He – " She stopped. She couldn't think of the word, but she made an 'OK' sign by touching her right thumb to the tip of her index finger.

I tried to think what she meant. "Good? Good looking?"

"Yes! Boyfriend good looking."

I laughed and put my arms around her. For the next hour, we did our best to talk to one another, and, despite our language difficulties, we became friends. Then Mr Soames knocked on the dressing room door. "We're resuming play, girls. Five minutes."

When I walked back out onto the court, I couldn't believe he had decided to resume play. The rain had stopped, but the grass was soaked. Maybe 20 minutes of daylight remained. At the rate Anastazja and I were going, we wouldn't even finish the first set before dark. To cap things off, the temperature had dropped. It was chilly, and I reached in my kit, took out Rachel's sweater, and pulled it over my head.

The umpire called out, "First set. Miss Hodgkin to serve. The games are 8-9. The score is 15 all. Resume play."

So there was nothing for it but to set up and serve.

A few minutes later, Anastazja had taken the first set and had broken my serve in the second set. I had fallen to pieces. I was saved only by the umpire, who, finally, suspended play for darkness. I thought it was easily five minutes past the time the daylight had become too weak to permit play to continue. Then the rain started again.

I picked up my kit, my rackets, and my pocketbook and shuffled toward the clubhouse. Once inside, I stood off to the side, shivering. I did not feel well. Rachel's sweater was cotton, and now that it was damp, it did little to keep me warm.

I missed Claire, I missed Rachel, I missed Bermuda, and above all, I missed my parents. Mark was nowhere to be seen. What in heaven was I doing here?

Mr Soames was standing, holding a clipboard, in the middle of a clump of players, each of whom wanted to know when her match would resume on Tuesday? On which court? Would there be practice time Tuesday morning? He was unperturbed, and I had the impression that this wasn't the first time he'd faced a group of anxious tennis players.

Once the crowd dispersed, Mr Soames turned in my direction and walked over to me. "It's Fiona Hodgkin, isn't it? Are you all right?"

I tried to stop shivering but couldn't. "I'm fine." I was nearly in tears, and I must have looked like a drowned mouse.

Mr Soames glanced at his clipboard. "You're from Bermuda. Where are you staying in London?"

"In Hyde Park Gate. With friends of my family."

"How are you getting to their home tonight?"

"The Upper Richmond bus to East Putney and then the Tube."

It was a walk of a kilometer up Priory Lane to Upper Richmond Street, in the rain.

Mr Soames called, "Mr Raymond!"

One of the tournament stewards appeared at Mr Soames' elbow.

"Mr Raymond, this is Miss Hodgkin. Please arrange for her to be driven to Hyde Park Gate, now."

"Yes, sir," the steward replied.

"Miss Hodgkin, Mr Raymond will arrange for you to be collected by auto in the morning. We'll need you here by noon, so perhaps the auto should come for you by 11."

I thanked him – gratefully – and walked away with Mr Raymond.

I let myself into 16 Hyde Park Gate, walked into the study, and flopped down in an armchair. I leaned forward and put my head in my hands.

There was no way I could defeat Anastazja.

Harold had heard the door open, and he came into the study. "Miss Hodgkin, young Mark apologizes to you, but he has already left for Miss Pemberton's party. He asked that I drive you to White's as soon as you dress."

"Harold, I'm not feeling well."

"Doctor Thakeham is at Miss Pemberton's party – should I call him home to see you?"

"Harold, thank you. There's no need to bother Doctor Thakeham."

"May I make you a cup of tea?"

"Yes please. That would be kind of you."

Harold left the study. I started sobbing.

The Thakehams had only a single telephone, which was in the first floor pantry. I heard the telephone ring in the distance.

Harold returned. "Miss, the telephone rang for you."

I walked back to the pantry, still crying, and picked up the receiver.

"What happened today?" It was Claire, who didn't bother with saying hello. "The BBC said you're down a set."

"I can't win." I bit my lower lip in an effort to stop crying.

"Complete twaddle. Pull yourself together. Certainly you can win, and you will. Did you play any of the second set? The BBC didn't say."

"Yes. She broke me. Then play was suspended."

I sensed that even Claire was concerned by this news. But

she said, "Don't worry about it. Eat something and then go to bed. Then get the break back tomorrow and win."

"Harold says I'm supposed to go to a party."

"Who is Harold? Don't tell me you've met *another* boy."

"Harold is – " I hesitated. It dawned on me that I had no idea what Harold's position was in the Thakeham household.

Harold had come into the pantry with my cup of tea and overheard me. "I'm Doctor Thakeham's gentleman."

"Harold is Doctor Thakeham's gentleman," I told Claire.

"Fiona, you're at Roehampton, damn it, you're not a character in a P.G. Wodehouse novel. You're not going to a party tonight. Hit the ball where she isn't. Just do that 30 times, and you've won. A break is nothing. Play your own game, and she can't beat you."

I felt better after talking with Claire.

Harold's response to any problem, including a weeping female houseguest, was to call for Miss Hanson. She appeared, wearing a worn, blue bathrobe. Miss Hanson took one look at me and turned to Harold. "Miss Hodgkin is not going out tonight, Harold. You may as well go to White's now and wait there for Doctor and Lady Thakeham."

Miss Hanson took me by the hand and led me into the kitchen, where I'd never been. "Sit down at table. I'll make you a sandwich, and then I'll draw your bath. I want you asleep in your bed in half an hour."

TUESDAY, 19 JUNE 1962
FIRST ROUND LADIES' QUALIFYING MATCH
ROEHAMPTON

I was alone at breakfast Tuesday morning. Mark either was still asleep or else he had already left for hospital. In any event, he didn't appear at breakfast. A young lady served me tea, toast, and a boiled egg, and Harold brought me the morning papers. At exactly 11, an auto from Roehampton was in front of 16 Hyde Park Gate.

The weather on Tuesday was still overcast, but it wasn't raining, and it didn't seem as though rain was imminent. It was warmer. Rachel's sweater stayed in my kit. When Anastazja and I knocked up at noon, the grass was nearly dry and less slippery than the evening before.

The umpire called the score: "The sets are 1-love in favor of Miss Banaszynski. Second set. Miss Banaszynski to serve. The games are 2-love. Play."

It wasn't even close. My volleys began to click, and Anastazja couldn't reach them; I just volleyed to where she wasn't. I took her break back early in the second set and then I broke her again. I won the second set easily. In the third set, Anastazja faded. I started taking even more chances at the net, and most of the time my gambles paid off.

There was no room between the courts for spectators, and there were hedges behind the fences at either end of the court. The only place for spectators was a grassy bank at the other end of the row of courts, closer to the clubhouse. I doubt anyone other than the umpire could see my match with Anastazja.

I took the third set. The umpire called, "8-10, 6-4, 6-3, Miss Hodgkin wins game, set, and match."

Anastazja was already at the net when I ran forward. I extended my hand but then saw she was on the verge of tears. I leaned over the net and hugged her. She put her head on my shoulder and began to sob.

I returned to Hyde Park Gate in time for tea, which was attended by 20 or so young ladies. The only ones I had met before were Catherine and two of my cousins on the Spencer side of my family. Several of the guests distinctly reminded me of Madeline Bassett, a humorous character in the P.G. Wodehouse 'Jeeves' novels.

I was in the second round at Roehampton.

Tuesday evening, 19 June 1962
Elizabeth Spencer's Party
Brown's Hotel

Harold drove Mark and me to Brown's in the Bentley. Catherine and Lady Thakeham were going to another party, and Harold would return to Hyde Park Gate to collect them after he left us at Brown's. Mark was polite but distant.

I was thinking only of my second round match. When we had left home, the BBC was reporting that the two girls in my bracket were still battling it out on a court at Roehampton, even though it was almost dark. I would play the winner in the second round. Defeating Anastazja had given me a much-needed boost of confidence, but still I was so nervous about the second round that I was almost wringing my hands.

I knew how Claire would deal with the uncertainty. She would ignore it. 'There's nothing for you to do about it,' Claire would say. 'So why worry?' I tried not to worry but couldn't help it.

As Harold pulled the Bentley to a stop at Brown's, I worked at pulling myself together for my cousin's party. My dress was a long, pale green gown that had last seen service at a dinner dance at the Mid-Ocean Club years ago. I was certain Mother would receive letters from my relatives giving detailed, and critical, accounts of my dress and, most important, whether I had been seen talking with – or, better yet, dancing with – any good husband candidates. Harold came back and opened the door on my side, and I stepped out. Mark was already out of the Bentley, and he took my arm.

Mark was wearing white tie, and he looked dashing. We swept into Brown's side by side.

I was getting used to the routine of a party during the season. First, there were cocktails, conversation, and paying respects to the hosts. Then dancing. Finally, breakfast, always well past midnight. After breakfast, many of the young people would pile into autos and go off to a nightclub or café to finish the evening.

This schedule was a contrast with Bermuda, where the island is usually closed, locked, and asleep by 11 o'clock at the latest – *maybe* midnight during Cup Match, the two-day cricket meet each July between Somerset Parish and St. George's Parish, which originated as a celebration of the abolition of slavery in Bermuda. During Cup Match, everyone wears the colours of one team or the other – red and navy for Somerset, pale blue and dark blue for St. George's – and gambles at Crown & Anchor, while the entire island throws a huge party.

I had been surprised that Mark did not know as many of the guests at the parties we had attended together as I had expected.

"Not my crowd, now," he said. "Too young. My friends are going down from university and beginning to find places in the City or the FO" – he meant the Foreign Office – "or somewhere else in Whitehall. Most of them have already found the girl they want. No reason for them to attend the season."

"So why haven't you found the girl you want?" I couldn't help asking.

He didn't rise to the bait. "Medicine. I'm still in university." The medical course of study at Cambridge was five years; Mark had one more year to complete before he began his internship.

"But," he went on, "there are the nurses."

I rolled my eyes. "I hope you're trying to be humorous and simply failing."

"Not at all. The nurses are wonderful people."

"I'm sure you've made the acquaintance of many of them."

We made our way to our hosts. When I had been 12 or so, my parents and I had spent a long weekend with the Spencers at their house in Devon. The house was so large that I had been given my own room – during the English Civil War, a small army of Cavaliers had been quartered in this house, apparently quite comfortably – but after Elizabeth and I had played in the garden for two hours on Friday afternoon, we had decided to move me into her bedroom. Together we had a delightful weekend, of the flashlights-under-the-covers variety. I hadn't seen Elizabeth again until I arrived in London for the season, but we had exchanged Christmas cards for years, and we liked one another.

I said hello to Elizabeth's parents – I couldn't begin to explain how we were related, except that it was through English Grandmother – and they asked after my parents. I introduced Mark, and I could tell my relatives were impressed that a young colonial – me – had snared such a prize.

Later, after the dancing started, I lost track of Mark for a few minutes, but I saw Elizabeth talking with a young lady, a bit older than us. She was an exotic creature, in a stunning gown, with a figure that made me feel as though I was a Boy Scout. Her hair was dark, and swept up, and her eyes were a shade of green I don't think I'd ever seen before. I went over to Elizabeth, who introduced us. Her name was Margarite. She was Spanish, but her English was fluent, with only a slight accent.

Elizabeth was called away by her mother, and Margarite turned to me. "I see you are escorted by Mark."

"Mark Thakeham, yes," I said. "You must know Mark?"

"We know one another at university."

"You were at Cambridge, then?"

"I am at Cambridge. I went down last year, but now I'm a fellow at Trinity."

Even I knew that going straight from being an undergraduate to a fellowship at Trinity College wasn't something that happened every day, or even every decade.

"Are you in medicine? Is that how you know Mark?"

Margarite smiled. "No, I'm not in medicine. I could never stand the messy parts. I'm in mathematics."

The only other mathematics fellow of Trinity I could recall was Isaac Newton. Good thing I hadn't mentioned to Margarite how relieved I was to be finished with freshman calculus at Smith.

Now Mark reappeared at my side. Neither he nor Margarite said hello to one another. Instead, Mark put his hands on her shoulders, and they kissed one another on both cheeks. She murmured something into his ear, and Mark chuckled. I imagined that she had told him something about me, probably something witty, in a Cantabrigian way.

It dawned on me that Margarite and Mark had been lovers – perhaps, for all I knew, they still were.

Mark asked me, "Have you been introduced?"

"Yes. Elizabeth introduced me to Margarite."

Margarite said, "You two should be dancing."

"No," I said. I had the sense that Margarite did not have an escort for the evening. "Mark, you should dance with Margarite."

Mark did not require further encouragement. He took Margarite's arm and led her onto the dance floor. Before I could ask myself whether it had been a good idea to push them into dancing with one another, a young man I didn't know approached me and, after the usual nonsense about not having been properly introduced, asked me to dance – and he turned out to be quite an accomplished dancing partner.

Suddenly, it was one o'clock in the morning, and I needed to get to sleep, even though breakfast wouldn't be served for another hour or so. I found Mark and suggested we say our goodbyes.

"We really should stay for breakfast."

"I need to get some sleep, in case I get to play my second round tomorrow."

He wasn't pleased by this, I could tell. I said, "Mark, would it be rude for me to take a taxi home? Then you could stay for a bit longer, and we could see one another in the morning." To coat this pill, I gave him a kiss.

"You don't need a taxi. I'm sure Harold is waiting for us. He'll take you home, and I'll find my own way." Mark, I thought, had agreed to the idea of my leaving on my own more readily than I had expected.

So Mark walked me out of Brown's and, as predicted, Harold was waiting at the curb with the Bentley. Mark kissed me, turned around, and headed back to Elizabeth's party. I got in the Bentley, and Harold pulled away into the London traffic.

"Harold, did you by any – " I started but then stopped. I shouldn't give the Thakeham household even more reason to think my only concern was Roehampton.

"Yes, Miss, I did," Harold said. "Those two girls finished their match this evening in three sets. Your opponent will be the American. I think her family name is Johnson."

Wednesday, 20 June 1962
Roehampton – In the Rain

On Wednesday, it poured rain all day, relentlessly, across London. Not a single tennis ball was hit at Roehampton. I spent most of the day in the dressing room, which was crowded with girls. We had to be there in case the rain stopped and, somehow, the courts dried quickly enough for matches to begin. I tried not to be too obvious in looking around for my opponent, but finally one of the other girls said to me, "If you're looking for Charlotte Johnson, don't bother. She'll not be here."

"But we all have to be here."

The girl shrugged. "Johnson's parents have taken a flat in Fulham, close by. They've employed a former Roehampton steward to alert them by telephone if she's going to be called. Johnson can be here in 10 minutes. That way she doesn't have to wait in the dressing room for her match."

"Have you played Johnson?"

"Once, outside San Francisco, a year or so ago. I won in straight sets. But Charlotte's strong and, I think, getting better. Her coach is Teach Tennant."

"Tennant must be quite elderly."

"I suppose. But all the American girls, at least the ones from California, seem to want her as a coach."

At four o'clock that afternoon, I went to find Mr Soames, the referee.

"Mr Soames, I have a family tea at five. If it appears we're not going to play any matches today, might I be released?"

"I was just about to release everyone. Even if it stopped raining now – which seems unlikely – the grass wouldn't be sufficiently dry for any play this evening. Certainly, Miss Hodgkin, leave for your family tea."

I thanked him and walked back toward the dressing room. Then he called to me, "Miss Hodgkin!"

"Yes, Mr Soames?"

He was looking at his clipboard intently. "We may have drier weather tomorrow, Miss Hodgkin. If so, I'll have you and Miss Johnson out first. So please plan to be here well before 11 in the morning."

"I'll be here."

"If you win your second round, Miss Hodgkin, and if the weather holds dry, I'll have to set your third round for tomorrow afternoon. I'll try to give you a couple of hours rest, but I can't promise it."

"I'll be ready."

"You've attracted the Committee's attention, Miss Hodgkin."

I was startled to hear this. "Have I done something wrong?"

"The contrary, Miss Hodgkin. You defeated Miss Banaszynski. And under difficult conditions. The Committee expected you to lose."

I started to say something, but he cut me off. "Have a

good evening, Miss Hodgkin. Get a good night's sleep. I may give you a long day tomorrow." He turned away.

Catherine, Lady Thakeham, and I returned from tea around seven that evening. Lady Thakeham said, "You young ladies should rest and then dress for dinner at the Savoy. I've asked Harold to bring the auto around a bit after nine." I knew a formal dinner probably wouldn't conclude until midnight, perhaps later, and there might be cocktails at a café after dinner.

Catherine went upstairs to her room, and Lady Thakeham went into the drawing room and began removing her gloves. I followed her.

"Lady Thakeham, may I have a word?"

"Certainly, dear child."

"It's about Roehampton, Lady Thakeham. If the weather is better tomorrow, my second round match will be early, perhaps before noon. And if I'm lucky enough to win, then I'll have to play my third round match in the afternoon."

"Well, child, we're to be at Rebecca Hurst's home at five tomorrow for tea."

I hadn't thought of that engagement. I said, "I'm sure my match would end well before tea." I had no idea if this was true. For all I knew, my third round – if I got into the third round – might not even start until after five. But that wasn't my immediate problem.

"Lady Thakeham, because my match may be early tomorrow, I'd prefer to go to sleep early this evening. Do you think I might be excused from dinner?"

She stiffened. "Miss Hodgkin, our hosts are expecting us. And, without you, Mark would have no partner for dinner."

"I know, and I regret so much having to ask, but it's terribly important for me to play well in the morning."

Lady Thakeham was icy. "Miss Hodgkin, Mark is your escort for dinner, not me. You should discuss this with him."

She dropped her gloves on a side table and left me without another word.

Mark came home from his hospital rotation that evening after eight o'clock, and I raised the issue of my missing dinner with him in the front hallway as he was taking off his short medical student's lab coat.

He was silent for a moment and then said coldly, "Fiona, you should do as you think best. It makes no difference to me, and I doubt anyone at dinner would notice your absence."

He started up the staircase. I put my hand on his arm to stop him. "Mark. That's mean, and I think it's unfair."

He gently removed my hand from his arm. "I have to dress for dinner. Excuse me."

He went up the stairs.

I waited a moment and then went up to my own room. I didn't go to the Savoy for dinner.

Later, there was a sharp rap on my door. It was Miss Hanson. "You're reduced to sharing dinner with me in the kitchen. I've put out cold steak and kidney pie. Come along, you can't play tennis on an empty stomach."

We talked for a long time at the kitchen table over the cold pie, and we began calling one another by our Christian names. She asked me all about my plans for medical school and wanted to know how my mother and grandmothers had become physicians. I told Myrtle American Grandmother's story about Mary Elizabeth Garrett and the admission of women to the Johns Hopkins School of Medicine 'on the same terms as men.' She seemed fascinated.

I had the impression that Myrtle might have become a physician herself if this had been even remotely thinkable for her as an English working class girl in the late 1930s. But it wasn't, and so she became first the nursery nurse and then the manager and counselor for a great Dutch-English family.

THURSDAY MORNING, 21 JUNE 1962
SECOND ROUND LADIES' QUALIFYING MATCH
ROEHAMPTON

I was alone when I walked out on the court at Roehampton for the second round. No spectators, no boyfriend, no chair umpire, and no Charlotte Johnson. There were no benches to sit on, so I simply stood beside the court holding my pocketbook and rackets. At least it was a beautiful day; I bent down and put the back of my hand on the grass. Not dry, but just damp. In a half an hour or so, it would be dry.

Finally the chair umpire arrived. He had brought the tennis balls for our match, but he wouldn't let me practice my serve until my opponent arrived. I hadn't hit a tennis ball since Tuesday afternoon. The umpire seemed unconcerned that Johnson wasn't on the court.

After 10 minutes had passed, I asked him, "Does my opponent plan to appear, do you think?"

The umpire shrugged and didn't answer.

Finally, Charlotte Johnson arrived with her parents. She was dressed in a Teddy Tinling creation, a white dress with a pale red belt at the waist. The hem of the dress was quite short in order to show her knickers, which had alternating stripes of different shades of white and beige. I felt out of place in my plain tennis dress from Trimingham's on Front Street with the small Bermuda flag I had inexpertly sewn onto the breast.

Johnson not only didn't speak to me, she ignored me completely.

I said to her, "I'm Fiona Hodgkin."

Johnson didn't reply.

"I heard that Teach Tennant is your coach."

No reply.

"I ask, you know, only because I've heard so much about Teach, and if she's here with you, I'd like to meet her."

This time, at least, I got a reply. "Miss Tennant no longer travels to tennis tournaments."

"Oh."

I regret to say I never met Teach. Father and Rachel knew her and, while I doubt either of them liked Teach, they respected her as a tennis coach.

We started to knock up, but the umpire stopped us. Johnson's parents were standing beside the umpire's chair, where they apparently planned to watch the match. The grass courts at Roehampton are directly next to one another, with no room for spectators. The umpire advised them to walk back to the grassy bank and watch the match from there. They weren't happy about this.

Once we began play, I could tell that Johnson wasn't a contender for qualifying. Don't get me wrong – all the players at Roehampton were world-class amateurs. And Johnson was in the second round, after all. But still – in the first point, on her serve, she hit a perfect, hard backhand from her baseline. She finished with her right arm straight, racket face just past perpendicular to the net, butt of the racket straight down toward the grass, weight balanced on her right foot, head held steady, topspin on the ball – all exactly correct.

Then she looked up and, surprised, saw me a meter behind the net, just in the middle of my ad service court. Whatever was I doing there? Her backhand came straight to me. The shock of it hitting my racket twisted my chest almost halfway around, but in doing so all the kinetic energy of her shot drained away. I dropped the ball into her deuce service court. She wasn't anywhere near it.

Her other strokes were as beautiful as her backhand, but she couldn't knit her strokes together. It was over in 50 minutes. Straight sets, 6-4, 6-2. At the net, Johnson didn't exactly refuse my offered handshake, but she just barely touched my hand. She didn't acknowledge the umpire at all but trudged off toward her parents. I reached up to shake the umpire's hand; we looked at one another; we both shrugged.

I knew what Rachel would have done if she'd seen Johnson's incredible strokes. Rachel would have found a way to use them to win tennis games. If Johnson had spent two years – maybe just one year – with Rachel, that backhand wouldn't have landed conveniently in my racket. Johnson wouldn't have been surprised to see me at the net, and her backhand would have drilled a small, precise hole in the air just under my right arm. I would have stood there watching the ball go past me.

There were lots of differences between Johnson and me – thank heaven! – but the important difference was that I had Rachel.

I was one match away from Wimbledon.

Thursday Afternoon, 21 June 1962
Third Round Ladies' Qualifying Match
Roehampton

My opponent for the third round had been decided in another morning match, so I didn't have to wait to know whom I would play. The problem was finding an open court. Mr Soames told me that there was no chance we would have a court before three o'clock, so I left Roehampton, walked up Priory Lane, and ate lunch in a pub on Upper Richmond Street.

My opponent was going to be Martha Fellows. I had met her in the dressing room the first day of Roehampton, and she had surprised me by saying that Claire had mentioned me to her. Martha was about Claire's age, and they had played one another many times, including a match at Wimbledon – "Claire thrashed me!" Martha laughed. Martha was married – Claire had been one of her bridesmaids – and had a young son. She hadn't played tennis in international competition for several years. But now she was back.

If Martha wasn't enough of a problem, there was Rebecca Hurst's tea at five o'clock. My hope was that I could win my third round match in time to allow me to get to Hyde Park Gate, make myself presentable, and attend the tea. A three o'clock start held a shadow of a possibility that I could get to the tea. Three o'clock, unfortunately, came and went, with still no open court. The wait was nothing to Martha; she had waited for tennis courts many times before.

She brought her son – he was almost three – into the dressing room to show him off to the girls. Martha had him wearing a British sailor's suit, and each of us wanted to hold him, which was fine with him; he wasn't the least shy.

It was past five o'clock when Martha and I walked out onto the court where we would play our third round match. So much for tea at Rebecca Hurst's. I thought about placing a telephone call to Lady Thakeham to apologize, but I decided against it. It would probably just make everything worse rather than better.

Martha won the toss and her first service game. I dug in my heels and held my service. And so it went – each of us held her service more or less easily, and we traded games until, finally, on Martha's serve, with the games at 6 all, I got ahead in the count, 15-30. Then Martha, of all things, double-faulted, and I went ahead, 15-40. Unbelievably, though, I dropped the next two points; we went to deuce; and Martha pulled the game out of the fire. How could I have let her do that?

To make matters worse, she broke my service in the next game and took the first set, 8-6.

Wimbledon was slipping away from me. No – I had *thrown* Wimbledon away by not breaking her serve when I had the chance. I was furious with myself.

But at the first changeover in the second set, a remarkable thing happened: Martha got to the water tank before me, and she poured water into a paper cup. Then she handed it to me.

She said, so quietly the umpire couldn't hear, "Calm down. The first set isn't the match. The first set is over. Focus on this set." Then she walked to her baseline.

I stood there, watching her back with amazement. But I calmed down.

I had to make my volleys work against her – which they hadn't in the first set. Unless I hit a pure winner, which usually I didn't, Martha would simply put up a lob. Her lobs weren't perfect, and most of the time I could send them back, but then I'd be right where I started – or worse, I'd be smack in No Man's Land between the baseline and the service line.

Now I started punching my volleys harder, and deeper, and Martha began to wobble, just a bit. When she would serve wide, to keep me off the court, I started taking her serve on its rise from my service court and then rushing the net. Slowly, my game started to work better for me.

There was only one court between the court we were on and the grassy bank where spectators could sit. The match on the court closest to the bank had ended, and now the spectators were following our match.

At the changeovers, I could tell Martha was breathing hard. On her serve, I got ahead in the count, but she took the game to deuce. We were at deuce three times. Then, on my ad, Martha took my backhand volley on the rim of her racket, and the ball spun off the court.

I had broken her. The second set was basically over. In a few minutes, the sets were one all.

Martha got her second wind in the third set, and it took me extra games to beat her. But I did. We shook hands at the net, and she said, "Well played. Congratulations."

"Martha, thank you for calming me down at that changeover. I'll never forget it."

"Make it up by winning Wimbledon for me."

I laughed. "Well, that's not going to happen, not this year at least."

We were walking along opposite sides of the net to acknowledge the umpire. But Martha put her hand on my arm and stopped me. She looked at me seriously for a moment. Then she said softly, "I'm not so sure. You might go all the way."

Friday Morning, 22 June 1962
16 Hyde Park Gate

When Harold came into the breakfast room with *The Times*, I practically snatched the newspaper out of his hands. I rifled through the pages searching for the ladies' draw at Wimbledon. I found the men's draw; I had almost forgotten that the other sex also played at Wimbledon. Then, the next page carried the headline:

The Ladies' Singles Championship Draw
Holder: Mrs Richard Kershaw

Just under the headline, in the first line of the draw I saw, in bold type:

Miss Margaret Smith (Australia) No. 1 Seed

This wasn't a surprise; Claire had known since she had lost the Australian Championship to Margaret Smith that probably Smith would be the top seed at Wimbledon. I looked down at the bottom of the page and found Claire's name:

Mrs Richard Kershaw (Great Britain) No. 2 Seed

I ran my finger up the players above Claire's name – I wasn't there. I was frantic; had there been a mistake? Without thinking, and for no reason, I simply assumed that I would be in Claire's bracket of the draw.

Then it dawned on me that maybe I was in Smith's side. The Committee, after all, simply pulled the names of the unseeded players out of an old cloth bag to establish the draw. I looked up at the top of the page under Smith's name. Finally I found, in tiny letters, the most thrilling words I've ever seen in print:

MISS FIONA HODGKIN (BERMUDA) Q

The 'Q' meant Qualifier.

Unbelievably, incredibly, I was going to play in the Championships at Wimbledon.

And, I knew this wasn't likely, but it *might* happen – I could get to play a match on Centre Court.

Later that morning, Myrtle brought me a telegram:

POST OFFICE TELEGRAM

MEET SATURDAY 11 AM AELTC TO GET YOUR PASS AND PRACTICE COURT 8 STOP WILL PRACTICE SUNDAY HURLINGHAM STOP WHEN I PLAYED YOU LONGWOOD I KNEW YOU WOULD QUALIFY WIMBLEDON STOP

CLAIRE

Claire forgot to mention in her telegram that she had won the final at Eastbourne in straight sets.

Friday Evening, 22 June 1962
London, England

I didn't see either Mark or Lady Thakeham during the day on Friday. I assumed that I was *persona non grata* with Lady Thakeham and probably with Mark as well, because I had missed both my social obligations the day before. If Mark had gone to the party last evening, he must have done so alone, without an escort. Given his tone with me Wednesday evening, when I had begged off dinner at the Savoy, I expected that I was in a deal of trouble with him.

I went out during the day and sent my parents a telegram telling them that I had qualified for Wimbledon. In the few words of a telegram, I tried to sound as though it was just a minor thing I had managed to do on the side, in between parties and teas.

That afternoon, Mark came home from hospital just before tea and, to my surprise, he took me in his arms and congratulated me on qualifying for Wimbledon. When I apologized for failing to appear the evening before, he said, "Oh, Fiona, you've qualified for Wimbledon. That's the important thing. I'm extraordinarily proud of you." He sounded sincere.

"I know I left you without an escort last night, and I'm sorry. I was being selfish."

"It wasn't a problem," he said cheerfully.

I didn't like the way he said my absence hadn't been a problem. "Did you go to the party?"

"Certainly. Margarite has been in London all this week. I rang her. She dressed at the last moment, and Harold collected her in the Bentley."

For a moment, I couldn't think what to say. Finally, I said, "Well, do you want me to go with you this evening?"

"Yes, if you would like. But it's your decision."

"Perhaps you'd prefer to go with Margarite again."

"Now, Fiona. Don't be that way. I told you in Bermuda that I'd broken up with Margarite several years ago."

At first, this bewildered me. I hadn't heard of Margarite until earlier that week. Then it dawned on me. "She was your first lover? You told me about making love to her, your first time?"

Consternation crossed his face. He must not have recalled that he had told me that the unnamed girl he broke up with several years before had been his first – and somewhat unhelpful – lover. He hadn't meant to permit me to deduce her identity.

"Don't worry," I assured him. "Your secrets are safe with me. But if you'd rather take Margarite tonight, please do so. It's not a problem for me."

But Mark said he wanted me to go with him, and we went. The party that evening was for a girl I hadn't met, Elsabeth Norton; it was at Grosvenor House (where the Thakehams were giving Catherine's party the next week); and it followed the formula with which I was now quite familiar. To my relief, Margarite wasn't there.

Mark wanted me to have a cocktail with him before the

dancing began, but I declined, which displeased him. But I was determined, for once, to stay out as late as Mark wanted, even though I was meeting Claire at the All England Club in the morning.

As Mark and I were dancing, I couldn't help asking him, "Did you and Margarite go anywhere after the party last night?"

Mark laughed. "Fiona Hodgkin, I think you're jealous of Margarite!"

I must have turned red in my face, and I tried to break away from him, but he held onto me. "Fiona, I'm teasing you. There's nothing between Margarite and me. We're only friends."

I relented, and remained in his arms, but I said, "I certainly don't mind either way."

"I'm sure that's true."

We didn't arrive back at Hyde Park Gate until almost three in the morning. Once we were in the front hallway, to my surprise, Mark simply picked me up in his arms and carried me into Dr. Thakeham's study, where he sat on the couch with me on his lap. I put my arms around his neck and kissed him. He reached up to my shoulder and pulled the strap of my gown down.

"Mark!" I practically hissed. "What are you doing? Anyone could walk in here."

This made no difference to Mark. He said, "There's really no reason for you to be in your gown. Let's take it off."

"Absolutely not."

He kissed me and pulled up the hem of my gown. This, I thought, was rapidly getting out of hand. I tried to make a joke of it. I pushed away from him, put my hands on either side of his face, kissed him, and smiled at him. "Behave yourself."

He was exasperated, but he did stop trying to undress me. "Fiona, really – "

I put my hand lightly over his mouth. "Let's sit here and kiss for a few more minutes, and then go off to our rooms – separately."

"Fiona, you know I want you, and I think you want me."

"You're certainly right that I want you, but that doesn't mean I'm going to sleep with you tonight."

He lifted me off his lap and sat me on the couch. He stood up and said, "Well, then. I'll see you in the morning. Do you plan to go to the dinner party tomorrow evening?"

I stood up as well. "Yes, I'd like to go to the party with you, but I don't want you to be upset with me."

"I'm not upset with you, but I'm certainly unaccustomed to having a girl repeatedly turn me down when I want to sleep with her."

He was incredibly arrogant to say this, and I was angry. "I'm sure Margarite didn't just say, 'OK, of course,' when you first tried to get her into your bed."

"No, she didn't say that. Actually, Margarite didn't say anything. She reached behind her neck and began unzipping her dress."

He turned and left me alone in the study.

Sunday, 24 June 1962
Hurlingham Club
Fulham, London

When Claire arrived for our practice time Sunday morning at Hurlingham, I was already sitting on the bench beside our practice court. I must have looked awful, and I certainly *felt* awful. She put down her pocketbook and rackets and looked at me. "Are you all right?"

"No."

"I would never have guessed. Which bus ran over you?"

"Claire, don't make fun of me. I'm so ashamed of myself."

"You qualified for the Wimbledon draw. You did it on your own. So, what's there to be ashamed of? Every tennis player in the world would love to spend the Sunday before the fortnight at Hurlingham."

"Last night, Mark slept with me."

"Good! Finally! How was it?"

"Horrible. I was humiliated."

Now she knew I was serious. She sat down beside me and put her arm around me. "Tell me what happened."

"We were at a party, and I had three cocktails. I don't even know what was in them."

"Good preparation for the first round at Wimbledon."

"I know. I can't believe I drank cocktails. But Mark was drinking, and he said I should have one, and then another, and I wanted to please him."

"Have you had anything to drink before?"

"At Christmas dinner, my parents would always give me a glass of champagne."

"And that's it?"

"Yes."

"And last night you had *three* cocktails?"

"Yes. When we got back to Hyde Park Gate, I went upstairs and I was sick in the loo. I stretched out on the bed, and the room was spinning."

"I know the sensation well. Not pleasant."

"No, it isn't. But then Mark knocked on the door."

"Uh oh."

"He came in and got into bed with me."

"What did you say?"

"I told him to leave, that I was sick."

"I assume he ignored you."

"That's right. He was drunk. I told him to go away, to leave me alone, but I don't think he knew what I was saying."

"Well, he couldn't have been too drunk, if he did sleep with you. But maybe he didn't, really."

"He was certainly drunk, but I think he did."

Claire was dubious, I could tell. "This boyfriend sounds like a real piece of work. When's your period?"

I looked at her. "Early this week, I hope."

"Did he spend the night with you?"

"No. He went back to his own room.

"So what did you do?"

I didn't say anything.

Claire said, "You cried into the pillow."

I didn't reply.

She shrugged. "That's what I used to do."

"I'm worried sick that I'm pregnant. But there's something worse," I said.

"After what you've told me already, I'm bracing myself for the 'something worse' part."

"I promised Mother I wouldn't sleep with Mark. And she even warned me about drinking. I don't think I've ever broken a promise to Mother before."

I started crying.

"Fiona, now this I wouldn't worry about. Your mother will care first about you, and then, maybe, about some promise you made. You told him to get out and leave you alone. What more could you have done? Hit him over the head with your tennis racket?"

She paused. "I tried that once, actually. It worked pretty well."

I still had tears on my face, but I had to laugh at her. Then I said, "There's something more."

"Fiona, the good thing is that you'll never forget the weekend before your first Wimbledon match. What 'more' could there possibly be?"

"I woke up this morning and went down to breakfast. Mark wasn't there, but Lady Thakeham was having breakfast, and I sat down with her."

Claire, who loved eating, nodded. "A good English breakfast is important for winning a match."

"She threw me out."

"She did what?"

"She said she thought I'd be more 'comfortable,' that's

the word she used, with one of my aunts until I had finished with my tennis. To make sure I didn't misunderstand her meaning, she said she would ask Miss Hanson to have one of the girls pack my bags while I was here practicing with you. I'm to pick up my bags later."

"What does the boyfriend have to say about this?"

"I didn't see Mark. I don't know where he was."

"This is a really lovely family you've found. Have you considered engaging some master criminal? For a price, you could ensure they're never heard from again."

"Claire, don't make fun of me. My aunts wouldn't let me wear a tennis dress, much less travel across London without a chaperone. I don't have anywhere to stay."

"Certainly you have a place to stay. You'll stay with us."

"No, I'm not going to do that. You're going to win Wimbledon again, and you're trying to get pregnant. The last thing you need is having me sleeping on your living room sofa. Where do the girls in the draw stay for the fortnight?"

"I don't know. I've always lived in London, so I've always stayed at my own flat. But Colonel Macaulay will know where the younger girls lodge."

"Who is he?"

"The Colonel is the Secretary of the All England Club; I'm sure he'll be here at Hurlingham today. Here's what we'll do: let's hit a few tennis balls, then we'll go to the buffet and have a late lunch. I'll find the Colonel and ask where you might lodge. I have the Alfa here, so I'll take you to pick up your bags at your boyfriend's place. Shall we set fire to it while we're there?"

I had to laugh. She was irrepressible.

Claire was the perfect practice partner for me – it meant that I was practicing against the best there was. Plus, being Claire's practice partner attracted attention to me in the newspapers. Claire could have had Margaret Smith, or anyone she wanted. While we knocked up on one of the Hurlingham courts, I watched Claire from across the net and thought she must be one of the most beautiful tennis stylists of all time. It was humbling to be hitting with her. 'I'm out of my depth here,' I thought.

Finally, even Claire was ready to quit. "Let's go get you some lunch," she said. We walked back toward the Hurlingham tea lawn together. Claire held her rackets and pocketbook in her right hand, and she had her left arm draped casually over my shoulders. Everyone was watching me walk off the court with the defending champion. I was still sick with worry about myself, but I was proud to be the practice partner of such a great tennis player.

The tea lawn was noisy and crowded with tennis players of both sexes, plus an array of guests. There was an outdoor buffet where food was served, but it took us some time to get to the food because everyone knew and liked Claire, so she stopped to chat with people, and she was kind enough to introduce me to them.

Claire embraced a large woman who, I thought, looked not much older than me. The two of them shared some private joke and chuckled. Claire said, "Margaret, let me introduce you to Fiona Hodgkin. Fiona, please meet my friend and formidable opponent, Margaret Smith."

Margaret took my hand in hers. She was surprisingly gentle, but she towered over me; she was a powerfully built woman. I think she and Christine Truman, who was a year or so older than Margaret, were the first women to 'train' for tennis by lifting weights.

The men in Australia had been weight training ever since 1938, when Harry Hopman wandered into a gym in Melbourne's Little Collins Street and met a weightlifter named Stan Nicholes. Hopman was then on his quest to bring the Davis Cup back to Australia, and he saw in Nicholes just the way to accomplish that goal. Harry was right, but the Davis Cup was only for men. Margaret and Christine, to their credit, had understood that weight training was just as important for girls as for the men – maybe more so.

But to tell you how unusual this was at the time, in Stan Nicholes' gym, there was no ladies' dressing room – Stan would have to guard the door to the men's dressing room while Margaret took a shower after her weight session.

Claire said, "Maggie, I think you're up right after my opening match on Ladies' Day."

"Can you believe it? I drew Moffitt, the girl from the States."

"Have you played Billie Jean? I haven't."

"No, I haven't either. How she plays so well wearing those eyeglasses, I can't imagine."

Margaret turned to me. "You and I are on the same side of the draw, so I hope we'll meet in the third round. If the weather holds up, and we stay on schedule, that'll be later this week."

"That couldn't be good for me," I laughed.

"Don't say that," Margaret told me. "Wimbledon is a surprising place. You'll do well."

Margaret and Claire knew that almost certainly they would meet in the final, two weeks from now.

"Enough, Maggie," Claire said. "I need to get some food into Fiona."

Claire and I went to the buffet, where I got a salad. Claire eyed it suspiciously. "Fiona, a rabbit couldn't survive on that." She turned to an older lady who was serving at the buffet.

"Evie," Claire said, "could we give this young lady some roast beef?"

"Certainly, Claire. And potatoes?"

"Definitely potatoes. Your son, I hope he's doing well? He's what now – 25?"

Evie beamed, because a Wimbledon champion had asked about her son. "He's 27, married, and I'm a grandmother, as of last Christmas."

"A grandmother? At your young age? It's a scandal!" Claire leaned across the buffet and whispered to Evie, who reached up, put her hand on Claire's cheek, and smiled. I guessed Claire had whispered that she, finally, was trying to start a family.

Then Evie, turning to business, put a huge slab of roast beef on my plate and enough potatoes to feed an army for three days.

This was more food than I could possibly eat. I turned to Claire to protest, but she said, "Don't worry, I'll eat anything left over," and we went to find a table.

"I hadn't thought about meeting Margaret Smith in a match," I said. Claire was busily eating most of my roast beef.

"Don't think about it. It wouldn't be until your third round. Don't think about anything but your first round match – which is Tuesday afternoon. Win the first round and then think about what comes next."

Claire, having almost finished my lunch, pushed her chair

back. "I'm going to find Colonel Macaulay and ask him where you should stay."

I worked on the food Claire had left me, and after 20 minutes she returned with a slip of paper in her hand.

"Sorry to be away so long. Had a talk about Bermuda with the Colonel."

"About Bermuda? Why?"

"He thinks Bermuda is part of Great Britain."

"He's not alone in that. But why were you talking about Bermuda?"

"Well, you should be assigned to the upper dressing room, with me. You're the champion of Bermuda. The dressing rooms are close together, and there's not much difference, but I'd rather have you with me."

"That would be wonderful. Is there a problem?"

"No, the Colonel finally agreed with me. He was just confused because the LTA ranks me the number one girl in Britain, so if Bermuda is part of Britain, you should be in the lower dressing room. The upper dressing room is just for seeded players and national champions. But now he thinks you should be assigned to the upper dressing room."

"More important." Claire spotted a piece of beef I hadn't eaten and speared it with a fork. "Where should you stay? Albert House, in Alwyne Road. It's just a rooming house for young ladies. Ten minute walk down Church Road from the Club. It's so close that the Club doesn't bother sending an auto for you. Three girls in the draw are staying there. The Colonel knows Mrs Brown, who manages the place, and he rang her. There's a room for you. Not fancy, but inexpensive. Agreeable?"

"Not fancy and inexpensive is good."

"Yes! Let's go collect your bags and bring them around to Albert House."

Claire drove the Alfa like a wild woman along Kensington Road, and at the turn into the Frying Pan I waved to the bobby standing guard.

In front of No. 16, Claire stopped the Alfa. "Let's get your bags."

I hesitated. "I don't want to see Mark. What if he's home?"

She looked over at me. "Why don't I go in myself and get the bags?"

I reached in my purse, took out my key to the house and gave it to Claire. "Could you leave this?"

Claire ran up the front steps, rang the bell, and Harold answered the door. A moment later, Myrtle appeared like a Royal Navy dreadnought steaming out of Scapa Flow.

"I knew nothing about this," she said. (I'm sure she was thinking, 'Or I would have put a stop to it.') "If I speak to Doctor Thakeham, I'm confident he will insist you remain with us."

I got out of the Alfa and hugged her, and she hugged me back.

"I'm fine. I've found a place to stay, in Wimbledon, close to the All England Club. It's better for me."

Claire and Harold emerged, Claire lugging one of my huge bags, and Harold struggling with the other two. They dropped my suitcases on the walkway beside the tiny Alfa Romeo.

Claire said, "Fiona, I go to Australia for two months in the winter to play in the run-up matches to their championship, but I take my rackets, my pocketbook, and one suitcase. A casket is smaller than any one of your bags."

Harold cleared his throat. "Ma'am," he said to Myrtle, "I don't expect that Miss Hodgkin's baggage will fit into this small roadster."

"Good thinking, Sherlock," Claire said dryly.

"Harold, put Miss Hodgkin's luggage in the Bentley and follow them to Wimbledon," Myrtle told him.

Myrtle turned to me. "Fiona, you will ring me if you change your mind about staying with us, or if you need anything. I want your word you will do so."

I agreed.

Harold loaded my bags into the Bentley, and he followed us to Albert House. I doubt that a Bentley had ever parked in front of Albert House to discharge a guest's luggage.

Albert House was a small, dark red brick house, with two front bays. A handwritten note was thumbtacked to the door: *"Do NOT Ring Bell After 9 At Night Or Before 7 In The Morning."*

Claire and Harold helped me carry the bags and my tennis things upstairs. My room was so small that the bags, tennis rackets, Claire, Harold, and I just about filled the room to the ceiling. Harold, I could tell, was dubious about my new living arrangements.

Claire shooed Harold out, but as he left he said to me, "Miss, please ring if you want me to come back and return you to Hyde Park Gate."

"Thank you and goodbye, Harold," Claire said.

Claire said to me, "Are you all right? Do you want me to stay with you?"

"I'm fine. You've been wonderful to me, Claire."

I was sitting on the edge of the bed, and Claire sat down beside me. "Fiona, listen to me. You have to eat a good dinner tonight, and you have to sleep well. Will you do both of those for me?"

"Yes, don't worry, Claire."

"We can't practice at the All England Club in the morning. Colonel Legg, the referee, gives all the courts to the men for practice on the first day."

The first Monday of the fortnight was only for the men players. Then the first Tuesday – 'Ladies' Day,' it was called – the women played, with the defending champion leading off on Centre Court. So my first round match, and Claire's second round match (she had a bye for the first round) would begin on Tuesday at two o'clock in the afternoon – 'precisely,' as the Intended Order of Play always stated.

The 'precisely' dated back to some of the earliest minutes of the Committee's meetings in the 1880s. The minutes always recorded that the meetings ended 'precisely' at 3:30. So the word 'precisely' had entered the Club's traditions. Until, of course, it had been blown away by American television, which couldn't begin a sporting event precisely on the hour – because when would the opening commercial advertisements be shown to the television audience?

Claire said, "I expect that if we ask Queen's Club politely, they'll give us a court for a couple of hours to practice. Let's meet there in the morning. Say, 11?"

"Yes. Where is Queen's Club?"

Claire thought for a moment. "You take the Tube from Wimbledon to Earl's Court. Change there to Piccadilly, then just one stop to Baron's Court. You can see Queen's just down Palliser Road when you come out."

She kissed my cheek and said goodbye.

I was alone. I took off my tennis shoes and stretched out

on the bed in my tennis dress. I was numb. I couldn't sleep, and so I just stared at the ceiling for a long time.

Then, I heard a loud knock. I got off the bed and unlocked the door. It was Mark, who was wearing a dinner jacket.

"Go away," I said, closing the door.

"Wait! Fiona! We're having dinner this evening at the Westons'."

"I'm not. How did you know where I'm staying?"

"Harold drove me here. May I talk to you for a moment? This is important."

"Go ahead and talk," I said, still standing in the doorway.

"May I come in?"

I stood aside and let him walk in.

"This is quite a nice place," he said after he had looked around the room. I assumed he was being facetious. I hated being in the same room with him.

"Fiona, Mother has told me what she said to you, and I'm sorry. I had no idea she would do such a thing."

I was certain Mark had known; that's why he had been absent from the house this morning. "It's not important. I'm better off here. Now leave."

"Fiona, we are expected at the Westons'. This is an important dinner for Catherine. You must be there." The Westons, I knew, were giving the dinner for Catherine and the Thakeham family as part of the celebrations leading to her big party that Wednesday night.

"I couldn't care less. I want you to leave now."

"Fiona," he began, but I cut him off. "Mark, it's humiliating for me to even be in the same room with you. The least you can do is go away and leave me alone."

"You're not upset about last night, are you?"

"You took advantage of me. It was horrible. I'm ashamed."

"Oh, Fiona, don't be that way. I didn't take advantage of you. I just had a bit too much to drink."

"Go away, now."

"I think we should wait to talk about this when you're not so upset."

I was determined not to cry. I hated him.

"Mark, if you don't leave now, I'm going downstairs to ask Mrs Brown to call a bobby."

"Fiona, I really must insist that you come with me this evening. Everyone is expecting you. It will be embarrassing if you're absent."

"Even if I were willing to go with you, which I'm not, I wouldn't go out this evening, because I'm going to practice with Claire in the morning."

He scoffed. "Look, you can't be serious about this. I mean, it's exciting that you made it to Wimbledon, and we're proud of you. I'm especially proud of you. But you said yourself this is just a trial run, this year. They've put you up against a top seeded player. You have to be realistic, you can't get past the first round. Eventually you'll win Wimbledon; I'm sure of it. But your first year, as a qualifier, you don't have a chance. I don't believe any lady qualifier has ever come close to winning. This is just for experience. You can't win. So why not come out tonight with me?"

The worst thing anyone could have said to me at that moment was that I couldn't win. I slapped him as hard as I could; he staggered and his cheek turned bright red where I had hit him.

"Get out," I yelled.

He turned and left.

Monday, 25 June 1962
Queen's Club
West Kensington, London

I woke Monday morning and found I wasn't pregnant. It was like a huge stone had been suddenly lifted off my shoulders. I told myself not to cry, and I didn't. I had breakfast in a tea shop and then took the Tube to meet Claire at Queen's.

When I saw Claire parking the Alfa, I went over to her and said, "I'm not pregnant."

She smiled. "I didn't think you were. But I didn't tell you in case I might be wrong. Your boyfriend was drunk, wasn't he?"

"He's not my boyfriend. But he was quite drunk."

"Yes, well, I've seen that, plenty of times. And close up. They don't like to admit it, but when they're drunk, usually the most they can do is make matters unpleasant for the girl. They can't perform."

"What do you mean, 'can't perform'?"

Claire laughed. "Let's hope you don't have reason again to find out for yourself!"

Still laughing, she led me into the Queen's clubhouse, where she located the old groundskeeper in his tiny office. He was heating water in an electric kettle for tea.

The instant he caught sight of Claire, he said, "Absolutely not."

"I have a difficult draw on Ladies' Day," Claire said.

"I'm sure. Probably your Ladies' Day opponent is some hapless girl who's ranked number 10 in Mongolia."

"Tingay ranked me number 10 once."

"Yes, Lance did, back when you still wore your hair in pigtails and slept with your teddy bear under your arm."

Claire frowned. "I didn't have a teddy bear."

There was an ancient couch in the groundskeeper's office. The fabric was worn; the springs were poking out. The groundskeeper arched his eyebrow and pointed to the couch.

"A small, furry toy bear? You sound asleep after practicing with Rachel? Remember?"

Claire pouted, or pretended to. "Perhaps I did sleep with teddy."

"I'm not giving you a court. The grass is too worn from the tournament last week – in which you didn't compete. You, I noticed, were off somewhere else."

"Eastbourne paid my expenses. Queen's didn't."

"What expenses? Your flat is two stations on the Tube from here. We give you tea for free."

"I promise I'll never play at Eastbourne again. I'll always play Queen's the week before Wimbledon. If you'll let me practice today."

The groundskeeper snorted. "I don't believe you, but even if I did, the courts aren't in any condition for play."

She went over to him and kissed his cheek.

He shrugged.

Claire took his arm and hugged it to her right breast. She

stroked her finger slowly along his thin moustache. "Your moustache looks so dashing now that it's all gray."

"You've used that line with me before. It won't work."

I could tell his resolve was crumbling.

Still hugging his arm to her breast, Claire said, "Your wife is lucky to have such a vigorous man."

"I'll tell her you said so."

"Which court would you say is in the best condition?"

"Court 5 is probably the best of a bad lot," he grumbled.

"Good, I'll practice on Court 5."

Once we were on the court, and Claire was about to toss her racket and ask me to call it, I said, "Claire, was that appropriate? I mean, flirting with that older gentleman just now?"

"Fiona. Please. He loved every second of it. And we needed a practice court. Rough or smooth?"

Tuesday, 26 June 1962
Court 14
Ladies' Day First Round Match
All England Club Wimbledon

My first round match at Wimbledon was against a French woman, Michelle Lyon, who was seeded fifth. She was about 25, and 1962 was her fourth Wimbledon appearance. The year before, she had reached the quarterfinals at Wimbledon, and she had just played in the semifinals of the French championship at Roland Garros. Lance Tingay's World Rankings for 1961 had Michelle in the number six spot. Claire had played her twice, once on grass and once on clay, and had won both times.

"Michelle is more comfortable on clay than grass," Claire told me, "but her groundstrokes are strong. She's consistent. She's going to pass you at the net a few times. Just be steady. Don't get rattled."

"Can I beat her?"

"I'm sure you won't if you're asking questions like that. The question is *how* will you beat her."

"So how do I beat her?"

"You've only got one game. You attack the net. So, attack. But she'll have strong passing shots, and you'll just have to deal with them. And you can."

My match with Michelle was set for two o'clock on Court 14, which in 1962 was about as far away from Centre Court as it was possible to get and still be standing on a grass tennis court. (Today, the court known as Court 14 is just to the north of Centre Court, but in 1962 the ground north of Centre Court was beyond the Club's boundary.) Claire was playing the traditional opening ladies' match on Centre Court at the same time as my match with Michelle, so I was on my own. Claire had told me, though, that after her match she would come to Court 14 and hope to see the end of my match.

The first set went past in only 20 minutes or so; I lost 6-2.

I knew this was going to be a disaster. I would be out of Wimbledon in the first round. I cursed Mark for telling me I would lose; as much as I hated admitting it, I believed him. I absolutely had to pull myself together, right now, or Wimbledon would be over for me, quickly.

In the first game of the second set, I held my serve and played a couple of solid points at the net. Michelle won the first two points on her serve in the second game, but then I volleyed a ball back to her. It took a bad bounce on the grass in her deuce court, and her return went wide. So it was 30-15. Her first service went into the net.

This was my chance: I took her second serve on the rise, returned it down the line as hard as I could, and came in behind it. She got to the ball and hit it back crosscourt, but I caught it with my backhand and angled my volley short into her service court. There was no way Michelle could get to it. 30 all.

If I could just win the next two points, I would have broken her serve. I felt a little more confident; my volleys were working better for me now. Also, as I watched Michelle bouncing the ball, getting ready to serve, taking her time, I sensed she was thinking that she needed to get her first serve in, and hard, to keep me away from the net. I decided to take a chance: if she got her first serve in, and I could do anything with it at all, I would rush the net.

Michelle served. It was in. Beautifully placed wide but not hit that hard. I returned it down the line and came in. She had plenty of time to set up a passing shot. 'Probably she'll go crosscourt,' I thought, and I moved toward the centerline of the service court. No, she went back down the line, and her shot was the hardest she'd hit so far in the match. I lunged for the ball and volleyed it back. Then I slipped and hit the grass with a thud.

My volley wasn't the best, but at least it went deep and gave me a split second to jump back to my feet. Now she had to go crosscourt because I was at the net wide, and she did. But I caught the crosscourt shot and punched back a deep, hard volley. She had to lob.

I drifted back, picked out the ball against the sky with my finger and swung as hard as I could. Both my feet were off the grass when I made contact with the ball. Michelle charged for my smash and made it, but her return was wildly wide. My ad.

Michelle tried to do too much with her first serve and faulted. 'This is it,' I thought. She served a slice right into my body. I sidestepped, took it with my backhand, and started to run in behind it. But I stopped. I didn't have to come in. It was a winner. The games were 2-love. I had broken her serve.

The crowds that second day of Wimbledon were distracting because people were walking up and down on the narrow path between Courts 14 and 15 – 'St. Mary's Walk,' it had always been called, after the old church in the distance. It ran all the way through the outer courts to the covered gangway between Court 1 and Centre Court. Few of the spectators stopped to watch our match. It was a high seeded player against a qualifier nobody; it wouldn't last long and would be boring while it did. I did my best to pull a curtain around the court in my mind and focus on the game.

At the next changeover, I sensed that Michelle was concerned. She'd been in worse situations than this and pulled out wins. She was up a set, but still – concerned. My volleys were clicking now, my footwork was better, and, most important, I had forgotten that this was Wimbledon. Now it was just a tennis match that I had to win.

I cruised through the rest of the second set and took it 6-3. Now there was a crowd watching us – could this be a possible upset? And this unknown qualifier was from *where*? Bermuda?

Third set. Neither of us could break the other. We went to extra games. On my serve, I made two stupid mistakes and got behind in the score. It was love-30. Michelle smelled blood. She was experienced; she was going to make full use of this opportunity I'd just handed her on a platter. Two more points and she'd put her first round into a bag.

For once, I took my time getting ready to serve. I tossed the ball high and out, and swung through it with every bit of strength I could find. The instant my racket collided with the ball, I rushed the net.

But my serve was an ace, my first of the match. Michelle didn't get near it. 15-30.

On my next serve, I came in, and Michelle tried passing

me down the line. I got to the ball with plenty of time, but I punched it back and it went just long. Another careless mistake. 15-40. Two match points for Michelle.

I faulted on my first serve. Nerves. I decided to gamble on following my second serve in. I hit a good second serve and forced Michelle to try and pass me at net. Michelle hit her shot into the net.

One match point saved. 30-40. Michelle's ad.

Claire, meanwhile, had finished the demolition of her opponent on Centre Court. Now she was at Court 14 to watch the end of my match. The crowd made a path for her to the yellow rope along the side of the court; everyone knew Claire was my practice partner. The chair umpire noticed Claire's arrival and gave her a short, stern glance that meant 'no coaching.' So Claire stood there, arms folded over her chest, showing no emotion, and not applauding.

I had never been so glad to see someone in my whole life.

I served wide, to Michelle's backhand. She returned low, to my feet, but I made a good half-volley into her deuce service court. She ran up but couldn't reach it. Both match points saved. Deuce.

I won the deuce point and gained the advantage. I served, ran forward, caught her return on my racket and punched it back. She had to stretch to reach my volley, hit a weak return, and I put it away.

My game. The crowd roared with approval.

I lost the first two points on her serve. 30-love. But then she faulted on her first service. This was the wrong time to hand me a second serve. I got to the net, took her passing shot with my backhand, and angled it away from her. 30-15.

She took her time on her next serve, and it paid off. An ace, her third of the match. 40-15. I risked a glance at Claire, who had not a trace of emotion on her face. Suddenly what Mark had said Sunday evening, that I would lose, that I had no chance, came into my mind. I gritted my teeth; I was *not* going to lose this match.

Michelle served, and I took the ball on the rise, returned it down the line, and came to the net. She got to the ball easily and hit a beautiful crosscourt shot, which I cut off with a volley and sent back down the line. Again, Michelle reached the ball with plenty of time and fired a forehand straight back at me, hard. I caught it with my racket, let my hand and arm drain off the momentum from the ball, and angled it softy into the opposite service court. A stop volley. Michelle couldn't reach it. 40-30.

The crowd on St. Mary's Walk had grown.

Michelle put her first service into the net. The crowd gasped. Michelle seemed tired to me. She had to serve as hard as she could over and over just to try and force me to stay back, and now her serve began to fall off just a notch.

I stepped inside the baseline for her second service. She sliced the ball wide but not hard. I sent it back down the line. This time, she hit a sharply angled, perfect crosscourt shot that should have been a winner. But I raced across the court and hit the ball back crosscourt.

I was off the court when I hit the ball, and I slipped on the grass and fell on my backside. The crowd groaned. But at least I'd hit a good volley, and Michelle had to run to get it back. She was off the court as well, and she hit the ball down the line with her backhand.

I sprang to my feet; I could just get to the ball. I ran back across the court as fast as I could and volleyed the ball crosscourt. Now it was Michelle's turn to race across the court, which she did – Michelle was *fast*.

She had time to hit a groundstroke but she didn't; instead, she lobbed down the line. I was surprised. I wasn't in a good position to take this lob. I had to jump to reach it with my backhand. I angled my shot into the opposite service court.

This should have been a winner. But Michelle sprinted diagonally across the court and reached my ball. Amazing speed. She hit the ball crosscourt, but then slipped on the grass. Michelle didn't fall, but she did have to catch her balance rather than get back in position for my next shot. I knocked the ball with my backhand into the service court away from her.

Deuce. If I could just break Michelle's serve, I thought I could take the match.

I won the deuce point. My ad. Michelle took her time serving. She went down the middle, to my forehand. She'd had enough of my backhand for one afternoon. I took her serve on the rise and ripped the ball crosscourt, deep into her deuce court. She couldn't get to it. I had broken her. I would serve for the match.

The crowd cheered; even Claire decided it was permissible for her to yell "Fiona! Fiona!" Michelle, as a good sport, clapped her hand against her racket head in acknowledgement.

I was playing on autopilot. She took her time setting up to receive. I could tell she was struggling to make passing shots off my serve. I fell behind in the score, 15-30, because of a volley that went long. But I made it 30 all with a crosscourt volley, and then 40-30 after she lobbed one of my volleys, and her lob landed long.

Match point in my favor.

The crowd was hushed. I served and came in. She had to pass me. She went crosscourt, and by instinct I sidestepped and hit a backhand volley into the corner of her deuce court. She barely got to the ball and then hit another lob. She was tired. That's why I was getting all these defensive lobs.

I set up, found the ball in the sky with my finger, and whipped my racket through the air. Michelle didn't get near my smash.

Claire was jumping up and down yelling, "YES! YES!" I shook hands with Michelle and then with the chair umpire, who called, "Game, set, and match to Miss Hodgkin, 2-6, 6-3, 10-8."

I was in the second round of Wimbledon.

I shook hands with Michelle, gathered my rackets and pocketbook, walked off the court and slipped under the yellow rope where Claire was standing, or rather jumping. She hugged me. She was still yelling. "INCREDIBLE PLAY!"

There were people with cameras taking photographs of us, and several British reporters were asking me questions. Claire knew all the reporters, and she said to them, "Not now, boys. Fiona needs a bath and a cup of tea before she'll be fit to talk with the likes of you!"

Claire and I walked back along St. Mary's Walk to the upper dressing room. She had her arm draped over my shoulders. All she could talk about was my "spectacular" upset of the fifth seed; she didn't bother to mention her own victory on Centre Court.

"Claire?" I said softly.

"Yes?"

"I would have lost if you hadn't been there."

"Nonsense."

But I could tell Claire was pleased.

As we walked, Claire warned me not to talk with reporters, at least not unless I had plenty of time to think and was careful in what I said. "They'll twist anything you tell them."

"Do you talk to reporters?"

"I used to, all the time, but I haven't since I married Richard."

"Why not?"

"Richard prefers not to see me quoted in the newspapers."

"Why doesn't he want to see you quoted?"

"Well, I can understand his thinking. I'm his wife, and I'll be the mother of his children. He doesn't want to see me saying something outrageous that's been splashed across a newspaper."

Before we walked into the South West Hall of Centre Court, Claire turned her head to glance at the scoreboard that was against the stands for Courts 2 and 3.

She stopped instantly. "I almost can't believe it," she said in a whisper.

"What?"

She pointed at the scoreboard. "Billie Jean beat Margaret."

Results – Centre Court

Mrs R Kershaw (GB)   def Miss M Curzon (GB)   6-0 6-1
Miss BJ Moffitt (USA) def Miss M Smith (AUS)   1-6 6-3 7-5

I'd never seen Claire nonplussed, but she was now.

We went in the South West Hall and found Margaret, disconsolate, in the upper dressing room. Margaret dominated the first set, which took all of 18 minutes. Billie Jean took the second set, but in the final set, Margaret had been serving for the match with the games at 5-3 — and the score was 30-15. She had been just two points away from winning. Billie Jean fought back to deuce, broke Margaret's serve, and finally walked off with the match.

Every girl in the dressing room knew what this meant. Barring another, equally incredible upset, Claire would be the holder of the championship for a third year.

When I got back to Albert House late Tuesday afternoon, I had one task that I dreaded. I hadn't told my parents that I wasn't staying with the Thakehams any longer and that I was by myself in a rooming house. Which of these two facts would be more upsetting to my parents, I wasn't sure. Probably Mother would be angry with me for leaving the Thakehams, and Father would be angry with me for staying by myself in a rooming house. I didn't know if Lady Thakeham had told them; maybe she would have felt obligated to do so. In any event, I needed to send them a telegram, and now.

Mrs Brown told me where to find the Post Office; it was close by, next to the Wimbledon Tube station. I walked there, took a telegram pad, and wrote:

POST OFFICE TELEGRAM

WIN TODAY THREE SETS OVER FIVE SEED FIRST ROUND STOP HAVE MOVED TO ALBERT HOUSE ALWYNE ROAD WIMBLEDON STOP HOMESICK AND LOVE YOU STOP FIONA.

The 'homesick and love you' part was certainly true. Part of me wanted to return to Bermuda immediately and never leave the island again.

But another part of me wanted to play in the second round at Wimbledon.

I handed in the telegram.

When I walked back to Albert House, Mrs Brown presented me with a dozen red roses, and an envelope, which just had been delivered. I had a bad feeling about this delivery.

"Mrs Brown, I don't have anywhere to put these roses in my room. Could we possibly find a vase for them and put them here on the counter? Then all your guests could enjoy them."

Mrs Brown readily accepted this added touch of class to Albert House, and we went back into the kitchen to find a vase. Albert House, I learned, was not well equipped with vases, but we did find an asparagus cooker. So we sliced the stems at an angle, put them in the asparagus cooker, added water, pushed the roses around a bit so they were shown to best advantage, and finally placed them on the counter in the reception room. Mrs Brown was pleased.

I went up to my room, dropped my rackets, pocket book and tennis kit on the floor, sat on the bed, and looked at the envelope. I recognized Mark's handwriting – 'Fiona Hodgkin, Albert House.' I really didn't want to open this envelope; I guessed the contents would be about Catherine's party tomorrow night. And once I opened it, I found I was right.

I threw Mark's note away just after reading it, and now, decades later, I can't recall exactly what he wrote. The gist was, as I expected, that I should attend Catherine's party with him, tomorrow night. And, to give the devil his due, he apologized for Saturday night. But most of the note was to the effect that I was expected at Catherine's party, and that he would appreciate it if I would come with him. He asked that I ring him and let him know.

I sat on the edge of the bed. I crumpled up Mark's note. On the one hand, I never wanted to set eyes on Mark again. On the other hand, Catherine's party was the reason Lady Thakeham had invited me to London. If I didn't attend Catherine's party, and Mother learned that I hadn't, which she would, she would be angry with me. She might well decide that I was withdrawing immediately from Wimbledon. If Father backed her up, and he probably would, that would be that.

So I needed to show my face at Catherine's party.

My second round match was set on Court 2 for Wednesday, following a men's match that started at two o'clock. The men should be finished by four o'clock, or five at the latest, unless there was a rain delay, or the men got involved in some extra game death march. If I were on the court by, say, five, my match would be over by seven, or, at the worst, eight. My match couldn't possibly go more than a few minutes past nine o'clock because of darkness. Catherine's party would begin at Grosvenor House in Mayfair at nine o'clock, but I wouldn't be considered late if I arrived by ten o'clock or so. I would come back to Albert House straight after my match, dress, and catch the Tube to Marble Arch.

I went downstairs. There was a telephone off the entryway. I put in the necessary coins and rang Hyde Park Gate. Harold answered the telephone in the pantry. "Harold, this is Fiona Hodgkin."

"Yes, Miss. I'm pleased to hear from you."

"Harold, may I speak with Mark?"

"Miss Hodgkin, young Mark is not in at present. I think he plans to return for tea. May I ask him to ring you then?"

"No, Harold. I don't have a telephone that is easy for me to answer. May I ask you to give him a message?"

"Certainly, Miss."

"Will you thank him for the roses he sent me?"

"Yes, Miss."

"Please tell Mark that I will attend Catherine's party tomorrow evening, but I will come by myself."

"Miss, should young Mark come collect you in his automobile? At what time?"

Harold was not grasping the idea of my coming to Catherine's party by myself. "No, Harold, I will take the Tube. The Marble Arch stop is close to Grosvenor House."

"Miss, let me ask Miss Hanson if I may come around in the Bentley and collect you at Albert House."

He really didn't get it. "Harold, is Miss Hanson there? May I speak with her?"

"Certainly."

After a moment, Myrtle came on the line. "Fiona? Are you doing well?"

"Yes, Myrtle, I'm fine."

"Wouldn't it be better to have Harold come bring you back to Hyde Park Gate? I would send one of my girls with him to pack your clothes. I would – " She paused. "I would satisfy Lady Thakeham. You needn't worry about her."

"Myrtle, I'm comfortable where I am. And I promise you I would ask if I needed you to help me. But I want to ask you a question: Would I be welcome at Catherine's party if I came alone, by myself?"

She instantly deduced what had happened. "Did Mark mistreat you?"

I didn't reply.

"Fiona, the truth, now."

I didn't reply.

"Your choices are to tell me, or for me to assume the worst, immediately find Mark, and strangle him."

"I drank too much last Saturday night. That was my fault. I think Mark took advantage of me after we came back to Hyde Park Gate."

She paused. "Are you all right?"

"Yes. I got my period yesterday morning."

"That's good, but that doesn't mean you're all right."

I didn't reply.

"I'll strangle Mark."

"No, Myrtle, leave Mark alone. It's over and done with between Mark and me."

AMATEUR TENNIS IN 1962
ALL ENGLAND CLUB WIMBLEDON

I must tell you about Wimbledon and amateur tennis in 1962. Few people remember now; it was 50 years ago. And you can't understand this story about Claire and me, really, unless you know.

We were all amateurs then. That meant even Claire – the top woman player – could accept only her 'reasonable' travel and lodging expenses. If she ever accepted money for playing tennis, she would become a 'professional,' and professionals were barred from most tournaments, including Wimbledon.

When Claire won Wimbledon in 1960 and 1961, her prize each time was a voucher for £15. She could use the voucher for lodging and meals – or she could visit a bank and redeem the voucher for cash. Which is what Claire did. In case you're wondering, £15 in 1961 was worth about $300 in today's American dollars.

In 2011, when Petra Kvitova won Wimbledon, she took home £1.1 million (about $1.71 million). In cash.

Oh, I almost forgot. Claire also received a tiny replica of the sterling silver Rosewater Dish that has been presented to each ladies' singles champion since 1886 – and then promptly snatched back! Claire was allowed to hold the actual

Rosewater Dish for all of about five minutes, each time, just so the photographers could snap their photos. She put the replicas in the back of a closet in her parents' country house, along with her other trophies.

When I first met Claire, at Longwood, she was touring the private grass court clubs on the East Coast of the States – Westchester Country Club, Merion Cricket Club, Baltimore Country Club. Having a Wimbledon champion play an afternoon's exhibition match was a feather in the cap of each of these clubs. But none of them paid Claire to appear, because that would be paying Claire to play tennis. Instead, each club paid her a handsome *per diem* for her expenses, about half of which she saved and deposited in her father's bank in the City.

The French took a unique approach to the reasonable expenses of top amateurs. For playing at Roland Garros, Claire got *un forfait* for her expenses. A lump sum, that is, and the French tended to estimate 'reasonable expenses' in terms of how many paying spectators a player was likely to draw through the gates at Roland Garros. Claire was a tremendous draw, and consequently the French felt her reasonable expenses in staying in Paris certainly must be quite substantial. Another tidy amount deposited in her father's bank.

I've never asked Claire about her earnings from tennis (although if the shoe were on the other foot, Claire would demand to know my take down to the last shilling). But I'll guess she cleared about £2,000 each year when she was at her peak. That's about $40,000 in today's American dollars. Nothing to sneeze at, but an offer of $40,000 to one of the top women tennis stars today wouldn't even get her agent to return your voice mail message.

And for a nobody like me in 1962? You can forget my reasonable expenses. I was lucky the All England Club fed me lunch and gave me tea without charge – and I appreciated it!

Players in those days traveled without the entourages of coaches and others that are common today. There was no money to pay for an entourage. At most, a player might travel with a parent or a spouse. And in any event, 'coach' implied 'professional coach,' which was quite the gray area. The Committee was uncomfortable when Teach Tennant, who was a professional coach, came to Wimbledon with Alice Marble and later Maureen Connolly.

On Ladies' Day in 1952, Maureen – 'all tiny 17 years of her,' as Teddy Tinling said – marched into Colonel Macaulay's office; announced she was calling a press conference; and told the Colonel to assemble the sports journalists – immediately! She then told the journalists, in no uncertain terms, that Teach was no longer her coach. Maureen thought Teach had been saying that Maureen was injured and couldn't compete at Wimbledon. Maureen proceeded to win Wimbledon three times in a row – and the Grand Slam in 1953.

The Committee was pleased with the departure of a professional coach, if not with the idea of a press conference. But no one could decide which was more amazing: that an amateur tennis player had held a press conference, or that Teach would no longer be running Maureen's life.

In 1962, three of the major international tournaments were played at small, private grass court clubs: Kooyong, in Melbourne; Forest Hills, in New York City, and the All England Club. Only Roland Garros was owned by a national tennis organization. Today, Wimbledon – excuse me, I meant

'The Lawn Tennis Championships upon the lawns of the All England Club Wimbledon' – is the only 'major' played at a private club, and the only one played on grass.

In 1962, the ground of the All England Club was 13½ acres tucked into a small triangle between Somerset Road to the west and Church Road to the east. The Club had only 16 grass courts, including Centre Court.

Centre Court then wasn't at the center of the Club's ground; it was off on the north edge. So why was it called Centre Court? Because before 1922, when the All England Club was just off Worple Road in Wimbledon, the main court *had* been in the exact center of the ground, and it was logical to call it "Centre Court." When the Club moved to Church Road in 1922, but the new show court, with its 12-sided design by the architect Stanley Peach, was built on the north edge of the ground, it was still called, inevitably, "Centre Court."

This is England, right?

In 1967, the Club purchased 11 additional acres to the north of the original ground and eventually on that land built the new Court 1, the new Courts 14 to 19, and the new Aorangi Park practice courts. So now Centre Court is closer to the actual centre of the ground.

When I played at Wimbledon, the roof over the stands around Centre Court was lower by a meter (and the stands smaller by 1,000 seats) than it became after an expansion in 1979. Centre Court in 1962 was so small and enveloping that, when you played there, to see the sky you had to look basically straight up. The writer John McPhee once compared Centre Court in the 1960s to 'an Elizabethan theater,' like Shakespeare's Globe, and that's exactly how it felt. A player on court could speak to the chair umpire in a normal tone of voice and still be heard by most of the spectators. The sound of a ball hit hard by a racket – *THOCK!* – would echo under the low roof.

Margaret Smith, who was accustomed to the open, expansive stadium at Kooyong, which had space for two grass courts side by side, and no roof, said that Centre Court was like playing "on a postage stamp" (although maybe she was simply repeating something Tony Trabert had said years before).

The outside of Centre Court was draped in Boston ivy so thick you could barely see the building itself, and, once inside, you were in a labyrinth of dark, narrow corridors, some of which seemingly led nowhere, but one of which led, through a small waiting room and two swinging glass doors, onto Centre Court.

Even the grass was different in 1962. Back then, the Club's courts were planted with red fescue, mixed with a little Oregon browntop, which made for a soft, slippery, and unpredictable surface. In 2001, the All England Club re-turfed all the courts with pure rye grass, and a much firmer soil, which made the courts slower. The most noticeable effect of the new turf is on the bounce. The ball comes up much higher, partly because the soil is harder, and partly because rye grass, unlike fescue, grows in tufts and is stiffer than fescue. The ball is now about one tenth of a second slower over the 23.8 meters from one baseline to the other compared to when I played at Wimbledon in 1962.

The All England Club insists the 2001 change in the grass was made only to make the courts more durable. Maybe so. Some people say it was because American television wanted longer rallies. But it's interesting that Jack Kramer back in the 1970s predicted that the different court surfaces at the major tournaments would be changed to be more uniform in terms of speed. And the speed of the grass courts at the All England Club today seems similar to the composition courts at the Australian Open and the U.S. Open.

But if you ever want to play a set on the old, unpredictable, and fun Wimbledon grass, you can. Just pack your tennis whites and take the rail from Wimbledon station to Eastbourne – the trip is about an hour and a half. You can walk from the station to Devonshire Park. Ask the staff if you might play on Court 1. Why Court 1? Because early in 1997, the All England Club demolished its old Court 1, which since 1924 had been pushed up against Centre Court like a shed. Eastbourne asked – politely – if they might have the turf from old Court 1. And so 730 square meters of turf was carefully taken by lorry to Eastbourne and reverently planted on Eastbourne's Court 1 – it's still there!

I don't mean to sound so nostalgic for 1962. Professional 'open' tennis should have come to Wimbledon decades earlier than it did. The retractable roof over Centre Court, the new show courts 1, 2, and 3, and the practice courts in Aorangi Park, are welcome improvements. If American television needs longer rallies, and a longer time on the changeover for a commercial advertisement, so be it.

Still. Wimbledon in 1962 was a thrilling place for me. When I walked past the Doherty Memorial Gates, I would brush a fingertip lightly over the wrought iron. Maybe Laurie and Reggie would bring me good luck. The British military officer standing guard would say, "Good morning, Miss Hodgkin. Lovely weather today for a bit of tennis."

The Tennis Player From Bermuda

One morning, I was walking down Church Road in my tennis dress with its tiny Bermuda flag, with my pocketbook in my right hand and my rackets clutched under my left arm. When I excused myself and cut through The Queue of people standing in line since before dawn to buy tickets, I overheard one of them whisper to another, "She's the tennis player from Bermuda."

For an 18-year-old tennis player from Bermuda, life doesn't get better than that.

WEDNESDAY AFTERNOON, 27 JUNE 1962
COURT 2 ('THE GRAVEYARD')
LADIES' SECOND ROUND
ALL ENGLAND CLUB WIMBLEDON

I was moving up in the world; my second round match would take place, not on one of the outer courts, but on Court 2, a show court nicknamed 'the Graveyard' – it was considered bad luck for a seeded player to have a match on Court 2 because over the years so many top players had been upset there. The BBC covered matches on Court 2 on television.

My opponent was an American, Mary Ann House, who was seeded eighth. Although she was just a year older than me, House had been on the tennis circuit for two years and had made a serious run at Kooyong that winter until Margaret eliminated her in the fifth round. Claire had never played House but had watched her match with Margaret at Kooyong. "It wasn't a walk in the park for Margaret," was Claire's assessment. House's play at Kooyong is probably what had gotten her such a high seeding at Wimbledon.

House and I sat together in the upper dressing room while the men played their match in the Graveyard. To be honest, I didn't care for House. She ignored me and gave me the impression that I had no business being in the upper dressing room. I tried once or twice to make conversation on some neutral topic, the food in the buffet, for example, with no success.

The men took forever. It was almost six o'clock before a callboy summoned House and me to Court 2.

I decided I would blow House off the court, and that's exactly what I did. It took 44 minutes. 6-4, 6-2.

I played so totally by instinct that I don't even recall much of the match. On House's serve at one game apiece in the second set, she hit a beautiful, sharply angled crosscourt passing shot that bounced exactly on my deuce court sideline. As usual, I was camped out at the net, and it certainly looked as though House had successfully passed me.

Still, I gave it a try. I *ran*. The ball was already way off the court when I managed to catch it with my racket. At full speed, I hit the ball with my forehand. I didn't have time to aim – I just hit the ball on the run as hard as I could and hoped for the best. I was so far off the court that, at the instant my racket struck the ball, my right foot tripped on the tarp that was rolled up at the edge of the grass, just along the first row of spectators, ready to be unrolled over the court in case of rain. My racket flew out of my hand, and I pinwheeled over the tarp and slammed into the spectators' barrier with my legs in the air.

I heard a collective gasp from the crowd and then cheers and applause. I landed in a position that was not modest for a young lady, and the BBC and several photographers captured it all on film. I rolled over, got up on all fours, reached back, and pulled my tennis dress down over my backside. I found myself looking straight at an older couple in the first row of spectators. The man leaned over. "Are you all right?"

I replied, "Did you see if my shot went in?" The spectators who heard me all laughed loudly.

There's no rule in tennis that the ball has to go *over* the net; the ball is still in play if it is hit *around* the net – provided it lands within the opponent's court. The point was replayed on television over and over, and I could see that the ball went wide of the net but then bounced just in the corner of House's ad court. The newspapers the next morning all ran an almost indecent photograph of me on my back with my legs splayed above me.

When I walked off the court, there were so many people crowded around me waiting for an autograph or a photograph that finally a Coldstream Guardsman led me back to the upper dressing room.

Claire was there, having just finished the demolition of another hapless, unseeded player on Centre Court. She asked, "How was Mary Ann?"

"Not a problem. Straight sets."

"I'm impressed. I was worried she might be a handful." Then Claire said, "Well, we have two days off." The Committee hadn't yet posted the Intended Order of Play for Thursday, but probably we wouldn't play our next matches until Saturday. "Let's bathe, find Richard and go out for dinner. Don't worry, I won't attack him until he and I are back home in our flat."

"I can't. I have to go to a party."

"I forgot! It's the season, and you're a young, unmarried lady looking for a husband!"

I laughed. "My current state of mind is to spend my life as a celibate spinster. No, this is a purely social obligation."

"Meaning?"

"This is the party for Mark's younger sister, Catherine. Her party is the reason I'm here in London for the season. Lady Thakeham invited me to come to Catherine's party. All the other invitations followed. Mother would – well, I don't know what she'd do if I skipped Catherine's party, but it wouldn't be good. She might make me withdraw from Wimbledon. Now I have to run because I need to get dressed."

"You'll be careful at the party, and after?"

"Yes, older sister, I'll be careful." I leaned over and kissed Claire's cheek. "Can we practice tomorrow morning?"

"I have Court 12 at 11." Another perquisite of being the holder: Claire decided when and where she would practice, as opposed to being told by the stewards whether she would be granted any practice time on a particular day. "Too early after a party for the season?"

"No, I'll be asleep in bed, alone, by midnight. See you at 11." I ran off to Albert House.

Wednesday evening, 27 June 1962
Party for Lady Catherine Thakeham
Grosvenor House
Mayfair

I took the Tube from Wimbledon Park to Marble Arch, changing at Notting Hill Gate. I tell myself that I dazzled my fellow riders on the Tube that evening; I was wearing my new Tinling gown, and a small diamond necklace, which Mother had loaned me, and which reached down just to my décolletage – not that I had much décolletage to work with.

I had been eating so many meals with Claire, who was convinced that I should double my intake of food, that I had put on an extra kilo in weight. I worried I might not fit into the gown, but actually it fit better now than when Teddy had finished it.

I felt elegant and sophisticated, and I loved it. Several people on the Tube recognized me from the BBC's television coverage of my match and congratulated me.

Catherine's party was in the ballroom at Grosvenor House and breakfast was to be served at two o'clock in the morning. I planned, though, to stay just long enough to be polite, for which I thought about an hour would be sufficient. I would be civil to Mark and avoid hitting him again. I walked into the ballroom just before 10 o'clock. The dancing hadn't started yet, and the guests were standing around in groups, drinking.

A young man I didn't know turned to me as I entered the room, put his drink down on a table and began to applaud. He cheered, "Well Done!" Then others began applauding and cheering. They crowded around me, and someone called out, "Are you going to win Wimbledon?" Claire had told me how to answer *that* question, and I replied, "I'm only thinking about the next round."

One of the men in the crowd wore a formal Royal Marine uniform. He was tall, with blond hair, and I guessed he was about 30 years old. He walked toward me. "May I introduce myself? I'm John Fitzwilliam. I saw you play today."

"I'm Fiona Hodgkin. You saw the match on the telly?"

"No, I was there. My family has debentures for the first Wednesday. I was watching Claire Kershaw's match on Centre Court, but from the cheering your match on the Graveyard sounded exciting. So I went over to Court 2. Were you injured in your fall in the second set?"

I laughed. "No, not at all, except for my dignity." I reached out and tapped my finger on a small medal on his chest. It was a silver cross bearing the Royal Cypher – 'EIIR,' for Elizabeth II Regina. "What an interesting medal."

He looked at me quizzically. "Do you know the DSC?" He meant the Distinguished Service Cross, which Britain awards for gallantry in combat at sea.

"My father has one. He was a ship's surgeon in the Royal Navy in the war. I've only seen him wear the medal once or twice. He wore it when the Queen came to Bermuda in 1953. The Queen walked down Front Street, and we saw her. Father wears the ribbon sometimes. On Christmas Eve, usually."

"That's right, I've heard you're from Bermuda. Why was your father awarded the DSC?"

"I don't know. I asked him, and he told me he couldn't recall. But I don't think he was being truthful. For what service were you awarded the DSC?"

"I can't recall."

We both laughed.

"Are you on a ship?"

"No, usually not."

"Shore duty, then."

"No, not that, either. I'm a Captain in the Special Boat Section." This was, and is, Britain's elite, small, and secretive naval commando group.

I put my hand on his arm. "Captain Fitzwilliam," I started, but he stopped me.

"Please call me John."

"I will, if you will call me Fiona. But, John, I need to find the guest of honor and pay my respects."

"I do as well, but I don't know her. Will you introduce me?" He offered me his arm. I put my hand in the crook of his elbow, and we set off across the room. "How do you come to know the Thakehams?" he asked.

"My father and Catherine's father served together in the war, and they're friends. Lady Thakeham was kind enough to invite me to London for Catherine's party and for the whole season."

"So you must be staying with the Thakehams?"

"Not at the moment. How do you know the Thakehams?"

"I don't. My mother knows Lady Thakeham – I couldn't tell you how – and my parents were invited to Catherine's party. They're away in the country, and my mother insisted that I come instead. I'm too old for a party during the season, but Mother hopes I'll find a girl to marry." He laughed.

"Are you looking for a wife?"

"No, not at all. My career isn't compatible with marriage."

We arrived at the side of the room where the Thakeham family was standing in a row, saying hello to their guests. There was a short line, so John and I waited our turn. We came to Mark first, and I held John's arm to avoid the possibility that Mark might try to take my hand.

Mark turned to me and rubbed his left cheek. "Luckily the doctors were able to save my jaw."

"How regrettable. I hoped to inflict permanent disfigurement."

"You came close, though."

I felt John straightening out his left arm to drop my hand. He sensed he might be in a false position here, but I held on tight.

"John, may I introduce you to Mark Thakeham? Mark, this is Captain John Fitzwilliam."

Catherine was now free, and I kissed her cheek and gave her my congratulations. Lady and Doctor Thakeham were next, and I thanked Lady Thakeham for inviting me to Catherine's party.

"Miss Hodgkin, dear child, I've been so worried about you. You're in a hotel somewhere. That wasn't my intention."

"It's not a hotel. It's a rooming house."

Lady Thakeham was taken aback that I would be living in a rooming house, which had been my intent in telling her. "Dear, it would be much better for you to return to our home. I'll have Harold collect you tonight, after the party."

The Tennis Player From Bermuda

"I'm quite comfortable where I am, but thank you for the offer." I tried to say this in a tone of voice that would convey my intent to never set foot in her house again. I looked at John, whose arm I still had in a death grip. From his expression, I guessed he was thinking that I had an interesting relationship with our hosts.

"But your parents are coming. They'll be upset that you're not with your aunts, or with us."

"My parents? Where are they coming?"

"To London, of course. This Monday. I sent them a telegram telling them to stay with us, but your mother said in her telegram that they would be at Claridge's, so I imagine that's where they'll lodge."

"Why are they coming to London?"

John interjected, "To watch their daughter play at Wimbledon? No, that couldn't be it. It must be something else."

"Your mother said she had sent you a telegram to the address of your" – an aristocratic pause – "hotel." You haven't received it?"

"No," I said, but then I thought that I had rushed dressing for the party so quickly that there might have been a telegram at the desk, and that I missed it.

Lady Thakeham said, "Your parents are bringing a friend from Bermuda as well."

"A friend? Rachel Martin?"

"Oh, dear child, I can't recall a name. Someone from Bermuda."

Just then the music began. I had planned to make my exit before there was any dancing, but John asked me to dance with him. He put his arm around me on the dance floor and said, "Ah, yes. Sweetness and light in the Thakeham household, I think."

I laughed. "You don't know the half of it. But if my parents are coming to London, that's wonderful news."

"Not until Monday, though. So they'll miss your third round match?"

"Yes, let's hope I win. I don't want them to come all that way and then find out that I'm no longer in the draw."

"Oh, I think you'll win. You were impressive this afternoon. I wish I could come see you play. When's your next match?"

"I won't know until the morning, when they post the intended order of play, but probably not until Saturday. Are you on duty this weekend?"

"Not that I know, although when they want me to be on duty, they usually don't give me much advance notice."

"Then why can't you come? I'd like to have you there."

"The tickets for the middle Saturday are impossible. Except for the finals, it's the most popular day of the fortnight."

"I think I'm entitled to a guest ticket. If I could get one, would you come?"

He stopped dancing. He wasn't any good at dancing to begin with. "Yes, I would."

"Then I'll do my best to get a ticket. How may I reach you?"

He gave me a house number in Wilton Place, Belgravia. I asked, "You don't live in barracks?"

"No, it's quite a cushy job, actually. I come and go as I please, except when they want me to do something for them."

I shivered a bit listening to him say this.

It was well past 11, and I told John I needed to leave.

"Why so early?"

"I'm practicing tomorrow morning. I need to get to sleep."

"Yes, of course. I've heard that you practice with Claire Kershaw."

I smiled. "To be honest, I'm proud she would practice with me. Claire got me into the qualifying round, so I wouldn't be at Wimbledon in the first place without her. She's a wonderful person."

"I quite agree; Claire is wonderful."

I was a bit surprised by the way he said this. "Do you know Claire?"

"Claire is my sister."

The instant he said this I saw the resemblance between them; why hadn't I noticed it before? I was stunned.

"Claire told me to watch your match on Court 2, but I wanted to see her match on Centre Court. On one of the changeovers, she noticed me in our seats. She glared and gestured for me to get over to the Graveyard and see what was happening. We could all hear the cheering, so I went to see you play. I got to the Graveyard just in time to see your tumble. Quite an interesting way to see you for the first time."

Then he said, "Do you have an auto?"

"No, I'm taking the Tube."

"Let me drive you to your rooming house – I'm sorry, I mean your hotel." He smiled. "My auto isn't here at Grosvenor House, but it's in Wood's Mews, just around the corner. Before you say 'No,' I'll tell you I must insist. Claire wouldn't forgive me for allowing her practice partner to get home on the Tube."

"But I'm staying in Wimbledon, and you'll have to drive there and back."

"I'll survive the round trip. Shall we?" he said, offering me his arm.

His garage in Wood's Mews was so narrow that he had to back the auto out before I could get in. The auto was painted silver, with a blue cloth hood. It looked like an upside down bathtub, and the motor rasped as though it was out of breath. I'd never seen or heard one like this before.

"What is it?" I asked.

"It's a Porsche 356 Carrera from West Germany. I've only had it a year. I meant to race it when I got it, but I've been away on duty quite a bit recently, and I've only gotten to the track twice. Do you prefer the hood up or dropped? The wind might ruffle your hair."

"Let's keep the hood up."

He drove like a man possessed, weaving in and out of traffic. I said, "Now I know Claire wasn't joking when she said you taught yourself to drive."

We pulled to a stop in front of Albert House, and John got out to open the door for me – but I noticed he kept the motor running.

He said, "I must tell you that you're splendid in that gown. I hope I'll see you in your third round match." He shook my hand, said "Goodnight," and started to walk back around the Porsche. I was going in the door of Albert House.

"Fiona!" he called.

I turned around. "Yes, John?"

"If your third round match happens to be on Saturday, would that mean that you could have dinner with me tomorrow evening?"

I smiled. "Yes, it would mean that."

"Then I'll hope that the match isn't until Saturday. Will the order of play be in the news tomorrow?"

"It's always in *The Times* and *The Daily Telegraph*."

"If your third round is set for Saturday, I could pick you up here tomorrow at, say, seven?"

"I'll be here."

Thursday, 28 June 1962
St. Mary's Walk
All England Club Wimbledon

The order of play went up that morning. I would be on Court 2 again for my third round match, against an American girl, Anita Castro. But not until Saturday afternoon, which meant that I would be having dinner with John that evening.

After we practiced, I said to Claire casually, "I met your brother yesterday evening."

She looked surprised. "John? Where would you meet John?"

"I told you I was going to a party for Catherine Thakeham, Mark's sister. John was there, and he introduced himself to me."

Claire laughed. "Why would John be at a party? He's not exactly the party type."

"He said your mother wanted him to find a girl to marry."

"Mother's engaging in wishful thinking there. He's not getting married, at least not anytime soon."

"He told me his career isn't compatible with marriage."

She frowned. "I don't like it when John says things like that. I wish he'd resign his commission and find another job. Father has asked him to, twice, and offered to help him find a place in the City, but John just laughs."

"Claire, John asked me to dinner this evening."

That stopped Claire in her tracks. "Fiona, he's much older than you."

"It's just dinner."

"With John, I doubt it's ever just dinner."

"Well, he was a perfect gentleman last evening. He drove me back to Albert House."

We had to get off the court because two groundskeepers had arrived to prepare it for the afternoon's matches. Claire pointed out to them a small patch of grass just outside the sideline that she thought was still damp from the early morning dew. They went down on hands and knees and began patting the grass dry with cotton towels.

Claire took my arm, and we went along St. Mary's Walk toward Centre Court.

"Don't misunderstand me," Claire said. "I love John. I probably know him better than anyone else. But he dates a lot of girls. He's not interested in a relationship. I just don't want you to have your feelings hurt."

"I'm just going to have dinner with him. I doubt he has any interest in me."

"If he asked you to dinner, he's interested in you."

I was thrilled to hear her say this. "Do you really think he might like me?"

Claire rolled her eyes. "I can't believe this is happening. And in the middle of Wimbledon. If my brother throws you off your tennis game, I'll poison him. Just don't let him take you to bed until Wimbledon ends."

"I have no intention of going to bed with anyone."

Claire scoffed. "We'll see about that."

A schoolgirl in a blue jumper approached Claire and asked

for her autograph. The poor girl was so shy she could barely get the words out of her mouth. There was no 'security' for players then. A shy schoolgirl asking for an autograph was about the most dangerous thing that could happen at Wimbledon to a tennis celebrity like Claire.

To be honest, the girl wasn't as pretty as she could have made herself: her hair was curly and wild, and she was just a bit chubby – unusual for an English girl then.

Claire said, "How old are you?"

"I just turned 14."

"What's your name?"

"Edith Wright."

"Do you have a boyfriend?"

"Claire!" I said.

Claire said, "Edith, ignore Fiona. What's the answer?"

"No." Edith hesitated. "I'm not that pretty."

Claire turned to me. "What do you think, Fiona?"

"Edith's quite attractive. She might pull her hair back. Perhaps take up field hockey in school." I thought a season of field hockey would fix the chubbiness.

Claire handed her rackets to me, took Edith's head in her hands, and gently turned Edith's face this way and then that. Then Claire took Edith's hair and pushed it back from her face.

Claire said, "Edith has strikingly good looks. The boys will be after her in a year or so."

Edith glowed.

"Give me your programme," Claire said.

Claire turned Edith's programme to the ladies' singles draw. Printed at the top of the page was: "HOLDER: MRS R. KERSHAW." She wrote carefully on the page, "*To Edith Wright, who has a LETHAL forehand. Best Regards, Claire Kershaw."*

Claire thought for a moment. Then she wrote on Edith's programme, "*LIBerty 6152.*"

Claire handed the programme back and pointed to the number. "Edith, listen to me. That's my telephone number. If you have any worries about boys, or anything else, ring me. I'll remember you, and we'll talk."

She said softly, "Yes, Mrs Kershaw."

"Edith, call me 'Claire.'"

Edith glowed. "Yes, Claire."

Thursday Evening, 28 June 1962
London, England

John said to me over the rasp of the Porsche's motor, "Do you like Syrian food?"

"We just don't get as much good Syrian food in Bermuda as I would like."

"Are you teasing me?"

"Yes, I'm teasing you. I've never had Syrian food and have no idea what it's like."

"Are you willing to try it?"

"Certainly."

We went to a small lane in Ludgate Hill, then up a dark flight of steps, and into a tiny restaurant. A young man appeared from the kitchen and greeted John in what I took to be Arabic, and John answered back in the same language. They kissed one another on each cheek. There was no menu, and after John consulted with the young man for several moments, he ordered for both of us. "Do you mind eating with your fingers?"

"Not at all. In Bermuda, we regard using knives and forks as bad form."

"More teasing."

The meal was served in a series of small dishes – all

delicious. John taught me the name of each dish and showed me how to eat with a small, folded piece of bread in my fingers. He took a tiny piece of lamb in a piece of bread, put one hand under my chin, and with his other hand fed me the lamb. He shared Claire's dry sense of humor but none of her rambunctiousness.

"Is the language you were speaking Arabic?"

"Yes. My friend here speaks some English, but he's more comfortable in Arabic."

"Where did you learn Arabic?"

"I read oriental languages at Christ Church, Oxford, before I went down and took my commission in the Royal Marines."

"Oh."

After dinner, we left the Porsche parked near the Embankment and went for a walk along the Thames. There was a bit of fog, and I looked up at the night sky over London.

John said, "Are you worried about rain? You don't play until Saturday."

"We're right on schedule; there's been no rain this week. If it rained tomorrow and delayed the order of play, it could set back my match on Saturday."

We walked along, and I asked him, "How did you join the Special Boat Section?"

"One of my senior officers in the Marines once casually asked me if I'd ever thought about the Section. I replied it would be something I'd be quite interested in doing. But I heard nothing further about it. Then, a few months later, I was on a ship that's in port, not in Britain. Somewhere else. I'm on shore one afternoon on leave, and this uncouth chap in blue jeans and a tee shirt approaches me. He says he's a

Captain in the Section, and I'm to come with him. I don't believe him, do I? He's got no identification. Well, that's not true. He showed me an expired driver's license from the States. But he sounds to me as though he's from East London – which he was, in fact.

"So he asks, of all things, if I want to come see his helicopter. I say, certainly, I'll come see his helicopter, which of course I assume doesn't exist. We drive an hour or so to an airfield and damned if he doesn't have a helicopter."

He stopped. "Excuse me, Fiona, I didn't mean to swear."

"I'll survive."

He went on. "The helicopter was a sleek machine, in fact. I thought either this fellow is in the SBS, or he's stolen this helicopter, one or the other." John laughed.

"Was he actually with the SBS?"

"It turns out I was right on both counts. Yes, he was a Captain in the Section, and, yes, he had stolen the helicopter. He'd also stolen the car we'd driven to the airfield."

"How did you know he'd stolen the helicopter?"

"Just then, three fellows arrived at the edge of the airfield in an auto. They opened fire on us with small arms. I asked him why anyone would be trying to kill us. He said he thought they wanted their helicopter back. He could be quite sensitive to the feelings of others, when the mood was upon him."

"What did you do?"

"We got in the helicopter, and he said that there was an Uzi in the cockpit."

John stopped again. "An Uzi is a light automatic weapon."

"Thanks for clearing that up for me."

"So I said, 'You fly, and I'll find the Uzi.'"

The Tennis Player From Bermuda

"He was a helicopter pilot?"

"Not really. The first time he ever piloted a helicopter was when he stole this one. He was what you might call a 'self-taught' helicopter pilot. He had particular problems with landing; he never could work out how it was supposed to be done. So he just would get within a few meters of the ground and kill the engine. His landings were a bit rough."

John laughed again and shook his head. "Quite a chap."

"He must be a friend of yours."

"He was. A close friend. He's dead now."

My blood ran cold. We walked along the Embankment for a minute or so. "Were you with him when he died?"

John didn't say anything. I sensed he was trying to decide whether he could tell me, but finally he said, "Yes." He paused. "I carried his body back."

He wanted to change the subject. He stopped and turned to face me. "Why do you wear your hair in a ponytail?"

"My parents want my hair kept long. They think it looks feminine long. I want it out of my face, for tennis. So, a ponytail."

He reached around my head and held my ponytail in his hand. "Do you mind?" Then he gently pulled off the band that held my hair back. "Shake your head."

I shook my head, and my hair flew around my face. He took my left hand and slipped my hair band onto my wrist. It occurred to me that somehow he knew how a girl would use the band to tie her hair back. Then he pushed his fingers gently through my hair. I felt faint. He put his hand under my chin and kissed me.

He finished kissing me. "Do you want to have a cup of tea at my flat? I live in the ground floor of my parents' house."

"A cup of tea would be perfect. Why do you live in your parents' ground floor?"

"Well, it's convenient. When I have to go away on duty, they look after my flat. I don't have to tell anyone else that I'm on duty, which is good."

"What about Claire?"

"Oh, our parents tell her I've gone away for a bit."

His parents' home was one of a long, curved row of identical, white townhouses on a private square in Belgravia. I've returned to this home many times in my life, and each time I think about that Thursday evening during the 1962 Championships.

The door to John's flat was down a winding staircase from the sidewalk. It led to a door under the entryway to the main house. There were flowers in boxes on the windowsills of the house. John unlocked the door, swung it open, and turned on the light. It was just two rooms, a sitting room and a bedroom, joined by a hallway in which there was an old kitchen. The flat was small and windowless, with a few pieces of furniture covered in English floral-print cloth.

"Don't blame me for the decorating," John said. "My mother had the flat fixed up when I came back to live in London a couple of years ago. Not my preference but, as I say, it's convenient."

I sat on a sofa in the sitting room. I had half expected that the promised cup of tea would not actually be offered, but John busied himself in the hallway kitchen putting together a tea tray. He carried it out and poured us each tea. I was permitted perhaps two sips before John took my cup away. He kissed me again, and I kissed him back. He pulled me onto his lap, and I put my arms around his neck.

John said, "Do you want to stay here tonight, or would you rather I drive you back to Albert House?" Direct, but the perfect gentleman. My decision; no pressure.

I had my face buried against his shoulder. "Here."

"Good." He stood up, with me cradled in his arms. He was incredibly strong; he might as well have been holding a pillow.

He was carrying me though the hallway kitchen when he asked, "How old are you?"

"I'll be 19 on Sunday." The hallway was narrow; he had to turn sideways to maneuver me through. My answer, I could tell, had given him pause. No doubt I was much younger than his other girlfriends.

"Fiona, have you done this before?"

I knew Claire was still skeptical about exactly what had happened with Mark, so I answered, "Maybe."

He roared with laughter, then put me down on my feet. We were standing in the kitchen hallway. I could tell he was worried he had hurt my feelings by laughing, and he had, just a bit. He kissed me, which made me feel better.

"Fiona, I'm sorry. I didn't mean to laugh. But most people would answer that question with a 'yes,' or 'no.' It's not a question that often elicits a 'maybe.'"

I didn't say anything. I put my arms around his waist and leaned my head against his chest. I sensed his next question would be on a subject that he normally wouldn't concern himself with but that now, as a gentleman, he would feel obliged to raise. And I was right.

"Fiona, do you have a way to take precautions?"

"No. But it's not a problem." My period had just ended; I didn't think I could get pregnant that night.

He didn't say anything for a moment. Then he said, "Look, I want you very much. But this isn't a good idea. Let's wait."

So we got back in the Porsche, and he drove me to Albert House. He opened the door of the 356 for me, and when I got out, he put his arms around me and kissed me.

"John, may I ring you tomorrow?"

"I hope you will."

"Give me your number, then," I said. He popped open the glove box of the 356 and found a scrap of paper. "Turn around," he told me. I turned around, and, using my back for support, he wrote out his number.

Then he kissed me again, said goodnight, and stepped over the door of the Porsche into the driver's seat. He didn't bother opening the door to get in. He waved at me, threw the 356 into gear and raced off.

Friday, 29 June 1962
All England Club Wimbledon

Earlier in the week, the upper ladies' dressing room had been crowded all the time, with a constant babble of talk among the girls. Now the draw was much smaller. Each round sliced the draw in half. Claire and I were alone in the dressing room Friday morning.

Claire asked, "How was dinner?"

"Claire, I need a diaphragm. Can you help me?"

"I take it we're talking about my brother?"

"Yes."

"Yesterday you said you weren't going to sleep with anyone."

"I've changed my mind."

"It must have been quite a dinner. Fiona, I love John, but is this a good idea?"

"I know, I know. He has plenty of girls, he's older than me, I shouldn't fall for him, I'll get hurt."

"Well?"

"So I won't fall for him."

"I think you've fallen for him already."

"I've fallen for him already. Will you help me?"

"Did you sleep with him?"

"No, but only because we didn't want to until I can take what he calls 'precautions.' Or, more accurately, *he* didn't want to. I was prepared to be more flexible."

"See? I did teach my brother some things. Fiona, John is a good person, basically, but sometimes he toys with women. Maybe most of the time. He sees a lot of girls. A couple of them are movie actress types. He's not going to be interested in a relationship. And he's nine years or so older than you. I just think this is a bad idea for you to see him, much less sleep with him. I don't think you should get involved. I think you're going to get hurt."

I just looked at her.

"I'll ring my doctor now and see if I can get you an appointment today."

That afternoon, Claire took me to her gynecologist. She was sitting in the waiting room when I came out half an hour later. "Well?"

In reply, I opened my pocketbook and showed her the small blue plastic box inside. She embraced me.

"Excellent!" Then she said suspiciously, "Do you know how to use it?"

"Yes, my grandmother explained it all to me."

"Your grandmother told you how to use a diaphragm?"

"She's an unusual grandmother."

"I'll say."

When I got back to Albert House, I went to the telephone in the downstairs entryway and rang John. "May I come see you?"

"Are you at Albert House? Why don't I come get you?"

"No, I can easily take the Tube. The Friday afternoon traffic will be frightful."

"The Tube to Hyde Park Corner?"
"Yes."
"Come out the exit on Grosvenor Place. I'll wait for you there."

Two hours later I was in his bed.

I got up on my knees and whispered to John. "May I spend the night?"

John was dozing. "You're not going anywhere. You're staying close at hand and naked. I'll want you again later tonight."

I kissed him on his ear. "Now."

"Fiona, I am entitled to a break now and then. It's in my contract somewhere, I think."

I shook my head. My hair hung down over his face. "No."

"No? Don't you have an important tennis match tomorrow afternoon?"

"Yes, I have a match in the afternoon. And no, you're not entitled to a break." I kissed him again, and he reached up for me.

SATURDAY MORNING, 30 JUNE 1962
BELGRAVIA

We were sitting in bed with a tea tray John had made and reading the Saturday morning papers, which John had collected from his parents' front steps, when the telephone rang.

John picked up the receiver, listened for a moment, and said, "Claire, dear, what makes you think Fiona would be here?" Then he had to hold the receiver away from his ear. His sister was yelling at him over the telephone.

John held the receiver out to me. "Claire wants to speak with you."

Claire didn't begin with any pleasantries, like 'hello.' Instead, she said, "How much sleep did you get?"

I giggled.

Claire yelled, "I knew it. I can't believe John's done this. Let me talk to him."

I handed the receiver to John. "Your sister wants to talk to you."

"Claire, I wanted Fiona to get some sleep. This wasn't entirely my fault."

He had to hold the receiver away from his ear again. Claire said so loudly that I could hear: "Has she had breakfast? I mean, a real breakfast?"

"Well, I was just going to boil her an egg and perhaps make some toast."

He held the receiver away from his ear. I could hear Claire yelling, "A boiled egg? You couldn't boil an egg. You have no idea how to boil an egg."

"Yes, I do. You take a pot of water and – "

She cut him off. "You don't own a pot, much less do you have an egg. Let me speak to Fiona."

John handed me the receiver. "My sister wants to speak with you."

"Fiona, are you there?"

"Yes," I said meekly.

"Listen to me. I want my brother to take you to a tea shop, right now." She paused. "And I mean right now. No more fooling around. I want you to have a full English breakfast. Drink a lot of tea and water. Have John take you back to Albert House. Go to bed – alone. Ask Mrs Brown not to let you sleep past noon. Then I want to knock up at one o'clock sharp. We have Court 12. You'll be there? You're on the Graveyard at two o'clock. They'll call for you a bit before two so we'll have half an hour, maybe a little more, to practice."

"Yes, Claire. I'll meet you on Court 12."

"Fiona, this American girl, Castro – I've never played her, but she's not a lollipop. No one gets into the third round without being dangerous, extremely dangerous. You'll have to beat her. It could rain today. You might have rain delays. It could be a long day."

"I know. I'm fine. I can take her."

Claire softened her tone just a bit. "So, how was John?"

"Claire, he's sitting right here, so let's talk later. But he's a perfect gentleman. He took care of me."

"Good, I knew he would," she said, and rang off.

Claire had her own match on Centre court that afternoon to think about. Instead of worrying about herself, she was taking care of me.

With John listening, I didn't want to tell Claire that I was hopelessly in love with him.

SATURDAY AFTERNOON, 30 JUNE 1962
COURT 2 (THE 'GRAVEYARD')
LADIES' THIRD ROUND
ALL ENGLAND CLUB WIMBLEDON

There had been comments in the Saturday morning newspapers about the Committee's decision to set my third round match on Court 2, rather than on Centre Court, or perhaps at least Court 1.

I had been a bit disappointed when I had seen the order of play; I had hoped to play on Centre Court. The newspapers, to my surprise, commented that the Committee seemed to be trying to help me by keeping me away from the pressure and intensity of Centre Court. My third round opponent, Anita Castro, from Florida in the States, was in her third Wimbledon and had played twice on Centre Court. The bookies, according to the newspapers, were giving good odds in favor of Castro.

In the dressing room before the match, Castro was relaxed and friendly. The American girls I had met so far at Wimbledon had all been influenced by Teach Tennant, even those who had never met Teach. Teach felt strongly that a player should be hostile to opponents.

I said to Anita, "I thought Teach told the American girls not to chat with their opponents."

Anita laughed. "You mean the girls from the West Coast, from California."

"I thought it was everyone."

"No, Teach influences just the girls from the West Coast. I'm from Florida. Most girls in Florida have never heard of Teach."

Anita was a large, strong woman, and she played Jack Kramer's 'Big Game' – meaning that she served hard and rushed the net, looking for a quick volley winner.

I lacked the physical strength to play the Big Game. I had to serve spot on and then make a good approach shot off my opponent's return of my service. Everyone thought I took too many risks. But once you hit an approach shot, there's no going back. You can't stand there in No Man's Land, between the baseline and the service line. You have to go forward, into the service boxes, and take your chances. But when you go forward, you're stuck out in the open and vulnerable to a passing shot. You have only instinct to help you; there's no time to think.

Rachel had told me for years that my game, assuming I placed my serve well, depended on my getting into the correct position at the net. And this was a matter of centimeters. Six or so centimeters out of the correct tactical position, and I would miss the volley altogether, or the ball would ricochet off the edge of my racket into the stands.

There were dark storm clouds overhead when we went out on Court 2. I failed to concentrate in the first set and lost 6-2. Court 2 had been full at the start of the match, but I sensed the crowd had now decided that this was the end of my Wimbledon, and many of the spectators began to drift away. I had a sinking feeling that Anita was confident that she had this match in the bag.

The Tennis Player From Bermuda

In the first game of the second set, on my serve, Anita lunged for one of my volleys when, of all things, the hooks on her bra snapped, and she hit my shot into the net. Anita's bust was of a size that made the bra's demise immediately obvious to the spectators. Also, her bust made continuing play *sans* bra not an option.

Anita had a couple of spare rackets and a spare pair of tennis shoes. But a spare bra? No. The chair umpire – a man, naturally – had not previously been presented with this particular problem.

A lady in the crowd called out that she had a safety pin in her purse, if that would help. Technically, it violated the rules to accept the safety pin – spectators could offer no assistance to the players – but perhaps the rule hadn't been written with this situation in mind.

I turned to Anita, and we both started laughing. I went over to the stands, and the safety pin was passed down to me through several rows of spectators.

"Turn around," I said to Anita. "I think we can do this and still retain your modesty." I yanked her blouse out of the waistband of her tennis skirt and pulled it up in back. It took me a minute, but I got the back of her bra pinned together with the safety pin.

I said quietly to Anita, "Does that feel all right?"

"It feels great – thanks!"

The crowd started to applaud.

I picked up my racket and held it up in the air. "I think we should thank the lady who contributed the safety pin!" I said, loudly enough for all the spectators to hear.

The crowd stood and applauded even more.

The umpire – no doubt relieved that this feminine crisis

243

was over – said into the microphone, "Second set, first game, Miss Hodgkin to serve at 30-love."

He had awarded me the point.

Anita and I were still standing together, just behind the umpire's chair. I put my hand on her shoulder, leaned over, and said quietly, "I think we should play a let." I meant that we should replay the last point.

"That would be great. I'd appreciate that." Then she kissed my cheek.

We separated and walked back to our respective baselines.

I said to the umpire, "Anita and I have decided to play a let. The score is 15-love."

The umpire was taken aback and plainly concerned that I was taking over from him as the person in charge of this match.

The crowd roared its approval.

I held my serve, and then, in the second game, with Anita serving, the clouds opened and a heavy rain began. The groundskeepers ran to pull the tarp over the court, and Anita and I raced for the players' entrance.

When I made my way to the upper dressing room, John was standing at the door.

I kissed him quickly and asked, "How is Claire's match?"

"She's inside," he said, nodding toward the door. "She's just a game away. Easy for me to say, but I can't see that she's having any problem dealing with her opponent."

I kissed him again and pushed through the door.

The dressing room was crowded; all the matches in progress had been suspended at once because of the sudden rain.

Claire was sitting on a bench, and I sat down beside her.

I said to her, "You've almost won your match, John says."

"Yes, I don't think it'll be a problem – if we can resume play. I'd like to get this match over with. And you?"

"Not good. I dropped the first set, 6-2."

Claire stared at me. "What happened?"

"I wasn't paying attention. But I am now."

Anita was sitting just across from us. Mrs Ward had taken her bra and was sewing the hooks back on. Anita had a towel draped over her shoulders.

A rumor ran around the dressing room that it had stopped raining, and we would be called back onto the courts soon. Anita leaned over and said to me, "Fiona, I'm worried they'll call us back before my bra is fixed."

"Anita, I'm not playing until you're ready to play. The umpire can't default both of us."

I looked back at Claire, worried that she might think I shouldn't agree to a possible delay that might help my opponent. I whispered, "Was that all right to tell her?"

Claire shrugged. "Just fair play. Not worth winning otherwise."

The rumor was wrong. The rain delay ended up lasting longer than an hour, and then finally we were all called back to the courts.

Anita and I knocked up and resumed play on Anita's serve.

We played out the second set, and I was so focused that I didn't realize that Claire and John had found seats during one of the changeovers. I took the set at 10-8.

Third set; I finally noticed John and Claire in the stands. I held both thumbs up to ask, 'Did you win?' Claire smiled and held both her thumbs up. She was in the fifth round, or as we would say today, the quarterfinals. Or just 'the quarters.'

Anita and I were on serve in the tenth game of the third set when the rain began again, hard. I looked at my watch; it was almost eight o'clock. We ran to the players' entrance.

In the dressing room, Anita went to the loo, and Claire immediately took my shoulders in her hands. "How are you doing?"

"Claire, I'm exhausted," I whispered back.

"Fiona, she's exhausted too. You have to play out the third set. You'll win. You're so close."

Claire asked Mrs Ward for a cup of tea. When she brought it, Claire had to hold the cup to my lips. I couldn't even raise my hands.

I thought, 'How can I even play, much less win?'

Claire put her arm around my shoulder. She placed her lips close to my ear so she could talk to me privately. We were in a gray zone of the prohibition against coaching. "Fiona, you have to win before it's dark. You can't give her a day to rest."

"I can't play. I have to quit."

Claire took my chin in her hand. She shook my head, not hard, but not gently either. She spoke right into my ear so no one else would hear her. "You're a champion. Now's the time a champion proves who she is." Claire gave me another sip of tea. "Run her around."

"Claire, I've already – "

She cut me off. "Fiona," she whispered, "she's almost done in. Volley to one corner, make her run there, and then volley to the other corner. She's almost finished. But win before it gets dark. Don't give her a day to rest."

At half past eight, our chair umpire knocked on the door

of the dressing room. Mrs Ward answered the door, and the chair umpire asked, "May I speak with Miss Castro and Miss Hodgkin?"

We went outside the dressing room. The umpire said, "Well, Monday's going to be a train wreck of a schedule anyway with this rain. Colonel Legg just met with the Committee, and they'd like to finish your match this evening, if possible. It would make Monday a bit easier. It's not raining now, but clouds are so dark the light isn't perfect, I'll admit that. Colonel Legg told me that you'll both have to agree to play in the fading light. It's your right to have good light for play. If either of you don't want to play, well then, somehow we'll just do it on Monday."

There was never play at the All England Club on Sunday. This was to avoid disturbing the local churchgoers on their way to St. Mary's.

I looked at Anita. 'Claire's right,' I thought. 'She's even more done in than me.'

I reached over and put my hand on Anita's arm. "Anita, this is your decision. I'm happy playing now, but it's whatever you want to do."

Looking back on all the extraordinary things that happened to me at Wimbledon 50 years ago, what I remember best is Anita's reply that rainy evening.

She hugged me. "Let's play it out now, Fiona."

This, I knew, was her thanks to me for helping her earlier in the match. Anita was a sport. I had helped her. Now she would play even though I'm sure she knew she'd be better off waiting until Monday.

We went out on Court 2. The Committee's definition of 'not raining' was interesting, since in Bermuda we would have classified the weather on the court that evening as 'light drizzle.' The grass was slippery. Plus, it had suddenly turned quite chilly during the rain delay. Anita put on a cardigan, and I took out Rachel's old sweater and pulled it over my head, freed my ponytail from underneath the sweater, and walked out on the court.

There were five or six Australians in the stands, still in mourning over Margaret Smith's loss on Tuesday. When they saw 'KOOYONG' on my sweater, they were thrilled. From then on, I had a small but loud and boisterous cheering section.

I concentrated on making Anita run from corner to corner, over and over again, as Claire told me to, and it worked. After each point, I looked at the sky and the fading light. I had to win tonight and that meant winning quickly, before it became too dark.

But Anita was out of fuel. I could tell because she started hitting more crosscourt shots – she needed the additional margin of error a crosscourt shot provides.

I drilled down on my volleys.

I would have lost to Anita if the rain hadn't come. Or, probably, if Anita had elected to wait until Monday to finish the third set.

It was just luck.

But as it happened, minutes before the umpire would have had to suspend play for darkness, I broke Anita and then got a match point on my serve at 7-6. There were only a few spectators left in the stands on Court 2, including the Australians. John and Claire were there, both soaked to the skin, both shivering and both cheering for me.

What did I ever do to deserve these two people?

I tossed the ball, swung my racket and hit the ball down the center. Anita just reached it and hit a return. Not strong, but short and low. I reached the ball, bent so far down that my right knee was skidding on the wet grass. Out of the corner of my eye, I saw Anita shifting a bit toward the deuce court; she was guessing I'd go crosscourt. But I didn't. I flipped the ball over the net into the near ad court.

My point. My game. My match. One more minute, at most, and the umpire would have suspended play for darkness.

Now the umpire wanted nothing more than to get out of the cold and drizzle. He vacated the chair for cover as quickly as I've ever seen an umpire move. Anita and I embraced and then we stumbled toward the dressing room.

John was standing in the entryway, just under cover. I grabbed his shoulders and fainted. I went limp in his arms. Then Claire had her hands on my cheeks and was shaking me. "Fiona, wake up. Wake up."

I opened my eyes. The Australians had found us and announced their plan to carry me around on their shoulders in the rain. Claire told them, "Not tonight, boys. Fiona's knackered. Come back Monday, bring all your mates, and you can do whatever you like with her."

This satisfied the Australians, and they went off in search of beer.

Claire frowned. "Aussies can be so literal-minded sometimes. You might be a bit careful around them on Monday."

I said, "I'm going to be sick."

"Not here. The loo," Claire said.

There were photographers everywhere. Claire grabbed

me out of John's arms and hustled me to the ladies' loo just inside Centre Court. She took the back of my head and pushed me over the lavatory. I threw up.

I tried to straighten myself, but Claire said, "I don't think you're finished." I wasn't.

Finally, Claire took a paper towel, put water on it, and began cleaning off my face.

"Claire." I was choking, slightly.

"What?"

"Rachel told me not to play at Roehampton. I mean to try and qualify for Wimbledon. She said it would change me. Not for the better. That it would take too much. Is this what she meant?"

"She'll be here on Monday. Ask her yourself," Claire said, while she was wiping my face. But there was bitterness in Claire's voice.

I was in the fourth round.

Sunday, 1 July 1962
My Nineteenth Birthday
Belgravia

I don't remember how Claire and John took me back to his flat. I don't recall anything about that evening after being sick in the loo. But I do recall waking up Sunday morning in John's bed.

"Happy birthday!" he said. "Would you like some tea?" He had made a tea tray, which he put down on the bed.

"I would love some tea. And I'm famished. Could we get breakfast somewhere?"

"Claire and Richard are on their way here. Claire just rang. They're going to stop and buy breakfast. I can't imagine why they think I couldn't just make breakfast for us."

"Could you?"

"No, not at all," he laughed.

I held out my arms to him and, to be honest, I deliberately let the sheet drop below my breasts. I almost couldn't believe that John would respond to me, but he did, and it was wonderful. He caressed me, and then reached under the bed and brought out a small package that had been gift-wrapped.

"This is for your birthday."

I tore open the wrapping. It was a cheap cloth wash bag

from Harrods. It had two small initials picked out on the corner: 'FH.'

I loved it. I still have it.

John said, "Well, if you're going to be hanging around the flat, I don't want your things in the loo getting mixed up with my own." Since John – like Father – used a regulation Royal Navy shaving kit for his razor, there was little risk of our things getting mixed up.

I put my arms around him and pulled him down to me.

Unfortunately, it turned out that Claire not only had a key to the flat, but that she didn't bother knocking when she entered – which she did at that moment, with Richard in tow, and with plenty of bagels, cream cheese, smoked salmon, red onions, and an almond coffee cake.

Claire said, "Would you two please stop for just a bit? You both have to eat sometime."

John's flat had no place for four people to have breakfast, so we trooped upstairs to the Fitzwilliam house to eat. On the way, we collected all the Sunday newspapers that had been delivered to the front steps. Claire made tea, and I spread out the bagels and other things on the kitchen table.

Then we sat around the table, ate, and read the newspapers. John was engrossed in *The Times Literary Supplement*. Claire was wearing her eyeglasses – which she never did in public – and she had her left arm draped over Richard's shoulders in a proprietary sort of way.

I was wearing a bathrobe that belonged to John, which was ridiculously big for me. I lifted my legs and put my feet on John's lap. He didn't raise his eyes from the *TLS*. Instead, he simply pulled my feet closer to him and squeezed my toes with his hand.

We were all quiet. It was an ordinary Sunday morning. Wimbledon didn't exist. Someone asked, "Is there more tea?" Someone else looked into the teapot. "No, I'll put the kettle on for more."

For just a moment, I allowed myself one wild, impossible thought: this would be a wonderful family into which to marry.

Later that day, John and I went for a walk in Belgravia Square Gardens, which is private. John took a small key out of his pocket to unlock the gate for us. It was a beautiful day after yesterday's rain, but still quite cool for early July.

I said, "I have to go back to Albert House."

"Why?"

"I have no clean clothes. Mrs Ward looks after my tennis dresses, but I need to organize a laundry for my other things."

"Mother has a laundry room upstairs. You can use that. I'll drive you over to Albert House."

"John, I worry that I'm imposing on you at the flat. I'm sure you have other things to do than look after me. I'll stay at Albert House."

"You're sleeping at my flat. I want you available to me."

I liked the idea of being available to him; it made me feel feminine. "You're sure?"

"Don't be silly, Fiona. But I don't have the keys to the 356 with me. So we'll have to stop at the flat first before we head to Wood's Mews."

When we arrived at Albert House, there was a telegram for me from Mother and Father:

The Tennis Player From Bermuda

Post Office Telegram

ON BOARD THE SS OCEAN MONARCH BY WIRELESS

ARRIVE SOUTHAMPTON MONDAY AM LONDON PM STOP
CLARIDGES WILL SEND TO ALBERT HOUSE FOR YOUR
BAGGAGE STOP ALL TALK ON BOARD SHIP IS OF YOUR
WIMBLEDON WINS STOP LOVE MOTHER AND FATHER

I showed it to John. He said, "Do you think Claridge's will be delivering your things to my flat?"

"Doubtful."

There was one other item waiting for me. The Committee knew that several lady players stayed at Albert House, and so a steward that morning had hand-delivered copies of the Intended Order of Play for the next day.

I was to play on Centre Court Monday afternoon. At '2 pm precisely.'

Monday, 2 July 1962
Centre Court
Ladies' Fourth Round Match
All England Club Wimbledon

Claire sat on the bench beside me in the dressing room. "I've played Dorothy many times." My opponent Monday afternoon was Dorothy Fielding.

Claire went on. "She's a good friend of mine. She's British, so the crowd might favor her." Claire chuckled to herself. "But remember what Jack Kramer once said: 'The British would pack Centre Court to watch two rabbits play tennis.' I don't think Dorothy will be a problem for you. I'll be in the players' box watching with John."

She kissed my cheek. "Good luck, Fiona."

She stood and left the dressing room. Three minutes later she came back through the door. "Fiona, do you have Rachel's sweater with you?"

"Yes, it's in my kit."

"Well, put it on before you walk out on Centre Court."

"It's warm. I don't need a sweater."

"The Australians are here, and I mean in force. They're cheering for you already, and I think they want to see that sweater. It's never good to disappoint Australians – they don't like disappointment."

"What are they cheering?"

"You'll find out. Just put on Rachel's sweater before you walk out. You can take it off after you knock up."

She took my hand, squeezed it gently and left again. I pulled on Rachel's sweater.

The callboy came, and Dorothy and I walked to the waiting room and then out onto Centre Court. I was met with a wall of noise from the Australians: "*AUSSIE! AUSSIE! AUSSIE! FI! FI! FI!*"

Over and over again. They were calling me 'Fi.' They yelled this cheer until the umpire finally asked them to be quiet.

My first match on Centre Court. I wasn't scared, exactly, but it was a big moment for me. It was a world away from the Graveyard. No one – not even Claire – was permitted to practice on Centre Court. During the first week of the Championships, I had asked Claire to knock up with me on Centre Court, just so I could see what it was like. Claire – who would do just about anything for me – shook her head. "I can't take you onto Centre Court. You have to wait for the Committee to schedule you to play there."

A tennis player's first Centre Court match, like for me that Monday afternoon? – well, that would always be the first time that player had ever set foot onto Centre Court.

Fred Perry said once that a player could see the ball better on Centre Court because the dark green sighting walls (which screened the tackle used to raise the tarp over Centre Court) and the low roof put the ball against a uniform, dim background. On most of the outer courts, the ball would pop up into the player's sight against a bright, sun-lit, multi-coloured expanse of spectators. Fred thought this difference made players in their first time on Centre Court think they had more time to swing their racket. He was right about that: it took me most of the first set against Dorothy to adjust my timing.

Centre Court was *quiet*. I would close in to the net, volley, and then stop and wait a half-second for Dorothy's attempt to pass me. Centre Court, in that instant, was so strangely tranquil – I loved that moment in each point. You're an actor on the stage of Shakespeare's Globe, with the audience waiting for your next line – *When we have match'd our rackets to these balls, we will in France (by God's grace) play a set.*

But then, Shakespeare in *Henry V* was speaking of real tennis.

In the third set, Dorothy and I were on service at 3-4, me to serve, and we changed ends. I waited for Dorothy to get a cup of water from the tank and then got myself a cup.

While I was drinking, I turned around to glance at John and Claire in the players' box. Claire was standing and hugging someone, but I couldn't see who it was. Then Claire pulled away; she had been hugging Rachel.

I yelled, "RACHEL!"

Rachel smiled at me, and gave me a slight wave, but she wasn't going to do anything that the umpire might consider coaching. Just then, Mother appeared in the gangway to the players' box, with Father just behind her.

I yelled again: "MOTHER! FATHER!"

Mother and Father waved, smiled, and called back, "Fiona!"

I was so excited to see them, and so proud that they could see me on Centre Court, that I pointed back to the court with my racket. "I'M PLAYING ON CENTRE COURT!" As though this wasn't entirely obvious.

A ripple of laughter went around Centre Court, and I heard even the umpire chuckling. There was a bit of cheering.

Then someone stood and began to applaud. In an instant, every spectator was standing and applauding.

The Australians took up their cheer: "*AUSSIE! AUSSIE! AUSSIE! FI! FI! FI!*"

The umpire felt this had gone quite far enough. "Quiet, please, ladies and gentlemen. The sets are one each. Games in the third set are 3-4. Miss Hodgkin to serve."

I held my service easily.

Dorothy served at 4 all. She went up 30-love quickly, but then I followed in her second service and hit a forehand volley winner. 30-15. I looked over at Rachel. She was impassive, with her hands folded in her lap. Dorothy hit a strong first service, which I could only block back, but then she took my shot and hit her return long.

30 all. I was two points away from breaking her serve.

Dorothy took her time preparing to serve. Another strong first service, but this time I took it with my backhand and hit my return as hard as I could. I thought it might float out, but it just touched the outer edge of the line. Dorothy got to it, but hit it back wide.

The umpire said, "Advantage Miss Hodgkin."

Dorothy put her first service into the net. 'Nerves,' I thought to myself. She hit a slice second service. I hit my return right down the line and came in. Dorothy hesitated for a fraction of a second. I was on the centerline of my service courts. Dorothy decided to go crosscourt, but I cut off the ball easily and put it softly into her ad court. She wasn't anywhere near it.

The games were 5-4. I was serving for the match.

I held my service easily; my match; I was in the fifth round.

I sprinted for the net, jumped over it, touched Dorothy's hand, and ran toward the players' box. Halfway there, I remembered the chair umpire, Mr Hewlett, so I turned around and ran back to the chair, reached up, and touched my racket to the toe of his shoe.

"Thanks! Well called," I said.

Then I tossed my racket in the general direction of my pocket book, spare rackets, and Rachel's old sweater, which were lying on the grass next to the umpire's chair, and ran straight toward the BBC television commentary booth. This was a little shed at court level just beside, and a bit below, the scoreboard. The BBC commentator, wearing a sweater and his old-fashioned headphones, saw me racing toward him and looked alarmed.

I was just trying to reach my parents in the players' box above the shed.

I stepped into the first row of spectators and reached up to climb onto the roof of the shed, but it was too high for me. One of the ladies in the first row put her hands under my backside and pushed. Father reached down and grabbed my right hand, while John grabbed my left. The lady spectator pushed, John and Father pulled, and I popped up on the roof of the shed.

From there, it was an easy step into the box.

Father hugged me. "Darling sweetheart," was all he said. I kissed Mother's cheek and then hugged Rachel. I was thrilled to see all three of them.

Claire said, "Solid, impressive play."

Rachel nodded. In the earlier rounds, Claire had been

exuberant about my wins. Now she was a bit more careful.

I guessed what Claire was thinking. By Thursday afternoon, barring rain delays, there would be only two ladies left in the draw. Claire would be one; some of the London bookies were beginning to give odds I would be the other.

John was standing back, on the other side of Claire. Without thinking that every pair of eyes in Centre Court was on me, I slipped past Claire, put my arms around John, and kissed him. I don't mean I pecked his cheek. I gave him a full, 220-volt kiss square on his lips.

The Centre Court crowd was agog over the kiss.

I took John's hand and turned back to face Mother and Father.

Mother's eyebrow was arched at the kiss I had given John.

Father was wearing his DSC ribbon on the lapel of his jacket, and John was wearing his on the left breast of his khaki uniform.

"Mother, Father, please meet Captain John Fitzwilliam of the Royal Marines. John is Claire's older brother."

Then I said, "John, please meet my parents, Doctor Thomas Hodgkin and Doctor Fiona Wilson."

The three of them shook hands. Father glanced at John's DSC ribbon and then looked at John. I could tell he was gauging how old John was.

Father pointed to the ribbon. "Suez Canal?"

John nodded. "You?"

Father shrugged. "U-Boat attack east of Gibraltar. Ship all on fire."

And that was that. Father and John were friends.

Late Monday Afternoon, 2 July 1962
Claridge's
Mayfair

I sat on the edge of the bed in the room at Claridge's I was to share with Rachel. Mother was unpacking my clothes and putting them away, just as she did when we traveled when I was, say, 12. Rachel was downstairs having tea with Claire.

I knew that Mother was about to rake me over the coals for my behavior in the weeks since I had left Bermuda for London. I must have insulted the Thakeham family, after Lady Thakeham had been so kind to me. That's what Mother would say. I had been selfish. I had behaved completely contrary to the way I had promised her I would behave in London. And she would want to know what in heaven had happened with Mark?

Mother surprised me. She always did. She put the Tinling gown over Rachel's bed and told me that she would have the Claridge's staff brush it and then steam press it. "We dress for dinner on board the ship home, and you're old enough now to wear a gown like this for dinner. The other passengers will be amazed."

Then she said, "I take it you're seeing John Fitzwilliam?"

"Yes." Well, 'seeing' him was the polite word for what I was doing.

"Does he treat you well?"

"Quite well. He's a gentleman."

"That was my impression when I met him." She exercised her maternal prerogative: "Are you in love with him?"

"Yes. A great deal."

"Is he in love with you?"

"I don't know, Mother. Probably not. He likes me, but that's all. I'm about nine years younger than him. He may think I'm just a child."

"Are you protecting yourself?"

Other girls get to have mothers who would never think of questioning their daughters about sex and who instead assume their daughters simply aren't having sex. Me? No, I have to have for my mother a practical-minded physician who assumes that if her daughter is seeing a naval commando nine years her senior, sex probably enters into the equation.

"Yes. Claire took me to her gynecologist. But I don't want you to be angry with her for that. I asked her to."

"Since I would have done exactly the same for you if I had been here in London, I'd have a hard time becoming angry at Claire."

"Mother, I know I more or less broke a promise I made to you."

"I don't care about any promise you made. I care about whether you're safe, happy, and doing well."

That was exactly what Claire had said Mother would say.

Then Mother asked, "Are you careful?"

"Yes." I laughed a little. "John sets the pace, but he understands I need a minute or so."

I assumed she'd have no idea of what I was talking about, but instead she laughed as well. "Tell me about it."

I was amazed that she knew about these things, but apparently she did. She'd only slept with Father, she'd told me. Father set the pace the way John did? It didn't seem possible.

Then Mother said, "But if you're right about how he feels, that he's not in love, you need to be careful with your own feelings."

"I know."

"So, are you careful with your feelings?"

"No." I gave a rueful laugh. "I'm a mess."

"You're not a mess. You're a quite normal girl."

Mother held up one of my tennis dresses and frowned at it. I know I took five tennis dresses to England, and that sounds like a lot, but since I had arrived in London I had played tennis hard, almost every day, sometimes twice a day, and the tennis dresses, with the constant washing and pressing, were showing the wear and tear.

Teddy Tinling would have gladly – now that I was in the fifth round – given me fancy new tennis outfits for free, which I could accept and still remain an amateur. I knew, though, that Mother and Father wouldn't approve my accepting clothing, and especially not clothing that would, no doubt – Teddy being Teddy – include brightly coloured underpants and short skirts to show off the underpants.

Mother, still holding up the tennis dress, said, "Fiona, I think we need to go shopping for some new clothes for you."

Rachel and I were in our room when John rang that evening.

Rachel answered; she had known John since he was a teenage boy. Rachel replaced the receiver and said to me, "John's in the lobby. He wants you to come see him."

I got my pocketbook and walked over to the dresser. I opened a drawer slightly and pulled out a clean pair of knickers for the next morning and slipped them into my pocketbook. My washbag was in the loo in John's flat; I had everything I needed. I said, "Rachel – "

She cut me off. "You go with John. I'll think of something to tell your father." Rachel had been a teenage girl in love at Wimbledon herself. "But I want you to get a good night's sleep."

I laughed. "I'm not given much control over how much sleep I get!"

Rachel said simply, "John's waiting for you."

John wasn't in the lobby. He had parked the 356 on Brook Street in front of Claridge's. It was a clear evening in London; John had put the hood down. He was in his khaki summer uniform, with shorts and high socks. John was tanned and so fit that I could see the outlines of the muscles in his legs.

He was leaning against the 356, with his arms folded over his chest, chatting with a young London bobby. It sounded to me that they must have known one another in the Royal Marines.

I put my arms around him and kissed him. John opened the passenger door of the 356, and I got in.

The bobby said, "Captain, sir. That's a beautiful young lady you have there."

John said, "I entirely agree, Mike."

He jumped over the driver's door, started the Porsche and threw it in gear. With the motor rasping, we headed into the Mayfair traffic.

Tuesday Morning, 3 July 1962
Belgravia

The next morning, probably at about the same time Rachel was telling Father that I had decided to spend the night at Claire's flat, I got out of John's bed, pulled on a pair of his boxer shorts, and a grey, cotton t-shirt with 'SBS' in black letters across the front. Both the shorts and the shirt were too big for me by at least twice; I had to hold up his boxers with my left hand.

I went into the hallway kitchen and tried to make tea for John on the huge, ancient cast iron gas stove. At one time, perhaps back in the Dark Ages, this stove must have served the entire house. It had all manner of strange valves and knobs. I turned one of the knobs, struck a match, and lit the burner. Flames shot up to the ceiling.

"John!" I yelled.

John ran into the kitchen and turned off the main valve. We both looked up at the ceiling, which now had scorch marks on it.

He said, "Put your hands up in the air."

I stuck my arms up. He pulled the t-shirt over my head. Without my hand to hold them up, the boxer shorts fell down around my ankles. John scooped me up and held me in his arms.

"There's only one thing you're any good for," he said with an air of weary resignation as he carried me back to bed.

"That's not true!"

"Oh, I forgot. You can also play tennis."

"Right," I said and buried my face in his shoulder.

The Times that morning had a photo of me on Centre Court that the photographer had taken *through* the tennis net. The top of my head was well below the net cord, though my ponytail was whipped above it. I was so low over my haunches that my left hand was down on the grass, probably to keep myself from sliding into the net. The ball was a white smear in the photo, and my eyes were locked onto it – I looked demented, to be honest. I didn't recall the point, but judging from the angle I was holding my racket, I must have been just flicking the ball over the net.

There was a caption under the photo:

THE BERMUDA SURGEON ARRIVES IN HER OPERATING ROOM

Wednesday Afternoon, 4 July 1962
Tea at Claridge's
Mayfair

"I've invited Lady Thakeham to have tea with you and me this afternoon," Mother said to me.

I should have known this would happen. Mother had accepted the situation on the ground as she found it upon her arrival in London on Monday, but she would want to repair whatever damage I had done to the relations between the Thakehams and the Hodgkins.

"Mother, I – "

She interrupted. "We're not discussing it. Captain Fitzwilliam is not invited – even though I know it distresses you to be out of his sight for even five minutes. I asked Lady Thakeham to bring her son with her, if he can get out of hospital. "

"Oh, you didn't invite Mark!"

"We're not discussing it. We're going to have tea, we're going to be polite, and, if we've done anything for which we should apologize, that's what we're going to do."

"Mother – "

"Fiona Alice Ashburton Hodgkin, do you want me to ask your father to have a word with you?"

I didn't reply.

"I thought not," Mother said.

At tea, Mark did his level best to charm Mother and it worked. He complimented her frock, asked for advice on a difficult diagnosis he'd had that day in hospital, denied with a laugh her suggestion that I had been 'inattentive' as the Thakeham's guest and offered to pour her another cup of tea. "One more of these small éclairs, Doctor Wilson?" he asked, holding out a plate to her.

No female, not even one as practical as Mother, could resist him – except, apparently, me.

I was left to chat with Lady Thakeham. I would rather have swallowed a lizard.

After we finished our tea, Lady Thakeham and Mother went off to the ladies' loo together. Mark and I stood looking at one another in the lobby of Claridge's while we waited for them.

"I don't want you to hit me," Mark said cheerfully.

"I'm not going to hit you. I shouldn't have hit you and I apologize."

"Not at all. You were entirely justified. I didn't treat you well, which I regret very much. And I was certainly wrong when I said you would lose the first round at Wimbledon."

"Actually, your telling me that I'd lose helped me in my first round match. It made me so angry that I was determined to win. Anyway, the mistakes were all my own."

"Well, I'm proud of you. As is everyone."

"Thanks. I appreciate that a great deal."

"Fiona, perhaps before you return to Bermuda we could have dinner together."

"Mark, I can't. You're kind to make the offer. I'm sorry.

I'm seeing someone else, and I probably shouldn't go out with you for dinner."

Here I was stretching the nature of my relationship with John. I'm sure John would have been surprised to hear that I thought our relationship had any element of exclusivity.

At first, Mark was surprised. Then it dawned on him. "Is this the fellow who was the lucky recipient of the kiss?"

The newspapers had all printed photographs of me kissing John and had called it, in huge headlines, "THE KISS."

"I doubt he considers himself lucky, but yes, it's him."

Mother and Lady Thakeham now reappeared. Mark put his hands on my shoulders and leaned over and kissed my cheek. He pulled back and said, simply, "Friends?"

I smiled at him and replied, "Friends."

Then we shook hands, and I noticed that he held my hand with a gentle pressure just an instant longer than I might have expected.

Then Lady Thakeham put her hand in the crook of her son's arm and they swept out of Claridge's lobby.

An objective observer – Mother, perhaps – might have said that I was turning away a handsome and charming boy, close to my own age, who I liked and who shared and accepted my plans to become a physician. He was, after all, the scion of an old and aristocratic, not to mention wealthy, English family. His children would bear titles.

I had the impression that, if I wanted, in a few years it probably could be arranged for me to be Mark's wife and then the mother of his children. If I wanted, someday I could be mistress of 16 Hyde Park Gate and Thakeham House. If I wanted, Myrtle Hanson might agree to be my children's nursery nurse.

But I was giving Mark up in favor of an older man who never would be interested in an exclusive relationship with me – or so Claire said emphatically, and she knew her brother quite well. John himself had said nothing that could lead me to think otherwise.

So I was just fooling myself. But American Grandmother used to say that people are only biological organisms. They don't do what they should do; they do what they want to do.

Thursday Evening, 5 July 1962
Claridge's
Mayfair

When John arrived at Claridge's in the 356, Rachel was waiting in the doorway, with her arms folded over her chest, and an unusually grim look on her face. I was beside her. There was a small crowd of tennis fans waiting for a glimpse of me, and there were news photographers with the same goal.

That afternoon, I had won my semifinal match. My win had created a wild sensation in the tennis world. I was the first lady qualifier to ever advance to the final.

Claire had also won her semifinal match that afternoon. She would be my opponent on Saturday.

John got out of the Porsche and opened the passenger door for me with a flourish.

Rachel said, "John Fitzwilliam, I want her back this evening. I want her to get a good night's sleep, both tonight and tomorrow night. Do you understand?"

John smiled. "Yes, Rachel, I'll bring her back tonight."

"This is serious, John. She's playing the final on Saturday afternoon. I'm sure Claire is at home, resting."

"Or something," I said.

Rachel went on. "I don't want Fiona out late, and I don't

want her to come back – " Rachel paused, trying to think of a polite term. "Tired. I don't want her tired."

John laughed. "Why isn't anyone ever worried about *me* being tired? But I promise – I won't bring her back tired."

I got in the Porsche, and we left with the motor rasping. I turned backwards and kneeled on the seat to look back at Rachel over the hood. I leaned my elbows down on the folded, blue hood, and gave Rachel a huge grin and two thumbs up.

I couldn't believe that in less than two days I would play to win Wimbledon.

Rachel slowly put out her hands and gave me two thumbs up in return.

I looked back at her in surprise. I could tell from her face that she was sad. No – she wasn't just sad; she was about to begin crying.

She had wanted to win Wimbledon herself so much; she had come so close that July afternoon in 1939. But Rachel loved Claire. She probably realized the first time she saw Claire play that Claire could win Wimbledon for her.

I remembered the first time I served for Rachel in July 1957, when I was 14. I didn't know Claire existed.

But that same Saturday afternoon in 1957, Claire had lost a long, desperate final on Centre Court against Althea Gibson. At the moment I was serving for Rachel, Claire was back in her flat in London, crying. She was in Richard's arms and telling him that she worried she'd never win Wimbledon.

Then in 1960, at long last, she'd held up the Rosewater Dish on Centre Court for the first time.

After I served for Rachel, I didn't keep going to the net. Instead, I turned and glared at her with my mouth open. I wasn't crying anymore, and I wasn't scared. The ball I had served was still in the air above South Road, just beginning its arc back down onto the court.

Rachel looked back at me coldly. She had said only "Like that" and then left.

I was still kneeling backwards on the seat of the 356. John reached his left hand over to brace my back. "Careful," he said. Then he made a racing change down into third gear, and the Porsche howled off through the London traffic.

How could I not have understood? That afternoon in 1957, Rachel must have known that she would teach me to play tennis, that she'd never again tell me to stay back on the baseline. I had, or would have after years of work, the serve I needed to take me to the net.

Rachel had known that first afternoon. I had wondered why she seemed to dislike me, as though teaching me to be a champion was the most difficult thing she could do, but it was something she was obligated to carry out as best she possibly could. The irony was that Rachel had come to love me in the same way she loved Claire. That's why she had looked about to cry as I pulled away in my lover's Porsche.

Somehow, she'd known from that first serve at Coral Beach that, eventually, someday, I would play Claire for the Championship on Centre Court.

And I might win.

Friday Morning, 6 July 1962
Breakfast at Claridge's
Mayfair

At breakfast, I sat beside Rachel, with Mother and Father across from us. Father was reading *The Times* intently. After a few minutes, he folded the paper to display a particular column and then pushed the paper across the table so that it was between Rachel and me. He took his fountain pen from his lapel pocket and used it to point to a headline in the paper:

An All-Martin Ladies' Final At Wimbledon

I looked at Rachel; she was as baffled as I was. We began to read the article together.

> Twenty-three years ago, on the eve of the war, this reporter, as a young man, covered for this newspaper perhaps the most thrilling ladies' singles final ever played at Wimbledon. An American, Miss Alice Marble, supported by her formidable coach, Miss Eleanor ('Teach') Tennant, defeated a teenage girl from the island of Bermuda, who was then known as Miss Rachel Outerbridge, 6-8, 12-10, 10-8.

> The match was played under metaphorical clouds of war (it was the last Wimbledon until 1946) and real clouds of rain. There were two rain delays, the first of half an hour and the second of almost two hours, and the match was completed only late in the evening as both twilight and drizzle fell on Centre Court.
>
> In the weeks before the final, the English public had become well acquainted with Miss Outerbridge, because she often had been romantically linked in the society pages with the handsome, debonair, and brilliant German player, Gerhardt von Schleicher, from Berlin's famed Rot-Weiss tennis club and a member of Germany's Davis Cup Team. The couple had just quarreled, or so the society pages the morning of the final said, over Miss Outerbridge's strong and quite outspoken anti-Nazi stance.

My jaw dropped. Years before, Rachel had once mentioned the Rot-Weiss club to me. I looked at her, but she was still reading.

> Although Miss Marble ultimately defeated Miss Outerbridge, this reporter has not seen any other tennis player with the electric energy and dynamic play of Miss Outerbridge. That is, perhaps until now. One of the lady finalists tomorrow is another teenage girl from Bermuda, Miss Fiona Hodgkin. Miss Hodgkin is slightly built but runs like the wind and appears utterly fearless on Centre Court. She has charmed the spectators at this year's Championships

with her good-natured humor, sportsmanship, and youthful insouciance.

I looked up. "Father, what does 'insouciance' mean?"

"He means you appear to be unconcerned. He's complimenting you, sweetheart."

> Miss Hodgkin has won over the Wimbledon spectators by showing her allegiance to the tiny island she represents. She appears on Centre Court with the Bermuda flag sewn onto her tennis dress. Miss Outerbridge, this reporter recalls, wore the Bermuda flag on her dress as well.

"Why do they always say that Bermuda is a 'tiny' island?" I asked. "It's not as though it's a speck."

"It's just the English, dear," Mother said. "Their idea of a good-sized island is Australia."

> Yesterday, in her semifinal match against Fancy Pants La Bueno (also known as Maria Esther Andion Bueno), Miss Hodgkin was unperturbed by the loud commotion on Centre Court each time Miss Bueno's short skirt flipped up to reveal her dazzling pink panties designed by the irrepressible Mr Tinling.
>
> Miss Hodgkin plays a wild serve and volley game and accepts risks in making her shots that no doubt many more experienced players would avoid, but in doing so she makes her matches extremely exciting to watch. Indeed, Miss Hodgkin reminds this reporter of no one so much as Miss Outerbridge herself.

Perhaps this reporter should not be surprised, because Miss Hodgkin's amateur coach is Mrs Derek Martin – formerly known as Miss Rachel Outerbridge.

The other finalist is the defending ladies' champion, Mrs Richard Kershaw, who many tennis fans may still recall as Miss Claire Fitzwilliam. Mrs Kershaw is a classic English beauty. Few women tennis players of the top rank regularly appear on the covers of leading women's fashion magazines, as Mrs Kershaw did before her marriage.

I said to Rachel, "Is that true? Has Claire been on the cover of magazines?" Rachel snorted, didn't answer, and kept reading. I don't think Rachel kept track of the women's fashion magazines.

The talented Australian girl, Miss Margaret Smith, has challenged Mrs Kershaw recently, but in this Wimbledon Miss Smith was eliminated on Ladies' Day by the doughty American, Miss Billie Jean Moffitt. Mrs Kershaw has a clear path to her third Wimbledon championship.

There is, however, a delicious irony. This reporter has learned that Mrs Kershaw, when she was a teenager, was also coached by Mrs Derek Martin, and that Mrs Kershaw's interest in tennis, and her competitive spirit, began during her time spent with Mrs Martin.

So, on Saturday afternoon, the spectators on Centre Court will see two ladies battle for a championship for which they have both been prepared by the same coach.

It has been striking to this reporter during the Wimbledon fortnight that Mrs Kershaw and Miss Hodgkin are close friends, as well as tennis practice partners. Centre Court this past Monday afternoon was treated to a memorable kiss Miss Hodgkin gave a handsome Royal Marines officer, who happens to be Mrs Kershaw's brother.

'Oh, great,' I thought to myself. 'Mother will be pleased as punch that I've managed to get my private life into the newspapers again.'

Mrs Kershaw is stronger than Miss Hodgkin, far more experienced in international tennis competition, and has a game that is better balanced than that of the diminutive Bermudian girl. At the top level, however, tennis, to a greater degree than other sports, is more about character than skill or experience. Both these players have character that seems to have been shaped by their common coach, Mrs Derek Martin.

Saturday will be, as it were, an All-Martin final.

I was staring at Rachel, amazed. This was the most incredible story I'd ever read.

Rachel said, "Don't believe everything you read in the papers."

MAY 2011
BERMUDA ROSE SOCIETY GARDEN
PAGET PARISH, BERMUDA

I planned from the start to include in this narrative Rachel's love affair with the tennis player who broke up with her the night before her Wimbledon final. It seemed to me to be part of my own story – even though I hadn't even been born until four years later. But to include Rachel's story I first had to worm the facts out of her.

I dug out my clipping of the old newspaper article that had been published the day before my Wimbledon final with Claire. The fellow who broke up with Rachel, this Gerhardt von Schleicher, had been a member of the German Davis Cup team. Bill Tilden had coached the German team. Rachel had met Tilden at Kooyong. Rachel had met von Schleicher at Kooyong.

I could put two and two together as well as the next pediatrician. Tilden probably introduced her to von Schleicher.

Now Rachel is elderly and frail but completely in command of her faculties. Let's face it – elderly people enjoy reminiscing. So on a recent May afternoon, I left my clinic, took my auto, collected Rachel, and drove her to the Bermuda

279

Rose Society Garden on Harbour Road, which I knew she appreciated. It's a beautiful place.

I took her walking cane from her and hooked it on the side of a bench in the garden. Then I took her arm and helped her sit down on the bench. She was anxious to make sure she could reach her cane, and I showed her where it was. There were Bermuda roses in bloom all around us.

I was subtle in the way I approached the subject of 1939. "Rachel, how did you meet Big Bill Tilden? What was he like?"

Rachel snorted, found her cane, slowly managed to stand, and walked, unsteadily, to a rose bush. It was a 'Mrs Dudley Cross.' She put her fingers around one of the stems, carefully, to avoid the thorns.

"I'm not telling you anything about Gerhardt."

Friday Afternoon, 6 July 1962
The Queen's Visit
All England Club Wimbledon

Before the men's singles final that afternoon, Claire and I stood in a line inside the clubhouse entrance to Centre Court with the men's finalists, Rod Laver and Marty Mulligan. Colonel Macaulay was going to present us to the Queen, who was making her first visit to Wimbledon since 1957.

I was in my tennis dress, but Claire had put on a frock. Claire was known to be a Palace favorite, and she felt a frock might be more appropriate.

With us in line were my parents, and, at the end of the line, John. Colonel Macaulay escorted the Queen into the entrance and, one by one, presented us to her. The Queen stopped to talk with Claire for a few moments.

Colonel Macaulay said, "Your Majesty, this is young Miss Hodgkin, from Bermuda."

I dipped my knee. I was awestruck.

"Good luck tomorrow, Miss Hodgkin."

Colonel Macaulay and the Queen moved onto Father and Mother. The Queen greeted Father, and then the Colonel said, "Your Majesty, this is Mrs Hodgkin."

Mother curtsied.

"It's actually 'Doctor Wilson,' isn't it?" the Queen asked Mother.

I don't know who did research for the Palace, but the Palace must have been world class in this department.

"Yes, Your Majesty, I'm called 'Doctor Wilson' in my clinic."

"I'm told your daughter plans to become a medical doctor as well. You must be proud of her."

"Quite proud indeed, Your Majesty."

Colonel Macaulay turned to John. "Your Majesty, this is Captain Fitzwilliam, of the Royal Marines."

"Captain, we have met before."

"Yes, Your Majesty."

"When you were awarded your Distinguished Service Cross, I believe."

"Yes, Your Majesty."

The Queen smiled. "That was before you took up your" – the Queen paused – "current duties."

John grinned and bowed his head slightly. "Just as Your Majesty says."

The Queen looked back at Father. I sensed that she had meant to say something to Father that she had forgotten when greeting him. "Doctor Hodgkin, I understand that your DSC was awarded at sea."

"Yes, Your Majesty," Father replied. "I was lucky to be above water at the time."

Everyone, even the Queen, chuckled at this – except Mother. She shuddered at how close she and I had come to losing him.

Then the Queen said, "I know my father would have regretted not awarding it to you personally."

Father bowed slightly. "The King favored me with a letter soon after the war, Your Majesty."

I had never seen this letter or even heard of it. A letter from the King wouldn't have simply arrived in the post at Midpoint. The King's Governor General of Bermuda would have delivered it in person, and such a letter would have been the talk of Bermuda for weeks. The Governor General would have quietly implied to his friends over cards and Black Seal rum at the Royal Yacht Club on Hamilton Harbour that the Palace had consulted him directly in the matter. But I had been just a small child then.

"I knew he did," the Queen said.

She turned back to John and placed her hand on his arm. This was a sign of royal favor. "I'm told I can expect even more great things from you in future years, Captain."

I would have thought that neither of the Fitzwilliam siblings would ever be at a loss for words, but I could tell that John had no idea of what to say. So he was silent.

Then Colonel Macaulay led the Queen up to the Royal Box on Centre Court.

Claire and I had decided to practice on Court 14 during the men's final, since the reporters and photographers would be otherwise occupied watching the Queen, while Her Majesty watched Rod dismantle Marty in straight sets. Claire and I could practice in peace and quiet for once.

Claire had to visit the dressing room to change out of her frock – "I can't recall ever wearing a dress at Wimbledon," she said. John and I walked hand in hand to the outer courts. John was going to watch us practice, and then he was going to drive me back to his flat. With John driving his Porsche, we hoped we could evade the reporters.

John and I couldn't have tea out because of the reporters and photographers, so I planned to make him something to eat in his flat. This was risky; I desperately wanted John to like me, and I hoped to show him that at least I could make his tea. Unfortunately, I had inherited American Grandmother's inability to cook.

Claire appeared on the court, and we knocked up. She was about to toss her racket onto the grass when we saw Colonel Legg walking rapidly toward us on St. Mary's Walk. This was astonishing: for Colonel Legg to leave Centre Court during the final between Rod and Marty, especially with the Queen present, was unthinkable.

Claire and I both assumed that, for some unimaginable reason, he was coming to talk with us, but instead he went straight to John and spoke quietly. I couldn't hear what he said.

John turned and said to Claire and me, "Someone's trying to reach me by telephone. I'll be back in a few minutes." He waved to us and left with Colonel Legg.

Claire and I tried to play, but our hearts weren't in the game. Something was wrong, we both knew.

About 15 minutes later, John returned. He was trying to appear casual, but I could tell that he was in a hurry.

"What is it?" I asked.

"I have to leave now."

"Why?" Claire and I both asked at once.

"I have to go away for a bit."

Claire's face instantly turned ashen.

"Where are you going?" I asked.

"I don't know."

"You'll be back for our match tomorrow?"

John laughed. "No, Fiona, I'm going to miss your Wimbledon final. But you'll be in other Wimbledon finals, I'm sure of that."

Claire said nothing.

"But when will I see you again?" I insisted. I was thinking only of myself. I was just 19.

"Fiona, I don't know when we'll see each other again."

Claire said to John, "Tell her, you fool."

Then I knew what he was going to tell me. He was going to say that perhaps it would be better if we didn't plan to see one another again. He was going to break up with me.

John said nothing.

Claire said, "John. Tell Fiona. Now."

My knees were giving way. I started to faint.

John said, "I've fallen in love with you."

I was standing just in front of him. I put my left arm around his waist, then took my right hand and began fiddling with a button on his khaki uniform shirt. This was the only way I could avoid bursting into tears. I just managed to whisper, "I'm in love with you as well."

He put his arms around me.

Claire said, "Why don't I leave the two of you alone?"

John said to her, "Stay here with Fiona. I have to leave now."

"John," I said. I was looking at his chest, not his face. "When you come back, I may be in Bermuda, or in the States."

"I'll find you, wherever you are."

The Tennis Player From Bermuda

Claire said, "Are you two sure you don't want me to go somewhere else? This sounds as though it could get mushy."

John and I ignored her. We were kissing.

Then I said, "John, will you marry me?"

Claire said, "Fiona, you know, usually we wait for them to ask that."

John said, "I'm definitely going to marry you. Should I speak to your father?"

"No, my parents are old-fashioned, but I think they're past that. I'll talk to them."

John asked, "How many children do we want to have?"

"Two or three? I'm an only child, and I don't want to have just one."

"Three sound good to me," John said.

Claire said, "Children are expensive, keep that in mind. School fees. The nursery nurse. The weekend country house. Holidays at the sea." Claire looked at me. "Well, Bermuda, maybe you have the holidays at the sea included."

"Three would be perfect," I said.

Claire said, "The way you two go after one another, you should expect a minimum of three."

John looked at Claire. "Mother and Father need to know about this, and I'll be away."

"Fiona and I will tell them."

John took my chin in his hand gently and lifted my face so that we were looking at one another. "The moment I come back, we'll make love to celebrate our engagement."

"I won't think about anything else until then."

Claire said, "I *knew* this was going to get mushy!"

John laughed and kissed Claire on her cheek.

Then he kissed me quickly, just brushing my lips, and said

softly, "I love you." I clutched at him, but he broke away.

Then I watched him saunter down St. Mary's Walk.

As soon as he came to Court 3 and thought he was out of our sight, he broke into a dead run toward the auto park and the little silver Porsche 356.

Claire and I walked back to the dressing room without speaking. Once in the dressing room, we were alone. The draw now was down to just the two of us.

Claire said, "John's gone off like this perhaps half a dozen times since he joined the Section. He always comes back." Her face was still ashen.

I looked at her but said nothing.

"He has promised me, as his sister, that he always will be careful."

"Do you believe him?"

Claire grimaced. "No. I don't."

"Neither do I."

"But he always comes back. Don't worry."

Neither of us spoke for a minute. Then Claire said, "John told me that he's in love with you. But he didn't know how you felt." Claire shook her head and laughed softly to herself. "I said to him, 'What? Are you blind?' I told him he was a fool not to tell you."

"Claire, I want the Kershaw children and the Fitzwilliam children to grow up together."

"They'll be cousins. Certainly they'll grow up together. I told you that I met Rachel at my parents' house in the country. The tennis court there is old – it must date from before the first war. The lines have been picked out with chalk for so many years that the lines are raised like ridges above the court. The grass is rough; my parents don't take good care of it. That's where I first played with Rachel."

She laughed. "We'll turn Rachel loose on our children on that old tennis court."

She leaned over, kissed my cheek, and we embraced.

Claire said, "We're going to be sisters-in-law."

I gathered my rackets and my pocketbook and left the dressing room. As I walked down the hallway, I saw Richard Hawkins, the long time Chief Groundskeeper – this was a senior position in the complex All England Club hierarchy. Last Tuesday, Rachel had surprised me by stopping to talk with Hawkins; he had been a ball boy at her final with Alice Marble in 1939. Except for the war years, he had been at the All England Club ever since. He and his family lived in the Lodge beside Court 1.

Hawkins stepped aside for me and said, "Good day, Miss Hodgkin."

Twelve days before, no one at the All England Club had known me. I had been ignored. Claire had to show me where the buffet was, where the dressing room was, where the order of play was posted, and how to obtain a competitor's pass. The only reason I didn't have to stand in line to request a court for practice was that Claire simply announced when and where she preferred for us to practice.

Now this gentleman stepped aside for me.

I knew exactly what Claire would have said to him, so I decided to say the same thing.

"Mr Hawkins, may I call you 'Richard'?"

"Certainly, Miss Hodgkin."

"And I would be happy if you would call me 'Fiona.'"

He beamed. "Thank you, Fiona."

"Will you be here tomorrow, Richard?"

"Yes, of course, to look after Centre Court for your match with Claire. I'll be sitting on the court, to the side of the players' entryway. If you have any problem with Centre Court, just motion to me."

"Then I'll look forward to seeing you tomorrow, Richard."

"Good luck, Fiona."

I smiled at him and continued on my way down the hallway.

He called out to me. "Fiona!"

I turned to look at him. He said, "We haven't had any lady like you here since Claire first came to us."

"Thank you, Richard. You can't know how much it pleases me to hear you say that."

SATURDAY, 7 JULY 1962
ALL ENGLAND CLUB WIMBLEDON

Mother, Father, Rachel, and I walked out of Claridge's to the auto that was going to drive us to Wimbledon. The auto had a small pennant on its radiator in the colors of the All England Club – mauve and green. When we came out, we could see a huge crowd of fans, reporters, and photographers. There were five or six bobbies waiting to escort us to our automobile. Mother held my hand tightly. The crowd cheered wildly, and the bobbies linked arms to protect us while we walked the few steps to the auto.

Mother clutched Father's sleeve. "Tom, I don't like having our daughter exposed in this way."

"Let's get in the auto and be off, Fiona." He was speaking to Mother, not me. We got in the auto, with Father in the front and Mother, me, and Rachel in the rear. We would pack Claire and Richard in the rear as well; there were small jump seats.

The crowd was large and noisy. A bobby knocked on the side window where Father was sitting. Father rolled down the window. "Sir," the bobby said, and then saw the DSC ribbon on the lapel of Father's suit coat. He said "sir" again, meaning it this time. "We're going to use a siren to get you out of here. Is that agreeable, sir?"

Father said, "As you think best, officer."

We roared off behind a police auto with its siren blaring.

The fans and the press hadn't thought that the challenger would be giving the defending champion a lift to Wimbledon, so no one was waiting on the street in Knightsbridge where Claire and Richard lived. They were standing in front of their flat. Claire had her pocket book, tennis kit, and rackets; her blond hair was neatly held in place by her barrette; she was calm, relaxed, and confident.

She sat in the jump seat, leaned toward me and took my hands in hers.

We arrived at the Doherty Memorial Gates to a mob scene. There were dozens of people, both men and women, jumping and screaming, on Church Road just outside the gate, plus all the photographers. There must have been ten bobbies trying to keep the crowd back. I looked over at Mother; she was as unnerved as I. She was holding Father's arm tightly.

Rachel said, "Fiona, let's go." I didn't move. Claire took me by the arm, not gently, and pulled me out of the automobile, with Rachel following me. Two military officers snatched us and hustled us through the gates. I just managed to touch the iron of the gates with my fingers. I felt I had to brush the Doherty Gates, if for just an instant, to have even the slightest chance of winning Wimbledon.

Then the auto with Mother and Father pulled away, with the bobbies slamming the door as the automobile left.

I had no idea they would drive off. My parents, in an instant, were gone. I yelled, "No! Mother! Father!"

Rachel said to me, "Fiona, you'll see them in the players' box in an hour. Don't worry." Then Claire half-dragged me down South Road to the South West Entrance to Centre Court. Neither Rachel nor Claire seemed bothered by the wild scene.

Then it occurred to me; they both had done this before.

As if she could read my mind, Rachel turned to me and said quietly, "You wanted to be here. This is what it's like."

Colonel Macaulay had offered Claire to move me to the lower dressing room for the final, so that we each could have privacy, but Claire had declined. Claire sat me down on the bench in the dressing room, while Rachel asked Mrs Ward for tea.

We drank our tea in silence. Finally, the telephone rang. It was Colonel Legg asking us to come to the waiting room. The three of us stood.

Rachel turned to me. "Stay in the point you're playing. Don't think of anything else. Win each point one by one."

She put her hands on my shoulders. "Fiona, you'll win Wimbledon this afternoon if you make your volleys work for you." Then she kissed my cheek.

Rachel turned to Claire. "Put your first serve in, hard and wide. Fiona's inexperienced, but she's dangerous if she can rush the net."

Claire nodded.

Rachel paused. "Claire, Fiona will win Wimbledon someday, I'm sure of it. But don't let her win today. She's just 19, she's a finalist at Wimbledon; no one could want more than that."

Which was all Rachel had gotten for herself.

Then Rachel kissed Claire's cheek and left us.

I walked down the narrow, dark corridor, carrying my rackets and my pocketbook. Claire followed me. In the waiting room, Colonel Legg was holding two large bouquets of flowers, one from Colonel Macaulay for Claire and the other from himself for me.

Colonel Legg said to us quietly, "Are you girls all right? I was at El Alamein under Monty with the gent in the Ministry of Defence who rang for John yesterday. When he told me he needed to speak with John immediately – well, it's an open secret that John's a senior officer in the – " And then he stopped.

Claire had her arm around my shoulders. She said, "Colonel, we're worried, but we're fine. John will come back. He always does."

I nodded.

Claire kissed my cheek. "Good luck, Fiona."

"Good luck, Claire."

The stewards lined us up, me first, then Claire several steps behind me.

Colonel Legg said, "Well, girls, we'd better get on Centre Court."

The doors to Centre Court swung open and sunlight suddenly flooded the small waiting room.

Claire called, "Fiona?"

I turned to look at her. "Yes?"

"Let's give them a final they'll *never* forget."

"Definitely, Claire."

I walked out into the brilliant sunshine on Centre Court. Two people – Mother and Father – cheered for me. Even the Australians were waiting for Claire. When she walked out on the grass, the crowd roared and stood to applaud her. We

The Tennis Player From Bermuda

turned together and dipped our knees for the Royal Box.

Minutes later, Mr Watson, the chair umpire, pulled the microphone over, turned to Claire, and said, "Mrs Kershaw, are you ready?"

Claire, confident and relaxed, called back, "Ready."

He turned to me. "Miss Hodgkin, are you ready?"

My heart was in my throat. "Ready."

Mr Watson picked up his stopwatch. "Mrs Kershaw to serve. Play."

PART THREE –

CENTRE COURT

Saturday, 7 July 1962
Two O'clock in the Afternoon Precisely
Centre Court – First Set

Traditionally, the spectators on Centre Court tend to cheer for the older player, especially when the older player is popular. The younger player will have plenty of chances to win. The older player? Perhaps no more chances.

And Claire wasn't just popular. She was beautiful, and her face might as well have had 'Made In England' stamped on it. She was a perfect sport: whenever her opponent made a remarkable shot, Claire would raise the face of her racket into the air and tap the strings lightly with her fingertips in appreciation. Claire could make this simple gesture elegant. She never challenged line calls, but if her opponent challenged and there was even the slightest question about the correctness of the call, Claire would simply raise her racket in the air – meaning that she conceded the point.

The loss of even an important point was nothing compared to the roar of approval Claire would get from an English crowd. People would turn to one another and say, "That's our Claire!"

Before she was married, Claire had the incredible knack of saying to the press things that were just outrageous enough to make everyone chuckle and say, "That Claire!" but never outrageous enough to make anyone say, "Our Claire shouldn't have said that."

And then she married Richard at St. Margaret's in Westminster. The wedding photograph that was in all the newspapers showed Claire, stunning in Teddy Tinling's off-the-shoulder white gown with her silver hair swept up, pale blue eyes looking straight at the camera, and her usual impish grin, as though she'd just pulled off a piece of mischief. Richard, handsome in a morning coat, his head cocked to one side, holding an empty Waterford champagne flute in one hand, had her hand in his. Once she was married, she stopped talking to the press.

Popular? The English crowds *loved* her.

Her first serve went straight past me.

Claire held her serve in the first game; I won only a single point. Worse, in the second game, she broke my service at 15-game. In two games, I had won only two points. I was terrified. Probably Claire would defeat me in just 30 minutes. Claire was relaxed and in her element. She was hitting perfect passing shots effortlessly. After breaking me, she held her service again in the third game, although at least I made it to game-30.

I served in the fourth game with Claire ahead 3-love. I began to steady myself, just a bit, and got the score to 30-15. I served and headed for the net. Claire returned my serve straight down the line. I lunged with my backhand but only managed to get the top rim of my racket on the ball, making it ricochet off into the stands. I was too far out over my feet, and I fell to the grass.

Claire came up to the net as I was getting up. "Are you all right?"

"I'm fine. Thanks."

Then Claire held up her racket as though she was straightening a string. Her racket then happened to cover her face. Quietly, so that no one but me could hear, she said, "Slow down. Take more time before you serve."

"I know, I know," I said, equally quietly. I kept telling myself, 'slow down, slow down.'

The game was even at 30-all. We went to deuce, but I got the advantage. My serve into her ad service court was sharply angled and drew her wide. Claire's only sensible option was to go crosscourt, which she did, but I was there and cut off the shot with a backhand volley for a winner. I had held my serve, so Claire was to serve the fifth game, ahead 3-1. But at least I was on the scoreboard. Gradually, I was calming down, and my volley was beginning to work for me. Just a bit.

It was Claire's advantage in the fifth game. She served, I chipped my return to her feet, and she hit a hard shot down the line. I split stepped well inside the service line and just managed to catch her shot on my racket. I sent the ball back crosscourt but not hard or deep. Claire had no difficulty reaching it, and she hit a hard forehand to my backhand side. I raced across the court and volleyed her shot back into her ad service court. Again, I didn't manage to hit the ball hard, but my shot was sharply angled.

This time Claire had to run hard to get my ball, but she did, and she threw up a perfect lob over my head. I couldn't get it with an overhead, and I had to turn and run back to my baseline. I got there, barely, without time to turn around, so I swung at the ball while I was still facing away from the net.

The crowd gasped in surprise that I even got to Claire's lob.

My ball fell softly right in the middle of Claire's service court. She could do anything she wanted with it. I ran toward the net, which was a stupid thing to have done just then. She came up to the ball and hit a forehand viciously hard to my backhand side. I lunged for it and got the ball back across the net.

Now Claire and I were facing one another across the net, less than two meters apart. She volleyed my shot at the level of her waist; the ball didn't get anywhere near the grass.

I volleyed back.

The ball went across the net twice in a split second. The crowd held its breath.

Claire volleyed crosscourt, and I volleyed back. The ball had been across the net four times in, maybe, two seconds – *THOCK! THOCK! THOCK! THOCK!*

With the crowd silent, the sound of our rackets colliding with the ball echoed back and forth under the low roof of Centre Court.

Claire then lobbed far over my head, and I had to turn and run for my baseline. I got to the lob only by leaping out over my feet, and my only option was to hit the ball up as high as I could and hope it would land somewhere in Claire's court. Then I fell flat on my face and slid across the grass.

Claire probably thought the point was over. Now my high lob forced her to run back to her own baseline. The ball bounced right on the line. The crowd gasped again because I had gotten off the grass and, like a fool, run to the net, when I should have remained on the baseline to have any chance of staying in the point. My tennis dress had grass stains on it from sliding along the grass.

Claire set up for an overhead, but my lob took a bad

bounce on the line and didn't come up as high as Claire expected. She had to adjust in a fraction of a second and hit a weak shot at her shoulder level. I volleyed it back with my backhand. It was hard and deep to Claire's backhand. Claire hit another lob, but her skill failed her for once. Her lob was high but not deep.

Claire, me, the crowd, Rachel, everyone knew this incredible point was about to end.

I had all the time in the world to set up. Living dangerously, I didn't wait for the lob to fall far. I jumped so that I was well off the grass when my racket made contact with the ball, with my left leg out in the air for balance – a skyhook. I put every single ounce of me behind the racket. I've probably never hit a tennis ball that hard before or since. *THOCK!* The ball smashed into the sideline of Claire's ad court so hard the chalk puffed up and hung in the air for seconds. Claire wasn't anywhere close.

The crowd was on its feet, cheering. I looked over at the players' box. Mother had forgotten herself. She was standing and yelling, "FIONA! FIONA!" Then I turned to look at Claire. She was facing away from me, walking back to her baseline. But she was holding her racket face in the air and tapping her finger tips against the strings.

Deuce. Claire got back to ad and then held her serve. But I was feeling far more confident, and my volleys were clicking into place. I held my service easily in the sixth game, so the games were 4-2 in Claire's favor.

Mr Watson said, "New balls, please."

The ball boys who had been kneeling at the centre posts stood and went to the small Lightfoot refrigerator on Centre Court, removed two cans of new balls and rolled the new balls along the grass to the ball boys at the ends of the court.

On my serve in the eighth game, Claire took me to deuce twice, but I got the advantage and volleyed the ball crosscourt, just out of her reach. The games were 5-3 in Claire's favor, and she was to serve for the first set.

She held her service, and Mr Watson said, "First set to Mrs Kershaw, six games to three. Second set, Miss Hodgkin to serve."

Saturday, 7 July 1962
Two Thirty Five O'clock in the Afternoon
Centre Court – Second Set

One thing that makes tennis so fascinating to me is advantage scoring – meaning that a player must be two points ahead to win a game, and two games ahead to win a set. Some points are much more important than others. Take the first set in the final I played against Claire, for example. The most important point in the set was in the second game, on my serve, when Claire went ahead of me in the score and then broke my serve.

Now, this was before the advent of the tie-break at Wimbledon in 1971. In 1962, having been broken once by Claire, I would have to break Claire *twice* to win the set. I'd have to get Claire's break of my serve back and then break her again to win. And the server has such a large advantage. Neither player could win without breaking the other's serve.

I was down a set to Claire. I had to win the second set. I couldn't allow Claire to break my service. If she did, I'd probably lose the championship. I might be able to break Claire once, but could I break her twice? Doubtful. So I had to hold my service.

303

I served to Claire and followed my serve in to the net. Claire was a master of slyly waiting just that fraction of a second to force her opponent to commit to one side or the other and then firing the ball back to the side the opponent *didn't* pick. She could be diabolical. I came to the net in my ad service court. Claire smashed her return crosscourt to my deuce sideline. The instant I saw her begin her swing, I guessed what she would do, and I moved to my deuce side. Her return was perfect and would have bounced exactly on the deuce sideline, except that I was standing at the net to cut it off and send it back straight down the sideline. Claire ran hard, but she couldn't reach my shot. I held my service easily in the first game of the second set.

Then Claire and I traded games, one after another, 1-1, 2-1, 2-2, 3-2. In the sixth game, I took Claire to deuce four times and got the advantage twice. But both times, she won the point. Finally, she got the advantage and hit a perfect stop volley that fooled me. I gave it a try and ran for it, but it bounced twice before I arrived on the scene. Her game.

4-3, 4-4, 5-4, 5-5, 6-5, 6-6, 7-6, 7-7, 8-7. Just when I thought to myself that this could go on all afternoon, I looked at the scoreboard clock. Almost four o'clock. It *had* gone on most of the afternoon.

Then Claire served with the games at 8-9 in my favor. Her first serve was straight down the line, and I hit back a clear winner. She served again. She chipped my return directly to my feet as I came in. I half volleyed back – I was so low that my right knee and the bottom rim of my racket face were both touching the grass. Claire ran, caught my volley, and sent it right back. I volleyed to her deuce court, deep. Claire ran. I volleyed to her ad court, deep. Claire ran. But she didn't get to my volley. love-30. I was two points away from taking the second set.

Claire served. She could usually serve an ace when she needed to and that's what she did. I didn't get my racket on her serve. 15-30. I won the next point, but she won the two points after that. Deuce. I was furious at myself for losing those two points. Claire got the advantage twice, lost it twice, but then won on her third advantage. The games were tied at 9 apiece.

Then she broke my serve. 9-10 in her favor. The crowd was completely silent. Claire had her third Wimbledon singles championship in the palm of her hand. I was exhausted and on the verge of tears. I looked at Rachel and my parents. All three of them looked grim.

Serving for the match, Claire quickly got the score to 40-15. She had two championship points. Our match was almost over. I was falling apart.

I returned her serve and came in. Claire hit a passing shot straight down the line on my backhand side. I lunged for it and hit one of the best volleys I've ever hit – although I fell and hit the grass just after I struck the ball. Claire raced for the ball but got only the rim of her racket on it. The ball shot off into the row of photographers on the side of Centre Court.

My parents were standing and yelling, and – finally! – the Australians decided I needed some encouragement: *"AUSSIE! AUSSIE! AUSSIE! FI! FI! FI!"* Claire tapped her racket face with her fingers. Mr Watson turned and glared at the Australians and they slowly quieted down.

Ad in. Second championship point. Claire served hard,

straight at me. I returned wide to Claire's backhand, trying to push her off the court. I came in behind my return. Claire was pulling her racket back for a passing shot.

"*Fault!*"

Claire looked up in surprise and, instead of swinging her racket, caught my ball in her left hand. I stopped and turned to the linesman who had called Claire's serve out. He was pointing to the service line, meaning that he had called the serve long.

I turned back and called to Claire over the net. "It looked well in to me, Claire. I returned it. Let's play a let."

She motioned to me to meet her at the net. She put her hand on my shoulder and her head beside mine so that she could talk quietly.

"You don't want to play a let on championship point," she said. "It's never been done on Centre Court."

"Well, I don't know what else to do. Your serve was good. The call was late."

Mr Watson turned off his microphone, leaned over, and said to us, "Might I participate in your conversation?"

The spectators closest to the umpire's chair overheard him, chuckled, and turned to tell those further up in the stands what he had said.

Claire said, loudly enough for everyone to hear, "Just girl talk, Mr Watson. Party frocks and babies."

The crowd roared with laughter.

I backed away from Claire and said to Mr Watson, "Claire and I have decided to play a let. Her serve was clearly in. Claire has the advantage and first service."

"I call the score, Miss Hodgkin, not you," he said stiffly.

Claire said, "Well, call it then."

Mr Watson hesitated. "Advantage Mrs Kershaw, first service."

The crowd stood, applauded, and cheered.

Maybe everyone there realized that Claire and I didn't need a chair umpire. We were opponents, but we were best friends. We were going to be sisters-in-law. This match was just between us, and we were going to see it through by ourselves.

Mr Watson, as far as we cared, could have gotten up, gone home, and let us decide which of us would be the Wimbledon champion.

Claire served, again straight at me. I stepped back and ripped my forehand down the line into her deuce court. She got to the ball, barely – and hit it into the net.

Deuce. Both Claire's championship points gone.

I looked over the net and saw why Claire was such a great champion: she was relaxed and calm as she set up to serve to me at deuce. No looking back. It's just another tennis game at deuce. She was serving; she could pull it out.

But for once, she didn't. I won the deuce point, and then, on ad out, I won the game. The games were 10 apiece. We were back on serve.

I had never seen, or rather heard, staid Centre Court like this. Everyone was standing and cheering loudly; today, my granddaughters would say the place was *rocking*. The Australians were the loudest – they were taking full credit for getting me out of the deep hole I had dug for myself. Maybe they deserved it.

I held my serve. On the changeover, as we were drinking cups of water, Claire said quietly, "Well played, Fiona." As I was walking to my baseline, I glanced at the scoreboard just to the left and below the Royal Box.

PREVIOUS SETS		SERVER	SETS	GAMES	POINTS
6	Mrs R Kershaw	—	1	10	
1 2 3 4					
3	Miss F Hodgkin		0	11	

At two o'clock, when we had walked out onto Centre Court, the sky had been brilliantly clear, but gradually clouds had appeared, and now rain threatened. I knew I had to get this set into the bag before it rained. If Claire had a chance to rest, she would come back and win the championship in straight sets.

Claire took her time setting up to serve. Another ace. I walked across to my ad court. I was tired. I needed to put this set behind me. Claire served – and it went into the net. Second service.

"Fault!"

Claire had double-faulted. 15-all.

I won the next two points on volleys. 15-40.

Centre Court was dead silent. My lips were parched; I licked them.

Claire served, I returned and came in. She hit a passing shot, and the ball nicked the net cord and dropped on my side of the net. I lunged, hit the grass, just barely got my racket under the ball, and flipped it back over the net. I was face down on the grass. Claire ran but couldn't reach my stop volley.

The crowd roared.

Mr Watson said, "Second set to Miss Hodgkin, 12 games to 10. The sets are one all."

Then, as though we were in a theatre where everything happened on cue, torrents of rain came down. Richard Hawkins didn't give Mr Watson a chance to declare that play was suspended. He immediately signaled to his groundskeepers, and they leaped onto the court, tore down the net, and unfurled the huge tarp over Centre Court.

Claire grabbed my arm, and we ran to the players' entrance. In the dressing room, we slumped down on the bench together. We didn't say anything. Mrs Ward wheeled in a tea cart, and she poured cups of tea for us.

Claire took one or two sips. "This is beyond doubt the best cup of tea I've ever tasted." I agreed.

Mrs Ward said that, if either of us wanted to bathe or have a massage, we had to do so now. Colonel Legg had told her he expected the rain to last only a few minutes. Claire shook her head. Mrs Ward looked at me.

I said, "Mrs Ward, if I got into the bath now, I wouldn't get out until tomorrow."

I needed to change my tennis dress, but I could barely reach around to my back to reach the zipper. Mrs Ward helped me. I stepped out of the dress and handed it to her. I was embarrassed; my dress was soaked with sweat and covered in grass stains. Claire's white Tinling dress was immaculate. She didn't spend any time spread out on the grass. I found a clean dress in my kit.

I had forgotten that I had one white tennis ball tucked under my knickers. I dropped it out onto the floor.

Claire said, "I was wondering why the ball boys could find only five of the balls."

We sat in the dressing room for 15 minutes. We spoke a couple of times, but we mostly left one another alone. I was thinking about John; she probably was as well.

Saturday, 7 July 1962
Five O'clock in the Afternoon
Centre Court – Final Set

The rain stopped.

When we walked back out onto Centre Court, I turned and looked at the scoreboard.

PREVIOUS SETS		SERVER	SETS	GAMES	POINTS
6 10	Mrs R Kershaw		1	1	
1 2 3 4					
3 12	Miss F Hodgkin	–	0	1	

"Final set. Miss Hodgkin to serve. Resume play," Mr Watson said into his microphone.

I served and quickly went up 30-love. On my next serve, Claire chipped to my feet. It wasn't a difficult half volley, but I carelessly hit it too low. The ball hit the net cord and fell back into my court. 30-15. I served and faulted on my first serve. I saw Claire take one step into the court, even though she knew I usually wouldn't take anything off my second serve. I decided to teach her a lesson for stepping in, and I hit a hard second serve. But it went long.

My first double fault today. So much for trying to teach Claire a lesson.

The crowd gasped. Claire was at 30-30 on my serve.

I served, came in, and volleyed Claire's return for a winner. My advantage. I served and followed my serve in. Claire had been chipping her returns, but now she hit an incredibly hard return down the line. I watched the ball go past me from about a meter away. Deuce.

The crowd had gone completely silent. Everyone knew what was at stake: the next two points might well decide the championship. If Claire broke my serve, all she had to do was hold her own serve, and in a few games she'd be serving for the championship.

I lost the deuce point and then, on Claire's ad, I tried a risky stop volley that backfired on me. It landed too deep into the service court. Claire raced to the drop shot, made it, and passed me at the net.

The crowd was cheering for Claire; she'd broken my serve; they thought she just about had her third straight championship wrapped up.

Claire held her service, and then I served with the games love-2 in her favor. I held my service, Claire held her service, and so it went. In what seemed like no time, Claire was to serve for the championship, with the games at 5-3.

The crowd was silent. This was almost over. Claire had told me once how quickly things happened on Centre Court; now I knew what she meant.

I was scared. I looked over at Rachel, but she was

impassive. I looked at Mother.

Suddenly, Mother jumped to her feet and yelled as loudly as she could, "FIONA! BREAK HER SERVE!"

The crowd all laughed, but in a good-natured way, and then, all at once, they stood and cheered. Mr Watson looked around to make sure that Rachel wasn't saying anything.

Mother wasn't my coach and so was free, like any other spectator, to yell anything polite she wanted between points. Claire looked at Mother, lifted the face of her racket, and then, still looking at Mother, Claire smiled and lightly tapped the strings with her fingertips.

I thought, 'I am *not* going to lose this match.'

Claire served, and in few minutes we were at deuce. It went to her advantage, which was championship point, but I won the point, and we went back to deuce. Claire hit her first serve into the net, and then set up for her second serve. I returned it, hard, down the line, and came in. Claire hit crosscourt, but I cut it off for a winner. My advantage.

Claire served down the middle, a classic, beautiful Claire serve. I got my racket on it, just barely, at about my shoulder level, and hit it crosscourt into her ad court. But it wasn't a strong return. Any sane player would have stayed on the baseline, but I went to the net. Claire had plenty of time to decide what to do, and she had plenty of good options. She went down the line on my forehand side, trying to thread the needle between the sideline and my racket.

I caught her shot and volleyed it back crosscourt, so Claire had to chase it down, which she did, but I cut off her return with my backhand. She raced for the ball, but she was too late.

I had broken Claire's serve.

The games were now 4-5, with me to serve. If I held my serve, this set would be tied at five games apiece.

Claire had turned her back to me. She was looking at the strings on her racket and shaking her head. She had three championship points, two in the second set and the third just now, and she had lost all three.

I looked over at my parents; Mother and Father both gave me two thumbs up and huge smiles.

I held my serve. The games were tied 5 all. Claire held her serve, so the games were 6-5 in her favor, with me to serve. Claire and I changed ends and stopped for cups of water from the tank under the umpire's chair. Claire smiled and whispered, "Long afternoon." We usually weren't given much time on the changeover, and you could forget sitting down to rest. It would be 1975 before there were chairs for the players on the changeover.

But this changeover was one of those moments in a long tennis match where the crowd thinks, 'This isn't ending anytime soon. Best visit the tea lawn, stretch our legs, and get a cup of tea or a pint'. Many of the spectators took advantage of the changeover to leave their seats. Mr Watson recognized this fact of tennis life and allowed a bit of extra time for the changeover and the partial clearing of the stands.

I held and tied the games again 6-all.

It was past six o'clock. The first evening shadows were approaching Centre Court. Our match had started longer than four hours ago. I gave myself one moment to think about John while I pretended to look at the strings on my racket.

Then I put him out of my mind. I would think about John after I defeated his sister – or she defeated me. But not just yet.

Claire held her serve, and then I held my serve. The games were 7 apiece. Then the games became 8 apiece. Then 9 apiece.

I sensed that Claire's serves were slowing down just slightly. To win, I had to break her again. It was Claire's service. I knew that this was probably my only chance; I was exhausted. If I let this match last longer than a few more games, I would begin to crumble.

I knew the only way to break Claire, at this stage, was to make her run from one side of the court to the other. Over and over. If I could break her serve now, then I would be serving at 10-9. Then, if I held my serve, the match would be finished, and I would win.

Claire served. Yes, I had been right; her serve *was* slowing down. Not much, but maybe just enough. Claire was tired too.

I returned her serve to her ad court and charged the net. Claire ran to catch my return and, again, she made a safe crosscourt shot, which I volleyed back for a winner.

We went to deuce twice before I got the advantage. I set up to receive and looked across the court at Claire. She served, and I hit a solid return and came to the net. Claire hit a beautiful, sharply angled crosscourt shot that went under my forehand before bouncing on the sideline.

So back to deuce again. I had thrown away my ad point.

"*Out!*" A way late call.

There was a dull roar from the crowd; everyone knew the ball had landed in – except apparently the line judge. I looked at Mr Watson. "That was a late call. Did you see the shot?"

"Miss Hodgkin, I cannot overrule." In those days, the

chair umpire wasn't authorized to overrule, although sometimes an umpire would give a line judge such a withering stare that the judge would change the call.

I held my racket in the air. "I concede the point." I looked back pointedly at the line judge. "Claire's shot was well in."

The crowd roared its approval.

I looked at Claire. She had already moved back to her deuce court before I had conceded. She had known I would concede the point. Then she served an ace; I wasn't even close to it.

Ad in. She was about to escape one more time.

Then, suddenly, I felt a cramp in my right thigh. I rubbed it and looked at Rachel. She shrugged. Nothing to be done. I was finished if I began cramping badly.

I returned Claire's service, took the net and volleyed deep. She just got to my volley, but her shot was weak, and I simply put the ball away for a winner. My advantage again. I worried about the cramp in my thigh. It hurt, and I couldn't move well.

Claire served, and I hit my best return of the afternoon. A winner. I had broken her serve. The games were 10-9 in my favor. I would be serving for the championship.

But my cramp was getting worse. I looked at the scoreboard clock. Coming up on seven o'clock.

We had been on the court for hours. We had played 50 games of tennis. We were exhausted.

SATURDAY, 7 JULY 1962
SEVEN O'CLOCK IN THE EVENING
CENTRE COURT – THE CHAMPIONSHIP

I hadn't thought for years about the end of my match with Claire – or, more accurately, I hadn't recognized that I have little recollection of it. I know the final score, and I remember playing the first two sets, and most of the third set, but I can't recall the end.

I wrote to the Committee of Management to ask if there was a film of the final that day and, if so, might I have a copy. The Committee graciously replied that there was indeed a black and white film made by the BBC of its live television broadcast, and they enclosed a copy of the film on a DVD.

After I watched the DVD, I knew why I couldn't recall the ending. My head had hit the court twice within seconds, and hard both times. I probably suffered a slight concussion. It reminded me that, after I had finally gone to sleep that evening at Claridge's, Mother had woken me to ask if I felt at all nauseous. She had held my head in her hands and shined the bed table light into my eyes. Now I realize she was making certain my pupils hadn't dilated, which might indicate a serious concussion. But I was fine, except that I couldn't recall much about few, dramatic moments in my life.

I watched the DVD in our living room. My granddaughters watched with me. One of them asked, "Bermuda Grandmother, why was your racket so small? It looks like it's made of wood or something." Remarkably, I see myself on Centre Court, barely aged 19, in the third set. I'm serving for the championship.

On the film, I look confused. I push my hair out of my face — somehow my ponytail has come undone, and for some reason I haven't put it back in order. How could I even see to hit the ball? I reach down to rub my thigh. When the television camera focuses on me bending over my thigh, there's sweat dripping from my forehead.

Mr Watson is speaking into his microphone. "Deuce."

I serve. It goes over the net and into the service court, but that's about every good thing you could say about it. Claire, though, doesn't put it away. She makes a good return but not a winner. I'm out of position and off balance, and I hit my return shot into the net.

Mr Watson says, "Advantage, Mrs Kershaw."

Break point. If Claire breaks me now, I'm done for.

The film is grainy. I rub my thigh. I look as though I'm in pain from the cramp. I serve. Again, it isn't much of a serve, but at least it's in play. Claire is determined to win this point. She blasts her return down my deuce court sideline. I just get to her return and send it back down the same line. This time, Claire goes crosscourt. I'm on the centerline of my service courts, and with my backhand I catch her shot on my racket face and drop it into her deuce service court.

Mr Watson says, "Deuce."

On my first service, I fault. The crowd gasps. Giving Claire Kershaw a second serve is never a good idea. I set up.

I serve a wide, sharply angled serve to Claire's forehand. My serve pulls her off the court. I'm in my ad service court when her return comes over the net, and I volley it deep into her ad court. She runs but can't make it.

Mr Watson says, "Advantage, Miss Hodgkin."

Championship point. Centre Court is silent.

My serve is weak and poorly placed. It bounces in the center of her ad service court. She can do anything she wants with it. Still, I rush the net. Claire waits a fraction of a second for me to commit, and I drift slightly to my right, betting she'll go down my deuce sideline. Then she blasts the ball crosscourt.

I lunge wildly for the ball with my backhand and hit it back, barely. I get my ankles tangled together, and I fall on my back, outside the sideline. The back of my head hits the ground so hard it bounces off the grass.

My backhand shot goes over the net but it's a sitting duck for Claire. On the film, I see Claire set up perfectly: she has all the time in the world. She split-steps, takes a short, precise backswing, and hits the ball softly into my deuce service court. She's taking no chances. Just hit the ball far away from me. I'm flat on the grass off the court. I can tell what she's thinking: take away the championship point, get back to deuce, and then win this game.

I watch this part of the film over and over. I push up with my left hand; I still have my racket in my right hand. I'm on my feet as Claire's shot crosses over the net, but I'm so far off the court that I could chat with the spectators in the first row of seats – and her ball is heading to the other side of the court.

On the film, I see myself shifting my racket to my left hand. It's my only chance. I switch hands by instinct.

When Claire's ball bounces, it barely lifts off the grass into the air. I'm sprinting across Centre Court, and my right foot lands on the centerline just as the ball begins its downward trajectory.

I'm a meter away from the ball. There's nothing else I can do.

I launch myself into the air, push out my racket in my left hand and barely get it under the ball. I whip my left arm up, just as my forehead slams into the grass. The racket flies out of my hand.

My face skids on the grass, and now, watching it 50 years later, I can almost taste the grass, dirt, and blood. My nose is bleeding.

Claire has already turned away, heading back to the baseline. She thinks she's saved championship point; now she's at deuce; she's back in this game.

My shot goes over the net by a centimeter and falls onto Claire's court. The spectators jump to their feet with a huge roar. She hears the cheering, looks down, and sees the ball rolling past her across the grass. Her mouth is open. I know she's thinking, how? It's impossible that I could have gotten to her shot.

Looking at Claire's face on the film, I can see that she's devastated. But she drops her racket, jumps across the net, comes over to me, and kneels on the grass. I slowly get up onto my hands and knees, but I'm dazed, with blood dripping from my nose. Claire puts her arm over my shoulders, she says something into my ear, makes me sit up on my knees, and helps me stand up. She's pinching my nose with her fingers to stanch the bleeding, and she's saying something to me, but it's inaudible on the soundtrack, and I can't recall anything she said.

I've never asked Claire about this moment; it must have been terrible for her.

Mr Watson on the film begins the traditional recitation of the score: "3-6, 12-10, 11-9, Miss Hodgkin wins game, set, match, and" – here there's a slight pause for effect – "championship."

Claire leads me to Mr Watson's chair, where I reach up to shake his hand, tentatively, as if I'm still not sure where I am, and then Claire walks me to the water tank under the umpire's chair and pours me a cup of water.

Watching the film, I see I never shook hands with Claire, which, I'm sure, is unique in Wimbledon finals – although maybe it counts for a handshake when you would never have made it off Centre Court without your opponent's arm holding your shoulders tightly.

Claire finds a towel to hold against her face. It's not audible on the soundtrack, but now I can recall the sound of Claire crying softly, covered by the towel.

A ball boy hesitantly comes up and offers me a bottle of Robinson's Barley Water and a towel. I take both, sip some Robinson's, wipe off my face, and pinch my nose with the towel.

The film shows the players' box, with my parents and Rachel standing and applauding – they look so young! Then the camera pans down to me, and I suddenly use the remote control to freeze the film.

A news photographer had taken a shot of exactly this scene, and the photo was on the front pages of all the London Sunday papers the next morning. The photographer, later that summer, sent me a print of the photo, which I've kept on my dressing table ever since. It's still in a cheap, plastic frame I bought in Hamilton just before I returned to Smith that September. I've glanced at it most mornings of my adult life.

In the photo, my tennis dress, with its small Bermuda flag, is streaked with grass stains, dirt, and sweat. There are smears of blood and dirt still on my face; my hair is a tangled mess. I'm standing there holding the Robinson's bottle in the air pointed toward the players' box. I have a huge gamine smile on my face, and I'm looking straight at my parents and Rachel. It had been the greatest ladies' singles final ever.

I had won Wimbledon.

SATURDAY EVENING, 7 JULY 1962
CLARIDGE'S
MAYFAIR

That evening, Mother vetoed for me the Wimbledon Ball at Grosvenor House, so Rod Laver, the gentlemen's champion, had to dance with Claire rather than me. To be honest, I didn't want to go to the Ball. Mother and Father had decided my nose wasn't broken, but already I had a bruise appearing on my face. Mother had held an ice pack on me for 15 minutes. All I wanted was to have a bath and tea in the room I shared with Rachel and go to sleep.

Claire rang before she left her flat for the Ball to see how I was feeling. We talked for a couple of minutes about our match. I held an ice pack to my face.

Claire asked, "Have you told your parents about you and John?"

"No. Not yet. I haven't had time."

"Well, you need to tell my parents. Before you sail for Bermuda." My parents and I were sailing for Hamilton from Southampton on Wednesday. Rachel was staying in England to visit her relatives in the Midlands.

Claire said, "Here's what we'll do. Tell your parents tomorrow. Then you and I will meet for lunch on Monday.

Let's go to The Goring, on Beeston Place. We can talk then." Claire said this in a conspiratorial tone, as though we were planning a bank robbery. "But tell your parents that my parents want to have them for tea Monday afternoon. I'll arrange that with Mother and Father. Then, during tea, you can tell my parents."

I replied quietly, because Mother was still in the room. "That sounds as though I, by myself, have to tell both sets of parents."

"Well, you're the one who's engaged to John, after all."

So I agreed to Claire's plan.

Claridge's delivered a wonderfully full tea tray to our room, and, wearing only my bathrobe, with my wet hair hanging down my back and a nascent bruise on my nose, I stepped outside into the hall to hold the door open for the lady who was delivering the tea. I looked down the hall toward the lift and saw a London bobby standing there. He was the same bobby that John had been chatting with earlier in the week. Even though I was wearing just the bathrobe, I let the door to our room close and walked down the hall toward him.

"Good evening, Officer," I said. "I think we've met, but my friend John Fitzwilliam failed to introduce us."

The bobby smiled. "Well, Miss, perhaps the Captain was more interested in seeing you. Congratulations to you on your win today."

"Thank you, and I'm glad to see you, but why are you here?"

"Just to make sure that anyone who gets off the lift belongs here, that's all, Miss. Normal procedure for us. I'll be here for a bit, and then one of my mates will take my place."

He meant he was there to protect my privacy.

"Officer, may I bring you a cup of tea?"

"That's not necessary, Miss."

"I'm bringing you a cup. Milk or lemon?"

"Milk, Miss, please."

I returned to the room, and Rachel opened the door for me. "Do we have an extra cup?" I asked.

"The lady brought two extra cups, for your parents, I expect."

I poured a cup of tea, put milk in it and said to Rachel, "I'll return in one moment."

I went back in the hall. I looked ridiculous barefoot, with wet hair, a bruise on my face, wearing nothing but my hotel bathrobe. I carried the cup of tea to the bobby. I could tell he was looking at my legs. I hoped he didn't realize or imagine that I was naked under the bathrobe. "Here you are."

"Thank you, Miss."

I started to go. He said, "Will Captain Fitzwilliam be here this evening?"

"John has been called away on duty."

"Just as you say, Miss," the bobby replied stoically. He knew what that meant.

I walked away.

"Miss!" the bobby called out.

I turned around.

"I served directly under Captain Fitzwilliam in the Royal Marines for the better part of two years. He was the finest officer in the Marines."

"Thank you, Officer. I'm happy to say he is my fiancé."

"Well, my congratulations to you both."

Sunday, 8 July 1962
Afternoon Tea at Claridge's
Mayfair

Winning Wimbledon certainly increases the invitations a girl has to lunch and dinner dances. On Sunday, Mother fielded four invitations for me to have lunch on Monday, and I think five invitations for dinner dances on Tuesday evening. She turned them all down.

When I walked out of Claridge's, there were photographers, but my bobby friend would shoo them away when I came out. Father was approached by an American businessman who had plans for 'promoting' me in the States. Father's curt response was decidedly negative. I knew Mother and Father were proud of me, but I sensed that the attention now being paid to me at age 19 made them uneasy.

At tea that afternoon, my parents launched their coordinated attack. They said that my winning Wimbledon had been extraordinary, they were proud of me, but they hoped I wasn't going to forget my medical studies. Like the good mixed doubles partners they were, first one talked and then the other about my future and my responsibilities to Bermuda, but I cut them off in mid-sentence. I told them that I would be back at Smith in September to continue with pre-med.

I had gotten what I wanted from tennis.

I reached into my pocketbook and pulled out a telegram I had received the evening before. The author of the telegram suggested that, although I was an amateur, still there were certain financial arrangements that could be made, if need be, to induce me to compete at Forest Hills that August. I handed the telegram to Father. "May I ask you to reply to this for me?" He took the telegram in his hand.

"Mother, Father, there's something you should know." I don't know why it is, but the phrase 'there's something you should know' coming from a child instantly grabs the attention of parents.

They both looked at me intently. They weren't going to like this, not at all, and I dreaded telling them. I knew what they would say: 'What about medical school? Aren't you too young to make a decision like this? Isn't he a bit old for you? Have you had time to think about this carefully? You've only known him for a few days.' I didn't have any answers for those questions. I didn't have an engagement ring. I didn't even know where John was or when I would see him again. I was a pathetic excuse for an engaged daughter.

Anyway, I told them; I just blurted it out. "I'm engaged to be married to John Fitzwilliam."

In the middle of Sunday tea in the dining room of Claridge's, they both hugged me at once. They were from old, established English families, and they probably knew half the people having tea that afternoon at Claridge's. Knew? They were probably *related* to half the people at tea. But still, they forgot themselves. Mother started crying. Father said, "Darling, sweetheart."

Mother said, through her tears, "That is so wonderful."

Father said, "I hope the plan is to be married in Bermuda?"

Mother wiped her eyes. "We should have the wedding in the garden of Midpoint. That's where your father and I were married."

Father said, "Captain Fitzwilliam is perfect for you."

"Fiona, you should wear what you want, of course. If you want to wear my wedding dress, we still have it at home."

Mother's wedding dress had been English Grandmother's wedding dress in 1917, during the Great War. One afternoon in 1942, in the middle of another war, my two grandmothers had hurriedly altered the dress to fit Mother. I can imagine English Grandmother that afternoon watching the sweeping, wild loops of thread American Grandmother was using to stitch the dress back together. English Grandmother probably said dryly, "Fiona, dear, we're all so pleased that you didn't let William Halsted talk you into becoming a surgeon." After my parents' marriage, the dress had spent two decades in a humid Bermuda closet, ripe with mildew.

It was not, shall we say, a Teddy Tinling wedding gown.

"Mother, I plan to wear your dress when I marry John."

She began crying again. Father put his arm around me. "In a few years, several grandchildren would be welcome additions to the family."

As planned, I met Claire in Beeston Place for lunch on Monday. She simply left the white Alfa with its hood down, smack in front of The Goring, handed the keys to the doorman, and kissed his cheek.

"Darling young man," she said to him. He looked to be around 70. "You will take care of my Alfa?"

"Certainly, Claire," he replied, tipping his bowler.

She took my arm and whispered, "Now I'm *sure* I'm pregnant!"

I giggled.

A press photographer standing across Beeston Place caught this scene, with Claire speaking to me and me giggling. A morning newspaper the next day ran this photo on its front page under the caption, 'WIMBLEDON FOES CHATTER IN BELGRAVIA!'

We walked out on the hotel's veranda, looking over the gardens, and took a table. I ordered a plate of cucumber and salmon sandwiches for myself, all of which Claire proceeded to eat. After lunch, we went to her parents' home to prepare tea; she had told her mother not to worry about tea, that Claire and I would take care of it.

Wednesday, 25 July 1962
Statement By The Lawn Tennis Association
London, England

For Immediate Release

The Association has received an inquiry from the United States Lawn Tennis Association in regard to whether arrangements could be made for Mrs Richard Kershaw and Miss Fiona Hodgkin to enter the United States National Championships upon the lawns at Forest Hills in New York City. In light of the intense public interest in a potential re-match between Mrs Kershaw and Miss Hodgkin, and the continued speculation in the sporting press, the Association has concluded to issue this statement in reply to the inquiry.

Mrs Kershaw has advised the Association that she and her husband are expecting their first child, and therefore she will not be in a position to compete at Forest Hills.

Dr. Thomas Hodgkin, D.S.C., father of Miss Hodgkin, has advised the Association that his daughter's pre-medical studies at college will cause her to limit her tennis competition to collegiate matches in the New England area of the United States. Consequently, Miss Hodgkin will not compete at Forest Hills.

* * * * *

After our Wimbledon final, neither Claire nor I ever played tennis in international competition again.

Part Four

St. Margaret's

OCTOBER 1962
ST. MARGARET'S
WESTMINSTER
LONDON, ENGLAND

October came, and I was back at Smith as a sophomore premed student immersed in organic chemistry. I had told the tennis coach that I would still play on the team, but that I no longer wished to play in the number one position. I said that my chemistry classes and labs would prevent me from giving the tennis team the time it deserved if I remained in the first position. This was half true. If I could have left the team altogether without disappointing my teammates, the coach, and Smith generally, I would have done so. But for Smith to have a Wimbledon champion on the team was sensational, so I played.

By late October, Claire and her parents had still heard nothing from or about John. I had been sick with worry about him, but slowly, in my heart, I came to feel John was dead. Otherwise, by then, he would have come back to find me. One day, I walked back to Emerson house through the New England fall afternoon and found a telegram addressed to me from London on the hall table. I picked it up and walked back outside to read it.

There was a bench about a hundred meters from the house, under a small copse of trees, and I walked to the bench and sat down. There were the red and gold leaves that New England trees produce in the fall on the ground, and there was a slight breeze that blew the leaves around my ankles. I looked at the telegram envelope for probably 20 minutes before I opened it. I knew exactly what the telegram would say.

WESTERN UNION

LEARNED TODAY JOHN DID NOT SURVIVE STOP HIS REMAINS NOT RECOVERED STOP NO OTHER INFORMATION STOP SERVICE ST MARGARETS NEXT WEEK STOP COME LONDON SOONEST STOP

LOVE CLAIRE.

I didn't cry. I was numb with sadness. Although I've led a happy, privileged life, and, after a long time, I finally said goodbye to John, even today a part of me has never left that bench under the trees, where I sat mourning him.

I went back inside my house and made the arrangements to make an international call to my parents. I sat down while I waited for the call to go through and held the telegram between my fingers. When the call came through, I picked up the receiver. Mother spoke first. She was crying. "Fiona, we know. Claire sent Rachel a telegram."

"Claire has asked me to come to London." I knew this would be a large expense for my parents, and going to London would take me away from Smith for at least a week, perhaps longer.

Father said, "You have to go to London. I'll make your flight arrangements in the morning. Flying from Boston probably would be best."

It was too late that day to send a telegram from Northampton, but in the morning I cut an English class and walked into town, where I sent Claire a telegram.

POST OFFICE TELEGRAM

ON MY WAY LONDON STOP LOVE FIONA

Claire met me at Heathrow. She was visibly pregnant. We embraced, and I asked, "Tell me how you feel?"

"Tired and nauseated. The baby has moved in and completely taken over. I wanted to be this way?" We half laughed and half cried.

I stayed with Claire's parents. The day after I arrived, Claire and I undertook the task of clearing out John's flat. There were few personal things there; maybe, I thought, he had deliberately kept his life simple, at least until he met me. Out of the corner of my eye, I saw Claire discreetly pull a pair of lady's knickers from John's laundry and put them in her pocket.

"Claire, you look exhausted. Sit down, and I'll make you a cup of tea." John had shown me how to operate the huge stove to make tea.

Claire sat on the couch without protest. When the tea was ready, I handed her a cup. "May I have the knickers?"

"What knickers?"

"Claire, they're mine."

"Oh," she said. "I was just concerned that – " She

stopped, reached into her pocket, and handed them to me. "You and John must have been quite compatible in bed."

"Yes, quite compatible, in all ways."

I got myself a cup of tea and sat down beside Claire. She said sadly, "We'll never be sisters-in-law."

I nodded.

"When I was a girl," Claire said, "I looked up to John. I followed him around, at least when he would let me. But I always wanted a sister. I wanted someone to talk to."

She didn't say anything for a moment. "I don't remember the Blitz well. This house wasn't hit directly. It was damaged, but we could stay here. We were lucky. One night, Mother and Father told John and me that the next day the two of us would be leaving for Canada, for Quebec City, on the St. Lawrence. Father had a business friend there. He and his wife were going to take us in. Mother and Father worried about the sea travel, but they must have decided it was worth the risk to get us to Canada. Father had gotten us passes for a train to Liverpool the next morning – that wasn't easy to arrange. John and I were going to go by ourselves. Father started to explain to John how to get us from the train to the ship in Liverpool."

"I never knew you and John were evacuated to Canada."

"We weren't."

"Why not?"

"John told Father, 'I won't leave London while the King is here, you and Mother are here, and we're being bombed.' Father said to him, 'Son, this is the best thing for you and your sister.' But John said, 'Father, I'll run away, live in the Tube, and take Claire with me.' Mother started crying and saying that we had to leave, how could we question our parents. But Father looked at John and said, 'If you stay here, you and Claire both could be killed.'"

There were tears streaming down Claire's face. She wiped them away with her palm. "John told Father, 'I won't leave London, and Claire won't either.' Mother was saying we would have to leave the next day, but Father motioned to her with his hand. He looked at me: 'Do you know what your brother is saying?' I didn't, but I told him, 'I'm staying with John.'"

"So you didn't go to Canada?"

She shrugged. "All four of us stayed in this house. We weren't evacuated. We lived here, on the ground floor, for awhile."

She looked around. "This used to be a coal bin, before Mother had the flat made for John."

Then she changed the subject. "Fiona, you and I could decide to be sisters."

I said, "Yes."

I put my arms around her, and we held one another. We talked for a long time, and finally she fell asleep on my shoulder. I lowered her head onto a pillow on the couch, stood up, got the blanket from the bed I had shared with John and gently covered her with it.

The day before the memorial service, an equerry from Buckingham Palace arrived with a letter and a small wooden box. The letter was from the Queen, in her handwriting. She had awarded John the Victoria Cross posthumously "for exceptional valor in defending the realm." The VC was in the box. Legend had it that the VC medals were struck from the barrels of canon used in the Crimean War.

I saw John's father open the box, glance at the medal, close the box, and shove it onto the mantelpiece. It's still there today. I don't think it has ever been moved or maybe even touched.

The memorial service was full of military men, many tennis players, and friends of Claire and her parents. There were also a half dozen or so men in dark business suits, but none of them seemed to have a name. Just before the service began, Prime Minister Macmillan slipped into a pew in the back of St. Margaret's. Claire asked me to read the twenty-third psalm, which I did.

As I walked out after the service, I saw Mark Thakeham, who had left the church and was waiting just outside.

"Hello, Fiona. I know you cared about him. My condolences."

"Mark, thank you for coming to the service. It's thoughtful of you."

"I saw in *The Times* obit that he was awarded a VC. For 'defending the realm,' without any more detail."

"Yes. Maybe some of the people here today know what happened to John, but I don't."

The brief obit in *The Times* had also said that it was "rumored" in Whitehall that John had been one of the senior officers of the secretive Special Boat Section. It said he was survived by his parents and by his sister, Claire Fitzwilliam Kershaw, who had been the 1960 and 1961 Wimbledon ladies' champion – and that his "frequent companion" had been the 1962 Wimbledon ladies' champion, Miss Fiona Hodgkin, of Paget, Bermuda. The newspapers didn't know we had been engaged.

"Are you going to stay in London?" Mark asked.

"No. Claire asked me to stay here and transfer from Smith to University College. She wants me in London. I've thought about it, but I've decided to go back to Smith. I've already been away from my classes for a week and a day. I need to get back to Smith. I leave tomorrow for the States. But I've promised Claire I'll come back to help when she has her baby."

Then I asked him, "How is medical school?"

"I go on rounds and, after a resident presents a patient, I'm occasionally asked for my diagnosis. I give it and everyone chuckles. Then the consultant gives the correct diagnosis. So it's going as expected, I suppose. You're taking organic, I recall?"

"Yes, and, as you said, it's rough. But it is interesting. I hope I haven't gotten too far behind."

"I never had the opportunity to congratulate you on Wimbledon."

"Well, now it seems like a very long time ago, but I guess it actually was only last summer."

We stood looking at one another for a few moments. Finally, he reached out, and we shook hands. His hand lingered on mine for just a second longer than would be customary.

"Well, again, my condolences to you. Keep in touch."

"Certainly," I said. "I will do so." And we parted.

Part Five –

Johns Hopkins School of Medicine

1968
Johns Hopkins School of Medicine
Baltimore, Maryland

At Smith, I never got around to having a boyfriend. I worked hard at chemistry, and I enjoyed it, but it didn't leave me with much free time. Just before I left Bermuda for my senior year at Smith, Mother sat me down. "Fiona. The time has come when you need to be open to meeting new people. You have a life to lead. You need to find a boy you like."

She didn't say what I knew she was thinking, which was that I needed to forget John Fitzwilliam. The problem was that I didn't want to forget John.

I promised Mother I would try to find a boyfriend, and I did make an effort. I went out with two or three boys, but nothing was serious. I even let one boy sleep with me, but that was a mistake. He had slept with other girls before me, but he hadn't learned anything from his other girls. When we were in bed together, and I suggested to him how to go about pleasing a girl – specifically, *me* – he was offended.

I knew exactly how it should be done; John had taught me.

So not having a boyfriend was my fault; I just wasn't interested.

I was in the spring of my second year at Johns Hopkins medical school when an intense, young pediatrician on the faculty lectured to my class on childhood vaccines. He was thin and wore tortoiseshell eyeglasses. I went up to the front after the lecture to ask him some question – I can't recall what it was – and we talked for two or three minutes.

I thanked him and was leaving the lecture hall when he called me back: "Doctor?" he said. This was a purely courtesy title; I was two years away from my M.D.

I turned back to him. "Yes, Doctor?"

"Do you have a chemistry background?"

"I majored in chemistry in college." Maybe whatever question I had asked reflected some knowledge of chemistry.

"I need a lab assistant. To assay an antibody. It's part of a research grant I have, but I haven't had time to do it myself. There's a stipend. But not much. Do you want the position?"

That was easy. The medical students who got the few lab assistant positions were stars who had been marked by the faculty for Great Things. But I had gotten this offer by merely asking a question after a lecture.

The antibody turned out to be for chickenpox. My first afternoon in his lab, I asked him, "How do I get a sample of the antibody?"

"Did you have chickenpox?"

"Yes, when I was five or six."

"Stick a needle in your arm. You'll find plenty of the antibody. Your immune system never forgets chickenpox."

A month later, I was working at my bench in his lab, and he stopped as he passed by. I expected him to ask how my work was progressing, but he didn't.

Instead, he said simply, "Will you go out with me this Saturday night?"

I said yes.

That August, just after my summer rotation, and just before my fall rotation at Hopkins began, the lease on the flat in Charles Village that I shared with three other women medical students was about to expire, and so he and I spent a Saturday morning packing up my belongings to move me to his flat.

He said I might as well move in since I spent most nights there anyway.

While we were packing, he found the photograph of me just after I had won Wimbledon, in its cheap plastic frame. I had never mentioned this part of my life to him. As far as I knew, he'd never held a tennis racket.

"What's this?"

"It's a tennis match I won. A long time ago."

"You look awful."

"Thanks."

He and I worked together, sitting side by side at the lab bench. His bench skills were far better than mine, and he took the time to show me how to conduct delicate assays without contaminating the samples.

Then he taught me how to prepare a scientific paper on my findings. I sat at my typewriter drafting the paper, revising it, revising it again, and again. Late at night, over our usual dinner of take out Chinese food, I reworked the text and tables of data until, at last, I submitted it for publication.

In early 1968, my paper finally appeared in *The New England Journal of Medicine*: 'Humoral immune response to ∞ herpesvirus 3. Hodgkin FA. From the Johns Hopkins School of Medicine.'

For a medical student, life doesn't get any better than that.

A week or so after our paper came out, I was walking down the main hallway of the hospital when the imperious Dean of the medical school passed me going in the other direction. I had never spoken to him, and I assumed he had no idea who I was. The Dean generally did not acknowledge the existence of individual medical students.

But he stopped. "Miss Hodgkin?"

"Yes, Doctor?"

"An interesting piece of work."

He didn't need to tell me that he meant the paper that had just been in *The New England Journal*. "Thank you, Doctor."

"I asked my secretary to check on your marks. She tells me you're near the top of the third year class."

"Yes." I didn't know what else to say.

"Your plans?" This was medical school code for what specialty I planned to go into.

"My father is a pediatrician, and I hope to be a pediatrician as well."

By pure luck, the Dean was a pediatrician himself. But how could he possibly treat children without frightening them? He certainly frightened *me*.

"Good. An interesting piece of work. Keep it up – " He paused for an instant and then said, "Doctor Hodgkin."

Purely a courtesy title. He turned and continued walking down the hall.

One evening during my pediatrics rotation, I came into my boyfriend's lab. I had spent the day being trained in how to care for ill children, and now I had hours of lab work in front of me.

I sat down beside him at our bench. He had made lemonade for himself, and he poured some for me into a glass beaker. We routinely ignored all the signs that warned against taking food or drink into the biomedical laboratories; we barely had time to eat as it was. He no longer saw patients but supported himself (and me, for that matter) entirely with research grants.

"Don't you miss treating children?" I asked.

He shrugged. "My clinical skills aren't strong."

I was included in his circle of research friends at Hopkins. Probably most of them had never heard of Wimbledon; that wasn't part of their lives. I never mentioned it. Our friends and colleagues assumed that my boyfriend and I would eventually marry and spend our careers at Hopkins. This was a compliment to me, because it implied that I had what it took for a career of research at Hopkins.

My boyfriend would be at Johns Hopkins permanently; he was a research star.

Late in the spring of my third year, my boyfriend took me out to a fancy dinner at a new restaurant in Baltimore, Tio Pepe. This was out of character for him, and I should have known something was up. In the middle of dinner, he asked me to marry him. He had even bought an expensive engagement ring for me. I told him that I was only 25 and wasn't ready to get married yet, or to make any commitment, which I intended as a gentle way of saying, "No."

I thought to myself guiltily that I had been plenty ready to be married when I had been only 19, and that the difference between then and now wasn't my age, but that I had been in love with John. I wasn't in love now. My boyfriend was disappointed and hurt, and so after dinner, even though I was tired, I took him by the hand, led him back to the flat, took off my clothes, and did my best to make it up to him.

Nearly two decades later, I was making dinner for my daughters, and I happened to turn on the television to catch the evening news. I was startled to see on the news a lecture room at Hopkins that I knew well from my medical student days. He was standing in the front of the room, just as he had the day he lectured to my class on vaccines. But now the lecture room was full of reporters, not medical students. He was still thin, but his hair was gray. He was just as intense as ever. He wore stained khaki trousers and a ragged sweater.

Earlier that day, the Karolinska Institute had awarded him the Nobel Prize in Physiology or Medicine for his work on childhood vaccines.

I hadn't seen him since I had taken my M.D. in 1969. We hadn't spoken since the late Saturday afternoon in July 1968 when I had talked with him by telephone from Claire's kitchen in Belgravia. When I returned to Baltimore, he already had left for 10 days to give a seminar at the Cold Spring Harbor Laboratory on Long Island. We had planned to make that trip together. I let myself into the flat and packed my medical textbooks, Rachel's old sweater, the framed photo of me after my final with Claire, and my other things.

As I was leaving, I locked the door and pushed my keys to the flat and to our lab through his mail slot.

I was going to chuck my career at Hopkins to become a pediatrician on Point Finger Road in Bermuda.

A reporter asked, "How did you start this research?"

He blinked his eyes for a moment. "I began this work with a colleague, Fiona Hodgkin, who was a medical student here at Johns Hopkins at the time." He stopped to think. "We used her blood as a starting point. She had chickenpox as a child. She published a paper about the antibody in her blood. In '68, I think. In retrospect, an important paper. Doctor Hodgkin deserves part of the credit for this prize they've given me."

Later, I read in the newspaper that he had never married.

July 1968
London, England

After I finished my third year at Hopkins, Father helped arrange a general surgery rotation for me over the summer in London at his hospital, Guy's. Claire picked me up at Heathrow. Her parents had retired to the country, and Claire, Richard, and their children had taken over the house in Belgravia. I was going to stay with them.

Claire had reluctantly given up her Alfa Romeo roadster for a Jaguar sedan that could hold her children. When I opened the passenger door, I had to brush the Animal Cracker crumbs off the seat before I could sit down.

Claire looked at the crumbs ruefully. "I dole out Animal Crackers to young Fiona to keep her occupied when we drive to the country. Richard says we have to leave off calling her 'young Fiona,' or else the double name will stick, and she'll be burdened with it for the rest of her life."

I laughed. I was young Fiona's Godmother.

"So," Claire asked, "how's your love life?" She had met my boyfriend on a trip to the States and made no secret to me that she didn't care for him.

"He's asked me to marry him."

"Oh, no! What did you say?"

"I told him I wasn't ready to make any commitment."

"Good! Fiona, he's not right for you. Has he ever been to Bermuda?"

"No," I admitted. Not only that, I thought, he'd never expressed the slightest interest in visiting Bermuda.

"And I don't think you should spend your time holed up in a laboratory."

This wasn't the first time Claire had said all this to me. Even though I knew the answer, I asked anyway: "Why shouldn't I do research? It's important."

"You need to be around people more. I want you to promise that this summer you'll be open to meeting new people. It's time. I'll find you someone else who's better for you." She left unsaid an important part of what she meant, which was that she would find someone *English* for me – not American. Claire and my Mother hadn't spoken to one another about me, at least as far as I knew, but they both said exactly the same things.

"I promise I'll be open to meeting people."

"Fiona," Claire said when we pulled up in front of the house in Belgravia. "You have a choice. We have a guest room on the third floor, or John's flat on the ground level is empty. The two boys are on the third floor, and they've been known to make a great deal of noise. You're welcome to stay in the flat if you like."

I thought for a moment. "I'd prefer the guest room, Claire. The boys won't bother me."

My first day at Guy's, I scrubbed and walked into an operating room to observe one of the senior consultants operate.

The Tennis Player From Bermuda

The consultant looked up when I came in. He wore gold-rimmed eyeglasses with a strip of white adhesive tape holding them to the bridge of his nose. "Well, a new face," he said.

The members of the surgical team chuckled. This was a small joke; with my surgical mask and cap, my eyes were the only part of my face visible.

The consultant asked, "Who are you?"

"Fiona Hodgkin."

The consultant went about his work on the patient and after a moment said, "There was a girl with that name some years ago who won the singles at Wimbledon."

"That's me."

"You've had quite a change in vocation, haven't you?"

"Yes, I have."

"Where are you training?"

"Hopkins. I start my fourth year in September."

At the name 'Hopkins,' he looked up at me. "You're English. Why train in the States?" He looked back down at his patient.

He thought I was English because I speak with an English accent. "I'm actually Bermudian. Both my grandmother and mother trained at Hopkins."

"A family of medical women, I see." He said this not entirely with approval. "So why are you here at Guy's?"

"My father did his internship here just before the war. He arranged for me to take my surgery rotation here."

"What's your father's name?"

"Thomas Hodgkin."

This got him to look up again from the patient. "Quite a famous medical name."

"My father is descended from the younger brother of the famous Thomas Hodgkin."

"Is your family Quaker, then?" The famous Hodgkin had been a Quaker.

"No, my parents are Church of England."

"Well, Miss Hodgkin, where did the famous Thomas Hodgkin train?"

"At St. Thomas's and Guy's medical school."

"Correct. And what is the second thing for which Hodgkin is famous?" The consultant was making another small joke. Hodgkin is best known for characterizing Hodgkin's disease, a lymphoma, in 1832.

"In 1822, he advocated the use of the stethoscope here at Guy's."

"Correct. For some reason we were reluctant to take up that handy device. Can't imagine why." Then he stepped away from the patient and asked, "Miss Hodgkin, are you scrubbed?"

"Yes, Doctor."

The consultant glanced almost imperceptibly at the senior anaesthetist, who checked the patient's vital signs and nodded to the consultant. The patient was stable as a rock, and a few extra minutes on the operating table for the training of a medical student would make no difference.

The consultant said to me, "Miss Hodgkin, have the heirs of William Stewart Halsted at Hopkins taught you to suture?"

"Yes, Doctor."

"Then come over here, and we'll see if you can suture as well as you can hit a tennis ball."

Then I knew that, even though I was a woman, I had been accepted.

Mark Thakeham was a Senior House Officer at a different hospital, but he heard I was in London through the medical grapevine. His schedule as an SHO was hectic and exhausting. Wimbledon was on, and Mark called the Club and got two seats in the players' box one afternoon during the first week. It was the first 'open' Wimbledon – that is, it was open to professional players. He rang me at Guy's and asked me to come with him.

I hesitated. I hadn't spoken to Mark in years, and I hadn't been back to Wimbledon since 1962. I was on the verge of saying 'no.' I would give the excuse of work.

But Mark said, "Fiona. Centre Court."

He was right; I couldn't pass up an afternoon on Centre Court.

We took our seats between matches, and there was a ripple of applause around Centre Court, which Mark joined.

"Why are they applauding?" I asked Mark.

"For you."

After the last match of the day on Centre Court, Mark and I went out to dinner at an Indian restaurant in SoHo. In the six years since I'd last seen him, he'd adopted the calm, unflappable, seen-it-all-twice demeanor many physicians have – I recognized it because I was in the early stages of trying to adopt the same demeanor myself.

When we walked back to the Tube after dinner, he asked me to have dinner with him again that weekend, and I accepted. I met him Saturday evening in Ken High, we had dinner in a pub, and then went on a long walk in Kensington.

One night the next week, he made dinner for me in his flat. He had become quite the chef. I was standing in the tiny kitchen of his flat, drinking a cup of tea and watching him make dinner, when I mentioned that I planned to spend a week in Bermuda with my parents at the end of my surgery rotation.

Mark said, "I need to go to Bermuda myself, but I haven't found the time. I haven't been there since we met. But I liked Bermuda. Mostly because of meeting you." He smiled at me. Mark could be charming when he felt like it; there's never been any question about that.

"Why do you need to go to Bermuda?"

"Do you remember Tempest? Where we met the first time?"

"Certainly, yes."

"My aunt passed away last year, and I inherited Tempest. It's standing empty, and I want to check on it."

"Oh, Mark, I'm sorry she's gone. I hadn't known. How did she die?"

"I was her physician. I could say she died of CHF." He meant congestive heart failure. "That's what I put on the death certificate. But probably it's just as accurate to say she died of old age."

I thought that Tempest perhaps wasn't the grandest house in Bermuda, but it was certainly in the running. The land tax alone on Tempest was probably more than the National Health Service paid Mark as a medical resident. But then it occurred to me. The upkeep on Tempest was no doubt looked after by some clerk at the Thakehams' firm of solicitors in the City. Mark probably hadn't the slightest idea of what it cost to maintain his house in Bermuda.

That week I found some reason or other to ring Mark just about every day, and we took to eating hurried lunches together in hospital canteens, and talking about our patients. I noticed, a little guiltily, that I never mentioned that I had a boyfriend in Baltimore. But Mark never did anything that would have forced me to make that choice. One day at lunch I was telling Mark about a surgical site infection in one of my patients that, personally, I thought could have been avoided. While listening to me, he reached across the table and took my hand. I took my other hand, put it on top of his and went on talking.

Thursday, 4 July 1968
London, England

On the second Thursday of the fortnight, the Club Secretary rang me at Guy's and invited me and my guest to the ladies' final that Saturday. I accepted and telephoned Mark twice at his hospital to see if he could arrange to be off Saturday afternoon to come with me, but I couldn't reach him either time. He was busy with patients; he had been on duty since Wednesday morning, working flat out the entire time. I finally got off from Guy's around nine that evening and decided to stop at Mark's hospital on my way back to Claire's house.

I took the lift to Mark's ward and asked a nurse where I could find him. She said he was asleep in the House Officers' lounge, and she pointed me down a hallway toward a closed door. 'Lounge' was an overly grand name for this room. It was the size of a closet, and the only furnishing was a plain Army cot. There was a door to a tiny loo on the side of the room across from the cot.

A row of hooks was on a wall, with a doctor's lab coat hanging on one hook and a pair of trousers hanging on another. I was relieved when I saw a mop of strawberry blond hair spilling out from under a sheet on the cot; at least I had found Mark and not some other sleeping SHO.

I closed the door, went over to the cot and sat down, uncomfortably, on the side rail of the cot. I put my fingers into the mop of hair, and Mark slowly came around. He looked at me and smiled. "Hello," he said.

"Hello yourself."

He reached up, put his hand on the back of my neck, and pulled me down to his face. I stopped him and said, "Mark, I'll kiss you, but only after you clean your teeth. What in heaven did you have with your tea?"

He laughed. "I think it was lunch, actually. Didn't get to have tea. Let me up, then."

I stood, and he peeled back the sheet, got off the cot and stumbled into the loo. He was wearing only his boxer shorts. I took off my short medical student's lab coat and hung it on a hook beside Mark's long lab coat. His coat had in script on the left breast 'Mark Thakeham, M.D., Cambridge Medicine.' Mine had, 'Fiona Hodgkin, Johns Hopkins School of Medicine.' Each coat had a stethoscope hanging out of the side pocket. I stood there looking at the two coats hanging side by side.

Mark came out of the loo. He put his arms around my waist, I put my arms around his neck, and he kissed me. "To what do I owe the honor of this night time visit?"

"I wanted to ask you something, but now I can't recall what it was."

"I'm sure you'll think of it." He kissed me again and put his hand on my breast. I put my hand over his and pressed his hand to me. He took this as an invitation – and maybe that's what it was. He reached behind me and fumbled with the zipper on the back of my dress.

"There's a small hook at the top of the zipper," I said,

trying to be helpful, but he couldn't manage the hook and zipper.

After a moment, I said, "Maybe you should let me do this. Get back on your cot." He did.

I unzipped my dress, stepped out of it and hung it on one of the hooks. I went over to the cot and sat down again on the side rail. He pulled me down to him, kissed me, then reached behind me to the hooks on my bra. He stopped, looked at me, and said, "Is this all right?"

I laughed. "Yes. Can you manage it by yourself?"

He undid the hooks on the bra, pulled it away from me and dropped it on the floor.

He said, "See? I got your bra off without any help."

"I'm sure you've had lots of practice with bras."

I stretched out beside him, half convinced the cot would collapse, but it didn't. I said, "How exactly are we going to do this on a cot? It's too narrow."

He pulled the sheet over us and said, "Perhaps I should be on top of you. That might work."

It worked exceptionally well.

Afterwards, we were on our sides, with my back snuggled against him. He was holding one of my breasts in his hand.

He said, "I've wanted you for so many years. You have no idea how much I've wanted you."

"So how was it, at long last?" I was trying to mock him, but I didn't quite bring it off.

"Perfect."

I felt his hand gently caressing my breast. I said, "I'm small on top."

"You're perfect on top. Just what I want."

"Now I remember what it was I wanted to ask you."

"If talking about your breasts reminded you of what it is, I can't wait to hear."

"Don't be silly. No, I've been invited to the ladies' final on Saturday. I wanted to know if you can get out of hospital and come with me."

"I think so. That would be great. I can check and make certain in the morning that I can get that afternoon off."

"I thought we might take our tennis whites to the final. The outer courts are closed for play after the fortnight, but if we're discrete we can probably get away with playing a set or two after the final. No one is likely to be around to stop us."

Although Mark had been a member of the All England Club probably since the day he was born, and I was an honorary member because of my championship, even members were not allowed to play on the outer courts after the fortnight until Richard Hawkins and his crew had repaired the courts, which took weeks.

Mark didn't reply. He rolled me over onto my back and took me again, and while he was touching me I cried out so loudly that he cupped his other hand gently over my mouth and whispered, "Let's not wake the patients on the ward."

Friday, 5 July 1968
Belgravia

I spent the night on that wretched Army cot, and in the morning I took the Tube home to Hyde Park Corner and walked to Claire's. When I arrived, Richard had left for the City, and Claire was chasing her boys around, trying to get them ready for the swimming camp they attended on Hampstead Heath. Young Fiona was in her booster seat at the kitchen table, eating a bowl of porridge.

Claire was taking the boys out the front door to wait with them for the van that picked them up when she called back, "Fiona, will you see if young Fiona wants banana with her porridge?"

I sat down across from young Fiona and said, "Do you want me to slice some banana for you?"

She nodded solemnly, and I sliced half a banana into her dish.

I asked, "Is the porridge good?"

She nodded again. "Mummy made it for me. Will you read to me?"

Claire and Richard kept a pile of old children's books on the kitchen table. "I will read to you but finish your breakfast first. Then pick out the book you want to read."

Claire returned and looked at young Fiona with an appraising eye. "Do you need to visit the loo?"

Young Fiona nodded solemnly.

"I'll take her." I lifted young Fiona out of the seat and carried her down the hall to a small powder room.

When we returned, I put her in her seat, and she went back to eating her porridge.

Claire looked at me. "In whose bed did you spend the night?"

I was a bit disheveled. "Is it that obvious?"

"Obvious? You might as well have 'Just Had Sex' written in red lipstick on your cheek. So who was it?"

"Mark Thakeham."

"Now there's a name out of the past. How was he?"

"He certainly knows what he's doing. I'll say that for him."

"He treated you well?"

"Yes. Quite well."

"Did he make you come before he did?"

"Claire, you really are awful."

"Just curious. What's the answer?"

Young Fiona held up an old Raggedy Ann book and said, "This one." The book had belonged to Claire and John when they were children; it was held together with Scotch tape; either Claire or John, or maybe both, had scribbled in it with crayons.

"Can you get down from your seat?" I said to young Fiona. "Come get in my lap, and I'll read to you."

"So?" Claire said.

"Yes, he took care of me before he came." I smiled. "Both times."

Young Fiona said, "Raggedy Ann has red yarn for hair."

Claire cleared young Fiona's dish. "Interesting that Mark Thakeham appears on the scene after all these years. Is he in love with you?"

"I have no idea."

Young Fiona said, "Uncle Clem is Raggedy Ann's friend."

Claire said, "You could answer 'yes,' or you might say 'certainly not,' but if you say, 'I have no idea,' that means you think he's in love with you."

She was right, but I didn't answer her. Four centuries before, Claire definitely would have been hanged as a witch. I did think that Mark was in love with me.

Young Fiona settled herself in my lap and opened the Raggedy Ann book. I began to read: "*One day Daddy took Raggedy Ann down to his office and propped her up against some books upon his desk . . .*" I used my finger to point to each word as I read to young Fiona. I leaned over and kissed the top of her head.

Claire said, "So if he's in love with you, are you in love with him?"

I stopped reading. "I'm not in love with anyone."

Young Fiona asked, "Is Raggedy Ann just a doll, or is she real?"

Claire answered, "She is just a doll, but she's a real doll."

I read: "*Daddy wished to catch a whole lot of Raggedy Ann's cheeriness and happiness . . .*"

Claire said, "You're not in love with anyone because you don't want to let go of John. That's why you have this laboratory fellow in Baltimore, because you're not in love with him, so you can still hold on to John."

I was stricken. This was the worst thing anyone could say to me. My lower lip started trembling, but I managed to whisper, "That's not true."

Young Fiona asked, "Is Uncle Clem a real doll?"

Claire said, "I think it's completely true. I think when you're in bed alone, you imagine making love to John. Then you cry to yourself. You want to do that for the rest of your life, don't you? But you can't if you fall in love with someone else."

I started sobbing.

"That's exactly what you do, isn't it?"

She paused. "At night, when I go upstairs to make sure the boys are under their covers, I hear you crying."

I had tears running down my face. I nodded.

Claire came over to me, reached down, picked up young Fiona and stood her on the kitchen floor. Then Claire pulled me up and put her arms around me. "Fiona. Listen to me. You can tell John goodbye, and it won't be as hard as you expect."

Young Fiona looked up at me with a frown. "I want you to keep reading Raggedy Ann to me."

SATURDAY, 6 JULY 1968
COURT 13
ALL ENGLAND CLUB WIMBLEDON

It didn't take Billie Jean King too long to defeat Judy Tegart, and then Mark and I went to the dressing rooms to change. We agreed to slip out separately and meet on Court 13. The outer courts were deserted and eerily quiet. When I walked out on the court, it dawned on me that this was the old Court 14, where I had played my first match at Wimbledon six years before. (In 1964, it had been renumbered 'Court 13,' but it was the same court.) In my mind, I could see the crowds and Claire yelling and jumping up and down. It had been beside this court that John told me he was in love with me. I felt it had all happened in another lifetime.

Mark arrived, and we played a set. The day was perfect, and while the court was badly bruised from two weeks of play, it was still an old-style Wimbledon grass court – fast, unpredictable, and fun. We were changing ends when Mark said to me, "It's just like old times." And I agreed.

We were both thirsty after our set, but there was no water on the court. A stray ballboy, apparently off on a frolic of his own, happened to walk past, and I asked him if he might find us some water. A bit later, he reappeared with not only one large thermos of water but also another thermos of hot tea with lemon.

Mark and I sat down on a bench and poured each other cups of water, and then tea. Mark leaned over and kissed me, and I kissed him back.

He pulled away and said, "You don't remember where we kissed the first time, do you?"

"Yes, I do. I had made a picnic lunch."

"We were at that lighthouse. What's it called?"

"Gibbs Hill Lighthouse."

Then he kissed me again, and I put my arms around him.

He stopped kissing me. "Fiona, will you marry me?"

I took my arms away in surprise. "Are you serious?"

"Quite serious. I want to spend my life with you."

"Are you in love with me?"

"Very much so." He paused. "Always have been, actually."

"Mark, I can't marry you. I'm Bermudian, and I'm going to spend my life in Bermuda. You're English; you're staying here, in England. I don't want to call England my home." I was surprised to hear myself say so emphatically that I was going to return home to Bermuda, but once I had said it, it suddenly seemed obvious to me.

"I've thought about that," Mark said. It must have seemed obvious to him as well. "When I finish my term as SHO, I won't take a Registrar's position. I'll come to Bermuda and practice medicine there. We'll have our family in Bermuda."

I thought for a moment. "Well, there's another problem. I have a boyfriend in Baltimore. I live with him. He's asked me to marry him."

Mark was plainly put off by the news that I had a

boyfriend. I could tell he hadn't considered this possibility.

"Am I that unlikeable?" I asked. "I can tell from your face that you didn't expect me to have a boyfriend."

"You're likeable," he said. He reached over and put his hand on my cheek. "I've liked you since I first met you."

"To be honest, I've always liked you as well."

"What did you tell him? Are you engaged to him? I hope not, since you and I slept together."

"I told him I wasn't ready to make any commitment."

"Are you in love with him?"

"No. I'm not."

Neither of us said anything for a few moments. Finally, Mark said, "You asked me about being in love with you, so I'm entitled to ask you in return. Do you love me?"

I simply said goodbye to John. Claire had been right – it wasn't as hard as I expected. John didn't disappear; he merely took one step further back in my memory. Now in my mind, he was covered by a fine mist, as though I were looking at him from across the Serpentine in Hyde Park early on a damp morning.

I thought for a long moment, and then I shook my head and gave a short, rueful laugh.

Mark said, "Is there something humorous here that I've missed?"

"Oh, Mark, I'm sorry. I didn't mean to laugh. But I was just thinking about the flat in Baltimore that I share with my boyfriend. I suppose that both you and he would insist that I move out."

"I don't understand."

"It's all right. I could find a place of my own for my last year at Hopkins. Or maybe I could move in with one of the women in my class."

"What are you saying, Fiona?"

"Well, we couldn't get married now, could we? We would have to wait until I have my M.D. And I've taken my medical boards in the States. You agree? That would mean next summer, at the earliest.

"Yes, of course."

"So, you wouldn't want me living with my boyfriend this year? I mean, my former boyfriend?"

"Certainly not," he replied in a shocked tone.

"Well, then." I sat back against the bench. I was pleased to see that I had completely befuddled him.

"Mark, we're going to be away from one another for most of the next year. I'll be at Hopkins, and you'll be in London. I don't want you to so much as look at another girl. I'm not going to sit in Baltimore and worry about what you're doing."

"Fiona, I'm committed to you. I'm not going to look at any other girl."

"Good."

"Fiona, I'm in love with you. I want you to marry me. Are you saying you will?"

"I might work out my internship so that I could be in London. I like Guy's; maybe they'll take me in even though I've trained at Hopkins."

"Fiona, please give me a straight answer. What are you going to do?"

I sighed. "I guess I'm going to go back to Claire's and place an international call to Baltimore. I don't know if I'll be able to reach my boyfriend on a Saturday. If he's in our lab, I can get him, but maybe he'll be out and about." I looked at my watch. It was past five in London, so it was early afternoon in Baltimore.

"What are you going to tell him?" Mark asked.

"I'll probably begin by saying that I'd rather eat a lizard than tell him what I'm about to tell him."

"Which is what?"

"That a long time ago in Bermuda, I met someone, and this summer in London I've met him again, and I've fallen in love with him. And that I'm going to marry this person."

He leaned over and kissed me. "Let me come with you to Claire's."

I smiled. "No. I'll be upset after talking with my boyfriend. Claire would put you out on the street before she'd let you see me upset."

I thought for a second. "I don't mean to keep calling him my boyfriend. He's not any longer. So don't take that the wrong way. But I do have to tell him myself, and that'll be a sad telephone call. I can't help that. You're all right with my making that call? This just has to be all unwound, and it's unfair to him for me to wait even a day to tell him."

Mark said, "But you will marry me? You won't change your mind?"

"No, I'm not going to change my mind. I'm in love with you, and I'm going to marry you."

"Tonight you could stay over at my flat."

"No, give me an evening by myself. I need to move from one part of my life to the next. Claire will want to talk to me. And I have to write to my parents. Are you in hospital tomorrow?"

"Yes. I'm due to be off at seven Sunday evening, but you know how that works."

"I'll go to market tomorrow and buy something for us

for dinner tomorrow night. Do you hide a spare key to your flat?"

"Yes," Mark said. "It's under an empty milk bottle in the hallway."

"That's not an original place to hide a key."

"If I put it in an original hiding place, I wouldn't be able to remember where I put it."

"I'll let myself into your flat and make dinner for us tomorrow. I have to warn you that I'm not much of a cook."

"Will you spend the night?"

"Yes, I'll stay over. I'll bring some of my things. I have to be scrubbed at Guy's by seven Monday morning."

"We could make love again."

"Maybe. We'll see." I smiled at him. "I like keeping you in suspense. We'll be making love to one another for a long time once we're married."

"I look forward to that. I promise to make love to you when you're a grandmother." He's kept this particular promise.

He leaned over to kiss me again, but just then, someone called out loudly, "Hallo! You there!" I looked up to see Richard Hawkins, the groundskeeper, standing on St. Mary's Walk across Court 13 from us. "This court is closed."

Then Richard recognized me. "It's good to see you again, Fiona," he said. "And I'm sorry. But you know the outer courts are all closed. I have to begin working on them."

"Richard, we're not playing tennis," I said. "We've just become engaged to be married."

That stopped Richard in his tracks. "Oh. Well, then. Fiona, my congratulations." And he walked off.

Summer 1969
My Wedding
Bermuda

The afternoon before my wedding, we had a family picnic on Warwick Long Bay. Mark was holding me against his chest as we sat on the beach, when he suddenly pointed down the beach.

I looked. Fifty meters or so away, Myrtle Hanson had rolled up her skirt and was standing in the Atlantic surf, holding young Fiona's hand. When the surf rolled out, Myrtle found a fragment of a pink shell for young Fiona, and the two of them bent over to marvel at the bit of shell.

Claire's head popped up. She had been sitting in a beach chair talking intently with Rachel. From the way Claire had been twirling her index finger, I could tell they were talking about how a tennis ball spins in flight. As though there was anything more to be said on that topic. Now it was almost dusk, and Claire wanted to locate her children.

Her boys were climbing some rocks at the far end of the bay.

Myrtle carried young Fiona back to our beach encampment. She had fallen fast asleep on Myrtle's shoulder. She put her down on a beach towel and then covered her with another towel.

The only way to tell there was a little girl curled up under the towel was the blond hair spilling out from under one end of the towel, and the tiny left foot sticking out the other. Claire reached down and pulled the towel to cover her daughter's foot.

I can't recall which of us asked the question. Maybe it was me, but looking back – it might have been Myrtle.

"Will she be a Wimbledon champion?"

Rachel replied, "Yes."

And so, the next morning I married Mark in the garden of Midpoint. I wore Mother's wedding dress. She had altered it to fit me, just as my grandmothers had altered it to fit Mother, and she had gotten most of the mildew off it.

Father gave me away, and Claire and Rachel stood beside me. Myrtle Hanson was holding young Fiona. They had taken a liking to one another.

The sky that morning was the blue that you see only in Bermuda, and during the short service, I turned my head to hear the soft clop, clop of an old farmer's horse-drawn cart far below on Harbour Road.

EPILOGUE

KOOYONG, 1987

January 1987
Australian Open
Kooyong Lawn Tennis Club
Melbourne, Australia

Late afternoon. A sunny day in Melbourne but cool for January. Claire, Richard, Myrtle, Mark, and I were having a late lunch on the balcony just outside the members' bar of the Kooyong clubhouse. The Australian Open was on, and there were huge crowds milling about on the lawns below us. I was amazed at how well the Aussies were able to stage a global tournament at such a small, private grass court club. But this year would be it. In 1988, the Australian Open would leave Kooyong forever and move to the composition courts at Flinders Park in Melbourne.

Young Fiona and Rachel were in the media tent for the (mandatory) post-match press conference. Earlier that afternoon, young Fiona had won her quarterfinal match at Kooyong against a top seed in three sets. She was in the semifinals of the Australian Open.

Just after young Fiona won, Claire had said to Rachel, "Will you go with her to the press conference? Keep her from saying anything shocking on television."

"Any suggestions on how to do that?" Rachel asked.

Claire thought for a moment. "Nothing comes to mind. But you're her coach, you'll think of something. Clap your hand over her mouth perhaps?"

Rachel snorted.

For lunch, Claire and I both ordered chicken salad sandwiches, and when the waiter set the plates in front of us, Claire, without a word, reached over with her knife and fork, cut my sandwich in two, deftly transferred the larger part to her own plate, and began eating.

I didn't bother objecting. Claire would eat everything in sight, even if the food in question happened to be on my plate. She would never change.

My twin daughters appeared on the balcony.

"Mom," one of them whispered. "You have to come see something."

"I'm having lunch."

The other twin clutched at my sleeve. "Now, Mom. You have to see this."

Myrtle looked at the twins with her head cocked to one side. Usually, one look from Myrtle was enough to cause the twins to back down from whatever mischief they were up to, but this time they persisted.

I sighed. "I'll be right back."

The twins practically dragged me inside the members' bar.

One of them thrust out her teenage hip and pointed at the wall in an exaggerated way. "Who is *that*?"

"That's the Club's portrait of Harry Hopman."

The twins rolled their eyes.

"Not the portrait, Mom. The *photo* next to it."

The old black and white photograph hanging on the wall showed a shy young girl clutching her racket to her chest.

"Oh. That's your tennis coach." The twins had grown up playing with Rachel on the grass court at Tempest, our home in Bermuda.

The twins looked at one another with their usual where-did-we-find-this-mother expression.

"Mom," one of them said. "It's not Rachel."

"It looks like her, though," the other said.

"But it couldn't be. The girl in the photo is a teenager."

"Yeah, it's not possible."

I laughed. "I have news for you two. It's a photo of Rachel after she won the championship here at Kooyong. May I return to lunch?"

The next day the twins played one another in the Australian junior girls' final. Claire and young Fiona knocked up with the twins before the match. Claire almost never hit tennis balls in public, and I could hear the excited whispers running through the crowd: "Claire Kershaw is practicing on court 8." Minutes later, the sides of the grass court were thronged with spectators.

It was even cooler that day in Melbourne, and young Fiona was wearing Rachel's ragged Kooyong sweater. I had given it to her the year before when she had been invited to play at Roehampton, where she had qualified for the Wimbledon draw.

It can be chilly in London in June, and I felt better knowing young Fiona had something warm to wear.

A steward arrived to take the twins into the old Kooyong stadium. The twins had Mark's strawberry blond hair and good looks. They were beautiful, really. I had sewn small Bermuda flags on their tennis dresses.

Young Fiona gave them each a hug. The twins adored young Fiona; to them, she was their older sister. Rachel said to the twins, simply, "Good luck."

Once we took our seats, Mark said to me, "I can't watch," and he put his head in his hands.

The chair umpire switched on her microphone and turned to her left.

"Lady Rachel Thakeham, are you ready?"

"Ready!"

The umpire turned to her right.

"Lady Claire Thakeham, are you ready?"

"Ready!"

"Lady Rachel to serve. Play."

Young Rachel tossed the tennis ball high and out, cocked her racket deep behind her shoulder, went up on her toes, whipped the racket forward, slammed the ball and ran toward the net.

Acknowledgements

On Saturday, 7 July 1962, the ladies' singles final at Wimbledon – in reality – was between Vera Sukova of the former Czechoslovakia and Karen Hantze Susman of the United States. Mrs Susman won 6-4, 6-4.

In 1961, the singles final was between two of the greatest British players, Angela Mortimer and Christine Truman. They played a classic three set match that Miss Mortimer won 4-6, 6-4, 7-5. Miss Mortimer (now Mrs Barrett) gave a thrilling description of this match in her book *My Waiting Game* (Frederick Muller, London 1962).

Anyone interested in the history of tennis should visit the Wimbledon Lawn Tennis Museum at the All England Lawn Tennis Club, where Mrs Barrett's racket – and her trademark tennis shorts designed by Teddy Tinling – are displayed, along with many other engaging items from the history of Wimbledon.

The tennis columnist and historian Bud Collins called the great and graceful tennis player Maria Bueno of Brazil the "São Paulo Swallow." She won Wimbledon in 1959, 1960, and 1964. In 1962 she lost in the semifinal to Mrs Sukova 6-4, 6-3.

In 1939, at Kooyong, Emily Hood Westacott defeated Nell Hall Hopman in the Australian championship final 6-1,

6-2. (Both Mrs Westacott and Mrs Hopman were Australian.) At Wimbledon, Alice Marble of the United States defeated Kay Stammers (later Mrs Menzies) of Great Britain 6-2, 6-0. Eleanor ('Teach') Tennant was there as Miss Marble's coach.

In October 1962, the Committee of Management "laid it down quite firmly that players must wear white throughout," as Lieutenant-Colonel Duncan Macaulay said. He described the Committee as "long-suffering" on the issue of ladies' undergarments. *Behind the Scenes at Wimbledon* by Duncan Macaulay with Sir John ('Jackie') Smyth (St. Martin's, New York 1965).

Alan Little, the Honorary Librarian of the Wimbledon Lawn Tennis Museum, has written fascinating books on the history of Wimbledon that have been invaluable to me. Mr Little's *Wimbledon 1922-2009: The Changing Face of Church Road* (Wimbledon Lawn Tennis Museum, London 2009) was especially useful. Also, Mr Little's *Suzanne Lenglen: Tennis Idol of the Twenties* (Wimbledon Lawn Tennis Museum, London 1988) is an important and quite enjoyable book on one of the greatest tennis players.

Audrey Snell, the Assistant Librarian of the Kenneth Richie Wimbledon Library (which is part of the Wimbledon Lawn Tennis Museum), has been extremely kind in arranging for me to do research in the Library.

I have relied on Christine Truman's *Tennis Today* (Arthur Barker, London 1961); Maureen Connolly's *Forehand Drive* (MacGibbon & Kee, London 1957); Teddy Tinling's *White Ladies* (Stanley Paul, London 1963); Susan Noel's *Tennis in Our Time* (W.H Allen, London 1954); *We Have Come a Long Way: The Story of Women's Tennis* by Billie Jean King with Cynthia Starr (McGraw-Hill, New York 1988), and *Court on*

Court: A Life in Tennis (Dodd, Mead, New York 1975) by Margaret Smith Court with George McGann. *The Bud Collins History of Tennis* has been indispensable.

Kathryn Drury was my first, and superb, editor. Terri Gaskill – a great tennis player and coach – gave me invaluable suggestions. My close friends Mark Eaton, Beverly Hodgson, and Linell Smith read the manuscript. Their detailed and helpful comments improved my writing so much more than I like to admit. Richard & Christine Jones of The Tennis Gallery Wimbledon, www.thetennisgallery.co.uk, found old tennis books and Wimbledon programs for me and gave me great encouragement.

This novel is fiction, but I have tried to recreate the atmosphere of amateur tennis at Wimbledon in the early 1960s. The many mistakes that I'm confident I've made are all my own responsibility.

Fiona Hodgkin
'Tempest'
Bermuda
March 2012